RESOLUTION

A FACTIONAL NOVEL

JOHN COLE

Grosvenor House
Publishing Limited

This book is published by
Grosvenor House Publishing Ltd
28-30 High Street, Guildford, Surrey, GU1 3EL.
www.grosvenorhousepublishing.co.uk

A CIP record for this book
is available from the British Library

ISBN 978-1-78148-581-1

About the Author

John Cole was born in 1935. He was educated at Taunton School and subsequently studied Medicine in London, before spending forty years as a country family doctor. His passion for music has been another huge aspect of his life. As a student he sang in a famous City church choir and took part in university revues. Alongside his medical life he performed many opera roles, started an operatic society, directed several choirs and founded a professional symphony orchestra. Love of imaginative writing and recording life events has culminated in this book, which is a fiction concerning the changing world of modern womankind. He finished writing it just after being diagnosed with Motor Neurone disease, so it is a fitting tribute to his total career and life's work. He lives in a converted Chapel with his wife and springer spaniel.

Author's Note

This book describes the lives of three twentieth century women, a first generation immigrant thrust into the disruption of World War, a product of the 'swinging sixties', and a modern girl born and brought up in adversity. It explores their attitudes to the woman's place in society, their gender roles, their careers and their families.

The story is told against a backdrop of modern history, the three lives being inextricably entwined with major national and international events as well as some almost forgotten minor ones.

All of the major characters are fictional, as are their personal events, though of necessity, historical figures are unchanged.

Please do not cheat and explore the last chapter prematurely.

John Cole

12.04.2012.

Acknowledgements

To Rhuwina Goodridge Griffiths for her Editorial help; to Anne Sharp for the Cover design; to Shanti Bygott for her assistance bringing this book to publishing level; to Helena Cole for her internet skills; and to my dear wife Linda for her encouragement throughout the whole process. Also special mention to Angela Heylin for her inspirational guidance.

Contents

1

1940 Enemy Aliens

The tall, handsome young man stood at the top of the grass mound that is Primrose Hill in North London. He had a sombre expression, in keeping with his black, Brylcreemed hair and dark suit. The city glistened in the summer sunshine. It was a beautiful day, the date; 10th June 1940. Enrico Bellini however, was all darkness as he composed himself for the dreadful moment ahead.

After what seemed an age, he straightened, walked the short distance to his restaurant and up the stairs to his private quarters, where Rosanna his wife sat on the floor, building houses of toy bricks with their daughter Maria.

As he entered the room, he paused and regarded his wife. 'Bellissima!' This vibrant young wife, so warm, so loving, so intelligent, seemed to Enrico to be a wonderful gift from God, one he often felt he did not deserve, but for which he would always be grateful. She smiled as she always did, but the smile faded quickly as she noticed his expression. 'What is it Caro?' she asked. 'You look frightened!'

He sat down in his chair and drew her towards him, still kneeling and rested his head on hers. 'It is as we feared, my love', he whispered. 'We may have managed to evacuate the troops from Dunkirk, but today Mussolini has declared war on Britain.' He paused for the enormity of this news to register with her. She said nothing, but her body stiffened which told him that she completely understood.

'This means that we Italians have suddenly become enemy aliens here. I think we may be interned, or at least I may be. They say that women and children will not be arrested, but we shall see if that is true. Rumours, rumours, everywhere is rumours!' His exasperation broke over him and he sat back in order to be able to look her directly in the eye. His right hand repeatedly thumped his thigh in despair and frustration. 'I fear we might lose everything we have worked for over the past ten years.'

They stared at each other, absorbing the import of their situation. Little Maria, aged five watched them, knowing that something was wrong, but not understanding how important this was to all of them.

In 1930, Enrico and Rosanna had fled fascist Italy after Mussolini's cronies had beaten Enrico severely because he had protested at their treatment of his neighbour. The thugs had torn Jacob's wife's blouse from her and shaved her head in front of the frail old man. They then held Jacob himself under water in his own farmyard water butt, until it seemed he must drown. But they were distracted by Enrico who, in response to the commotion, came running out of the little trattoria in which he waited at table, yelling to the villagers for help as he ran across the road. The thugs paused long enough to viciously punch and kick him for his trouble, before riding away with Jacob's prize pony. All this was because Jacob was a Jew. Even the beautiful hills around Lake Orta were no longer safe from these gangs who were little better than bandits. Jacob had not died, but he left for America on the next boat. He visited Enrico in hospital where he was recovering from his injuries, advising the young man to do the same, 'You must run Enrico! You resisted them so they will come back for you!' he cried. A little while later, home from hospital watching Jacob's cart pull away at the start of their emigration, he recalled the old man's words. Even though Enrico was a good Catholic, not a Jew, he guessed that Jacob would be right. Enrico never recovered the sight of his left eye.

Rosanna came from a region in the North East, near the little town of Bardi, marrying Enrico there in 1926. She had been a receptionist in the hotel in Verona, whilst Enrico was a waiter. Both had some training as chefs. They had pursued a classically long courtship among the wonders of Verona with its Roman Amphitheatre, its opera festival, and the tourist attraction of Romeo and Juliet. These same tourists, coming from all over the world, needed to be housed and fed, so catering for them was a major industry in Verona. Enrico and Rosanna therefore learned their business very well and were quite accomplished by the time they married.

Behind the glamour of tourism however Italy was not happy with itself. At the time it was divided politically into Fascist and Anti-Fascist elements, the former believing in strong authoritative, single party government. The Fascists fought on the Allied side in World War 1 and enjoyed some support in the upper echelons of European society. The problem was that they sought to stifle any individual entrepreneurs or non conformist individuals, and were quite prepared to back their will with violence. Small business men, those in the arts, academics, and professional people came to fear them. They were particularly strong in the towns, especially large towns with employment problems and poverty. It was for this reason that Enrico had taken his new bride home to Orta, high in the Italian lake district, perhaps the most beautiful and restful place in the world. There, they felt free of this sort of unrest; free, that is, until the gangs came.

The gangs consisted mostly of frustrated, testosterone laden young men without jobs, who blamed the rest of the world for their own problems, and were encouraged to do so by their leadership. Everything that was wrong was somebody else's fault, especially the paucity of jobs. The Jews were seen as unfairly successful in business, and so the party became extremely anti- Semitic, a creed that allied them to Hitler's Nazis in Germany. At that time Italy was poor, and was struggling to feed its people. They were making babies much faster than they were producing food to feed them. Indeed, the most important export of Italy by far was not goods, but human beings.

And so the young Enrico and Rosanna Bellini had made their way to London, chosen because there were good relations between Italians and the British, and because Rosanna's elder brother Andreas ran a grocery in Rosebery Avenue, part of Clerkenwell, London's 'Little Italy'. Once in London, Enrico had worked as a waiter until an uncle died and left him some money. With this he opened his restaurant in Primrose Hill, just on the junction of Primrose Hill and Regents Park Road. Rosanna gave birth to little Maria in 1935. His restaurant became popular with the celebrities of north London and life was very good. They loved the cafe culture of Primrose Hill, and enjoyed nothing more than walking as a family across the enormous expanse of grass so close to their home, and, from there, surveying the great city before them. The population was so cosmopolitan that they never felt themselves to be foreign. Now, suddenly, at the stroke of some bureaucrat's pen they were enemy aliens in the country they had adopted and loved.

They spent the rest of that day planning how they might keep the business going without Enrico. Most of the men had been called up or had volunteered to fight, so they relied on the women that had been left behind. But in some ways this was a blessing, for the ladies were dependable, knew how to run a kitchen and made a good team.

The police came at four the following morning. They were very polite, making it quite clear that they were not enjoying carrying out their instructions, but the new Prime Minister Mr Churchill had decreed that all Enemy Alien men must be rounded up and placed in camps. Enrico was given 10 minutes to pack a bag of belongings and to say farewell to his tearful wife and daughter. Then he disappeared into the night, not knowing where he was being taken.

Mr Churchill had a big problem. There were about 80,000 so called Enemy Aliens and so few places to corral them. Many were Jews who had fled Nazism, Italians who had fled Mussolini's Fascism, or Germans, who were often senior academics or contributors to the arts world. Many were of advanced years and others had spent almost all of their lives in Britain. Few could be described as a risk. All were rounded up. There was a general fear of a so called Fifth Column, an enemy within the gates, and Churchill was determined to take no chances.

They were categorised into three groups. A was a small group of about 600 people thought to be high risk. B was a group thought to be medium risk. This was by far the largest contingent. Category C people were considered to be of very slight risk and were eventually allowed to remain free. Enrico, being young and energetic was considered to be a B risk. He was herded onto a train and taken with many of his compatriots to Warth Mills, in Bury, Lancashire. The buildings formed an old industrial site with no furniture and few facilities. Even before the men arrived it was overrun with vermin. Conditions quickly became intolerable and overcrowding extreme. Other large camps had been established in the north of the country. One was at Huyton, Liverpool, and was on a half completed large council estate. Here each unfinished small house, often littered with builder's rubble, would be occupied by twelve men; some were obliged to sleep in hastily erected tents in the gardens. Treatment was not good, and there was considerable hardship.

Enrico had not long arrived in Warth Mills when he was hailed loudly and, turning to see who knew him, found his brother in law, Andreas, who had also been rounded up. They embraced warmly and decided to share quarters. 'How is Rosanna?' asked Andreas.

'She is very well, and I think very strong also.' said Enrico. 'I feel sure that if any woman can manage she will. But I do worry about how she will run the restaurant and look after your niece, Maria.'

'Don't you have any friends or neighbours?' Andreas asked.

'Yes, of course we do, I expect the Greeks next door will help. He has his old mother living with them and they are not being treated as enemies,' Enrico replied.

'It's all the fault of that madman, Mussolini. If I could put my hands on him he would not last long'. Andreas, one of the world's gentler souls, was a very large and powerful man and for a moment Enrico smiled wryly at a mental image of the dictator held, squirming, in the air, by this man.

They went on talking about Andreas' life in Clerkenwell. Although he was older than Rosanna he had never married, saying that he had not found anyone as good as his Mother, which was perhaps true, thought Enrico. Italian men tend to idolise their mothers in a way the British would never understand.

Evidently 'Little Italy' was very upset with the British Government about the round up. Their venom was particularly bitter against Mr Churchill. Most of the inhabitants of those streets had lived in London for many years and had come to occupy important and respected niches in the capital's life. There were lawyers, doctors, hotel managers, shop keepers, ice cream makers, and restaurateurs in abundance. Andreas reported that there had been a very large attendance at St Peter's Italian Church in Clerkenwell for Mass on the evening of the announcement of internment. The mood was an odd mix of piety, acceptance and anger, but most of all, that of a community gathered together in adversity. The two men envisaged the unnatural quiet that the absence of so many would create. Enrico was kept only a week or so in Warth Mills and then taken to the docks for transportation on 'The Lady of Man' to the Isle of Man. There he found himself in camp M in the town of Peel.

Camp M being a collection of Victorian houses at the end of the Promenade which had been surrounded by barbed wire. Here conditions were much better than on the mainland. Overcrowding was still a problem, but they were not ill treated and the main issue for busy intelligent minds was boredom. The internees quickly organised activities designed to keep them busy and to prevent the unrest they knew would come with so many men, all crammed together. In a very short time catering and cleaning rosters were established. Within two or three weeks educational and sporting activities had been organised and a primitive system of social support was in place.

Letters were allowed, but females were not allowed into the camp. Women and children were not interned. Perhaps the government still had bad memories of the British Concentration Camps in the Boer War decades previously, in which thousands of the women and children of the Dutch farmers in South Africa had died, not of actual maltreatment, but mostly of poor nutrition and sanitation, bringing disaster through neglect and disease.

Back in London, the government became concerned that such a mass of men that had been rounded up could not satisfactorily be housed on mainland Britain. Churchill negotiated with Canada to send many Enemy Aliens there. A ship was chartered to take them across the Atlantic. Many of those men were taken from Warth Mills just a week or so after Enrico had been moved away to Peel.

The SS Arandora Star, once a Caribbean cruise liner left Liverpool on 1st July 1940, carrying 1,200 of the 8,000 Enemy Aliens deported from Britain at that time. At about eight o'clock the morning of 2nd July she was torpedoed, just off Ireland, and sank in 30 minutes. She was painted grey and was not flying a Red Cross ensign. It was thought that the German U boat considered her to be a naval vessel. Of the 1600 men on board 800 prisoners, crew and soldiers died. Some were German Jews, among them some senior scientists who would have been very helpful to the war effort. Others were non Jewish Germans, both pro and anti- Nazi. The Italians had been housed on a lower deck and could not escape. 485 of the 700 Italians drowned. Fifty were from the little Italian town of Bardi, population 2700, Rosanna's home. One of them was Rosanna's brother Andreas.

In August 1940 a summer storm washed hundreds of bodies ashore from the Arandora Star, a few were identified, but many were not, their graves unnamed along the coast of northwest Ireland.

2

1940 Evacuation

Rosanna was both tired and sad. She was doing much of the cooking in the restaurant because her main cook had slipped off the edge of a pavement on the way home a week ago and broken her ankle. Such injuries were common now that there were no street lights and all the windows were blacked out. It was fine to walk home on a moonlit night, but the restaurant worked until ten in the evening, so if the night was cloudy, the streets were very dark indeed. Clara had fallen on just such a night. She clearly would not be back at work for a couple of months.

Old Mrs Mikolos from next door had agreed to sit with Maria whilst the restaurant was open so that Rosanna could keep an eye on things and do some cooking herself. In fact, Rosanna took her turn at all of the jobs including mopping the floors. In order to open at noon it took several hours of work just to clean the place and prepare vegetables.

And that was another problem; food was getting scarce, just as the business was becoming busier than ever. The government had introduced rationing right at the beginning of the war, but not on restaurant meals. Primrose Hill, being in an affluent area, not too far from central London was a good place to run a restaurant. Hungry Londoners, who could afford it, ate out more than they used to. She was busy, oh so very busy, and she missed Enrico very much indeed. They had always been a touching, loving pair, and she missed her night time hug.

And then there was Andreas. Andreas, the big brother, who went to church on Sunday, had never done any harm to anyone, who worked hard, paid his taxes and was liked by everyone, but who died because of a piece of paper saying that he was born in Bardi, Italy; died because this stupid government thought he might be a threat and sent him to the bottom of the sea without even a proper burial or goodbye. Rosanna knew that Clerkenwell's 'Little Italy' was very angry indeed and would never truly forgive.

'Oh God,' she raged in her thoughts, 'Why Andreas? What have we done to deserve this?' But, whilst such angry thoughts tore at her very being, she had to remain smiling and pleasant to all, because, after all, she was an enemy alien too, and she knew that, in some parts, shops and restaurants belonging to Italians and Germans were the subject of vandalism and riots. It did not seem likely in the cosmopolitan atmosphere of Primrose Hill, but she was aware she must not provoke hostility, come what may, especially now she was on her own. But when the hours of dark arrived and she lay in her lonely bed, the evil thoughts took control and she experienced both anger and distress the depth of which had hitherto been unknown to her. Consequently she was hollow-eyed and found it very difficult to dress each morning: Maria's childhood smiles and chirpy laughter often rescued her from the throes of real depression.

In fact, apart from Maria, the only good thing about life was that the bank balance was growing faster than ever before. Fewer staff, with the waitresses earning a little less per head than their absent male counterparts, and many more meals being served, had made the restaurant a little gold mine.

But, little Maria was being very difficult, throwing tantrums and was uncharacteristically disobedient. Rosanna knew that this was her fault, not Maria's. A six year old is right to expect her Mamma's attention, especially with Papa missing too. Rosanna had to admit that recently she had been preoccupied running the business and that Maria's company was not as high a priority as it should have been. The walks on the hill had almost been abandoned, and the book at bedtime only seemed to happen on Sundays when the restaurant was closed. Still, Mrs Mikolos seemed to be very fond of her and there had been a big increase of drawing and writing recently, so maybe Maria was not suffering as much as she feared. She was also learning a lot about ancient Greece and its role in civilising the World. It always amused Rosanna to think that London has more Greek Cypriots than Nicosia, but then, if Italy had continued to send her children away, the same might soon have been said of Italy too.

As she cleaned the front step of the restaurant that morning in the first week of September she noticed a few brown leaves and thought. 'Autumn has come early this year'. On her knees, polishing the brass threshold with her bottom waving in the air in time with each swing of her arm, she jumped when it was rudely pinched in a very Italian manner. Turning her head in outrage and straining against the sun to see who could be so cheeky she saw a thin, bearded man. It took a brief moment only to realise it was Enrico, standing there with his tired old suitcase beside him and with a grin big enough to drive a bus in.

He swept her into his arms and off her feet, carrying her upstairs to celebrate his homecoming in a proper manner, despite the hour being just about ten in the morning. Afterwards she asked him by what miracle he had come home. 'I think that Whitehall is reacting to the bad publicity of the Arandora Star sinking' he said. 'I was called to a tribunal much earlier than I expected, and because I have been here ten years and had come because of the injuries the Fascist thugs gave me, they decided that I should be reclassified. I am now a C and at liberty! So here I am, just 12 weeks after I left.'

The Bellini family's rejoicing was to be cruelly short lived, for on the very next day, Saturday September 7th 1940 Hitler threw the Luftwaffe at London in earnest. 364 bombers, protected by 515 fighters crossed the Channel to attack the

Port of London. Just 41 British Hurricanes rose from the home shores to face them. The attack began in the late afternoon, and was followed by a further 133 bombers that night. They did not really need pathfinders for the fires could be seen many miles away. Nonetheless many bombs fell on residential districts so that by the next morning 436 Londoners were dead and 1,668 injured.

Some planes completely missed the target area and dropped their bomb loads indiscriminately. One fell close to the Bellini home in Primrose Hill and shook the house severely. Plaster dust covered Maria's bed, but the anxious parents noted that she slept through as if nothing was happening. Later, Enrico stood on the hill and watched the city burn. It was an awesome sight.

Weeks previously the so called Battle of Britain had begun, the Royal Air Force doing battle with the might of the German Luftwaffe, mostly in so called dog fights between fighters, and often over the English Channel. Several attempts by Goering's air force to destroy the British radar early warning stations had not made much difference to the British efficiency in locating the invaders just long enough before they arrived to rush the defence planes into the air. Thus was coined the word 'scramble', an apt description of the rapid deployment of fighter aircraft to meet the enemy. The British fought bravely in their Spitfires and Hurricanes, winning the fight at a ratio of two to one, but they were being bled to death by the simple arithmetical weight of numbers and by September had lost over two hundred fighter pilots. Attacks on the south coast airfields, especially on August 18th, the so called 'Hardest Day', had severely weakened the British capability.

For this reason, when Goering turned his attention to civilian targets and brought large flights of bombers across the channel, the decision was made to oppose them in small numbers only. Encouraged by the lack of opposition Goering increased the size of his bombing raids to enormous numbers; at times several hundred aircraft packed the sky like a swarm of angry bees.

But the British were not beaten. Goering had made a major misjudgement in turning from the air fight to destroy the civilians whilst the RAF still had men and machines. The painful interlude was used to full effect. Airfields and planes were repaired and men transferred, so that by September 15th, the British were ready. It was a beautiful late summer's day with bright sunshine and excellent visibility, except for some early autumnal fog. Air Vice Marshall Keith Park, a New Zealander, commanding 11th Squadron sent his Spitfires up to dive out of the sun onto the German fighters, distracting them from protecting the bombers, who droned on towards the mainland cities. There they met Douglas Bader's 10th Squadron of Hurricanes who harried and burned them all day. One hundred and seventy six German planes were shot down by the RAF and a further nine by anti aircraft barrage. Just twenty three British planes were lost. That day became known as The Day of Reckoning. Churchill was at the command centre in Uxbridge during the day, and as he left, muttered to his companion, 'Never in the field of human conflict was so much owed by so many to so few.' It was a foretaste of his famous parliamentary speech a few days later.

Hitler continued his bombardment of Britain until May 1941, by which time 43,000 civilians had been killed, half of them in London, and a million homes had been destroyed, but never did the intensity equal that first few weeks. Hitler had been warned that any invasion would be a disaster unless the skies were clear of allied aircraft. Although he apparently accepted that advice he nonetheless prepared the invasion. Firstly planned for October 1940, then for December 1940, then finally consigned to history.

However, none of this was known in London at the time. On Monday the education authorities and the government decided that children should be evacuated as soon as possible and sent to safer parts of the country. The rationale of course was that children are an investment in the future. There had been a similar edict in September 1939, but the long silence of the so called Phoney War led to most children returning to their homes. Enrico and Rosanna agreed to the Evacuation Scheme and signed the documents. Maria came back from school one evening with a note requiring her to go to school next day with a small suitcase of personal clothing and toilet articles, her gas mask and, if possible, a stick of barley sugar, which was intended to ease the hunger of a long and uncertain journey. She did not know where she was going, but promised to write as soon as possible. She was not yet seven years of age. Children under school age were evacuated with their mothers. Those of school age could take their mothers with them, but, of course, many mothers could not go. Rosanna was one of these because of the demands of the business.

A tearful Rosanna took her to school next morning and stood alongside all the other mothers waving whilst a fleet of buses took the children away. Nobody seemed to know where they were going. Each of the children was labelled just like a postal package. Each was experiencing a torrent of emotions, fear being uppermost but excitement also. In keeping with the times, behaviour was excellent though there was some sobbing.

Maria's bus took her to Paddington Station in West London where she and her school friends joined a great number of other children for the journey, which was to take them through Reading and then, south of Bath via Westbury, to Taunton in Somerset. Taunton had no strategic value and was not a town of any special historic or architectural interest. In fact it was distinguished by its very lack of distinction, except that it is one of England's more peaceable places. That is of course, precisely why it was chosen.

At the station they all stood in line whilst a billeting officer called them one by one to meet the families who had agreed to take them in. They made a sorry spectacle, some of them already thin, many lacking warm clothing, some already covered with sores from impetigo, which had been painted with a purple antiseptic. Maria was pleased when the sweet boy, named Walter, who had travelled with her all the way, and who smelt horribly of stale urine, was led away by a cheerful lady and a short bald man, who seemed to call everyone 'My Dear.' An expression she had never heard before, but one which would become quite familiar in the next few years.

But, at the end of the wait, there seemed to be nobody to collect Maria. Eventually the billeting officer himself turned to her and said. 'Young lady it looks as if I am to take you home with me.' And with that he lifted Maria's case and led her to a large but elderly motor car which was parked in the station yard.

They drove out of the town and along a main road for about five miles before turning left onto a side road. Quite soon they were going up a drive to a very large house where Mr Lloyd, as everyone called him, helped her down and took her inside to meet his wife.

There were several children in the house and Maria came to understand that Mr Lloyd was in the habit of picking up the strays who had, for whatever reason, not been collected. Failure to collect was not uncommon, especially among the better off, because the receiving host families who had promised support for the scheme, quite often made their own arrangements with family or friends of family, and the officials had failed to remove their names from the list. Fortunately Billeting Officers were often well to do, public spirited men, prepared to pick up the pieces. So it was that Maria began an entirely new and not altogether unwelcome or unpleasant life. Her lodging was delightful, her hosts quietly authoritative, but very kind and caring. There was good company of her own age.

There was a great shortage of school places, and indeed of school teachers, since most of the male teachers had been called up to fight. The village school at West Buckland was overcrowded despite the fact that nearby a special school for evacuees had been opened. Eventually a place for Maria was found in a small village called Nynehead. The school was very old fashioned but the teaching was remarkable. Maria did not know that this tiny establishment boasted the best primary school results in Somerset. She stayed with Mr Lloyd's family for the remainder of the war. There, she learned about the countryside, about farming, and about animals and birds. She gained a love of dogs and horses, and understood the seasons for the first time. Importantly, as a restaurateur's daughter, she learned where food came from.

A great sense of freedom came when she learned to ride a bicycle, and Enrico sent the money to buy one of her own. This enabled her to ride around the almost empty country lanes, sometimes with the other children, but often quite alone. Nobody seemed to mind. Nobody thought for a moment that this was unsafe. She saw very little of the war, except one day there was a fight between aeroplanes in the sky above, which they called a dog fight. One German plane came down, but the pilot parachuted safely. He was caught by the Home Guard, a uniformed army of local men too old to go and fight. There was great excitement about this in the community.

But, perhaps most of all she learned about the British. Her London home had been so cosmopolitan that the ordinary residents of these islands were not commonly to be seen, at least not in the particular gentility that pervaded that home in Somerset. Mr Lloyd and his wife were wonderful examples of civilised, well educated folk. Yet, like many of their sort, they were not snobs and treated everyone with the same degree of respect. Maria learned from the housekeeper that when they went to their church there was no singing, and quite often there was nothing at all, not even reading from the scriptures. Maria, used to the pomp of Mass in a great London church, thought this very odd. She had never heard of Quakers.

At the little school she shared a desk with a tall farm boy called Harry. At first she could hardly understand him, because of his strong Somerset accent. They became very good friends except that he had an alarming tendency to pull her pigtails; not hard really, but enough to be uncomfortable. It took her a long time to realise that this was a form of affection. This friendship was very important because some of the local children were not altogether kind to the evacuees, especially ones with foreign names. Harry was her protector during the awkward initial term. He lived very close by, so a lot of time was spent on the farm looking at the animals, learning about milk and eggs, cows and chickens, and even bulls and geese, though these she treated with great care. Harry's mother would take a huge pan of milk and put it to simmer very slowly on the great stove, until all the goodness had risen to the top, and was skimmed off to be served as clotted cream. She made the butter too, in a big churn in the dairy. The cows were milked by hand and had to be fetched twice a day from the fields to the milking parlour. Before she returned to London Maria had become quite adept at doing this.

There was a massive shire horse called Ben, who used to pull farm implements and carts for Harry's father. Ben was so huge as to appear like a house to little Maria, but she was encouraged to pat him and eventually found the courage to do so. When she knew him well he would come and nuzzle her for some titbit such as a carrot that she took to hiding in a pocket, ready for just this. Ben became Maria's first real animal friend,

Of course, living in dairy country, rationing was not so great a problem as in the towns, but the only fruit available was what they grew themselves, and many houses had turned their lawns into vegetable patches, so that they could produce all their vegetables at home. There were no bananas or pineapples. Clothes were a problem though, especially for a girl living as she did, coming home muddy and bramble torn from her romps on the farm. The whole country was beginning to look dowdy, living on 'hand me downs'. Fortunately Mr Lloyd was better placed than most since his business made cloth.

Academically she did very well. Miss Elson the headmistress believed in learning by rote, so Maria was very soon able to recite her tables and then to do sums in her head. She enjoyed reading to the point that Mrs Lloyd learned to check every night that she had in fact settled to sleep or she might have read all night.

Gradually she lost her puppy fat and became quite tough, a strong runner capable of keeping up with the boys. She bicycled everywhere, to school, to the farm and back to the great house. Sometimes, with her friends, she would cycle out of the valley onto the surrounding hills, where there was a great monument to a previous war.

Maria was returned her to her real parents in 1945 a very different person; one who knew how to behave, how to converse and most importantly how to think for herself. It was many years before Maria appreciated that her happy experience of being an evacuee was not shared by all. Some three million people, mostly children were evacuated in World War Two, perhaps the biggest migration in modern history. Many had wonderful experiences like Maria, but sadly about 12% reported problems, ranging from social difficulties to abuse of all sorts. Part of this stemmed from cultural differences. Many of the evacuee children were from very poor urban communities and had no notion of hygiene, or of manners. Many had never had a bath. Large numbers had no soles to their boots, which were just uppers tied on. Toilet behaviour was a major problem. They had not seen clean sheets or an eiderdown, had never sat up to table to eat, did not know how to hold knives and forks, and seemed to speak a foreign language. It was hardly surprising that traditional, rural England tried to absorb them but reeled under the impact.

Back in Primrose Hill, Maria's parents, reunited, but grieving over their absent daughter, faced life in a city in turmoil. Enrico, despite the demands of the restaurant, joined the ARP (Air Raid Precaution) service as a warden, one of almost a million citizens to do so. He patrolled Primrose Hill at night wearing his black helmet with a large W on its forehead, sealing lights that were potentially visible to the sky, helping people to air raid shelters and guiding emergency services to sites where there might be survivors of a bomb. Central government recommended portable prefabricated shelters called Morrison, or Anderson shelters, which folk erected in their gardens or in cellars within their houses. In London some 172,000 people sought safety from the bombs in tube stations, which were not really suitable for the purpose, often becoming horribly insanitary as a result. On his 'patch' there were some purpose built larger public shelters. In April 1941 one of these took a direct hit. When Enrico forced his way in over the rubble, he found some 70 people all sitting, almost as if nothing had happened, but all dead from the blast.

And then in May 1941, suddenly, there was no raid, no fire, no death. They waited night after night for the bombers to return but they did not, at least not in a major way. The RAF had won. There would be no invasion. Hitler, running short of fuel and with no natural oil supply, had turned his eyes eastwards, to Russia, seeking to annex the great oil fields lying on the other side of the Volga River, beyond Stalingrad. Londoners had a two year respite, until the rockets of 1944 began to rain upon them.

Rosanna watching her husband exhaust himself working both day and night, resolved to make things as easy for him in the business as she could. She took on all of the financial management and proved so good at it that they found themselves becoming quite well off, even rich. Their customers were people of good connection and large wallets, so it was little surprise when one of them whispered in Rosanna's ear that a famous restaurant in Soho, the new centre of Italian interest in London, was coming on the market. He recommended they think about buying it, maybe in partnership with him. They agreed, becoming proud owners of Bellini's in Wardour Street in 1944.

At the end of April 1945 they thought it safe enough for Maria to return to them in Primrose Hill. They still lived over the original restaurant, because they just loved the neighbourhood. They waited for the train to pull into Paddington but could hardly recognise this young lady, so grown up and so composed. Rosanna wept for joy as she hugged her daughter, but the tears also fell for all the years of Maria's childhood that she had missed. When she spoke they found she had lost her domestic Italian accent; none remained, just a correct, rather formal English, tinted with a hint of the long brown vowels of the West Country. Maria missed the great house and the farm, especially Harry and Ben, but she was very glad to be at home with her very own Mamma and Papa. She settled back into the household quickly and easily, making an especial fuss of Mrs Mikolos next door.

And so it came about that on May 8th 1945 a greying, slightly rotund 45 year old Enrico, wearing a large Hunter watch over his prosperous ampleness, stood in The Mall with his still glamorous, vibrant 38 year old wife, and their 11 year old daughter; 'the enemy aliens', as enthusiastically part of the madly excited crowd as any native, waving to the King and Queen on their victorious Buckingham Palace balcony, Later they walked back through Piccadilly to the Soho restaurant for 'one hell of a party' with their many friends.

3

1946 Canons

Dr Kathleen Anderson riffled through the pile of papers on her desk. She was filling her mind with information about some four hundred and fifty girls who wished to come to her school. Just seventy would be successful in their application, and Kathleen Anderson was acutely aware that the process of selection was perhaps the most important act of the year for her, in her role as headmistress of The North London Independent Collegiate School for Girls (or NICS as it was inappropriately known).

The school had been founded in Camden by the great Victorian champion of female education Frances Mary Buss, immortalised by the verse 'Miss Buss and Miss Beale Cupids darts do not feel'. It started in 1850 in Frances Buss's own home but quickly grew both in numbers and reputation until, in the 1930s, the school had moved to the Duke of Chandos' house, 'Canons', in Edgware. The magnificent buildings, set in a large acreage of fabulous grounds quickly became perhaps the finest girls' day school in England. The list of alumni was indeed impressive, including a comprehensive array of academics, sporting personalities, celebrities and senior politicians.

Kitty Anderson had been appointed headmistress in 1944, a difficult time in war torn Britain. Staff were not young, materials were hard to come by, and the school needed to increase its numbers and its facilities rapidly to stay in its pole position in the educational firmament. That depended significantly upon maintaining and indeed improving the expected academic standards, which was why this new, dynamic headmistress, who would become almost as much a legend as the school founder, was being so very diligent over selection.

The selection process at NICS was a little unusual for its time. Of course there were academic papers appropriate for eleven year olds but in addition there were very extensive interviews with senior members of staff, who were looking for the tell tale markers of true excellence, a fine mind and an independence of spirit. This of course involved the ability to discuss, even debate, issues with the best minds the staff had to offer. After all, these girls would eventually be the movers and shakers of the world, and must therefore be nurtured in that atmosphere from the start. This is not to assume that the school was some sort of tropical plant house for blue stocking girls. It was nothing of the sort. In fact it was reassuringly normal and human, treading the line between good order and free expression, and between self awareness and awareness of others. Dr Anderson wanted above all for her girls to be human beings not automatons.

Being situated in close proximity to the metropolis, the applicants, even in 1946, came from a variety of cultures and religions, with many languages being spoken. Catholics met with Protestants, Jews and Muslims in a great soup of intellect.

Their examination was not the more accepted Common Entrance exam used at aged thirteen by many private schools, but a searching exploration of talent, designed to identify real potential. Although fees were high, the applicants were by no means restricted to the upper classes of British Society. Successful middle class business people, émigrés, even some very bright children from less affluent families, sponsored by scholarships, moved cheek by jowl with the old money of the British Establishment. Providing the fees were paid, the elite nature of the school rested upon ability, not upon family.

After the written papers, about one in four of the candidates were shortlisted for interview, and of these a little more than half were accepted. So, of the original cohort only about 15% were successful. The interview stage was critical and very tense for all concerned, not least the staff and headmistress. Today was the last day of interviews and Kitty had a very good idea by now where they were heading. Some seventy girls had already been identified as outstanding, but there remained another ten to interview. If two or three of those were of the highest calibre, they would be oversubscribed, and a further pruning through staff room discussion would be needed. Quite obviously there would be debate and, perhaps, some heated argument between the examiners this evening, because a few really bright students would lose out in the competition. Kitty encouraged this debate, although the final decision would, of course, be hers. It was her practice always to be the last person to interview the likely candidates. Everyone knew that she was the last hurdle in the process.

She selected one of the papers from the pile in front of her, and read it with increasing interest before walking to her door and into the sitting room outside. Three eleven year olds were sitting in the soft chairs pretending to be relaxed. 'Which of you is Maria Bellini?' She asked in a neutral tone.

A smartly dressed, dark haired girl with Mediterranean features stood and nodded, saying 'I am Maria, Dr Anderson.'

'Good morning Maria, do come with me,' said the headmistress, shaking her by the hand and then leading her by the elbow into the inner room. Once there, they sat opposite one another in front of the fireplace, a low coffee table between them. Kitty eschewed the formality of sitting at her desk, with the image of power that always comes from that.

She started by asking about Maria's family, and of course about her wartime experiences. She was already in possession of one of the best examination papers in a particularly good year, so was fascinated to learn that Maria's early education had mostly been in a village school in rural Somerset. When she learned about the evacuation household, and the milking of the cows, followed by a bicycle ride home in all weathers, she realised that she had a very determined young person of considerable strength of character. She also noted the finely honed sporting body.

She probed the Italian family background and eventually came around to asking about the experience of being regarded as enemy aliens in Britain. 'It was not very good, Dr Anderson. My family had been here for ten years. I was born here. We have a restaurant business you know in Primrose Hill.'

'Yes, I do know Maria. I have eaten there myself.'

They smiled at each other at this exchange.

'Well, Papa was sent away early in the war, not for long. But it was very upsetting for Mamma, especially because my Uncle Andreas was drowned on the Arandora Star, which was a ship carrying immigrants considered to be at risk to the British during the war. It was torpedoed on its way to Canada.'

'Yes, I remember it very well. We were all sad about that tragedy. I imagine it was not well received in your community.'

'No it wasn't and some of the older ones are still angry about it.'

'What do you think yourself Maria?'

There was a pause, and a wrinkled forehead before Maria replied. 'Well, it was cruel, and Andreas was a lovely man who had done no harm to anyone. But I understand that it was not intended, and that the government did need to make sure the country was safe. I also understand that some of the men had to go abroad. So, to me it was just a terrible accident and I do not blame anyone.'

'Does your Mother agree with you?'

'I think her head does, but her heart does not. She is still very angry and very sad.' Another pause. 'But you know, she thinks herself to be British now. She has worked here for sixteen years, having escaped those nasty people in Italy. She has very many friends, and feels that she belongs. I laugh at her sometimes, because she is more British than the British.'

'I am quite sure she does belong, and am glad she thinks so too Maria.' Kitty said quietly, thinking that her recent exchange showed a maturity and understanding which would fit very well in the school.

A few days later, a formal letter arrived in the Bellini home offering Maria a place at North London Independent Collegiate School. She started there the following September and blossomed in that environment. She showed excellent social skills, probably from her upbringing, living over a highly fashionable eating house and meeting the customers. She proved very adept at natural sciences and languages, as well as singing a lusty soprano in the school choir. But perhaps it was on the sports side that she most excelled. At a time when girls did not embrace running very enthusiastically, she became the winner of the school cross country at sixteen, and was encouraged to join an adult athletic club of national standing.

Of her friends and contemporaries, a staggering forty nine per cent went on to university, and many filled very prominent roles thereafter. This was at a time when only three per cent of the populace went to university, and only ten per cent of those were girls. Years later Dr Kathleen Anderson became Dame Kitty Anderson, perhaps the foremost educator of her day.

4

1954 The Interview

Maria entered the hospital through the casualty doors, as, it seemed, did many others, since there was a great deal of activity with people coming and going in all directions.

The nurses wore a confusing variety of uniforms; the younger, apparently junior ones, were dressed in a pin stripe pink and white with a small cap and a heavily starched apron, kept in place by a wide black belt which had a splendid buckle. The belt gave them a figure enhancing sensuality, made more so by the rustle of stiff under slips.

The more senior nurses wore exactly the same uniform, but in pale blue and white, and with a wonderful royal blue Maltese cross pinned to their bosom. These were staff nurses and the cross proclaimed them to be fully fledged Nightingales, as the nurses from St Thomas' were known all over the world. A few, more senior still, were in plain blue dresses. These were known as charge nurses, and were the deputies to the matriarch of a hospital ward or department, the sister in charge. The word 'sister', Maria thought, with her Catholic upbringing, was probably a residue from the time when Nuns would do nursing work. The sister in Casualty was quite little and was dressed in a grand navy blue dress with white dots on it. Her hat was much larger, adding several inches to her diminutive frame. One had the impression that this sister was not to be trifled with.

Working with the nurses were a few young men with full length white coats whom Maria wrongly took to be doctors because many of them sported a stethoscope around their neck. Actually the junior resident doctors wore white jackets not full length coats. Maria's young men were medical students. There were injured people sitting on benches in the department, and a considerable number of cubicles screened by curtains. Prominent in the room was a large metal tank which hissed all the while. She had no idea what that was for but it felt very threatening.

Passing through into the hospital main corridor she was taken aback at the very size of the place. The corridor seemed to go on for miles, an impression which, though far from true, stemmed from the fact that it did indeed stretch about half of the way from Westminster Bridge to Lambeth Bridge. The old hospital had been built in seven huge high buildings, each one larger than many provincial hospitals of the time. They were linked by smaller office blocks, canteens, outpatient departments, operating theatres etc. The whole was embellished with Victorian architectural features which, though not very attractive, imparted a sense that the whole thing was a grand palace, as was fitting for its position directly across the river from Parliament and Big Ben.

About half way down this thoroughfare there was a great open space with a very high ceiling and with panelled walls covered with portraits of famous surgeons and physicians of the past. This was the Governors Hall, home of the head porter and his team who in reality kept the whole place running. The whole effect was so overwhelming in its grandness that Maria quailed, fearing that the whole idea of being a student here was a great mistake.

The Dean's Office was on the main corridor close to this grand concourse, and so it was with trepidation that she pushed open the door and walked to the desk at which was seated a woman not much older than herself.

The Dean's Secretary, for this is who she was, looked up from her desk as Maria approached and beamed a very bright reassuring smile. 'Good afternoon and welcome to St Thomas', Miss Bellini,' she said. 'You are a little early and they are running a few minutes behind time, but never mind. There is a comfy seat over there. You will find reading matter to occupy you.'

Maria stammered her thanks and went to sit in the generous sofa indicated. She was quite unbalanced, both by the warmth of her reception, and because the secretary knew who she was, without her having to announce herself. Later she learned that this girl memorised the photographs of every applicant and every student, along with their personal details, so that everyone felt they had a friend in the Dean's Office, which indeed they did.

As she sat absorbing her surroundings, she became aware she was not alone in the waiting area. A young man was studying her intently from the other side of the room. She smiled at him and he smiled shyly in return. It seemed they were both waiting for admission interviews. Maria asked him the time of his appointment.

'I've come all the way from Devon and my train was early.' He said. 'So I'm here well ahead of time.'

Maria was relieved, her anxieties about having to spend even longer waiting to be called in to interview unfounded. As a matter of fact, his company made the time fly by. Very soon she was summoned into the interview.

As she crossed the room, the young man stood up. 'My name is Ian Plowman.' He said, 'I hope to meet you properly next term.'

Three men were sitting in the inner office. Each stood, when Maria entered, shook her by the hand and introduced himself. There was the Dean, the assistant Dean and a University observer. The Dean took control of the interview, inviting the others to ask questions periodically. They enquired into her academic achievements, her family, her interests and the reason she wished to study medicine at St Thomas'. They seemed very interested in her success in the school cross country run, and her explanation of how a young woman of Italian family would want to study in England. Very soon she stopped feeling nervous or threatened, and actually enjoyed the questions, probably because of the courteous and gentle way they probed. When the interview was over she found a telephone and reported to her mother that she thought it had gone well.

It clearly had for, just a few days later, the postman delivered an offer of a place starting the following October, provided she managed reasonable grades in the public exams. She was the first year to do the new A levels, which replaced the Higher School Certificate, so nobody quite knew what to expect.

So, when only about one in three hundred girls went to university, this shy, first generation immigrant Italian won her place at one of the most prestigious medical schools in Britain. At the time more graduates from St Thomas' were going on to be consultant specialists than from any other medical school in the land.

5

1954 St Thomas' Hospital

Ian Plowman made his way along the long main corridor to the Dean's Office, checked in with Sally, the Dean's Secretary, and thereby started his life's work.

Sally welcomed him warmly, just as she had at the interview all those months previously. She gave him a schedule of lectures and tutorials, checked that his lodging arrangements were satisfactory, and offered some advice about student and hospital social activities. He strode off down the remainder of that long corridor, out into the sun for a short distance, and then found himself entering the Medical School, which was the last building of the huge hospital site. The medical school was not far from Lambeth Palace, the official home of the Archbishop of Canterbury.

The physiology laboratory was on the left, just as one entered the building, and then came the museum, a grisly place full of anatomical specimens pickled in formaldehyde. There were all sorts of macabre sights demonstrating some of the extreme things that can happen to human beings.

Worse was to come, for after a brief introductory lecture they were led to the Anatomy Department where lay nine adult corpses, Each had been preserved and so the whole room smelled of death and formaldehyde, a pervasive stench which the students soon enough got used to, but which, for the next eighteen months, they would carry about their persons wherever they went. They wore white coats whenever they went in there, but the coats soon became vile with grease from subcutaneous fat, which added more than a little to the general air of disgust.

The thirty two students on Ian's course were each directed to a table, four to each body, two on each side. Each student had a bag of dissection tools, scalpels, forceps etc. and each table had some larger equipment such as saws. There were dissection manuals and the famous Gray's Anatomy which everyone was advised to buy for themselves, since there would need to be much homework in preparation for the frequent written and aural tests that were to come.

The corpse that lay between them would be their preoccupation for a whole eighteen months during which, little by little, they would dissect out every muscle, blood vessel, nerve and bone, as well as every organ, including the brain, until, by the end, little would remain of the body. What did remain was, Ian was told, carefully and reverentially disposed of according to the instructions in the will or from the family. Ian noticed that despite rumours that bodies were bought cheaply in Asia, all of these people seemed to be Caucasian, and all were of normal build. All were adults, but a few seemed quite young. Both sexes were there of course. The students were several weeks into the course before they stopped hiding the more personal bits under the covering sheet.

The department was run by a Professor, a Welsh rugby fan, who lavishly decorated the department with daffodils every St David's day. He had a few lecturers on his staff, whose job included helping the students with their dissection, not by doing it for them, but through verbal guidance, which Ian noted was freely and courteously given.

The students themselves were a strangely mixed bunch. Several had accents which immediately spoke of very expensive backgrounds, but a few were clearly from ordinary homes. One of these was an enormous Welshman, who not long after commencing his medical studies had an international rugby trial. Another, even larger and stronger was already a famous young oarsman. There was a delightful smiling man of Caribbean background, and there were six girls. Ian found himself paired with a tall Jewish boy called Maurice. On the other side of the table was a very chirpy, small statured lad named Peter, and the Italian girl, Ian recognised from the day of their interviews, called Maria. Ian found her extremely attractive. She stood very straight as if her parents had always instructed her to sit upright at table, which, by the way, they certainly had done. She had a lovely warm smile, twinkling eyes and black hair which flounced as she walked. She was trim, perfectly female and shapely, but definitely trim, thought Ian. He did not know then that she had a passion for running.

The majority of the students had already known each other for a year having done a preclinical First Bachelor of Medicine (MB) course. A few, including Peter, Maria and Ian, had joined a year later, having scored well enough in their school courses to be admitted directly to the second MB course. This meant that it would take them five years to qualify instead of the more usual six.

Although content with the choice of companions, none of them on that first day would have realised that this awful place would become a store of happy memories, or that the people sharing the corpses between them would acquire a bond, never to be totally broken.

At the end of that afternoon they were released early, because there was much book shopping and equipping to be done. Ian made his way on foot over Westminster Bridge, up Whitehall, across Trafalgar Square, and into Charing Cross Road. There, near the top of the road, stood Foyle's Bookshop, a world famous emporium of literature and other academic paraphernalia.

He bought himself copies of Gray's Anatomy, Dorling's Medical Dictionary and one or two other books. He also bought a skeleton, not a replica skeleton, but a real one. He could not carry the whole load so he took the skull and arranged to collect the remainder next day.

His lodgings were in the YMCA headquarters on the corner of Tottenham Court Road and Great Russell Street. Here he shared a room with two other medics, one from King's and the other from Guy's Hospital. The skull lived on the top of his small dressing table, and did so until he married quite a few years later. The accommodation was basic, but wholesome and cheap. It also had the virtue of being very central. There was a truly silent library, and a large common room where the whole household tended to gather for coffee. Ian and his roommates generally met there in the middle evening, having done a couple of hours in the library. Three ladies of indeterminate age often entertained, playing piano trios. There was no piped music in the building and Ian often smiled to think that these three, playing to young men of totally different tastes, nonetheless created a homely enjoyable atmosphere with their music. Money was not plentiful but some pleasures were important, so Ian took to smoking a pipe, which was very fashionable at the time. Even when he was obliged to put up with soup and a roll for his main meal, he still smoked his pipe of Gold Block.

The lads, almost penniless though they were, loved to soak up London life. At the weekends, especially, they had time to notice their surroundings. Ian would always remember awaking on Saturday mornings to the sound of a Barrel Organ, worked by an old man turning a handle. The man had a monkey, dressed in a waistcoat, who held a cloth cap out to passers by. He was pretty well rewarded for so doing. The music came in through the open window with the smell of hot rolls and coffee from a new shop around the corner which sold cappuccino with a dusting of chocolate on top. Ian had never met this before, so it soon became the habit to go there for breakfast on Saturdays.

On Friday and Saturday evenings they sometimes went to a film in the West End or, if funds would run to it, they went to the theatre. Walking back from Piccadilly to The YMCA involved passing through Soho, at that time the home of London's sex trade. Prostitutes were hounded by the police, but pretty ineffectually. One Saturday evening the boys were accosted one hundred and sixty times in the 30 minute walk home. Curiously none of them was ever seen to accept the invitation, but from then on the count was made regularly as a sport between them.

Ian's parents, staunch Methodists in Plymouth, repeatedly enquired as to which church he was attending, In fact the answer was both none and all. He was carrying out his own enquiry, visiting the Reverend Dr Donald Soper at Kingsway Hall, the Salvation Army Regent Street Citadel, where the band was superb, Westminster Abbey and even, once, Westminster Cathedral, which for a nonconformist was a huge leap to make. Actually Donald Soper captured Ian's imagination greatly, which led to the boys going often to Speakers' Corner in Hyde Park where Dr Soper, known as Dr Soap Box, dealt skilfully with the hecklers, which made for great free entertainment. He often had several hundred people around him.

However the matter of church was settled for Ian by his great love of music. He played the piano and had been encouraged to go for a King's College Cambridge Choral Scholarship. However, this would have entailed a significant delay in medical qualification, and he did not feel justified in increasing his dependency upon his parents a day longer than was necessary. Nobody in the family had trodden this path before him, so nobody pointed out that he would be missing out on a great experience.

However he did join the St Thomas' Hospital Choral Society, run in those days by Wilfred Dykes Bower, brother of the organist at St Pauls Cathedral. Wilfred, having heard him sing for a few weeks, was very supportive when Ian asked if there was a good small choir that he could join. This led to an introduction to All Saints Margaret Street, a marvellously hideous church designed by Butterworth, just behind Oxford Street, which had its own choir school. So Ian became a high Anglican, much to his parent's dismay. He sang there until the day he qualified in medicine. The choir was one of the finest in London, and sang a full liturgical mass every Sunday. The men would see the music for the first time on Friday evening, so Ian's reading skills were very quickly honed.

Ian's Aunt Jane, an awesomely large woman in every sense, had introduced him to a young lady, the daughter of a naval officer, who played the piano at least as well, perhaps a bit better than Ian. They had promised to meet in London since both were students; she at the Royal Academy of Music, but neither had got around to following up the suggestion.

Their meeting happened to be one of chance. The Dean's Office often had tickets for theatres and concerts at reduced prices. One evening Ian managed to get one of these for a concert at the Royal Albert Hall. He was standing in the queue for a drink when, from behind, somebody covered his eyes with their hands and said 'Hello, do you know who this is?'

He did not need to think about it, the voice was so distinctive. 'Hello Daphne', he replied laughingly, 'How lovely to see you, or at least it would be if I could'.

She laughed with him, removing her hands so he could indeed see her. He turned and saw that she was looked radiant. She was dressed in a skirt and pullover with a very loose roll neck on it so that it almost, but not quite slid off her shoulders. Nonetheless there was an alluring amount of skin to be seen and for the first time Ian realised how good a body she had. Daphne watched him appraising her and wondered why it had taken him so long to realise that she was a real woman.

'What are you doing here?' They asked each other simultaneously, giggling at the stupidity of the question.

'I am here to listen to Rubenstein play,' said Daphne. 'He is my idol and as he is getting so old now, I thought I should come whilst there is still the chance to hear him, other than just on records.'

'Are you living here in London?' he asked.

'No, I have a relative in Esher and live there in term time. She has a good piano for practising, so I am comfortable and well looked after. And you?'

'Oh, I live in the YMCA here in town, which is also ideal. But how do you travel? Do you drive up, or get a train?'

'I stay up for an evening most Wednesdays just to see some of the sights and go to concerts and things. Otherwise it would be possible to have a whole degree course and never be part of London. When I stay for an evening I catch the last train from Waterloo.'

'And when is that?'

'11.48 precisely.'

The bell went for the second part so each had to return to their seat. They arranged to meet in the same place after the concert had ended. Ian was not concentrating very well during the second part, because he felt suddenly drawn to this girl and wanted to see more of her. He spent the time planning what he might sensibly suggest. Concerts do not usually go on very late and this was no exception, so in fact they had a couple of hours together before the last train.

In the end he took her to a nearby Lyons Corner House for a coffee and pastry. They talked at speed and with enormous attention to each other. Each was looking intently at the other as if unable to tear their eyes away. Their knees were touching under the table and, hands apparently accidentally rested against each other from time to time. It felt very good, so good in fact that they arranged to meet the next Wednesday on the pavement outside Swan and Edgar's at the bottom of Regent Street. He escorted her back to Waterloo and waited with her until the train left, before receiving a little kiss, and then walking all the way back to Tottenham Court Road. He fell into bed at just before one o'clock, very tired but quite uplifted.

And so began a rich time in Ian's life. He had work in abundance with people he liked. He lived in the very centre of a great city, which, though dirty and still recovering from the damages of war, was beginning to regain its vibrancy. He had his Sundays busy with a truly great church choir, which incidentally paid him enough to eat rather better and to have an occasional treat. He could, and did, walk the West End with his YMCA pals until he knew central London as his home turf, and he had a talented beautiful girlfriend who, fortunately in a way, was only available one day a week, and so never became a distraction from the business of learning medicine. Swan and Edgar became their regular meeting place. Life was good.

But Ian and Daphne were both lusty young people who never saw each other in private places. Indeed other than renting a hotel room, something which would not have occurred to either of them, there was no hope of privacy. Women were not allowed, except in the public rooms, at the YMCA. There were no private places in the Academy and they were not dark alley people. They did have an occasional short time together if Daphne had managed to wangle an invitation for Ian to her Aunt's house over a weekend, but basically that led to such urgent fumbling as to be an embarrassment for both of them, especially with the ever present likelihood of aunt's premature reappearance. And so they took to park benches, which was of limited success. A quiet corner of Hyde Park on a summer evening did permit some limited petting and even an inquisitive exploration of Daphne's more private parts once or twice, but a cold frosty winter's evening with the hoar frost on their breath was, they found, a bit discouraging if for no other reason that access was rather difficult through all that clothing.

One Wednesday they considered going to the Festival Hall, but being very full of music and feeling quite lusty they opted for a film. At least one could be very friendly in the warm darkness of a cinema.

And so it happened that they were walking arm in arm across Hungerford Bridge to catch the train at Waterloo when they ran into a great swell of people coming in the opposite direction. Ian perceived that this was the audience from the Festival Hall, but the time was at least an hour later than should have been. Eventually he stopped a couple and enquired what had happened. They replied in some rapture that Albert Schweitzer, the great organist and medical missionary, had been at the concert and had played the organ for an hour afterwards. Of course almost all of the audience stayed to listen.

Not long afterwards Daphne and Ian were on a bench high above The Embankment just beside the Royal Festival Hall. Nobody else was in sight. It was about eleven at night and they had been very close that evening. They were kissing passionately and Daphne suddenly swung herself astride Ian in an overtly sexual manner. Her voluminous skirt had ridden high, exposing white thighs and she was busy rubbing his very erect manhood with her warm sex. In fact he still had his trousers buttoned and she still had her knickers, but nonetheless it was the nearest they had ever got to comprehensive love making, Daphne was rhythmical in her movements and was making soft noises in her throat when suddenly there was a loud cough just beside them, and there was a policeman leaning over the rail staring out over the river. Of course they stopped what they were doing and resumed a more demure position. After a minute or two the policeman moved off. He had said absolutely nothing, but they both knew that they had been warned. Things went downhill after that. Daphne became irritable and Ian was moody, so within a few weeks she broke it off. They never met again, but Ian did later learn that she had married and moved abroad, where she had a good concert career.

In the medical school, friendships were being forged. One of the problems with a London teaching school was that there was no student accommodation as such. There was indeed a students' club, St Thomas' House, but that was not used in the evening much by the preclinical students who were not required in the evenings except for social events. The club had changing rooms and toilets in the basement, a passable student restaurant on the ground floor, and a large lounge with a bar with a stage on the first floor. Several times a year the lounge was converted for a few days into a theatre or into a dance hall. The Temperance Seven, a new extraordinary dance band with wonderful music allied to an amazingly contrived air of decadence, was engaged to play there for one of the dances. Ian with several of his pals, none of whom danced very well anyway, having attended boys only schools, sat, mesmerised, and watched.

For about a fortnight at Christmas time the upper room became the home of St Thomas' Christmas Show, written by and played by the students themselves. Ian had heard a lot about this and knew it to be quite famous in its own right. But nothing quite prepared him for the standards displayed that first Christmas. There was a truly brilliant lady pianist who was obviously in some sort of relationship with one of the lead performers. He, it seemed, had written much of the work. Ian had no experience of the genre of Revue, but quickly became aware that many of the assembled company were familiar with it and had even performed with such august companies as The Cambridge Footlights. The humour was broad, heavily dependent on slapstick or on satire, but it was the musical standards which amazed him. He noticed that his dissecting room companion Maurice was sitting in the band playing a clarinet, and that another of his peer group played the saxophone.

The hospital had a sports ground at Cobham in Surrey and it was here that Ian spent most winter Saturday afternoons. Rugby was his game and the hospital rugby cup was a matter of huge pride to all concerned. He never quite made the first team regularly, possibly because he was a bit too light to play at senior level in the position he had played for so long at school, but he did play second fifteen games, and occasionally found his name on the first team list, if the large Welshman was not available for whatever reason.

It was on one such occasion that he received two injuries, one of which would remain for life. It was a game against the Metropolitan Police at their ground, and it had been a very wet week. The Police prop forward was the current England international and, although he was not in any way a dirty player, he was hugely fitter and stronger than Ian, giving him one of the most memorably uncomfortable afternoons of his life.

At one point Ian was tackled and both he and his opponent slipped in the deep mud, the tackler's hand riding up to the side of Ian's head. The hand was absolutely full of a cake of mud which became slapped over Ian's right ear. That evening in the customary bar camaraderie between the two teams Ian, feeling a little dizzy and still somewhat deaf, caused considerable amusement by accidentally blowing smoke from his pipe out through the right ear. Clearly the eardrum had been broken by the muddy impact. It never fully recovered.

In the same game he received a hefty kick directly on the top of his left thigh. Whilst this did not trouble too much that evening he found he had an enormous leg the next day and was admitted to the ward for treatment. There he was cared for quite beautifully by the nurses, one of whom, an ample young lady, turned out to be a close relative of Ian's idol Donald Soper. Later in their time at the hospital Ian would ask her to dance, and was delighted to find that she was magically light on her feet and quite the best dancer he had ever met.

On another rugby occasion the hospital had just won a cup match against St Mary's, which was no mean feat since St Mary's had a strong side, littered with internationals and Oxbridge blues. There was a good pub at the top of Victoria Street, not far from the bus station and the medics gathered there that evening to celebrate. Peter, Ian's classmate had been their scrum half that day and had, for some reason, become separated from them when they went to the pub. As he approached on foot, very pleased with himself no doubt, he bumped into a group of boys walking in the opposite direction. It never became clear what exactly happened, but they took exception to Peter and beat him up. They wore long draped coats, had narrow trousers and sported very greasy hair moulded to a 'quiff'. They were Teddy Boys, well known for causing trouble. On this occasion they were out of luck, because the commotion attracted the attention of those in the pub and in no time at all a great fight broke out in which several of the

Teddy Boys were hurt. Peter suffered some nasty bruising, but luckily sustained no serious physical injury.

But, despite the social distractions, this period of a medical student's life was the hardest part of the whole course, not so much because of the need for abstract reasoning or very high intelligence, but because of the graft required in committing a huge number of facts to memory. Most of the students became very dedicated, increasingly programmed in a pattern of work which involved five days working eight hours during the day and two each evening, as well as some reading over the weekend. The relentless pressure of work was more than one or two could cope with, so a few people dropped out of the course just before the hurdle which was the 2nd MB examination. This test of knowledge in Anatomy, Physiology, Biochemistry and Pathology would determine access to the clinical training three years. Ian found himself with a few odd habits such as deliberately humming out of tune whilst shaving in the morning, and piling his clothes for the next day in a very precise pile before going to sleep. It was a mild form of obsessive behaviour common to many of them. His weight fell away dramatically during this time, causing his mother much concern when he slipped home for a short break. Thereafter food parcels arrived regularly and were shared amongst his roommates.

And then, suddenly, the examination was upon them; long written papers, practical sessions in the chemistry and physiology labs, and aural tests with familiar professors and an independent external examiner also.

6

1956 Clinical Medicine 1

That two year long part of the course concerning itself with anatomy, physiology and biochemistry, known as Second MB was recognised as one of the hardest of all university programmes, simply because of the vast number of facts crammed into such a short space of time. Second MB came and went very quickly and only caused a minimal drop out from their number. All of Ian's friends remained for the rest of their degree course. Its main effect was to transfer their centre of activity from the medical school to the hospital itself. Also there was an intake from Oxford and Cambridge who had done their own second MB, but who came to St Thomas' for their clinical training.

Suddenly the YMCA seemed claustrophobic, so when the opportunity came Ian joined five of his colleagues to rent a large flat in Westbourne Street, just opposite one of the northern entrances to Hyde Park. The three bedroom flat, on the first floor, was comfortably furnished and had a large kitchen diner as well as a splendid lounge.

It quite soon became not just the home of the lads living there, but a social centre for meals and for parties. One of the weekend habits they acquired was to walk with their friends, often female, in the park and then return for tea. This involved toasting crumpets on the gas fire, using a long fork, and serving them with lashings of butter. These gatherings were accompanied by a great deal of enjoyable banter which sometimes became horseplay. After tea the party would go out to whatever evening function they had separately, or collectively, arranged. As the resident students found themselves with girlfriends, the remaining, unattached members, of which Ian was one, sometimes felt a pang of regret for their lack, but for the most part the gang was very mutually supportive and had an eye for embracing anyone who was feeling a bit left out. Attachments were most often with Nightingales, simply because they were the girls the lads saw mostly, that is except for their own peer group. Curiously, initially, there seemed to be a lack of association socially, or sexually with the peer group girls, possibly because they were thought of as being part of the 'lads'.

The professor, in an initiating lecture, informed them that, having spent their time so far studying mostly normality of structure and function, they would from now on be dealing with abnormality of both structure and function, and that this would involve meeting and dealing with the live human beings who are the sad possessors of these abnormalities, and dealing with their relatives, which is often more difficult than dealing with the patient.

'You must therefore from this moment cease to be long haired, greasy, unsavoury, students with a relaxed view of life, and become young doctors overnight, properly attired, and clean, especially the finger nails. You must wash your hands frequently, particularly after every contact examination. You must show proper respect for all of mankind, irrespective of age, gender, race or social status. You must not only care about them, but you must, by your behaviour, create in your patients the sure knowledge that you care.'

'However, when one deals daily with heartbreak in others, it is difficult not to be swept into the 'slough of despond' oneself. It is therefore crucial that you do not become too emotionally attached to those you are trying to help. A carefully nurtured balance designed to produce a high level of care, whilst retaining professional objectivity, is one of the main aims of this school. Personally I find the Nightingales are superb examples of how to achieve this.'

'You will almost certainly become deeply upset at some time in your training when a senior doctor elects not to treat someone who in theory might be treated. This will most commonly be when, in the judgement of that doctor, an individual is very close to the end of their life. At that point further treatment should be directed not at cure, but at comfort. We call it palliative care. It is new title for a process that has been accepted for centuries. To quote William Osler 'Thou shalt not kill, but there are times when thou shalt not strive too hard to keep alive.' Most importantly of all, live by the maxim 'do unto others as you would be done unto by them.' That way you will become more sensitive, more polite, and you will learn much more, because your patients will unburden themselves much more readily. Sometimes you will be shocked by what they say. Try not to show that, because it easily becomes judgemental. You will be obliged to perform embarrassing tasks of an intrusively personal nature. Learn quickly that embarrassment is an infectious condition. I know that you will be embarrassed, but if you show that to your patient you increase their embarrassment greatly. If you are dealing with a member of the opposite gender be sure that you offer a chaperone. Your patient may not accept your offer, but it should nonetheless be made.'

It was a lecture, which even years later, Ian was able to remember almost word for word.

The tuition was organised into groups or 'firms' in which a group of perhaps eight students would be attached to a special unit and its consultant. They would admit the patients, write up their notes, organise the relevant investigations and do examinations, all under the very watchful eyes of the resident doctors, and, through them, the consultant specialist. The Nightingales were ever present, whispering warnings when things were not quite being done correctly, soothing the fears of the patients, especially the women, and being very supportive.

Perhaps their greatest influence however was that their own code set such impeccable standards that the same approach rubbed off onto the students visiting their wards. In particular, decorum was observed with as much care as the situation permitted. No woman ever bared her breasts or pubes without a Nightingale to see that she was well cared for. Every now and again there would be a redistribution of firms, so that, by the end of their course, students had been given hands on experience in pretty well all aspects of the hospital's clinical work and life.

Consultants and registrars spent a good deal of time teaching, sometimes on so called teaching rounds where the whole firm - the students, all of the relevant qualified staff, and usually the ward sister, would go from patient to patient, with the consultant teaching, examining, and conferring as they progressed through the ward. Ian thought the patients often knew as much about their illnesses as the doctors after one of those sessions. Other teaching took place in lectures and seminars, at which the registrars were especially helpful. Perhaps because they did not quite have the mystique associated with a teaching hospital professor, they seemed much more approachable and therefore were often involved trying to improve understanding.

For the first year of clinical training there seemed to be more free time, perhaps because there was less daily home study to do. Second MB was famous for its hard graft, the sheer number of facts required being overwhelming. Also it came at the end of a huge sequence of public examinations, starting at aged sixteen and going on to age twenty one or thereabouts. Quite a few of them had a mild form of burn out by then, and actually needed a break from the examination treadmill. This first year in the hospital itself, offered just that, a break from continual examinations and a chance to live a little.

In the summer of 1957, very early in his clinical training, Ian was working in the Casualty Department late one evening when a slim man in a tail suit appeared. He had crushed a finger in his car door and needed a relatively minor repair. On filling in the needful documents Ian learned that the man was called Dennis Brain, perhaps the finest French Horn player in the world. It appeared that he had been playing a Mozart Horn Concerto in the Royal Festival Hall that evening, and the accident had occurred as he left. Ian was much too awed to do the repair himself and summoned his superior to do it, but stayed and watched, finding his idol an easy man to converse with, a person of charm and elegance. He was devastated when only a couple of months later on September 1st, Dennis Brain was killed in a car crash near St Albans, probably falling asleep at the wheel after an ill-advised long drive home in his sports car.

That particular summer Ian found himself exploring London's wonderful parks, and on one glorious Saturday morning went north from Regents Park to Primrose Hill, leaving the Zoo and the carefully tended flower beds for the higher, more open downs and broad walks of the grassy knoll that overlooked the city. He sat on that grass, smoking a pipe of Gold Block, trying to identify landmark buildings in the city below, when he suddenly noticed a runner coming up the steep hill towards him. It was a woman in a light shirt and running shorts, looking as if she meant business. As she approached he thought there was something familiar and then he recognised Maria Bellini, his student friend from the other side of the anatomy corpse. She saw him also and, as she came level with him, she threw herself on the grass beside him, grinning broadly between her gasping breathing, waiting to be able to talk. She was sweating a lot and the sweet, straw smell of her was suddenly a powerful signal to Ian, who had hardly looked at a girl since Daphne had departed. She was also pretty lightly dressed and the sweat revealed more of her than would be normal, the material of her shirt clinging revealingly to her breasts. He could not help noticing her enormous nipples, at least an inch long, which were standing very proud just now.

'Hello Ian, and what brings you here on this lovely day?'

'Well, I just like to walk and have only recently discovered how splendid it is up here.'

'Yes it is, I know. I love it here, but you should come on a frosty day, or when the fog is over the city. It is very romantic then.'

'So you come here regularly then. Why is that?'

'I live just over there' she said, pointing to the houses at the corner of the park. 'I have lived there all my life, except for a bit during the war.' Ian remembered that she commuted from home, but had never enquired more closely. He recalled that they had once walked to Waterloo Tube station together.

'And why the running kit, Maria? You seem to be taking it quite seriously.'

'I suppose I do. When I was at school I found I could never go fast enough to win the short races but I did much better the longer the race, so eventually I ended up doing Cross Country. I just loved the battle with the pain and the exhaustion. I became addicted and so I joined the Harriers as soon as I could and have been running ever since.'

'You look as if you are pretty good. Which Harriers did you say?'

'Highgate Harriers, it is not far from here you see, so I can train quite often.'

'Highgate Harriers? That's a very famous club, you must be good to be one of them.'

Well, good enough perhaps, but not in the Joyce Smith or Ken Norris class.' She clambered to her feet. 'Look,' she said, 'I know it is a warm morning, but not when you are not wearing much and are evaporating a lot of sweat. I am getting cold, so I shall go on now. You see that corner over there.' She pointed about half a mile away. 'If you just go around that corner you will find a restaurant called, surprise, surprise, 'Bellini's.' By the time you walk there I shall have got home and had a shower. I'll meet you there for a real Italian coffee, and if you are good maybe a little bite to eat. If I haven't come down by the time you arrive, just tell the staff you are with me.' With that she was gone, loping off across the park at a very good speed.

Ian followed behind sedately. He was met by a cheerful young waiter who had clearly been primed by Maria, and was sat down before a cappuccino, which was rather better than the ones he remembered from YMCA days. The waiter muttered something about Italians not drinking cappuccino so late in the day, and sure enough when a wonderfully fresh Maria appeared in a flowery summer dress and a tight belt she ordered an espresso and a glass of water. The restaurant was clearly very smart, and obviously beyond Ian's student pocket.

Maria told him that her parents were at their Soho restaurant today and that she would be eating here alone a little later, inviting him to join her as her treat, meaning of course that she did not have to pay. He gently teased her that it seemed strange to eat in the restaurant when presumably there was a perfectly good kitchen in the private quarters above. She replied that she did sometimes cook for herself, and liked to do so, but enjoyed the company in the restaurant more. She said she loved people watching and that, if he stayed for lunch, in about half an hour he might have a surprise.

'In any case,' she added mischievously, 'nice Italian girls do not invite handsome young men into their homes alone, especially when they hardly know one another.'

Ian was about to retort that he had known her for about two years when he suddenly realised that this as the very first time they had been, as it were, alone together. One or other of the students had always been present before. It suddenly felt almost as if they were strangers, not knowing what to talk about. She felt the same for they were silent for several minutes, until he became aware that she was laughing.

'This is very silly isn't it?' she said. 'I like you, Ian Plowman, and have done since we first met, but I am naturally quite shy you see, especially with boys. I went to a girls' school and do not have brothers, so our talk has always been about work, or public things; never about each other. I have wanted to know about the real you, but have never had the courage to ask. So now, this morning, I stumble over you on Primrose Hill, persuade you to come to my home, and I still cannot talk with you.'

Ian's reply was lost because just then the waiter came over and placed a menu before each of them. 'Miss Maria.' he said, 'We are going to be very busy quite soon, so if you would please order early, Chef would be grateful.'

Ian said that he did not know what to order, explaining that he had no experience of Italian food and asking her to order for him.

'Do you like pancakes, and cheese and spinach?' she asked. 'It is delicious, but quite light. I eat my main meal in the evening, so this is just to refuel after the running.' She smiled at him encouragingly.

He did not know whether or not he would like those things but was perfectly content to let her be in control, so he nodded his assent.

'Giuseppe, I think we will have the Crespelle please, and a half bottle of Rosso Di Montpulciano. It is a bit lighter than the Nobile, and will not put us to sleep this afternoon.' She placed the order with all the aplomb of someone to whom these surroundings and these choices were every day events and always had been. To her it was normal. To Ian it was a new insight into this girl whom he had known, yet not known, for some time.

Whilst the meal was being prepared he learned about her parents'flight from Mussolini's Italy, her birth, right here in London. He learned about the war, including both her father's internment and her own evacuation to Somerset. She did not tell him about Uncle Andreas. That was still too tender to talk about. But she went on about enjoying Somerset and how difficult it was coming back to crowded, bombed out London, and to secondary school in Edgware. But then, she brightened and admitted that she had done extremely well academically, and said how very proud her father was when she got into medical school, especially St Thomas'. 'You see, nobody in our family had ever been to university before' she said. 'And here I was, a Mediterranean, Catholic girl being admitted to university here in London. It was not quite real.'

'And how was school in Edgware.' he asked.

'Oh, it was very good really. It is quite a famous school and I was lucky to get in, but I had a wonderful time. Compared with the homely atmosphere of a village school in Somerset it was just amazing. So many cultures there, full of Jews of course,' she said, smiling wryly. 'But, you see, we Catholics and Jews get on very well together. They are a warm and passionate people and very clever, many of them. I am sure they dragged me along with them academically. We even joined in each other's religious ceremonies, just to show we supported each other, I guess; each feeling like outsiders, especially the Italian children who were here in the war. It was not good to be Italian in London in the war.' She was silent awhile, her face, quite still. He did not wish to intrude upon her.

'And now, what about you Ian?' she asked, throwing her mood to one side and smiling again. 'I will order some real ice cream for dessert and you can talk to me whilst I eat mine and yours goes all runny.' They giggled and she ordered. The Italians gave many things to the world. One of the best was truly splendid ice cream.

'There is not so very much to say,' he began. 'Compared with you I have been a dull fellow. But we have one important thing in common, which is that I too am the first in my family to experience a university education.'

'I know only a few generations of my family, but we were fishermen in Devon and Cornwall, though my mother's maiden name was of French origin, I suspect from the Channel Islands some generations ago. I was brought up in Plymouth, in a street close to the docks and to the harbour, which is in an area called Plymouth Hoe. It was called Pier Street, which tells you exactly what sort of location. By the time I arrived my family had long since ceased being sailors and were civil servants and shop keepers. The street was of Victorian three storey houses, some quite small and a few quite spacious. My family was strongly

Protestant of the nonconformist kind, which is common in the West of England. They were quite strict, especially when it comes to alcohol.' He said, raising his glass to drain it before starting the dessert. In fact he had never tasted alcohol before becoming a student and was still not quite able to manage a whole pint of beer, even in the rugby club.

'I suppose we were Methodists. Certainly John Wesley was an important person in our folklore. I too was evacuated from Plymouth during the war, but with the difference that my parents came with me.' He smiled at the ludicrous suggestion that a five year old could control his parents' movements, but in fact, although he did not know it, he was not far from the truth. His father had accepted a work transfer specifically because he had young children and was too close for comfort to a big naval base.

'Anyway, we went to Cullompton in Devon, almost on the Somerset border, not more than 20 miles or so from where you spent the war. I was a very late baby. My mother was forty three when I was born and father was older. As a matter of fact they have just retired and returned to their roots in Plymouth. I went to a good state school in a nearby village, but I played the piano pretty well and because of that I won a scholarship to Blundell's School in Tiverton. There I learned enough sciences to get me here. I played rugby to a reasonable standard. Mostly though, I got involved in the school music and drama. I nearly did music for a living, but my pragmatic father did not think it was a good idea unless I showed much more promise than in fact I had. But, it remains my passion nonetheless, and I sing in one of the great churches here every Sunday.'

He paused reflectively. 'You should come and listen, good Catholic or not. All Saints is so High Anglican that the services seem to be straight out of the Vatican. I am sure you will feel quite at home.'

They both laughed again. In fact laughter was increasing dramatically in their corner of the room. Just at that moment Maria nudged Ian and nodded towards the door. 'I told you that there might be a surprise', she whispered.

Three people had arrived, two men and a woman. The woman, who was clearly attached to one of the men, seemed to be very lack lustre and almost dependent upon him. The other man, who had a trilby hat, spoke to Giuseppe courteously, but with a distinctly clipped English which seemed familiar to Ian, though he could not place it.

'Who are they?' he whispered back.

'Oh come on Ian, surely you recognise them?'

'No I don't', he said. 'The man by himself seems familiar, but I am not sure about the others. 'Who are they?' he asked again.

'Well, the man alone is Noel Coward and the others are Lawrence Olivier and Vivien Leigh, who as you know are married.'

'She does not look good.'

'No, she's not good. She has been unwell in the head on and off for some years I believe.'

'Do they come here often?'

'Oh yes, this is one of Noel's favourite haunts. Would you like to come upstairs now?'

The manner in which the invitation was made, attached as it were to the observation about the famous guests disarmed Ian, but Maria stood, and with an audible swish of her skirt, moved towards the stairs, passing right by Noel Coward's table.

'Good day to you Maria,' said Noel.

'And to you Mr Coward,' smiled Maria as she led the way to the private quarters aloft.

The sitting room was quite big and very heavily furnished. There was a large window overlooking the park and the city. A sofa offered a stunning view over London. They sat on it together, just a few inches apart, each acutely aware of the other. Ian could not recall ever having been alone with a beautiful girl like this before, and did not quite know what to do.

He slowly reached to take her hand in his and brushed the back of her hand over his face. She did not resist. Then, a little later, whilst they were talking about something totally unimportant he transferred the hand to his other one and put his arm around her shoulder easing her towards him so that both were looking out over the park with their heads almost touching.

After a while she turned and kissed him fully on the mouth. It was a sweet kiss, lacking in guile, which did not invite more, but was one of the most wonderful things that had ever happened to him. The kiss went on for a long time, until she broke it off, smiled at him, and went to the bathroom. When she returned he could smell a faint smell of sandalwood from her soap. They sat, looking at each other for a little awhile, and then he reached to her blouse and began to unbutton it. He was very slow and gentle, and although she would never say so, she was willing him to go faster. He reached inside and eventually it was there, a wonderful white breast with its enormous pink nipple, so big he just had to bend over and nibble it. There was a shuddering intake of breath, as if this was entirely new to her, which it certainly was. When he looked up she had her eyes shut, but with the most peaceful smile he could imagine and her breathing was short and shallow. She eased her body lower on the sofa slightly spreading her knees a little as she did so. They stayed just like this for what seemed a very long time, but then she opened her eyes, she sat up, quietly replaced her breast inside her bra and refastened her blouse, much to his disappointment.

'I would like to see you again Ian' she said. 'I would like to see you a lot, but you must be patient with me. I am not, how shall I say? I am not experienced, and I am frightened; not of you.' she hastened to add, 'But of myself. I am Italian, and we are supposed to be a hot blooded people. I certainly feel that way today, but enough is enough for now. Let's go out for a walk to calm down a little and talk about this evening.' And so they almost ran down the stairs and out into the park again.

Maria knew herself to be in love for the first time in her life. She felt like some precious flower just opening to the rays of the morning sun. For his part, Ian was completely besotted, enveloped in her whole being, in a manner so sudden and confusing that he felt himself to be an inarticulate idiot. In fact he nearly ended the whole thing right there by blindly walking out in front of a passing car. And so began their romance, an old fashioned courtship, conducted with great joy, but mostly in the company of others, and always with a sense of restraint, almost a fear of consequences. Although they wanted to shout from the rooftops they actually behaved in a very polite, rather constrained manner, avoiding excessive public displays of affection. Over the next few months they restrained their physical exploration of each other, so that each new thing was an important milestone. Each knew where they were heading, and each knew that the arrival at their destination would bring a life altering decision. This was not a casual dalliance. There was much hugging of pillows and personal examination in those solitary beds as the momentum increased.

Of course Rosanna knew immediately that her daughter was different and, upon finding the reason, demanded to know all about him. 'And when are your Papa and I going to meet this young man of yours?' she said, 'What is he like? Is he tall and dark, and is he handsome like a good Italian boy should be?'

No Mamma, he is not very tall though he is quite broad and strong. I think he is very handsome, but he plays a rough game called rugby quite seriously and has a damaged ear and his nose is a little to one side, which spoils his looks a bit. But Mamma, he is so loving and gentle, all the girls like him.'

'So, he is a lady's man, this Ian of yours'.

'No Mamma, I said the girls like him I did not say that he has lots of girlfriends. But you must meet him. Shall I ask him to supper?'

'Of course, but make sure that Papa is not due to be in Soho when he comes. Enrico will want to meet him too.'

And so Ian was summoned to Bellini's Restaurant in Primrose Hill, not of course to the public restaurant but to the inner sanctum above.

There, standing imperiously with his back to the fireplace stood Enrico, smoking his cigar. Rosanna, after a quick effusive introduction, busied herself in the kitchen aided by an unusually nervous Maria.

'Come in my boy, sit down,' said Enrico, rather as if he was interviewing a potential staff member. Ian shook hands and sat straight backed in the proffered chair. He accepted a glass of Prosecco, finding it very agreeable. Enrico enquired about the bruise on his cheek and was told that it had been acquired that afternoon on the rugby field. This broke the ice between them because Rugby had been played at international level in Italy since 1920 but never on the scale of other European nations. Lately however, perhaps because of the allied troops stationed in Italy after World War Two, the game was coming much more to the fore. The Anglophile Enrico dreamed of the day when the Azzuris, as they were known, would come to compete with the great rugby nations.

And so the evening got off to a good start. Rosanna excelled herself in the kitchen, Maria carefully trod a fine line between being the properly brought up daughter and the young romantic, desperate to show her parents that her young lover was a real star. Ian himself became quite relaxed with the laughter, food and wine, lost all his fears and was his charming intelligent self.

As Maria walked him to the restaurant door at the end of the evening Rosanna turned to her husband and said 'What a delightful young man. I could fall for him myself.'

'He is indeed a delight, just as you say, and I could like him well enough as my son in law, but we must always remember that he is a Protestant. My daughter will never marry a Protestant. Not as long as I am alive.' Enrico sat heavily, knowing the truth of his words and totally perceiving the difficulties to come.

Rosanna sat opposite him at the table, pausing for some time to consider his statement. Good Catholic though she was, she had not anticipated quite such a dismissive view, especially from her husband, who had in many ways left the doctrines of his youth behind. She understood that, living as they did in such a cosmopolitan society it was important to preserve the central core of their culture and faith, in order not to become faceless and rootless. To her, however, there was a great difference between keeping oneself on a path, and seeking to impose one's own powerfully held axioms upon others, even one's own, modern, multicultural daughter.

Maria, rushing in from her farewell to Ian, anticipating some favourable comment from what she felt to have been a very successful evening, found them in this state; her mother, clearly upset sitting with her father whom she loved dearly, but who was looking stubbornly determined as he faced her across the room.

She stood still, taking in the scene with concern rising within her. 'What is the matter?' she asked. 'Did we do something wrong. Did Ian upset you?'

Rosanna shook her head in denial of any misdeed and looked to Enrico for an answer. He cleared his throat and, gesturing expansively with both hands, said, 'This is nothing to do with Ian himself. He seems to be everything we would wish for you. On a personal level we would approve. But you must not entertain thoughts of a permanent relationship. Enjoy this fine young man as a friend if you wish, but please do not think of him as a husband. I cannot have a Protestant son-in-law. Also, please forgive me intruding so personally, but, since we are talking of such matters, I should remind you that you are a good Catholic too, so you do not use birth control. That means that you do not have intimate relations until marriage. A baby would be a complete disaster for you. Do I make myself clear?'

'Papa! Do not say such awful things!'

'I have no choice, Maria. I do not enjoy what I am saying. I love you and seek your happiness, but in this matter I have a duty to remind you that this is our way, and it will remain our way.' His voice was trembling a bit and his lower lip twitched, not with anger, but because of the situation he found within himself. He reached out to Maria to embrace her.

She however furiously brushed him away. 'I shall marry whom I please Papa!' she cried, 'You do not own me and you have no right to demand such things. I shall decide, not you. Actually he has not asked me, and the question is not yet to be answered. For all I know it might never be asked, but if and when it is I shall decide, not you!'

'If and when it is asked, do not ask me for my blessing. It will not be given.' He growled.

She looked hard at him, and seeing an implacable determination there she flounced out of the room to her bed where she lay weeping until, much later, her mother, in her dressing gown crept in and sat a long time on the bedside stroking her hair. Finally Rosanna suggested she took herself properly to bed and that things might look better in the morning.

The effect of this exchange on Maria and Ian was simply to make her invitations to him to come to her home in Primrose Hill much less frequent than she would have liked. Their centre of interest shifted to Ian's student flat, with all the tolerances needed to make a large collection of young men and their girls rub along well enough together. Maria did not explain nor did she need to, because Ian had accepted that her parents were lovely, that he had got on well, and did not need to enquire further. He never knew about her father's ultimatum.

Later that year Imre arrived. He had Slavic features, was very thick set, and did not smile very much to start with. Also his English was not very good. Maria found herself drawn to him perhaps because of her own origins and so, one lunch time, she made it her business to sit with him in the canteen, sharing their meagre lunch. Maria learned that Imre was Hungarian, studying medicine in Budapest when the Russians had re-entered Hungary in October. He was one of the lucky ones he said. 30,000 of his countrymen had died and some 200,000 had fled to the West. Imre had kissed his mother goodbye and walked 200 miles to the border, eventually being accepted by distant relatives in London and gaining permission to resume his studies. He soon became a popular figure, taking a very active part in hospital social life and in the Christmas Show. He made several passes at Maria, but each time she gently rejected him, knowing her heart was already given. She later laughed when she learned that Imre made similar passes to every girl in his environment.

7

1957&8 Clinical Medicine 2

St Thomas' Hospital Summer Ball took place in the Royal Festival Hall, just a few hundred yards away, along The Embankment, which was the name of the bank of the river between Westminster and Waterloo bridges. It was a truly grand affair which started at eleven at night and went on until six the next morning. There was a grand meal in the middle. Ian guessed that there might be a thousand or more people there, from the Dean and his wife, many professors and consultants, administrators, nurses to impecunious students. All were determined to enjoy themselves.

The men were mostly in dinner jackets, though some wore tails, and the ladies all had ball gowns, often seeming to sheath them from bust to toe like some Greek goddess, an effect which was enhanced by the way they piled their hair high on their heads and stuffed their bosoms into heavily padded and pointed bras. Maria looked absolutely fabulous in a scarlet dress which set off her dark hair and Mediterranean high cheeks wonderfully. She wore an antique cameo of the most intricate design on a gold pendant, which she told Ian was on special loan from her mother, having originally belonged to her grandmother.

Ian thought he might burst with pride at being with such a wonderful woman, and indeed they were very much an attraction that evening, with their friends almost causing a log jam of people in their desire to be with them.

Dancing took place in several areas, each one magically sound-proofed from the other so that there was no conflict. Victor Sylvester provided the main band, ably reinforced by the Royal Artillery Dance Band which was very good and, for those who fancied a contrast, there was the, now world famous, Temperance Seven, whom Ian noted had grown to nine in number in the years since he had first heard them.

Having danced until exhausted, the company took breakfast on the terrace overlooking the River Thames and watched the summer sun rise over the city. The occupants of Westbourne Street, with their partners and a number of other friends made their way back home to flop on beds, chairs, or even the floor for a couple of hours sleep. Several of them were expected at work by nine in the morning. Ian lay on his narrow bed, spooning with Maria, but in a very chaste manner since there were at least four others in the room.

The weather that summer was lovely and there were many happy social events as well as some increasingly intense work. Final examinations were not too far off and minds were beginning to focus on books and lectures. Quite a few sessions were taken actually working in hospital departments in the evenings and overnight. The students were involved in periods 'on take' when their firm would be in receipt of the emergency admissions.

Only a week or two later Ian and Maria found themselves alone in Westbourne Street. They had both been at the Hospital Sports day in Cobham, having driven there in Maria's car, but the others had wanted to go to a dance which somehow did not appeal, so they had made their way happily back to town, stopping only to have an early supper in Kensington on the way. It was during that supper that the easy public behaviour of the day subtly changed. The conversation became much more focussed on themselves, their likes and dislikes, their family relationships, and their declared attitudes to romantic matters. At one point Maria became animated. She clasped his knee between hers under the tablecloth, and her tongue seemed more visible than usual. For her part, Maria noticed that Ian touched hands, arms and face as if to enhance a discussion and once, briefly reached under the table quite high up her thigh. Subsequently Ian would look back on this meal and realise that both knew that their great moment had come.

After supper, they drove almost wordlessly home across the park and up to the flat. Ian took her gently by the hand directing her, not into the sitting room but, unspoken, to his bedroom. It was a midsummer evening, warm and still light. They stood facing, looking deeply into one another, smiling gently. He kissed her long and intensely and she responded, pressing her lower belly against him firmly. Very slowly he unbuttoned her dress, slid it off her shoulders so that it dropped to the floor and then unbuckled her bra. She was topless, standing with her hands at his neck with those wonderful breasts lifted and the long nipples he had known about since that chance meeting on the hill, thrust up towards him. He bent to kiss them and she gently pulled him to her, sitting and then falling together onto the top of the bed.

There she attacked his clothing in a wild, unrestrained manner, throwing off his shirt and undoing his trouser belt to explore below. In no time he was naked and she held him in her hand, the first time she had done such a thing, and marvelled, at his thing which was so firm, and which seemed reluctant to remain still. She knelt beside him, surveying her man, as if to fix this memory within her whilst he lay still and watched her. She noted the wavy hair, the wry smile, the deep blue eyes and the crooked nose almost as if seeing them for the first time, though they had been dating each other for a year. Then she bent slowly forward and kissed him on the belly, gently moving south until she took the great member into her hand, feeling the width of it and riding gently up and down it, but only for a few moments, because Ian suddenly said 'If you go on like that I shall pop much too soon.' and, laughing, he sat up, turning her onto her back on the bed.

In his turn to look and admire, Maria lay on the bed, feeling his gaze upon her, almost as if with a physical touch. Her instinct was to cover her naked breasts with her hands, but he gently eased them away placing them carefully one on each side of her head so that she appeared fully stretched. Her underwear was of white silk and he noted her knickers were not tight around her thighs, but the crutch was pulled high so that the material clearly showed the outline of her great divide. Somewhere in his mind he knew they were called French knickers. He kissed her again, a long, reassuring, loving kiss, and said 'Maria Bellini, I love you more than I ever imagined I could love anything.'

'And I too love you Ian, with all my heart.' she murmured in reply.

He began to caress her, wanting to register the feel of every bit of her, her hands, her arms, her neck and ears, the toes and feet. Ian made his way around this wonderful body, deliberately taking his time before coming to those knickers.

He slid his hand under the waistband feeling downwards until he had a lovely soft down under his fingers. Maria's head tilted backwards, the head rolling side to side as if in protest and her knees locked firmly together; her breath in short sharp intakes, as if in shock, but she did not actually resist.

He gently eased lower, around the corner and underneath, where he found her to be very warm and damp, a welcome that contrasted with her tight knees and thighs. Eventually, having caressed her for a little while he took her knickers off, with no resistance now he noted, and gently spread her knees, displaying her sex for him to see and to feel. Instinctively he felt for the little pleasure button he knew existed and was taken aback by her intense response when he touched it and started to rub in a gentle rhythmical manner.

'Oh God, Ian that is wonderful!' she gasped, 'Go on, go on, please.' Her voice trailed off in a great shudder and a few minutes later she was engulfed in a convulsion which went on for some moments and which led her to writhe completely out of Ian's touch. She cried out in some primitive, unintelligible cry that echoed around the room.

When she subsided she was sobbing in emotional release. All of those months of desire brought to a climax such as she had never experienced. It was just like a volcano erupting, releasing momentous tension from her inner self. She reached for him and hugged him to her as fiercely as she could and then guided his manhood towards its natural home. It slid past the dampness of her portal but just at the very moment when he must thrust inside her she suddenly cried out. 'No! Ian, no! I cannot do this. I am sorry my darling, so sorry, but I cannot do this.' and pushed him to one side. They lay side by side, a weeping Maria, truly upset at her outburst, and a now drooping Ian, puzzled and hurt by the rejection.

After quite a long time she said 'I promised to wait until my wedding. I promised, and at that last moment I knew I had to keep that promise, or at least to wait until I am engaged and with a wedding soon. Are we going to marry, Ian? I think we love each other enough, don't you?'

'Yes, we do,' he replied.

He lay there thinking carefully, just to be absolutely sure, then, finding nothing but certainty in his mind, he turned onto an elbow, looking her in the eye and said simply 'Maria Bellini, will you be my wife?'

'Yes, yes Ian. I will', she replied solemnly, and then almost as an afterthought. 'Of course you will become a Catholic.'

Ian was very still, feeling a great chill in his heart.

'No, Maria. I cannot do that. You know that I was brought up a nonconformist, and have travelled a long way, much to my family's distress, by attending a high Anglican church. To go further and embrace Catholicism would be to take me away from my family for ever. Please do not ask me to do that.'

'Don't you see Ian? It is not just me that asks. It is my family also. They would never agree to their daughter marrying a Protestant. You could take instruction quite soon and be accepted within quite a short time. I think I could wait for you until then', she smiled at her gentle humour, which was not funny to him at all.

He lay beside her, utterly desolate, knowing in that darkest recess of a mind which we call a soul, that despite their love they had reached an obstacle which would defeat them. 'No, Maria. Please accept once and for all that I cannot do this thing, anymore than you could make love to me just now. I am very sorry too.' It seemed to Ian that despite the 'just now' there was suddenly a great distance from what they had been to what they had become.

The two naked lovers were still for a very long time; their skins touching in places but their spirits shrinking into a truly desolate loneliness, until suddenly, Maria turned to face him and said 'Ian, we came very close in our passion to risking a pregnancy which would have spelled disaster for both of us. We were carried away because I do love you, and I know you love me. We both know that, but if God and family mean that we may not marry, then we must find a way of being friends.'

Ian looked up at her with the greatest sadness, 'What you ask is not possible for me, Maria. It would be like being in a sweet shop and never eating one, or like being totally deaf in a concert. I would go crazy. No Maria, we are defeated by our backgrounds and cannot bridge the gulf. Not now, not ever. This must be the end for us.'

She looked as if he had slapped her, but with a great sigh she rose, dressed quickly, and left without another word passing between them.

Very shortly after that a saddened, rather withdrawn Ian moved out of the wonderful flat that had seen so much happiness with his friends, and with Maria, and went into a bedsit just opposite the hospital. This was very convenient for he was at that stage of the course which was associated with much more involvement in the hospital's life at any time of day or night. The work intensity was building again towards final examinations, so easy access to the wards and to outpatient clinics was a great asset. He became something of a loner, except for regularly having a half pint of ale with his peers in St Thomas' House around six o'clock at night. He worked hard and perhaps neglected himself a bit, so when the Asian 'Flu came in 1958 he was an early victim, being so ill that he was admitted to the ward. One of his peers a couple of beds away died of that 'flu. He was one of the first fifteen rugby forwards, as fit as could be and as strong as an ox.

Ian was interested in surgery, becoming an adept assistant to the consultants and registrars, holding retractors, peering deep into open abdomens and learning basic techniques. He repaired wounds so neatly that eventually the surgeons allowed him to close some incisions on his own, with just a watchful eye from his tutor.

It was in the obstetric unit that he really felt at home. He related very well to the resident registrar, and to the senior midwives, so he learned quickly and well. The first baby he delivered was the seventh child of an older mother. The midwives chaffed him gently that he nearly dropped this slippery, grease covered creature who arrived so suddenly into the world that he felt a little like a cricketer fielding in the slips. He was soon to learn that this was not however, the usual way of things.

In fact he had a number of alarming experiences at that time, one of which occurred when attached for a week to the district midwife, attending a birth in a small terrace house a mile or so from the hospital. Home births were common at that time, especially for second and third babies if the first confinement had gone well. This lady had gone into quite a rapid labour with the baby's head still high so that when the waters broke there was a great gush and, to the midwife's dismay, there was a loop of cord showing externally. This was a potential disaster because, as labour progressed, and the head descended the cord would be squeezed tight, cutting off the baby's blood supply and causing a still birth. Ian was dispatched to the nearest phone box to summon help, and before long his registrar friend arrived in an ambulance and with a second midwife. The registrar quickly decided that a Caesarean Section was needed and so they loaded the mother into the ambulance and raced back to the Hospital, radioing for the operating theatre to be made ready as they went. In order to keep the pressure off the cord the registrar had his right hand inside mother trying to hold the advancing head up, a most difficult thing to do, painful for both the mother and the registrar. It was visiting time when they arrived and the party had to process rapidly, almost running, down that long corridor to the obstetric unit under the eyes of large numbers of hospital visitors. Despite the decorous use of blankets it did not take much imagination for the onlookers to understand what was happening. They managed to get a live baby, and a couple of days later a happy family celebrated with the registrar, midwives and Ian, laughingly saying that it was a story to tell their grandchildren.

Perhaps to ease his pain over the loss of Maria, Ian became more involved in his music. He had always found it to be a wonderful antidote to the emotional rollercoaster of the medical world. In his last year as a student he joined with many others to present a concert in the Royal College of Surgeons Great Hall. The United Hospitals Choir and Orchestra gave a programme under the direction of a young man called Colin Davis, which included a piece by the Russian composer Borodin, himself a medical man. Ian found the camaraderie of the rehearsals and the excitement of the performance lifted him somewhat from the pit into which his emotions had fallen. Much later he reflected that perhaps without this lift he would have found it impossible to prepare properly for his exams.

Maria meanwhile truly struggled. She had driven home on the night of the crisis in tears of hurt, anger and humiliation and with the utter desolation of great loss. There was no way to reach the private quarters that did not involve passing through public areas of the restaurant and since she could not walk through in the state she was in, she pulled into a bay in Regents Park. She sat there for several hours in the most abject misery she had ever known. Eventually, embarrassed by a caring enquiry from a patrolling policeman, she drove home. It was of course impossible to tell her parents the whole truth about the evening, but they needed to know that the romance with Ian was over and would not be renewed.

In the core of her distress was a seed of anger, anger directed partly at herself, a little at Ian for his intransigence, but, importantly, anger mostly directed against her father for being so stubborn that, in her eyes at that moment, he had spoiled her life. Maria knew perfectly well that, but for her father's loudly stated views, the outcome of the evening would have been completely different. Although she was cross with herself for listening, she knew that her twenty years of regarding Papa's wishes as the law had imprinted her too much to be resisted on so important a matter. But the spell was broken. She also knew that her relationship with her father would never be quite the same again, and that never again would his prejudices determine her behaviour. She would find somewhere to live. She guessed that even that suggestion would be opposed, but to her at this moment home was too stifling to contemplate.

In fact both parents were aghast at the state she was in and distressed for all concerned, including themselves, when they perceived that religion had fractured the relationship and that Ian would not be visiting again. They had come to value him highly and genuinely grieved the loss. As part of the new understanding they realised that their daughter had grown up and needed to be her own person with her own quarters, so they did not resist when Maria said she had found a small flat in Chelsea, right on the riverside.

Enrico, having checked the place out, helped her move and paid for the first six months rent. He drove home, sad that she did not say goodbye when he left her there to start out alone.

Maria did the only thing she sensibly could, she worked hard. Avoiding Ian at the hospital became an art form. She became very skilled at sensing his nearness, declining to lunch with the gang in St Thomas' house, deliberately choosing to do duty rosters which would not bring them into contact. But the problem was that this led to isolation from all of her old friends. She became something of a waif, always on the fringe of things, losing a lot of weight, not eating adequately and no longer doing her therapeutic running.

One day, after several weeks in this purgatory she was lunching on a sandwich whilst perched on a bench on a riverside walkway outside the hospital. She was watching the barges pulling huge cargos stacked on lighters going up and down the river. The Thames still being tidal at this point, it was easy to tell which way the tide was running. Heavily laden barges would struggle slowly against the tide, especially going upriver, but going with the tide and the stream downriver, they flew past at an amazing speed. Maria had always liked this seat, staring across the capital's commerce to its legislature in the Palace of Westminster. Sometimes she had crept into the Public Gallery to listen to debates. Today, as in previous weeks she could not rid her mind's eye of two naked bodies in Ian's bed and the pain of that awful parting. Her reverie was interrupted when she became aware that someone else was also on her bench. She looked up to see Peter Brown, the chirpy pal of Anatomy Room days surveying her with concern. They had never been close friends, but were always on good terms. Peter's sense of humour defied anyone to take him too seriously so he had become the unofficial jester of the group. As a result few had realised that his humour was a mask for a very sensitive, caring person.

'Will you come to the theatre tonight Maria?' he asked, having surveyed her carefully for a full minute. 'We have a spare ticket for Flanders and Swann doing 'At the Drop of a Hat'. Several of us are going and wondered if you would like you to come with us.'

She shook her head in refusal, saying that she had work to do, but his smile, her awful loneliness, and the knowledge that she would be among friends eventually enabled him to persuade her. She did not know that Peter had been 'volunteered' for the task by others who thought, correctly, that she was in trouble with herself, with the world and potentially therefore with her career.

And so the rehabilitation of Maria Bellini began. Gradually the others drew her back into their midst, always being careful not to create a situation in which Ian and Maria would have to face each other. Very soon the glorious Maria began to reappear. She even began to laugh and to put on a little of the weight she had lost. Certainly she became more like her old self.

Several of the unattached men tried their luck with her, some delightfully subtly with exciting invitations to events, a few quite crudely with invitations of an altogether more basic nature. Some attempted to put an arm around her. One tried to hold hands. All were unsuccessful, politely, but without a smile, rejected. Maria had a sign around her neck, hung so obviously as to be almost visible. It read 'I am not available'.

8

1959 Finals

Part of her rapidly increasing awareness led Maria to become a political person. She was rather left wing, at least in comparison with her more traditional peer group, but her trips to Speakers' Corner with Ian, and her close following of the parliamentary debates presented her with a very clear image of the world, a world which she felt was overdue for change.

The huge public issue of the day was Nuclear Disarmament. Western governments took the pragmatic view that nobody would start throwing 'Weapons of Mass Destruction', as they would be called forty years later, if such a thing would inevitably lead to self destruction through an overwhelming retaliation. Hence the great powers were busy arming themselves to the teeth with nuclear missiles, which were based in so many different sites in the world that it would be impossible to destroy them all in one strike. One of the problems with such a stance is that it was necessary to keep a fair number of these weapons on someone else's soil, simply because of the vast distances to potential and presumed targets, and there was difficulty in powering delivery vehicles, mostly rockets, to carry the destructive warheads. Five nations were known to have nuclear capability, United States, Russia, United Kingdom, France and China. They were engrossed in what the media called The Arms Race.

The Western powers' policies in respect of nuclear confrontation were not, however, universally accepted within their own boundaries. An increasing number of powerful voices expressed opposition to the government position. Aneurin Bevan from his Ebbw Vale constituency was initially a big voice in the anti-nuclear programme, but early in 1957 he changed his mind and supported the government's view of 'defence through strength'. His political place was to a large extent taken by Michael Foot, later to become for a short time the leader of the British Labour Party.

Foot gathered around him a large and influential cohort of academics, politicians, actors, musicians, and others who enjoyed a public presence, There was a large gathering in Westminster Hall followed by several thousand protestors outside Downing Street, and then over the Easter Weekend 1958, several thousands more people undertook a four day march from Trafalgar Square to The British Atomic Weapons Research Establishment at Aldermaston, over 50 miles away. From that movement the Campaign for Nuclear Disarmament was formed and grew into a national protest movement which exercised considerable influence for many years.

Maria, enthralled by the 1958 march, was determined to join the planned march for Easter 1959. This was despite the proximity of final examinations, which led most of her colleagues to forgo the holiday break in favour of study. On Good Friday, she duly presented herself, all kitted out with sleeping bag, anorak, walking boots, and spare socks to join the 60,000 who would, that year, undertake the journey. The vast procession wound its way slowly and peacefully from London to the Oxfordshire countryside. Periodic breaks were associated with passionate speeches from prominent people. The nights were in shelters such as church halls or schools. Conditions were primitive but not particularly unpleasant and the company was mostly good natured and intelligent. In fact intelligence was perhaps the one common denominator. They may have been naive, but these marchers were not stupid. They believed that the known world was under the extreme threat of global war which might destroy the human race, or at least the more advanced civilised states on Earth. They reasoned that political systems come and go; that governments, even in one party States, change and evolve as all human life does, and that the destruction of a whole civilisation was too great a price to pay to avoid one's political enemies. They adopted a symbol similar to the Mercedes motor company symbol, based on the semaphore for CND. Maria possessed an anorak emblazoned with that symbol right up to her forties. She found the common goal of the campaigners very therapeutic in her fragile emotional state, enjoying the undemanding company and the sense of purpose they all shared.

Enrico and Rosanna were busy trying their very best to reach out to her in her angry grief, and to mend fences with her. Slowly but surely they enticed her back into the family, firstly Rosanna met her on unemotional ground such as summer sporting events, or going for a meal after Sunday Mass at St Peter's in Clerkenwell. Then she made an emotional return to Primrose Hill for the after mass Sunday lunch. The healing, though far from complete, had truly begun. Rosanna and Enrico knew the tide had turned when Maria again went for a run on Primrose Hill.

Medical Final examinations in 1959 were spread over several weeks. There were, of course, not only demanding written papers in each of the subjects, but also the practical examinations, involving patients themselves, which were crucial. Ian was faced in one of these by an elderly man with a hard lump in the left lower jaw bone. It was obviously a tumour of some sort, but what sort? The man concerned did not look particularly unwell but admitted that he needed to get up at night quite often and felt sleep starved. Ian suddenly realised that he was talking to someone with a prostate cancer which had spread to his bones, in particular to the jaw. He was able to discuss the situation quite knowledgeably with the external examiner.

On another day his obstetric practical test involved identifying a breech baby just before birth time and a discussion about the issues of trying to turn the baby, or accepting the way things were, and deciding how best to deliver the baby.

All of the students had similar experiences. They realised that the examiners had collected interesting or unusual situations for them to use as a basis for question and discussion. They learned that if the patients related well to the student, they would drop little helpful hints about their conditions, but if the student got off on the wrong foot with the patient, no help was forthcoming.

The fearful day arrived when the results were posted on the notice board. Ian passed with a distinction in pathology. He could not but help look towards the top of the alphabetical list which clearly read Bellini, Maria E — Pass. Great was the celebration in St Thomas' House that night, but Ian was overcome with a terrible headache and retired to his lonely bedsit to sleep.

Hospitals around the land were geared to a regular influx of junior house officers in jobs that lasted just six months in most cases. Very often the start date was but a few days after finals results were declared. Unless one had considerable private means there was an absolute imperative to earn a living because any grant aid stopped immediately. So it came about that Ian was not part of the goodbyes. He missed out on the qualification celebrations and by the time he emerged all his peers had gone off to start their first paid jobs as proper doctors.

Many, if not most of the new doctors, had already applied for and been appointed to jobs. Some of the very best were retained in their own training hospital; perhaps half a dozen of the thirty newly qualified would stay at St Thomas'. The remainder were cascaded all over the land, and a few overseas. Two of Ian's peers went directly to Canada and remained there all of their working lives. Ian had fixed his job at the newly enlarged and redeveloped Freedom Fields Hospital in Plymouth, where he had family connections. The hospital, originally a work house, stood on top of a hill and Ian enjoyed unforgettable views from his window in the residents' block. He stayed there a year until the summer of 1960, when he returned to London to be the resident obstetrician/ gynaecologist in Lambeth, close by and with strong links to his alma mater at St Thomas'.

Maria was even more fortunate. She was appointed junior house surgeon at the John Radcliffe in Oxford. Neither knew what had happened to the other.

9

1960 John Radcliffe, Oxford

Maria settled well into the routine in Oxford. She was exhilarated to be on the staff of one of the world's great hospitals, brimming in innovation, at the very heart of medical advance. As a resident house physician she had a lot to do with the new Intensive Care Unit. This was an entirely new concept, or so it was thought.

The fact is that it was not new. In the Crimean War, in the 1850s, Florence Nightingale observed that battlefield injuries carried a forty per cent mortality. By inserting medical teams actually on the front, she reduced the mortality to two per cent. Somehow nobody had truly grasped the import of this until, in 1953, there was a major Poliomyelitis epidemic in northern Europe, an epidemic which was claiming a huge number of lives in Copenhagen.

The Medical Director there realised that a lot of people were dying of respiratory failure in the acute stage of their illness, simply because they could not breathe. He guessed that if they could be maintained alive for a couple of weeks many of them might survive. After talking to his anaesthetic department he instigated a regime of continual respiration through a tracheotomy, (an artificial hole made in the windpipe) and a rubber bag, rhythmically squeezed by a relay of volunteers. The volunteers were often medical students, who found the role taxing in every way. However, the result of this basic, simple procedure was that, of the hospital admissions with Polio, the mortality dropped from eighty to fifteen per cent very quickly.

The appreciation that there were many instances in which, if you can sustain life over the critical initial period, mortality rates might be amazingly improved, spread rapidly around the world. During the 1960s intensive care units sprang up in all major hospitals, and were used mainly for people with heart attacks, but also, for example, in cases of severe accidents.

Thus it came about that Dr Maria Bellini received training, and acquired expertise in the art of sustaining life during medical crises. It was a heartbreaking job, because the technology was unsophisticated, labour intensive, and she was often trying to achieve the impossible. But it was also perhaps the most exciting, emotionally rewarding job imaginable.

Late one evening Maria fainted on the ward. The other staff rushed to her aid, amongst them a young orthopaedic registrar, whose accident victim patient Maria had been trying to sustain alive for some twenty four hours. They carried her to a trolley and realised quickly that she was not ill, but was exhausted through lack of sleep and food. Her deputy was called in to carry on whilst Maria had a break and Michael O'Leary, for that was the registrar's name, helped her to her quarters. He arranged for some supper to be brought up before gently leaving her to put herself to bed. She slept for 14 hours.

When they next met, Maria thanked him for his care, and thus began a friendship that grew steadily over the period of her job.

Michael was very Irish, very clever and a little bit unpredictable, a trait which struck a chord with the Italian in Maria. Eventually he began to ask her out to meals in Oxford's numerous restaurants, and to the Oxford Playhouse, where they saw a Brian Rix Whitehall Farce. On one occasion, late in November, he took her to Covent Garden Opera House, London, to listen to the great Australian Joan Hammond sing Aida, with Michael Langdon as Ramfis. That night they stayed with Enrico and Rosanna in Primrose Hill, in separate rooms of course. Maria's parents were quietly pleased to see that she was beginning to live again, and especially noting that the new young man was an Irish Catholic. They observed, and hoped, that this time all would be well.

But Maria was not fully recovered from Ian. She still dreamed of him, still imagined him in highly erotic images which embarrassed her, but quietly pleased her also. She was physically slow to respond to Michael, and doubted if that would ever change. She told herself over and over again that this man was right for her. She enjoyed his company greatly, laughed at his jokes, had similar tastes to him, and liked everything about him immensely, but he was not Ian. The Earth did not move when he entered the room. She could take him or leave him. She certainly was not addicted.

Michael had a passion for inland waterways and kept a small boat on the Thames. When the weather was good they would go for an evening potter along the river, usually going upstream towards Fairford. There was a good pub there where they were sometimes to be found enjoying a meal in the open on the riverside. They were a very gregarious pair and soon became part of a large circle of friends, based both in the hospital, and on the university campus also. In common with their time, challenging conversation with like-minded people was a favourite occupation, so that it came about that they both felt comfortable, and that they became regarded as an item by their friends.

The work of John Charnley in Wrightington Hospital fascinated Michael. Charnley, an innovative, supremely talented, orthopaedic specialist had become frustrated with bureaucracy in Manchester, and had persuaded the authorities in Wrightington to set up a special unit for him to work on prosthetic hips. He perceived that much of the failure of previous attempts was due to friction between the elements of the new hip, especially of course between the head of the femur and its socket. Charnley was experimenting with plastic, and just now in 1960 he was working with Teflon. He was looking for a tough material with a low coefficient of friction. Michael knew that this was where his future must be and persuaded his Danish senior to let him do some work of his own on replacement hips. It was clear to Maria that her friend was a rising star in the orthopaedic world.

Inevitably they gradually became ever closer physically until, one evening, in his room, they had full blown sex, the first time in Maria's life. She did not cry out as she had in Ian's bed two years previously, and she could not honestly swear that it was anything particularly special, but she was pleased with the warm glow from the act of giving, and knew that she had pleased him also. But, in Maria's mind, perhaps because of her faith, it meant that she had crossed the Rubicon. There was no going back now. She was going to marry her very good friend Michael, who was safe. They would look after each other, always.

Her parents were delighted, as were Michael's. The wedding was arranged for June 21st 1961 in St Peter's Italian Church Clerkenwell, that church which had played so large a part in the Bellinis' life ever since Enrico and Rosanna arrived in 1930. It was the place Maria had worshipped all her young life apart from the spell in Somerset.

The Italian community in London turned out in force, to be joined by an almost equally numerous and outrageous crowd from Dublin. The service was conducted with all the ceremony appropriate for such an occasion. Maria and Michael took their vows in solemn sincerity, meaning every word they uttered. On the church steps for the photographs after the service Maria looked like a goddess in her long white dress with the train tastefully arranged around her. Michael was as proud as a peacock, as well he should be. Rosanna shed many tears of joy, surrounded as she was by all of the people she loved in this world. Some of her tears were for brother Andreas, who would never see such wonderful things again. Enrico too had a problem with his eyes, and needed to use his handkerchief once or twice. He could not help thinking of how long ago it seemed since he went to Jacob's rescue in Orta.

As a very wealthy fashionable Italian restaurateur, he spared nothing for the wedding breakfast. It was quite a party. Some of Maria's medical friends from St Thomas' noted that Ian was not present and wondered if he had been invited, but were too polite to enquire. In fact he knew nothing about it.

Michael and Maria honeymooned in the Italian lakes and did not fail to visit Orta, Verona nor even the little village of Bardi with its sad memories, just to see where the adventure had begun, thirty years previously.

As soon as she returned from her honeymoon, Maria's job in Oxford having come to an end, she obtained a junior post in the anaesthetic department in The Lambeth Hospital, Brooke Drive, London. Michael remained in Oxford, for his was a two year post. They knew that time together would be limited, but this was common to all of their young colleagues. They just did their best to arrange the duty rosters so that, at least, they had every other weekend together. Maria's job was for only six months.

Meantime, Ian was working hard in Plymouth, a city he loved, but which, strangely, always deprived him of energy, making even ordinary things feel like hard work. The city had suffered greatly in the war with complete destruction of the city centre. At the end of the war the wonderful Guildhall was just an empty shell and one could see all the way from Drakes Circus to Union Street and beyond, without a single building standing in the way.

Reconstruction meant an entirely new city centre with large shops like Dingles and a great dual carriageway, almost like central Paris, leading directly across the city behind the famous Plymouth Hoe. Ian's old family home in Pier Street, now owned by folk he did not know, had miraculously survived, though there were a number of gaps where houses had been bombed, one of them almost next door. On his evenings off, Ian loved to walk along the sea front, all the way from the Yacht Club past the old Ladies' Swimming Pool and the Lido to the Barbican, where he would stand at the Mayflower Steps, imagining himself to be a Pilgrim Father on his way to America. From there he could look out to sea past Drake's Island to the breakwater and the channel. There was a lot of naval activity, and just to his left he sometimes heard a deep throated roar as a flying boat lumbered across the sea and climbed out of the water like some giant aquatic bird. He certainly felt the pull of his sailor ancestry.

Shortly after his arrival he received an invitation to Sunday supper from his parents' long standing friends, the Lindsays. The Reverend John Lindsay was the Devonport Methodist minister and was also a keen musician. He used to play violin duets with his wife Charlotte as a young man, but by the time he was twelve, their eldest son, George was better than his father. So George was given the family position of first violin and took up the viola instead. Before long their second son, Jeremy, outperformed his father with the viola, so John Lindsay moved down to the cello. Before too long, Rachel their daughter became more accomplished than he with the cello. The Lindsay's youngest child played the French horn sufficiently well that Ruth Railton had admitted him to the National Youth Orchestra. By the time Rachel was twenty two and home from her three years study at the Guildhall in London, they had a splendid quintet, with John Lindsay, the founder of the dynasty, reduced to making the coffee and sandwiches. This they did regularly on Sunday evenings after church.

The invitation was not entirely without self-interest for the one thing they lacked was a good pianist and of course they knew from old that Ian was very skilled. Ian would always remember that evening, the first of many, and how hard they kept him at it; Schubert, Beethoven and Brahms, all played with great enthusiasm and enough skill to be enjoyable. He discovered that Rachel was already entered in a competition and was easily persuaded to play for her. She played the Brahms E minor Sonata Op. 38, a piece which taxed them both greatly, but which brought out a unity of musicianship beyond anything he had known before. Ian always felt that E minor was a melancholic key, and noted that Elgar's great Cello Concerto was predominantly in E minor, though occasionally changing to the much more effusive D major. He noted that the 'Cello, even in good hands, was less sonorous in E minor and seemed to laugh at the world in ringing release when the key changed to D major. Rachel taught music to teenagers in a local school, and also sang in the local Gilbert and Sullivan Society, appearing as an imperious Duchess of Plaza Toro in the Gondoliers, whilst Ian was there.

Ian became a regular and welcome visitor with the Lindsays, increasingly involved in their warm family life. But Rachel was the real reason for his attachment. The bond between them grew steadily with a remarkable match of compatibilities. Just two weeks before the end of his appointment Ian proposed to her and was accepted. He was keen get things settled before he went for another year to London, at the Lambeth Hospital obstetric unit.

10

1961 The Lambeth

Ian was perpetually exhausted and lay on his bed that evening wondering if he dare go to sleep. The professor had warned him at the job interview that quite a high proportion of the resident obstetric staff failed to complete their contract because of fatigue. Two residents shared a unit in which three thousand five hundred babies were born every year, all of them from pregnancies deemed, for whatever reason, to be of above normal risk.

There were huge antenatal clinics each with over one hundred patients taking place every morning. Three doctors, the consultant, the registrar and one of the residents, managed the clinic, whilst the other resident was in the unit itself, dealing with any confinements which required medical intervention. There were three consultants who were in charge of beds in that unit, each one having other appointments at the parent teaching hospital, St Thomas'. The residents therefore had three bosses, each of whom had slightly different procedures and preferences. Sometimes that created difficulties.

In addition there were gynaecological outpatients and thirty gynaecological beds to be serviced. There were, of course, regular admissions to those wards for planned surgery, but there were other, unplanned, emergencies as well. It meant very long days, with night work in addition, shared between the two residents. The duty resident hardly ever slept the night through. There was always something to get him up. Every other weekend was off duty.

In addition Ian always had Tuesday evenings off from seven until midnight. The professor, who was the senior consultant, told his staff never to hang about the unit during off duty times. They were so limited, that no matter how tired, he insisted the residents get out for some air.

The phone rang in Ian's ear. 'Yes, Dr Plowman here,' he said.

'Good evening Dr Plowman, it is Staff Nurse Dickinson from Casualty. Dr Bell asks you to come down straight away. He has a problem which is in your department.'

'I'll come now.' He put his shoes and his jacket on, hurried out of the door of his staff bedroom, down the stairs and along the long corridor to the Accident and Emergency department which opened directly onto Brooke Drive. The Lambeth Hospital had been a Victorian Workhouse, as were many similar units in Britain at the time. Although they offered vital space for the expanding demands of health care, they were inefficient in their use of space, leaving the staff and other services large distances to cover in their daily work. Distance was also time and, in Ian's work, time was quite often vital. For this reason he sometimes slept in a bath full of pillows on the labour ward, when he reckoned somebody would need his help in a hurry.

It was just about five minutes after the call that he arrived in Casualty and was directed behind a screen to a couch where his friend David Bell, the Casualty resident, was hurriedly putting a drip up on a young woman. She was very pale and sweaty with a very rapid pulse and low blood pressure. She was bleeding profusely. Too profusely Ian thought. The blood transfusion would surely not keep up. They must stop the bleeding and soon.

'What is your name?'

'Sarah.'

'How many weeks are you, Sarah?'

No reply.

'How many weeks since your last period?'

'About twelve.'

'So you know that you are pregnant?'

'Yes.'

'How old are you?'

'Seventeen.'

'Do our parents know about this?'

'No.'

'Do you live at home?'

'Yes.'

'When did the bleeding start?'

'Last night. It has been getting worse all day, and I got frightened'.

I'm not surprised, he thought. I'd be frightened too.

'Are you having pain, if so is it like period pain and how often does it come?'

'Yes. It was about every five minutes, but now all the time.'

'Have you passed anything other than blood Sarah?'

'No.'

'Well, I must have a look at you and then we shall decide what best to do.'

With his instruments Ian could not get a good view, there was too much blood, but the little round opening in the cervix was not quite tight shut.

'I'm afraid you are having a miscarriage. Has somebody helped you to do that?'

No reply

'Sarah, this is important. Did someone help you miscarry this pregnancy? Has someone stuck things inside you?'

'Yes, some sort of needle I think.'

'Well, I must get you into the operating theatre very soon and we shall tidy things up for you and stop the bleeding to make you safe. OK? I will need to talk to your parents*, have you got a phone number?'

'Yes, but they are away for the day, which is why I came alone.'

**please see appendix on page 306 for comments around age of majority and medical decision making for minors.*

She was cold now from blood loss, and began to shiver uncontrollably. She was obviously terrified of her situation, but determinedly trying not to cry. Ian squeezed her hand reassuringly and raised his eyebrows in question. She nodded assent and Ian left to make the arrangements.

She was one of up to 30 criminal abortions each week who passed through the unit's care following a 'back street' abortion. Some did not live. Some bled too much. Some died of infection. It seemed to him that it was a tragic lottery, this dicing with death at the hands of a criminal abortionist. Of course the girls never told him who it was they were seeing. They knew the hospital would be sending the police around if they spoke out. And who paid? Ian knew that it was usually the boys who had fathered the babe who salved their conscience with the £50 needed for the abortionist's dirty tricks. This was a month's pay to many people.

He took her to Theatre, tidied her inside which meant emptying the womb of its contents, a little human creature about the length of his index finger. Ian knew that this girl's abortion had been inevitable ever since the abortionist had thrust what was probably a needle through the cervix. All Ian had done was to make her safe from infection and from bleeding to death, but he hated this aspect of his work. He was often uncomfortably aware that in this particular role he felt himself to be on some sort of bridge; on the one side seeming to abet the destruction of life, but on the other side struggling, often against the odds, to introduce new life into the world. The moral dilemma could only be kept in place by constantly reminding himself that even in these awful cases he was, in fact, just saving lives, those of the sad mothers who had been driven to such depths of desperation.

'Abortion is illegal' he kept reminding himself. It may well also be immoral and was certainly contrary to all his childhood teaching. 'But what of the greater good,' his other self would say. 'Surely there must be a better way than this. Let's hope this new pill will be ok, and put a stop to all of this.'

As long ago as 1938 Mr Alec Bourne a most highly respected surgeon at St Mary's Hospital had aborted a 14 year old girl who had been raped in a London park by five guardsmen. She had presented at St Thomas' Hospital asking for an abortion, but had been turned away on the grounds that 'she might be carrying a future prime minister', and had come to St Mary's as a last resort. Bourne terminated her pregnancy and reported his action to the authorities. He was charged and tried, for at that time the only possible ground for abortion was if the life of the mother was seriously at risk. In fact he was acquitted because the court accepted that his deed, for which he did not charge his patient, was carried out in the highest interest of compassion, and was entirely compatible with the ethical standing of his profession. The case had the effect of bringing into the public mind the issues surrounding abortion, and paved the way for later legislation. Bourne himself was later to be a founder member of Britain's major pro life movement.

All this was never far from Ian's mind as he witnessed an endless stream of abject misery, associated with high risk to life and to future motherhood, attending his unit.

He gave Sarah some injections to make the womb shut tight and stop the bleeding, and put her on a course of antibiotics. The drip would stay up for another few hours to be safe. Sarah would live, but, as he wrote the notes, he lit one of his pipes and sat back thinking about what he would say to her parents. Sarah had told him they had no idea she was pregnant and that they were away for the day. She thought they would be very upset. He promised that he would ring them that evening and whilst he agreed they would be upset, he assured her that they would also be relieved that their daughter was alive and going to be fine.

It would be very easy, he realised, to think that this was all that young women ever did, but of course he was taking all of the emergencies from a vast urban population and that coloured the perception dramatically. Nonetheless he, who liked women very much, was distressed to find himself so involved with the sordid side of femininity. It was about midnight when he finally got to his bed. The phone rang again just after two.

The Lambeth maternity unit was a popular place for the Nightingales living in London to come for their babies, and so it was that one morning in the Antenatal Clinic Ian was met with the broad smile of an Indian Nightingale who had married an Englishman. Ian had been in the choir at their wedding. She was very advanced in her first pregnancy and was very well. They were delighted to meet in this way, Ian insisting that when she arrived in the labour ward she should ask that he be informed. He wanted to be present at the birth.

One Saturday afternoon a couple of weeks later all seemed very quiet, so he rang the labour ward to be sure that he was not needed, and then slipped across the street to a barber to have his hair cut. He told the hospital telephonist where to find him in an emergency. On his return he decided to stroll up to the ward just to see how things were and, to his horror, discovered his friend was not only in the ward, but was in deep trouble with a baby that was stuck in a poor position. When he enquired why she had not asked to see him she told him she had repetitively asked, but that the staff midwife, who was African, refused to disturb him. A quick assessment made Ian realise that he needed to turn the baby's head, and then do a very high forceps delivery, a difficult job. He preferred to have an anaesthetist present.

He was completely taken aback when the duty anaesthetist arrived and he saw that it was Maria Bellini. Maria smiled at him like a sister before greeting their patient. Immediately the two doctors settled down to the business of getting this reluctant baby into the world alive and well. Eventually Ian succeeded and, then leaving Maria to settle the sleeping mother, he went to tear a big strip off the midwife for not calling him. He shouted at her in real anger, accusing her of racial prejudice and professional incompetence. He was merciless in his rage, eventually reducing her to tears, at which point he turned on his heel and stomped off to the office to write up his case notes.

He was still seething when there was a light touch on his shoulder as Maria came into the room and sat in the chair beside his desk,

He noticed that she had a wedding ring, and that she had gained a little weight which suited her. She looked happy and serene. 'Don't be too hard on her Ian', she said. 'She is very capable, but she just thought that you were being taken advantage of by a silly patient, one of a race that are traditionally hated where that nurse was born and lived. That cultural background obscured her normally good judgement, that's all.'

'Yes, but that obscurity, as you put it could very well have cost my friend her life, and had I not by chance come into the ward it would certainly have cost her baby's life.'

'I know, but you can bet it will not happen again'.

'Hmm, I have not been so angry for a very long time. I'm very sorry. Anyway Maria, it is lovely to see you. How are you? Married I see. Tell me about the man who has taken my place.'

His smile robbed the remark of offence. None was taken.

'His name is Michael O'Leary. He is a fine man and an orthopaedic registrar in Oxford. But he has not taken your place or, if he has, it is only because you left it empty and available, remember?' The voice was low and the eyes penetrating.

Ian felt the old warmth stirring, exactly as he feared it might if they ever met, but now things were quite different. She was married and he was engaged to be. Both had chosen their paths. He sat, head down, for some time and then looked up and said sadly 'I simply could not do as you asked Maria. I have never been so sad or upset about anything, ever.'

'I know, but I could not do it either, could I, and I wept in anger and disappointment for weeks. You know I even blamed my wonderful parents for imprinting me too well, and became quite estranged for a while.' she smiled gently.

They spent about half an hour swapping information about their lives, until Ian's anger at the midwife had all evaporated, and he was quite at home with the world. Eventually Maria rose, kissed him chastely on the forehead and went out, pausing on the threshold to look back and say 'Now we can be friends.'

Soon afterwards Rachel came to London for the weekend. They stayed as a small hotel in Kensington, Ian deliberately embarrassing her by asking loudly over breakfast in the dining room if she took sugar in her coffee. They went to a concert on Friday evening and shopped for the home they were planning on Saturday. Then that evening, for the first time since Ian's parting from Maria, they once again dined with Enrico and Rosanna at Primrose Hill. This time the table laid for six. If anyone was uncomfortable with that arrangement it was well hidden, because all of them sensed that this was an important moment and wished it to succeed.

Maria and Rachel clearly warmed to each other immediately, and were quickly exchanging girl talk. Michael and Ian were slower to relax together, but once they got onto the subject of International Rugby the traditional respect and camaraderie associated with the game took over, and all was well. Rosanna fussed over them like a mother hen, whilst Enrico, taking an evening away from his more prominent restaurant in Soho, played host as only an Italian can.

After the meal, they all went upstairs to the private apartment for coffee, to the sitting room, so familiar to Ian. Rosanna and Enrico sitting on the same sofa that Maria and Ian had occupied that afternoon when she had been found running on the Hill. Enrico, reaching for Rosanna's hand said that coming to Primrose Hill was the third best thing he had done in his life, choosing his wife and partner was the best, and having such a wonderful daughter with her was the second. He declared himself to be happy and proud, and he certainly looked it. He was now quite grey and bald, and distinctly rounded, but his eyes were as sharp as ever, and his laughter rang around the apartment bouncing happily off the walls, as if life was a source of great joy to him. He charged everyone's glass with Grappa and toasted the four young people. 'Maria, my beautiful daughter, I wish to make a toast to you, for all that you have brought your mother and myself in joy, and tonight, for bringing your husband and your friends together into our home. I know I speak for Rosanna when I say that I hope this will happen again, and again. Thank you.'

Michael was encouraged to speak about his work with prosthetic joints and how he hoped he would be able to make Oxford his base for life. There was a senior registrar post coming up shortly and he intended to apply. 'If that happens I think we shall get into the housing market. There is a house in Lechlade, the highest point of navigation on the Thames, which we would love. I'm sure we could find moorings and have our own boat nearby. I am tempted to go for it, but the problem is that if I do not get the job we will be lumbered with the house.'

'Then I would like to see this house myself very soon,' said Enrico, much to everyone's surprise. 'I do not wish to interfere, Michael, but I think that such a house will command a good price and sell very quickly. If you wait until you know for sure about your appointment you might lose it. If I buy it now I promise to sell it to you at the same price when you are ready to buy. I can well afford to do that, and it would be a pleasure to help. If you do not get the job then I might decide to keep the house and we can all use it as a retreat.'

'Oh Papa, that would be lovely,' cried Maria, 'Let's ring them on Monday and make arrangements to view.' They all laughed with delight at the prospect, but as the laughter died down Maria held up a hand for silence.

'And now,' she said, 'to cap Papa's generosity, I have some news. Next January Michael and I are going to have a baby, so to have our own home would be just wonderful.'

Whilst everyone poured their congratulations and good wishes on Michael and Maria, Ian had just a small pang of regret that Maria's child would not be his child, but the moment passed quickly, and he was able to join in the general celebration.

Not to be outdone Rachel pulled Ian to his feet to declare that they had fixed a wedding date for Saturday March 31st

1962. For the briefest moment Maria and Ian locked eyes, each affirming their commitment to their marriages without denying their tie to one another.

The weekend ended on Sunday with all six of them attending All Saints, Margaret Street, where Ian had sung as a student. The music was Schubert in G. Ian could not help smiling that there, in his party, in this Anglican communion, were four devout Catholics and two Methodists, all bound together by love in all its manifestations.

11

1962 Adoptions

'But I can't let her go!' came the wail from the lying-in ward that week before Christmas 1961. The whole department could hear the fuss and was shaken and saddened by it, for everyone knew exactly what was going on.

To have a baby outside marriage was a social crime which besmirched the family concerned, and was simply not acceptable, especially to the middle classes. Young women of that background from the provinces, who were pregnant, had three choices. They could marry quickly, get an illegal abortion, or have their baby adopted. It has always been the case that many single mothers were ill informed, inexperienced and naive. Some thought they got pregnant from lavatory seats. The 'good girls' got caught. These same young women would leave home, on the pretext of a job in the city, come to London and maybe work in a temporary capacity whilst finding accommodation in a Home for Unmarried Mothers. They would work until too pregnant, stay and have their baby in the hospital, from which the baby was removed for adoption. Then having physically, if not emotionally, recovered they would return home. The neighbours and sometimes her parents were not told the truth.

The Lambeth Hospital serviced the needs of several such establishments and so Ian very often had a lonely, tearful girl in his care who did not get visitors, and for whom the experience of the Lambeth Hospital was anything but joyful. The midwives were, for the most part, very considerate of these young women, often putting them quietly in a side room if one was available, so that they would not be upset needlessly by the contrast between their sorrow and others' joy.

The adoption agency most often collected the child before any real bonding could take place, but at times, perhaps because they were busy, the mother and child had a few days of each other's company before 'the nice lady from the agency' came to take the baby away. When that happened some of the girls found the wrench unbearable and, as on this afternoon, cries of protest would come from the little room in which the drama was taking place.

In those days, perhaps because he was contractually tied to the unit for so very many hours, Ian used to do an evening round of his beds, just to check that all was well. With about 100 women in the obstetric and gynae wards, he could not of course spend a great deal of time with each person, but everyone got a 'hello, are you ok'. The ill or the distressed received much more time, however, and so on this particular evening Ian found himself very tired, with one hip sitting on the bottom of a very tearful lady's bed, hoping that the dragon of the night sister would not see him and tell him off for sitting on the bed. It seemed the right place to be.

Tonight the mother was a dark haired 24 year old university geography graduate, who had been in her first teaching job. She had fallen in love with another teacher, and was soon having a pretty steamy affair. He was married, of course, and had no intention of leaving his wife, so when the inevitable happened she had no choice other than to seek an abortion or have the babe quietly adopted. Abortion was an appalling thought, so she eventually found herself in Ian's care in The Lambeth. 'What are you going to do now?' Ian asked

'Oh, as soon as I am well I shall go back home and hopefully get another job there,' she said.

'Will that bring you into contact with your baby's father?'

'Maybe. It is a small town, so I expect that would be inevitable.'

'Is that why you want to go back there, so you can take up with him again?'

'I do not think that is any business of yours, Dr Plowman.'

'No, you're right, it isn't, except,' He paused in mid sentence. 'Except that I do not like to see lovely people, who have been through hell, deliberately court a repeat of that experience.'

She sat with her head looking out of the window. The unit was the top floor of six, so she could see a long away across the city from her bed.

'I love him you see, and I want him. I have learned a lot about love and sex, lust and wanting over all of this, and I know that I want him more than anything in the world.'

'You might find someone else, you know. It is simply not true that there is only one person out there.'

'What would you know about it, Doctor?'

'Oh, Stephanie, I know. I know better than most, believe me,' he said, as he shut the door quietly, leaving her with her thoughts and dreams.

On one of these evening rounds Ian passed the nursery and noticed something odd. A newborn, wrapped in a blue blanket had a tiny hand showing over the top. Ian was astonished for he saw that the hand had six fingers. Extra digits are not all that rare, but they are most commonly quite obviously extra bits that visually do not belong. This hand however had six perfectly formed fingers, something Ian had never seen before. He himself had examined this baby immediately after birth and had not noticed. Embarrassed and concerned, Ian examined the baby all over again and was relieved to find nothing else amiss. So he carried the tiny tot into his mother's room, sat solemnly by her bedside and confessed that her baby had an abnormality which he had missed. 'That's quite all right, doctor,' she said, 'so have I.' She thrust her own hand in front of Ian displaying six perfect fingers. Nobody had noticed that either. They both laughed, mother in genuine amusement, but Ian in relief. He asked her about her own experience and was told that she was a nurse who, because the hand worked perfectly, had decided to keep her extra fingers, finding that the only real disadvantage was in wearing gloves. They parted very amicably.

About a month before the end of his contract, Ian was contacted by his father to be told that there was a vacancy in the medical practice in Cullompton, Devon, and that perhaps he should apply for it. Ian considered this with mixed feelings. On the one hand he enjoyed being at the centre of things and working in a busy unit with exciting colleagues, but the pay was bad and he wanted desperately to settle down. Also he had to admit that he found the city noisy and dirty, even sometimes a lonesome place to be. A home in the country with a good income, somewhere to settle down with Rachel, and to bring up a family decently was a big attraction. Also he knew that the practice had its own maternity unit and cottage hospital, both of which were very advantageous. Ian and Rachel had discussed children enthusiastically and intended to have a clutch of them.

He arranged to go with Rachel to see the partner, Dr Davidson, on his next weekend off. The interview went well, Dr Davidson seeming a larger than life extrovert who loved his life, his patients and his glass of wine, though Ian was not quite sure in which order. Rachel adored the countryside, and learned that there would be professional outlets for her in the area.

He returned to London undecided, but a particularly foul week, bringing more than an ordinary ration of sadness and emotional fatigue, led him to wake up one morning quite certain of his future. He telephoned Dr Davidson, agreeing to start work on the 15th April 1962 just two weeks after his contract in London ended. Rachel and he would be married at the beginning of that break, so he would bring his bride to the new job. She would resign her teaching post in Plymouth at the end of the winter term and look for work in Cullompton, Uffculme or Tiverton.

Only a few days after he had made this arrangement, the Professor called him on one side at the end of a clinic to explain that his Registrar's post at St Thomas' would become available in April and that Ian would be well advised to apply. Ian duly explained that he had already accepted a post in general practice. The Professor was not pleased, never directly addressing him for the remainder of his job. Ian knew he had been in some ways stupid to turn his back on an opportunity to be the professorial registrar in a major teaching unit, with all that might arise from that in the future, but his background was such that he could not go back on his word.

12

1962 New Starts

There were thirty five Methodist Chapels in Plymouth and Devonport, and their history together had often been contentious to say the least, but John Lindsay was a popular figure and so the congregation for the marriage of his daughter Rachel to Dr Ian Plowman was a great event. On March 31st 1962 the church was full to the brim with locals from many of the chapels on the circuit, including, since the Plowman family also originated from Plymouth, many of their old friends, some having not met since before World War Two.

Rachel's music friends and Ian's medical ones poured into town and, since the Methodists knew how to sing a hymn, the service was heard well beyond the walls of the chapel. The Lindsays had always been friends with the Salvation Army at Plymouth Congress Hall, so they had contributed a band to lead the service. The family quintet, with locum cellist and pianist, would contribute later to the reception jollities, playing as the crowd waited to be introduced to the bridal party.

Rachel was dressed in white of course and contrived to look both beautiful and demure, arriving with her father in a gleaming old Rolls Royce, so silent that it seemed to glide along. Her bridesmaid was an old school friend, Sheila Green, with whom she had got into many scrapes as a child and who had gone into social work after completing a Sociology Degree. The choice of Best Man had been difficult for Ian, but he finally chose Peter Brown, the humourist who was part of the anatomy room quartet. Peter managed the unfamiliar scene very well and gave a very witty speech hinting at some unspoken dark past of Ian's.

Michael and Maria O'Leary sat near the door with 9 week old James in arms, having chosen their seats in case a baby's wail disturbed proceedings and necessitated an early departure. Maria told Ian that Michael had got his senior registrar job, that they were living in the house in Lechlade and that she would be starting in General Practice as a part time assistant in Cirencester just as soon as she felt able to manage both job and baby. When Ian expressed surprise that Maria was giving up anaesthetics she laughed and said that she preferred her patients to be awake.

The whole day was one of joy. Had anyone asked, Ian would have said that he had found peace at last.

Being a Methodist wedding, many of those present had 'signed the pledge' and the reception was therefore officially alcohol free, but Ian insisted that his medical friends had wine on their table, and provided it himself. Nobody seemed to mind.

After a very brief honeymoon in Cornwall, the newlywed couple settled into their new home, a small terrace house in the High Street in Cullompton. It wasn't much, but the surgery was close and there was an amazing shop selling the best ice cream anyone had ever tasted, just a little way up the street. Rachel commuted to a good girls' school in Exeter, teaching music there. Over the years she would take her cello pupils to remarkably high levels of attainment. Several played in the National Youth Orchestra. For fun she played in a good amateur orchestra in Exeter, and also went to sing in the big choruses that gave regular concerts in the Cathedral. One of their first pieces of furniture was an 1895 Bechstein semi concert grand piano, which occupied about half of their modest sitting room. It had a wonderful bass sound so suitable to the cello, although it needed the tuner from Tiverton Pianos more often than Ian would have wished.

One of the big problems with living on the main street in Cullompton was the holiday traffic. The post war increase in private cars and increasing affluence led to an enormous boom in holiday traffic to the South West. On summer weekends it might take over five hours to drive the 70 miles from Exeter to Bristol with enormous queues on either side of the towns on the route such as Cullompton, Wellington, Taunton and Bridgwater. The lives of the occupants of those towns were severely and miserably disrupted by not being able to move around their own communities.

Ian and his colleague entered into an arrangement with the local policeman that the 'on duty' constable would come to the surgery at about eleven on Saturday mornings simply to enforce a pathway for them to leave on their rounds. An emergency call would always be associated with a message to the police to help. All of the doctors bought flashing green lights that they could fix to their car roofs, but sadly most of the grockles (the local name for tourists) ignored the lights and did not allow them passage. Although the policeman was helpful for escaping the surgery, the police presence did not extend to helping residents leave their own homes, so in effect the young Plowmans were prisoners in their house from about five on Friday evening until eight on Sunday evening. They took to leaving their car up a side street so that they could get out, and became expert at navigating the minor roads and lanes to avoid the main road.

A related problem was noise and exhaust fumes. Neither Ian nor Rachel slept much on summer Fridays and Saturdays, which was a serious matter since both were quite drained by their week of work and needed the rest. Also Rachel showed signs of asthma, which she felt sure was due to the pollution. The local people were desperate for government action and were lobbying fiercely. Actually plans for major bypasses and fast roads had been discussed in Whitehall since the late 1930s but it would be 1968 before the motorway reached the town. Clearly they needed to live somewhere close by the town and the surgery, but not associated with the main road. Eventually they found an old cottage near Uffculme. It was close enough to Cullompton, would allow easy access to Exeter, and had wonderful views. There was a large cottage garden full of roses. They loved it.

That September, sitting on the patio of their cottage overlooking the colourful garden and with views across the valley over Halberton and Tiverton to the smudge of the hills behind, Rachel was overwhelmed by the serenity of the scene, and by the all-embracing feeling of rightness that her marriage to Ian had brought about.

She reached across to him as he sat reading the paper in the adjacent chair, and said. 'Ian, this is bliss. Please may it never end.'

He smiled over the rim of the paper, then put it down, filled and lit his pipe before saying 'We certainly have fallen on our feet. Somebody was looking out for our well-being.' But end it did, though not in the way that anyone might have foreseen.

On the evening of Boxing Day 1962 it began to snow. They had never seen snow like this before. It came down in such a thick blizzard that they not only lost their horizon but they could hardly see across the lane to their neighbours, who were quite elderly. It was not the usual West of England wet snow that quickly melts and disappears, but was fine dry snow, more like that of large continental land masses. It was bitterly cold. Sometime in the night the electricity failed so they awoke next morning to an almost dark house. It was still snowing.

Ian and Rachel were not alone in the house for Rachel's parents had driven up from Plymouth on Boxing Day to be with them. Ian's parents had been present on Christmas day, had shared a Boxing Day lunch with all of them, but had driven home late in the afternoon. Ian reckoned they would have reached home before the snow came.

That morning they lit all the fires in the house, found a reasonable supply of candles, and struggled across to their neighbours, finding them cheerful and well with a good supply of logs and lights. They lent Rachel a Victorian oil lamp suitably primed. It would provide light for some days. Fortunately, being the Festive Season, there was a large quantity of food in the house. It would take several days to run short.

Rachel, being a teacher, was on holiday but Ian was fretting because he could not get down the hill in his car to work, leaving his partner covering the whole practice. Eventually he telephoned the local garage owner, who was already a good friend, and an hour or so later a Land Rover arrived at the front gate to take him into town. George, the garage owner, insisted that the vehicle was his, free of charge, as long as it was needed; Ian only need pay for the fuel. As they made their way back to Cullompton that morning Ian noticed that there had been a lot of drifting. Some parts of the road just had a few inches of snow, but others were ten or even fifteen feet deep. Many houses had snow as high as bedroom windows. Of course the business life of the town was almost completely paralysed. As the days went by the commonest vehicle to be seen was a tractor. Outlying farmers could only get to town in this fashion, and so were sent by their wives for provisions, sometimes collecting food and other goods for a number of families.

Not far from the town the main road going northeast became a long hill. Heavy transport failed entirely to make it to the top, sometimes sliding off the road. Eventually there was a roadside queue of immobile lorries several miles long. The drivers clearly would have died if they stayed with their vehicles and so they found beds in the town. Very soon all the hotel and Bed and Breakfast accommodation was full, so the local populace helped out. A sort of siege ensued in which the community, like many others in the land at that time, learned to manage somehow without much communication from outside.

In his work, largely because he was the younger partner and had the loan of the Land Rover, Ian undertook almost all of the house calls. In fact for a number of weeks the attendance at the surgery was greatly diminished, partly because of the great difficulty in getting into town, but also because people with minor illnesses, or needing a routine check-up, chose to manage themselves for a while.

House calls took an enormous amount of time and effort, with Ian often guessing what medication would be required and taking it with him in a heavy satchel. He called at the local shoe shop on the second day to buy some boots. Several times he needed to walk across fields that were almost waist deep in snow to reach his patient. He had no concept of how difficult deep snow was until faced with the problem. On one occasion he nearly failed to reach his destination, being spotted floundering by a farmer who was attempting to feed his animals, he was ushered into the farmhouse and sat by the fire to recover.

After that Rachel would not let him go alone. Fortunately there was a strong young man who could not get to his work who volunteered to be Ian's co-driver. On one such occasion Ian left his vehicle at a farm and was driven further into the country by the farmer himself, who was expert at off-road driving. They winched themselves using hawsers tied to trees, and at one point found the upper corners of the windscreen was gouging furrows in the snow wall on either side. That one call took all day. The patient was not particularly ill when they got there.

The doctors quickly became exhausted trying to service their widespread community, but they were luckier than some. In a neighbouring practice one doctor had slid into a ditch late at night and struggled to walk to the nearest habitation. Close to exhaustion he knocked on a door only to be refused entry by the occupant. Fortunately, a few hundred yards further on, the next house he reached belonged to a member of his own staff. She later said he was blue, breathless and exhausted, with icicles hanging from his moustache and a cut on his neck where his icy scarf had rubbed. Another little while and he would not have survived. In a hilly practice between Cullompton and Taunton one of Ian's friends got through five cars that winter, trying to do the impossible.

The nearest Ian himself came to disaster was when he was visiting a half completed estate and backed into a side road before leaving his vehicle. Immediately he fell some six feet into a drain, which had been completely obscured by drifting snow. Fortunately he had company with him who dragged him out to safety. They had a good laugh at that one.

The extreme weather lasted until March. One nearby village was without mains water all of that time and depended upon tankers. One could still find ice under hedgerows up on Exmoor as late as July, when the weather was wonderfully warm, and dead sheep were to be found on the moors for months afterwards.

Ian joined local clubs, playing rugby for a couple of seasons, but then, unable quite to maintain the level of fitness required, he became a referee. This lasted several years until one day he was unsighted when a try was claimed in a local derby match. He realised he could not quite keep up with a fast moving game, and so surrendered his licence.

He also joined the local Round Table, a club for professional men under forty. They met at a local hotel, enjoying a meal and a talk from someone, often with a very interesting tale to tell. One meeting not long after he had joined was on November 22nd 1963. He was listening to his car radio on the way to the meeting when he heard of President Kennedy's assassination. He would never forget that evening.

Musically he found some fulfilment playing for Rachel but also being accompanist for the local choral society. More rewardingly, he joined a very small select chamber choir in Exeter, meeting a number of like-minded folk as a result. Rachel meanwhile was being noticed as a cellist of quality and so became very busy playing for orchestras all over the West. Most of these gigs were paid at Union rates, and so it became a significant addition to her income.

13

1963 South Cerney

George Troutmann puffed contentedly on his cigar, a particularly fine Havana, which had come in the excessively large Christmas parcel from Trumpsters the tarmac company. He sat back in the leather desk chair and surveyed his office with satisfaction, his elbows on the chair, arms and fingers steepled in front of his chest. He wore a Harris tweed suit and rather vulgar brown boots with patterns wrought in them. His face was round and pink, his hair sandy and beginning to thin on top, a minor deficiency for which he compensated by having luxurious sideburns. He exuded a sense of powerful self-satisfaction, as well he might, for he knew that he was well on the way to being rich.

George dug holes in the ground for a living, or, to be more precise, he owned a rapidly expanding company which excavated gravel. The demand for gravel was insatiable. South Gloucestershire had been extracting gravel since about 1920, providing a huge area of the country with it, for road making and building purposes. With the need for post war reconstruction demand had risen hugely. The young George, just 25 years old, seeing an opportunity, had used all his capital and a fair bit of the bank's money to buy a large piece of ground near the village of South Cerney just a few miles from Cirencester, and had set about doing his best to satisfy the demand. But the truth soon became apparent that he could not hope to do that, despite rapidly expanding the business through the purchase of new ground and more machinery. Now, some ten years on, he had a smart office in Dollar Street Cirencester and a fine house near South Cerney. Troutmann Aggregates' trucks rattled through the south Gloucestershire countryside from five in the morning until dark.

The only awkward thing about his business was water. There was water everywhere and for some time they had not quite known what to do with it. The area of upland plain where the gravel was to be found in quantities that would far outlast his lifetime constituted the head water of the River Thames, and the water table was very high. Digging the gravel very soon became a battle with the water. Originally they used wet digging but more recently they had decided it was better to dig holes, pump the hole dry by pumping the water into the nearby River Churn, and then dry extract the gravel. This process was much cheaper and therefore more profitable and was the main reason for George's increased prosperity.

Once a gravel pit was worked out they simply turned the pumps off, allowing the water to fill the great cavity, thereby creating a man-made lake. By 1960 there were a dozen or so such lakes, some with shallow shores suitable for swimming and small boating and others much steeper with deep water and good fishing. Some were being used for these activities already. It was clear to George that very soon the gravel pits would become a major leisure attraction and, who knows, an area of highly sought after residential accommodation. George also knew that there would be many more lakes before long.

But all this demanded permission; permission from landowners, local authorities, conservationists, and central government to say nothing of the local populace whose cottages stood in the way of progress. George became an expert negotiator, adroit in the backwaters of bureaucracy. He soon realised that a little give and take might be required, in that if he wanted to take he must learn to give. In addition he found himself in a position to do favours for others, who wanted some form of employ, or perhaps a road here and a plot there. Soon he found himself in situations in which roles were reversed. He was seen by others as the man in the powerful seat whose palm must be suitably crossed in some way. This became a cornerstone of his empire, hence the large cigar and the fine wines and spirits in his cellar, that he had neither the knowledge nor the good taste to truly appreciate, although he greatly enjoyed parading them at the frequent dinner parties at Cerney Manor. Those dinner parties were, he knew, an important step on his road to acceptance by the old money of Gloucestershire, where the aristocrats still reigned supreme.

As part of all this George had married Catherine Willoughby-Smythe, a most elegant, willowy, lady, from a good family, who cut her hair short and wore A line skirts in imitation of Jacqueline Kennedy, although at this moment she could not for she was pregnant and due to deliver very shortly. It never occurred to George that his wife was bisexual, preferring women to men, though he often thought she preferred the horse to his company, and even wondered how she had managed to conceive, so rarely did she permit any intimacy. Not that this mattered much as long as she continued to play the hostess to perfection, because there was always Elaine, his secretary, who was very good at other things, as well as typing and dealing with clients. In recent months he had needed to be away on business fairly often and took Elaine with him.

George sighed, tapped the ash off his cigar and rose. He had promised to take Catherine to the doctor for a check up this afternoon. William, their man about the house, who would normally have driven her, had 'flu and would not be at work for a day or two. Catherine would not be happy if he was late. He collected his hat, and, stopping only at Elaine's small office to give her a kiss on the nose and a little tickle of a nipple, just to remind her of better things to come, he went out to his car. It was an Armstrong Siddeley Hurricane Drop Head Coupé 1949, complete with its Sphinx on top of the radiator. George was very proud of this motor, feeling it was more in keeping for a successful business person than a Rolls or a Bentley, and since he was trying to play down the double 'nn' on the end of his surname, (inherited from a 19th century mining engineer who had come to Britain from the Ruhr), he had decided against a Mercedes. In any event, feeling still ran high following the recent war so German cars were frowned upon in Britain even though they might be admired.

George found Catherine waiting impatiently at home and they drove back to Cirencester together in silence, having had an irritated exchange about something totally unimportant. He resented the intrusion on his day's work, and she was just plain bored; bored with him as a husband, bored with the lifestyle she had so misguidedly embraced, and most of all bored with this wretched pregnancy.

They passed through the town and went about a quarter of a mile up the Tetbury Road before turning left up a long drive to the Querns Maternity Hospital. The hospital was very small, a minor country estate really. The main building was a house of Georgian appearance with a fine porch and a drive that swept into a turning circle before it. The grounds were quite extensive, probably ten or more acres and housed a number of staff in small bungalows, including the House Surgeon from the main Cirencester Hospital in Sheep Street, and the senior theatre nurse and his wife.

Mr Allenby, the gynaecologist, examined Catherine and pronounced that the pregnancy seemed perfectly normal, but that her blood pressure was up a bit. Since the due date was almost upon them he advised that she stay in the unit and be induced. George went home to fetch some toiletries, pausing only to phone Elaine in the office to say that he would be alone in the house that night if she fancied a little sport.

The next day an angry, exhausted, Catherine delivered herself of a baby daughter, pausing only as she gave her final push to hiss at the midwife. 'I hate him for this, and always shall. There will be no more babies.'

They called the baby Deborah. It was November 22nd 1963. Events in Dallas that day meant that nobody ever forgot Deborah's birthday.

14

1964 Rachel

All was going very well until, in early summer 1964 Rachel emerged from a visit to the bathroom, slumped on a kitchen chair and burst into tears. Ian, comforting his wife had no idea what the problem might be until she looked up and said 'I have just started a period. Yet again, another damned period!! No pregnancy Ian! Why am I not pregnant?'

He thought for a long while, realising that they had not avoided pregnancy for about a year, and had enjoyed a normal married life all of that time. He had been so preoccupied with building up his professional following that he had totally failed to appreciate his wife's concern. 'I am very sorry. We haven't been communicating very well, have we?'

'I thought we were communicating extremely well.' She smiled through her tears at her 'double entendre', and he responded with a nod.

'I do not think there is anything wrong with our behaviour, nor is there anything obviously wrong with either of us physically or mentally. For example, I did have mumps but it was quite uncomplicated as far as I remember.'

'OK,' she said. 'Where are you going with this?'

'Well, as a general rule if an apparently normal couple do not succeed in a year the medics would think it is time to investigate. That means attending a proper Fertility Clinic and being subjected to all sorts of personal enquiries and examinations, including some pretty intrusive tests. Many people back off, not being able to face all of that. What do you think?'

Rachel paused for quite a long time, getting up to make a cup of tea as she considered her response. Eventually, several minutes later, she replied, 'Before we married, we were both talking about enjoying a large family. In fact it was a cornerstone of our discussions and our commitment. If you seriously think there is a threat to that, we owe it to each other to try to sort out what, if anything, is amiss, and to adjust our thinking in the light of the answers. Do you agree?'

'I agree,' he said solemnly.

And so, they arranged appointments in Exeter with the Fertility Clinic, undergoing lengthy tests over almost a year. Finally they were summoned to the expert who sat them down courteously and said. 'Dr and Mrs Plowman, I have rather difficult news for you. We find nothing amiss with you Rachel. All of you seems to be in good working order.'

'But you, Ian, do have a problem. You are not infertile in that you do make live and active sperm, but sadly you do not make many of them, so in functional terms you are relatively infertile. We guess that your mumps did more damage than you thought at the time. It is our experience here that men like you may never become fathers, but that sometimes they do, often when they are least expecting it. I am very sorry if that seems a ridiculously imprecise answer to give you at the end of all the tests you have endured, but it is the accurate picture of your situation.'

Rachel began to weep silently and discreetly, trying not to show her disappointment in front of Ian. He of course knew perfectly well how severely this distressed her, and to think that it was himself at fault was hard. He sat head bowed for a little while. 'So what would you advise? Should we just keep on trying, knowing that the chances are slim, or shall we try to adopt a baby?'

'I think that time is on your side. It is now the spring of 1965. You, Ian are thirty one and Rachel is still only twenty six.

You have had all the upheaval of marriage, of settling into new lifestyles, new jobs, new home and had all the problems of that awful winter. All of these things are stressful. There is some evidence that this might make a difference. As I say, there is plenty of time. I think you would be well advised to let the turmoil of all this pass by and see how you feel in the future. You never know, you might progress in your careers and lifestyle in a way that children will seem less needed. Perhaps it might help if I tell you quite frankly that when I first got involved with Fertility Clinics in London several years ago, we would have advised couples like yourself that pregnancy is unlikely. However we did a follow up survey and found a significant pregnancy rate in couples to whom we had given that news. That survey somewhat modified my answers today.'

That night, in their bedtime cuddle Rachel told Ian that she did not yet want to think about adoption. He let it go at that. They continued to behave and live entirely normally.

It would be more than ten years later that Rachel returned to the subject of adoption. In the meantime they lived and played together each developing a network of activities in which they became truly established. Ian's practice flourished and grew in tune with the expanding local population. Their little town was at last bypassed by a new motorway and so became an oasis. As such, its proximity to Exeter proved an attraction for many, so building flourished.

Rachel, emancipated from the expectation of imminent motherhood, developed her career with enormous energy. In a couple of years she was helped in this by the motorway which facilitated her drive in and out of Exeter greatly. In 1970 she became head of the music department, taking her school choir to great heights in national competitions, and becoming a very established figure in Exeter artistic circles. She bloomed as a woman, looking magnificent and totally assured. Ian enjoyed the role of consort.

At home they became great gardeners and housekeepers also. The cottage was in a supreme position but was not cluttered by preservation orders, and so over the years they extended it significantly, so that they had a new sitting room opening onto a large conservatory, and thence onto manicured lawns. The original sitting room became the dining room and there were two extra bedrooms. Thus they were well equipped to entertain their friends. They also acquired a Springer Spaniel, a family addition which would follow them though several generations of dogs. Springer spaniels require exercise and so the Plowmans regularly walked the canal or the hills, where they could ramble for miles.

Socially they were very active, holding quite formal dinner parties about once a fortnight and enjoying other people's events in between times. They played host to visiting friends from both the music and the medical world. Peter, Ian's best man, now happily married, and with three rampaging small boys, would come at least annually for a few days, usually on their way to Cornwall for a holiday.

Michael and Maria O'Leary were infrequent visitors too. Michael was very preoccupied with his boat, and so spent most of his spare time pottering about on the river Thames. Young James, growing into a highly intelligent, self-assured, young man, had been joined by a sister, Maureen, who had Maria's eyes and hair, and was considered by Ian to be a real winner. Michael had acquired an international reputation as an orthopaedic surgeon and was being sent abroad on lecture tours from time to time. Life was very good indeed.

15

1980 Last Lap

The cistern in the girl's lavatory was the repository for Grass. Today Debbie was in need. She felt gingerly above the piping and found the small tin containing the spliff. A second, heavier, small tin was behind the first and was used for payment. The honesty box system seemed to work well. Certainly Debbie would not dream of cheating as she carefully placed her coins in it and retreated to a lavatory seat to enjoy her prize. Smoking Cannabis was strictly forbidden, but everyone knew where to get it and many people did so, including, Debbie knew, some of the staff.

That morning, yet another row with her parents, this time because she had taken her mother's car without asking, had led to Catherine and her daughter screaming at each other across the kitchen table. She had dented the front wing when she misjudged a low wall whilst turning into the woods. Debbie had known her mother would be very angry, but was unmoved.

'What did it matter anyway?' she thought, as she sat, inhaling deeply. 'We have plenty of money, and it wasn't as if some old lady had been run over.'

Catherine was in fact much more upset by her daughter's attitude than by the damage to the car, which would be repaired in a couple of days. There was also the serious matter of driving whilst unlicensed and uninsured. Fortunately, police were very rare in the country lanes around Cerney, but nonetheless Catherine could not understand how her own daughter could expose other people to damage without insurance cover. Nor could she understand Debbie's total disregard for the law.

She wondered yet again what it was that had produced this rebellious teenager, who had no sense of shame and little appreciation of right and wrong. What had she and George done to deserve this young vagabond? They were well off, and had given her everything a child could possibly want; first a pony, now a horse, expensive clothes, wonderful holidays, lots of parties and very generous spending money. They had promised her a car for her seventeenth birthday. They accepted that she was never going to win scholarships, and did not chivvy her about reports which rather monotonously said that 'Deborah could do better'. They turned a blind eye to the galaxy of boys who seemed to flock around her, and over whom she seemed to exercise amazing power. They even tried to smile sweetly when her sixteenth birthday party had turned into an alcohol fuelled rave in which hundreds of pounds of damage had been done. Even George admitted that perhaps they should have stayed at home for that one, especially when they found a condom packet behind the sofa. Debbie had said that she knew nothing of that, because she was in the kitchen and conservatory all evening. They had chosen to believe her, but had begun to realise that their little girl was growing up and maybe was starting to play with dangerous toys. Catherine had tried to persuade Debbie to go to the GP asking for The Pill. She had angrily refused, saying she was not at risk, and in any case would not talk about such matters to the family doctor.

George was seldom at home these days, spending more and more time on his travels, and Catherine was very busy at the fitness club trying to keep her wonderful figure in place. There was a lovely young masseuse there who liked jewellery and who invited her to her flat quite regularly. They shared a shower, and afterwards the deep sleep in the large bed they also shared seemed to revitalise her.

Catherine herself was becoming increasingly interested in antique jewellery and, with George away so much, and with their marriage not exactly prospering, she was seriously considering setting up her own business. Oxford, or even Kensington, seemed to beckon to her. She could imagine herself operating a small exclusive boutique shop catering for the very wealthy.

But for now, Catherine reasoned, the housekeeper was usually about and Debbie had free range of the house and paddock. She could bring her horribly spotty young friends home whenever she wanted. Nobody spied on her or curtailed her. She rode her horse very skilfully and successfully, excelled in gymkhanas, and was also a determined hockey player, whose ability to keep the stick close to the ground, and to run determinedly and fast might make for senior appearances in a few years. Why then could she not be happy and normal, instead of being so arrogant and manipulative? Catherine felt she never won any of the arguments these days and was increasingly being dominated by her own daughter.

She had never believed in punishment or even in discipline, having herself been educated in the period of the liberal educational revolution which began early in the 1950s, and by 1960 had altered the classroom profoundly. She hated her secondary education at a very expensive boarding school for girls; hated, that is, apart from Mary Hislop who had seduced her and who became her inseparable companion.

Having scant notion of discipline, indeed, having herself lived through the period of the late 50s and early 60s, in which the liberal educationalists had changed that word's meaning so profoundly from the positive acquisition of 'self-control', to the negativity of 'repression', Catherine had sought to gain co-operation from her headstrong child through bribery. She knew no better. Many times Debbie had been given presents as a reward for doing ordinary things that most children took for granted. She had always been inclined to be sulky and unco-operative, never joining in any household chores, never helping in the kitchen. Yet, when it came to her horse, she was very possessive, doing all the grooming and mucking out without complaint, actually resisting help when offered.

Catherine did not grasp, even now, that Debbie had understood from an early age that life was a trade. If she did what her mother wanted she could demand a prize in return. Debbie played the game hard most of her life.

Her spliff having finished, she felt quite a lot more benign and walked over towards the science block looking for her friends. Lessons had ended for the day and the grounds were full of young people strolling to the boarding houses or standing in groups talking, mostly planning some adventure, or intently discussing the forthcoming exams. The school was a co-educational boarding school with about half of the pupils living in and the remainder travelling, sometimes considerable distances.

Today, at the beginning of the summer term 1980, all the talk in Debbie's group was about public examinations. Everyone seemed completely overtaken with the need to perform well; as well they might, because the results would determine much about their future. Good exam results at age sixteen would lead to Advanced Level courses in a small number of specialist subjects, and thereafter to a good chance of university and a degree. Poor results would lead to early departure from formal education into a manual job or a trade. Everyone understood that the watershed was upon them. They were nervous and afraid and became quite highly strung and irritable with each other. Their parents who were behind them, pushing ever harder to get a worthwhile result from the years of investment in an expensive education, came in for a lot of irritable rebellion also. Debbie was not comfortable with all this talk of exams. She knew in her heart that her grades might not be good enough for her to go higher in the school, and had already been quietly weighing her options. None of them really appealed to her, though there was an interesting fruit farm over near Tetbury, which offered young people employ and seemed to be well run. She realised that this might be the last term of her education and so every moment became important, especially the end of term celebrations.

The school campus was large and the buildings quite magnificent, at one time catering for many more boarders than were now resident. The loss of the British Empire and the reduction in foreign commitments which resulted from that, meant that schools like this had lost a large proportion of their traditional source of pupils. Some had gone out of business, but many had adapted very well by admitting girls. Of course this had changed the school's character profoundly, but most people thought it was for the better. Discipline was noticeably less harsh, and those who were not good on the rugby field might find a sense of identity in gentler pursuits, one of which was the Debating Society, for which this school had acquired an international reputation.

These were decent young people, unconsciously intent upon adapting to the new wind that was sweeping the land, driven from Downing Street. Gone were the scruffy unwashed long haired youths of a decade previously. Going was the attitude that the comfortable State would provide for a future. Instead there was a new mood, a mood of change, of self-determination and self-reliance. The utter selfishness, which so marred the later Thatcher years, had not yet undermined the bright vision of how things should be, and how people should behave. It was a 'polished shoes, shoulders back, and stand upright time', and schools of this nature were revelling in it. Teaching had changed also to become more of a two way communication, in which pupils engaged with teachers in a way that previously would have been unthinkable. The staff, which a decade ago were worried about the spread of the American disease of youth drug habit taking, a disease which had certainly infected British cities, were more relaxed, not seeing any real evidence of serious problems. That is, except perhaps that they were much more aware of sexual activity in their young.

But even decent, sensible young people sometimes behaved badly, tears were not uncommon, the girls snapping cattily at each other and the boys squaring up in testosterone laden scraps, usually about nothing at all. This powder keg of hormone laden young under stress, would eventually blow up into the big emotional release of the year, the summer dance. Even here on the very English Cotswolds some were calling this event the Summer Prom, a term imported from across the Atlantic. There is no doubt that, across the land, this end of school year event, especially designed for those who might be leaving, or those going on to Advanced courses, was the social culmination of the whole school experience. Its importance could not be overstated. People went to extraordinary lengths to grab attention, through absurd dress, to amazing dancing exhibitions, even to strange forms of transport. Here in the depth of the country a reveller might arrive on a bedecked trailer pulled by a farm tractor, or even come in a horse and cart, though there were not many horses capable of doing that any more. The normal British understatement was put aside in favour of a brighter, brasher import. The bragging rights, which came from making a hit at The Prom, acquired a symbolism which would remain for many years in the minds of those touched by it. To see and, importantly, to be seen, was the overt need. To lie with, or to be laid, often for the first time ever, was quite a common covert need. But of course there was always the eleventh commandment –'thou shalt not be found out'. These young people were still under the jurisdiction of school rules at the time of The Prom. The staff turned a blind eye to many things but not to drugs, nor to being caught in a compromising sexual experience.

In this hothouse atmosphere, if someone was talented both on the sports field and academically as well as at the other activities, such as the school music or drama, they became a 'special one', almost deified by the other pupils, especially those a little younger. Daniel Hodges was just such a one. Excelling at everything he attempted, he was in the sixth form and was expected to win a state scholarship to Oxford or Cambridge. He captained the school at rugby and opened the batting in the cricket team. He was tall with a wide schoolboy grin and an easy manner which made him popular with staff and pupils alike. Debbie decided that she wanted him. She really wanted him.

She found him at the cricket pavilion, oiling a bat, the smell of linseed hanging around him. He looked up as she stood in front of him. 'Hello young lady' he said in mock formality. 'How are you today?'

'I'm fine thanks', she replied. 'I came to offer you some tea. That is if you would please take me home.'

She knew that Daniel had a battered old Morris Minor which he had been given for his seventeenth birthday. Of course he had passed his driving test in no time, and at almost eighteen years old he was driving himself to school every day. The request from Debbie was illogical in some ways since his home was in quite a different direction from hers, but he sensed there was some sort of promise in the suggestion, and he was not so deaf that he had not heard some rumours about her being a bit easy with the boys. After all, it was not every day that a pretty girl asked to be taken home. Their previous meetings had all been friendly and full of banter in the crowd that usually gathered around him. Once, when she stood very close to him, he had noticed a smell of newly washed hair and of something more intangible, but distinctive.

He looked her up and down, noting the summer school uniform dress, worn just a little shorter than regulation length, and the belt that was very tightly pinching her waist, showing her young figure to advantage. She appeared to him to be standing with her shoulders back thrusting herself upwards as if for display. She gazed at him very frankly and wore a gentle smile and a questioning expression. Daniel liked what he saw. Fraternisation on campus between his exalted peer group and a mere sixteen year old was not encouraged, but after a pause he nodded.

'I have some chores to do for about half an hour, but I could take you then if that suits you. Be at the front gate, preferably just outside'

'I shall be there,' she smiled and went in search of her books and her bag.

They drove to Cerney almost without speaking, except for her giving him directions. He had never been before, and was clearly impressed by the wrought iron gates, the long drive, the sweeping lawns and the creeper covered Georgian front of the house with its pillared porch.

They went inside, Debbie calling out to see if her mother or Annie the housekeeper was about. There being no reply to her call she took him through to the vast, farmhouse like, kitchen, with its racks of pans and large, hugely robust, central table. She put a kettle on to boil and, as she made the tea and found some biscuits, she asked him about his plans. She knew that he had another year at school, and that he was doing languages but had never asked him about his ambitions.

He told her that he hoped to get a good university place to read Modern Languages, especially Russian, so that he would be well placed either to go into government service or into business. His parents were comfortable but not well off, father being a clerk in the rent office of the local council and mother a part time primary school teacher.

'I do not want to go on being a charge to them,' he said, 'so it important that I win scholarships to help pay my way. In fact I am on a scholarship now.' He shrugged in a way that robbed the statement of any sense of boasting.

She had never considered the need to pay one's way before, and was horrified at the prospect. In her own life if she wanted something she simply asked for it and it was provided.

She took a tray of tea things through into the conservatory, placing them on a low table in front of a wicker sofa. She indicated to him that he should sit on the sofa rather than the adjacent chair, and having poured the tea, sat next to him. Black Cat, as he was called, immediately jumped onto her lap and snuggled there purring away as she tickled him behind his ear. Debbie had loved cats ever since she was a little girl, and whenever her relationship with her mother was particularly fraught, she took refuge with the current feline. They regularly slept on her bed and seldom left her alone for more than a few minutes whilst she was in the house. Black Cat was the latest in a line of such animals and was perhaps the most favourite of all.

'What does your father do Debbie?' Daniel asked, clearly seeking an explanation of the opulence around him.

'Well, you know all those grit lorries we see around here with Troutmann's Aggregates on the side? They belong to Daddy. He owns the pits and the trucks take the gravel wherever it is wanted. It seems to pay well enough,' she said, almost dismissively.

He was silent for a moment before replying that he would be sensible not to mention that in his home, where the hole in the ground seemed to be closer each day and the noise of the machines upset everyone.

She smiled at him and, as if to apologise for what he had said, he reached over to share the petting of the cat. Their hands touched for a moment, a little shock passed up his arm and he glanced up to her face, but she was looking down at the cat and did not seem to have noticed. He did not remove his hand.

'Are you going to the dance?' she asked.

'Why of course, it is the end of year big event. All of my friends will be there. You know that surely?'

'I would love to go too,' she said, 'but there won't be many of my friends there. They think it is too grand for them, and in any case there is nobody I would want to be with.' She consciously erased the image of Tom Whistler with his acne and crooked teeth from her mind. He would be upset to hear her say this.

Gently she took Daniel's hand away from stroking the cat and turned its palm towards her. 'Would you take me, do you think?' She stared at him intently, the sudden unexpectedness of the question taking him by surprise.

'Well, I, I am not sure. You are not in my year and do not know many of my friends. Wouldn't you feel a bit awkward?'

'But, maybe that doesn't matter' he added quickly as she brought his hand closer to her until it rested on her belly, quite low down.

'No I'm sure it would not matter one scrap.' She smiled, welcoming him towards her. She released his hand, put her arm around his neck and pulled him down to her for a long kiss. The cat escaped from her lap, made suddenly less welcoming for him, as she turned towards Daniel whose hand went wandering again, this time towards the top buttons of her dress. But as soon as he became too excitingly close to baring a breast she pulled away, stood, straightening her clothing, and said briskly. 'Well, that's settled. Would you like to come and have a look at my horse before you go home? We have won lots of prizes together.' She gestured to a number of ribbons and silver cups on a shelf as she spoke and, before he could protest, led him through the door and down the garden to the paddock.

16

1980 School Is Done

That summer term of 1980 was nearly perfect for Debbie. She felt herself more and more in control of her life. The exams were looming but did not seem such a fearful mountain now that she was acquiring a social status beyond her dreams.

She was happy at last, and as a consequence became much more relaxed, and agreeable. One might almost say that she was lovable for the first time in years. Certainly her parents were absolutely delighted to find that they had a supportive, cooperative daughter who kept herself and her room tidy, who whistled in the bathroom, and who exhibited such a level of simple joy that it came to pervade the whole house.

George found himself staying home more, enjoying his wife's new enthusiasm to cook, and the supper time conversations which involved a good deal of banter about the political issues of the day, in which his newly found daughter revealed a totally unexpected leftish view of the world.

Catherine felt proud of their achievement at producing this lovely young woman, something she had not expected to feel, and which gave her real pleasure. Both George's secretary in Cirencester and the masseuse at Catherine's health club were relatively deprived of their respective attentions. George actually found himself with his arm around Catherine's waist once or twice, a gesture that was, for once, not unwelcome to her.

All this wonder was, of course, entirely due to Daniel, who nowadays brought Debbie home from school more often than not, unless he was engrossed in a cricket match. Even on those days Debbie would, for the first time ever, often stay to watch the team play.

It was not just the change in atmosphere at home that Catherine noticed. Debbie was working consistently and methodically for her exams, bringing the same intense concentration to her books that hitherto had been reserved for her equestrian exploits. This was entirely new. The parents knew that this too was an infection caught from Daniel Hodges.

Physically Debbie was blooming. She had a remarkable growth spurt and became very shapely, with hips and bust to rival any of her peers. She had changed from girl into woman almost overnight, it seemed.

With it all came that magic ingredient called confidence. She was at ease with herself, and this translated into an ease with others, even with her parents' friends whom she had previously regarded as being too stuffy to bother with. She more than held her own with guests when they entertained, happily doing the little chores like admitting them and taking any coats they might be wearing.

Miss Henrietta Burchill was the most feared, yet respected of the teachers. She taught history and was formidable. Her fiancé had been one of the 1109 Britons who died in the Korean War in the early 1950s. It was a short but bitter conflict produced, like so many others, by Western powers artificially dividing countries of which they had little understanding, along some line drawn on a map. His needless death left a bitter young woman who had given all her love away, and apparently had none left for anyone else. She had an excellent history degree and spoke several languages but eschewed a potential diplomatic career in favour of teaching and living in the school. At first glance one would think that hers was a severely self-proscribed life, in which she took little pleasure in any activities outside the school campus. She was known for her wintry smile and withering stares directed at those who failed to reach her high standards. Even the staff treated her a little warily, for she was quite capable of making them feel very stupid in staff meetings. She was in her fifties, thin and wiry, with swept up grey hair, tied in a bun. She was the owner of a snappy little dachshund with which she patrolled the perimeters of the estate night and morning.

Yet this woman had the largest Christmas mail of all the staff, and quietly doted on some 20 godchildren, all of whom were born to her ex pupils. To those pupils, after leaving school of course, she had become known as 'Aunt Henry', the most affectionate term anyone could have imagined. Of course everybody in the school knew about this and totally understood the imperative to earn the right to call her Aunt Henry. It was not a privilege earned lightly, nor taken for granted. Henrietta Burchill was well on the way to becoming a legend in her own time.

As was her annual role, Miss Burchill had been watching the latest batch of young reach the watershed of O(rdinary) level exams, that hurdle which must be crossed successfully in order to progress to higher education. Her particular interest was not those who were clearly going to succeed, nor those who would sadly fail, but the small group in the middle for whom an erroneous decision could be so disastrous. Misjudgement here was potentially catastrophic. Henrietta was not so naive as to think that O level success or failure completely decided any young person's future, but it certainly was a significant predictor of success in life at least as judged by society's yardsticks. To her it was much better for an academically less able child who might have excellent hand eye skills, or a marvellously practical personality to be gently guided into vocational, rather than academic, paths and to acquire self-worth from doing something very well. She had become skilled in sensing what the best course of action might be for those on the bridge between the paths, rather than those clearly on either side of the divide. Pupils could be wrongly promoted, find themselves unable to adapt and perform effectively in the intellectually demanding world of Advanced Level work, subsequently lose all sense of self-worth, and end up considering themselves to be a failure. Even worse, someone who was just a slow developer could be consigned to the outer darkness of academia and never achieve their potential. Quietly and unobtrusively, she was building evidence in her mind to help marshal the arguments that came every school year, when the Head must decide whether a pupil who had not quite made the grade, should be nodded through to the sixth form or find the door closed against them.

This year, her attention had been arrested by the Troutmann girl, a selfish, manipulative, lazy and spoilt teenager, who seemed to have metamorphosed into something altogether more attractive. Her school reports had been unpromising both as regards her attitudes and her attainments. She had been marked down as a likely failure, and few of the staff would have disagreed with that judgement. But now, quite suddenly, Miss Burchill was not so sure. Certainly attitudes had changed, appearance and bearing were altogether more positive and the grades in the 'mocks' were improving all the time. But was it all too late? Miss Burchill did not yet know, but would continue to observe closely. She noticed that the odd smell which she though must be of cannabis had gone, and that smiles had replaced scowls in a remarkable manner. 'Love or Lust' she thought, and soon discovered that a young romance was blooming between Debbie and young Daniel Hodges. She smiled to herself but crossed her fingers firmly, praying that Daniel would have the good sense to manage this girl well.

For a long time her hope and faith in Daniel was well placed. He courted Deborah in an old fashioned and gentlemanly manner, assuming that although she had a reputation for being a flirt she was, like most of the other girls he had known, pure and virginal. Yes, he loved to feel and even kiss her young breasts and caress her stomach, even her bottom, but he never attempted to get inside her knickers and he certainly never expected her to undo his trousers. Little did he know how often, after he had gone home, she would flounce off to bed and there lie with her hands between her thighs caressing until that great moment of release came.

Daniel's family had always been encouraging and proudly supportive of him. His grandfather had played cricket for Essex and had enjoyed introducing him to the finer points of the game. His mother played the piano and sang in the local church choir. She had ensured that he could play a bit himself and could read music passably well. Father, not truly enchanted with his job, had expended his energy in the greenhouse and garden and was famous for his enormous long, straight leeks and carrots. He exhibited in the Flower Show every summer, usually coming away with a prize. This was a family in which there were few spoken demands, but in which one was expected to embrace one's chosen path with all of one's being. Nothing was half hearted about the Hodges family. But, the unwritten code was that each person should never bring shame or dishonour upon the house. This code was central to Daniel's success at school, both academically and on the sports field. His word was his bond and his credit was high with everyone. This was the reason for Miss Burchill's grounds for optimism.

Debbie's exams came and went in a blur. She described it as being a bit like going to the dentist. There was the increasing discomfort in advance, allied to a sense of apprehension. Then at the time it was not as painful or as long lasting as had been feared, and afterwards one was left wondering what all the fuss was about. She was not depressed about it at all because she knew that she had worked, and believed she had done better than anyone expected. She could hold her head up. The only question was whether she had done well enough to stay on at school, something she really wanted now that she had Daniel, who had one year still to go, and who had not had to face public exams this year.

Daniel's school programme also wound down quite early so they had more freedom than they had been accustomed to during the two weeks before the Summer Prom. They decided to enjoy a day or two away from the immediacy of home and school. Firstly they drove to Oxford and had a wonderful day viewing some of the colleges, soaking up the atmosphere of the city and then going to a farce at the Oxford Playhouse.

One Saturday Debbie persuaded Daniel to take her all the way to Bristol to the Hippodrome for a soft rock concert by Barry Manilow. She was thrilled to be there and screamed just as loudly as anyone present.

But perhaps the most wonderful thing they did was to persuade Catherine to pay for a boat on the Thames and to spend a long weekend travelling from Oxford to Fairford and back. Debbie was disappointed that both sets of parents insisted that they were not alone on the boat so George spent the Saturday with them and was replaced by Daniel's mother on Sunday morning. Debbie made sure she had a good relationship with Daniel's mother and actually did get on quite well with her, but this intrusion on their beautiful weekend was not well received by either of the youngsters.

But the Prom was now upon them and the excitement was almost unbearable. The girls discussed how outrageous they might be in their dresses. The 1960s miniskirt and the plastic mackintosh which had given rise to the description Dolly Bird had been replaced, at least for a while in the late 1970s and early 80s. Some thought it was because, as a fashion, the skirt 'could go no higher' and others thought it was because the feminist movement had understood that there was a need to restate femininity in a less overt manner. For whatever reason, skirts were at, or below the knees for this occasion, and a few of the girls actually went the whole way and came in formal long dresses of a classic nature. Punk had given rise to a resurgence of the skinhead culture, so some of the boys appeared close cropped and wearing jeans, some of them splashed with bleach, but more of them came dressed up like waiters in ill-fitting hand me down dinner suits, loaned for the occasion by a reluctant father.

They gathered in the school hall which had been thoroughly decorated with streamers and balloons and they danced to a rock band from Swindon, who were a passable imitation of The Clash.

By the time Daniel and Deborah arrived, Debbie having deliberately made them a bit late so as to make an 'entrance', the dance was in full swing, the floor was so crowded that they were all shoulder to shoulder and the noise was totally overwhelming.

They stepped inside the door, just as one dance was ending and stood there looking at the scene before them. Several friends were so adorned as to be hardly recognisable. Some looked ill at ease in garish teenage misjudgement of chic. Quite a number looked absolutely stunning, the boys tall and elegant, and the girls with tight bodice, shoulderless gowns and flared skirts, their hair groomed to perfection. The headmaster and his wife, acting as hosts greeted them and complimented Debbie on her exquisite dress. It had cost Catherine a great deal of money and came from a London fashion house, but the investment was well worth it. Many of the assembled crowd noticed and nodded their acknowledgement that the queen of the ball had arrived. For that is indeed how she felt herself to be that wonderful evening.

They danced almost all of the evening, just stopping once or twice to refresh themselves and to rest a little. Their friends, or rather Daniel's friends, crowded around them whenever they stopped, many to congratulate Daniel on the half century he had scored that afternoon.

It was about eleven when they quietly slipped out and strolled in the still, warm summer evening. It was natural for them to find themselves at the door of the Cricket Pavilion, for which of course as the captain, Daniel had a key. They slipped quietly inside.

Miss Henrietta Burchill could stand the noise no more. Being without any male attachment she never actually attended the Prom, and privately regarded is as a penance she somehow had to endure.

About 11.30 she set off around the grounds with Charley the Dachshund for his last exercise of the day. They walked from her rooms, across the front of the school with its tall clock tower, past the playing field, set out this term as the cricket pitch, and around the science block to the pavilion.

As she walked past the cricket pavilion she heard a noise from within and, fearing burglars she strode in, turning the main lights on as she stood in the doorway.

There on the mat was a naked Deborah Troutmann, both legs in the air, panting loudly as a rampant Daniel thrust manfully inside her. On the floor was a small packet of blue pills, later identified as MDMN or Ecstasy, and a half empty bottle of sherry.

'Oh My God!' thought Henrietta. 'I wish I had not seen this.' she muttered. She turned without a word and went out.

It was the end of the second week in August that the letters came, one to each household. They were identical in their wording except for the addressee:

Dear Mr Troutmann, 10th August 1980

It is with considerable personal sorrow that I must inform you that at the end of the recent summer dance your daughter Deborah was discovered on school premises having sexual intercourse. We believe she had also been using an illegal drug as well as quantities of alcohol.

You will I am sure appreciate that this behaviour was in contravention of several strict rules of conduct and that the Governors and myself have no choice but to censure both participants.

Regretfully therefore I must inform you that there will be no place for Deborah here next term, nor at any term in the future.

Yours sincerely

James Rowbottam.

Headmaster

George threw the letter down, stomped out to his car, and went to work, which of course entailed a visit to Paris with his new PA. Catherine made a beeline for the fitness club and did not return until middle evening. Neither discussed the matter with Deborah who spent the day in tears, having had her phone call to Daniel brusquely declined by his mother.

She did, as a matter of record, score sufficiently well in the now forgotten exams to have gone on to the Advanced Course. Instead she went as a clerk to a fruit farm owned and run by a business acquaintance of her father. It was between Tetbury and Malmesbury, and offered on site accommodation since there were dormitories for armies of fruit pickers, many of whom were foreign labour.

Daniel went to work as a bank clerk in Liverpool. He never went to university, never had his diplomatic career and never saw Debbie again.

Henrietta Burchill tossed and turned at night for many months, and became more wintry than ever. She had truly admired Daniel Hodges, and felt very maternal towards him. She felt her blind adherence to the rules had deprived a young man of his destiny. She would never truly come to terms with the fact that, in truth, she did not have any other option but to relate what she had seen to the headmaster.

17

1980 Tetbury 1

The farm at Tetbury was just half an hour's car drive from South Cerney, but her father George was so disappointed in her that he had not given her the expected birthday car, instead settling for a Yamaha 50cc Moped, which was very much the fashion for young people. It was a tedious journey on this so the decision was made that Deborah would live in the accommodation block on the farm. The moped was perfect for slipping the three miles into the town of an evening for a drink at the local pub.

Relationships with George were at a low ebb so Debbie was not too sorry to be away from home, and quickly settled into the routine of a major agricultural site.

The farm was owned by Major Mark McDougall who lived there with his wife, Elizabeth, and son, Robin. Robin was just twenty and worked on the farm himself, gaining experience in all aspects of growing fruit and vegetables on a large scale and getting them to market in good order.

Crops were rotated so that there were very few weeks of the year when some sort of harvesting did not take place. There was asparagus and broad beans, followed by strawberries, raspberries, plums, apples, pears, and then the corns followed by winter crops of swedes, turnips, parsnips and later, spring potatoes. Most of the harvesting involved backbreaking manual labour which was provided by a local staff of regular employees bolstered at peak times by large amounts of itinerant labour.

Major McDougall had attempted to use Travellers for the peak times but found them both unreliable and unproductive. Too few local people were seasonally available since all those who genuinely wished to work already had regular employ. The solution was to import labour from abroad at peak times. He embraced this with some trepidation since he did not wish to cross swords with authorities anywhere, was not sure about the legalities, or the practicalities, not least the practicalities of language. He started with a few caravans and a toilet block, but was so pleased with the system that before long he had a formal accommodation block with individual rooms, all well-equipped, and a large mess hall which doubled as a social centre. At peak times there might be up to a hundred temporary employees, often students, from all over Europe. Both genders were employed, but there was a great preponderance of boys, perhaps because the work was very hard. The foreign labour was administered by a highly regarded firm in London, so he did not need to source his own people, just look after them and pay them. But of course the work of the farm had become complicated, the European regulations were onerous and the market forces quite imposing. He therefore needed good office staff as well as a production team. Robin, his son, was taking an ever larger share of the production responsibilities, and was becoming reasonably fluent in several Eastern European languages, but his real gem was Mrs Krystyna Ramsbotham, a buxom jolly lady of about thirty five whose Polish father had flown in the RAF during World War Two, and who had married an English girl and stayed on. Krystyna, their daughter, born and bred in Gloucestershire, married a farm worker, and understood the way of the countryside. But her real value was that she was a good office person who spoke fluent Polish, German and Russian, as well as some Estonian. She also understood the Eastern European cultures.

It was she who was the glue in this business. Krystyna ran the nuts and bolts for the family.

Debbie worked in the office and was directly responsible to her. As the junior with very little experience she was initially little more than a filing clerk, but gradually she was entrusted with more direct dealings with the workers, helping them sort out problems associated with living in a foreign land. In addition she was given the responsibility of dealing with the paper work associated with visiting lorry drivers, who would come daily to collect produce for delivery all over the country. Not infrequently large juggernauts would park overnight to be loaded early in the morning and make their way to London, Birmingham, or other centres where they might deliver to restaurants and hotels, but mostly to produce markets and supermarkets. Some of these men travelled many miles and needed a stop over to satisfy the law which restricted the hours they were allowed to be on the road.

Many of the lorries had sleeping facilities in the cab, but the drivers would still use the mess hall and the bathrooms on site. The mess hall was well provisioned; food was good and plentiful as it needed to be for people burning huge amounts of energy during the day. Mark McDougall however was wary of alcohol on site. The idea of 50 drunken Russian students did not appeal, so alcohol in the mess hall was limited to beer and even that was strictly rationed. As a result, vodka and spirits in general were confined to the private quarters. Debbie soon found herself invited to small drinking parties with a few of the lads. Occasionally too much was consumed and then behaviour became much less inhibited. One of the lads, a quiet, bearded Eastern European, smuggled cannabis in occasionally, and his parties were noticeably more popular than others. Debbie, already accustomed to it, was happy to be involved, and to enjoy the relative loss of inhibition that accompanied the sessions. It did not take too long before sex became part of the menu.

Krystyna said to the Major one morning that the new office girl was clearly a great success with the visitors. He did not realise her irony, and responded by inviting Debbie to supper in the farmhouse. There she sat opposite Robin, a powerfully built young man who would one day inherit everything. There was no other offspring. Debbie found herself once again attracted by opportunity and power, almost in an unconscious manner.

Robin and Debbie offered to wash up after supper, leaving the older generation by the television. Talking together in the kitchen they found they had a mutual love of horses. Robin offered to show his to Debbie after work the next day and told her there was a spare mount for her if she would care to exercise with him.

After that they often went riding together. Robin hunted of course, and encouraged Debbie to join him, but she told him that she had a dislike for the sport which she could not quite explain, especially as she liked nothing better than a gallop over the fields, jumping the dry stone walls of the Cotswolds almost as if they were no obstacle at all. In fact at those times she felt a little mad with exhilaration.

One warm autumn afternoon, one of those days when the angle of the sun on the golden yellows of the old season's fields and hedgerows made everything seem to be very sharp edged, so that the scene stood etched in the mind, she threw herself to the ground in a secluded corner and lay there panting, laughing delightedly with the exertion of the ride.

Instantly Robin was sitting astride her, pinning her to the ground in his powerful thighs. He tore at her jacket, blouse and waistband until she lay there exposed, but with a grin on her face and a smudge of mud on her cheek. She gazed up at him and said 'Come on then. What are you waiting for?'

He did not need any further encouragement. Later Robin pointed out an old shed in a corner of the woods, saying he would put a few blankets inside for their future comfort. Over that winter Robin and Debbie became an established relationship as far as the family were concerned. Robin was invited over to South Cerney for dinner and both families saw in the New Year 1980/81 together. Nobody told the McDougall clan what had led Debbie to leave school when she did and, if Mark McDougall noticed a cooling of Krystyna's attitude towards Debbie, he chose not to enquire too much. Why should he? The office and the business were being well run.

Debbie however was sometimes looking a bit tired, was pale and occasionally irritable. Krystyna noticed a slight tremor in her hands on occasion, and thought her error rate instead of reducing was actually increasing. She was not the only one who noticed. One of the lorry drivers, a hard working, sensible young man, named William Mason observed the change one day when Debbie had failed to present his manifest properly.

Instead of complaining he took an early opportunity to whisper to Krystyna that he thought Debbie was not quite herself. The work rotation in his firm took him all over the southern parts of England, from Cornwall to Kent, collecting and delivering in his huge vehicle. He liked to stop off overnight in Tetbury when he could, largely because the facilities were so good. He could have a good meal, a small beer, a chat with some pleasant folk and perhaps most importantly a decent soak in a bath. His home was in Brighton, but Krystyna reckoned he could be there only a couple of nights a week. There was an old piano in the mess hall used mostly by the student Gennadi, who was a brilliant pianist, but when Gennadi was not present William would sometimes sit playing light music, mostly songs from the shows. He didn't need any sheet music for that. He had no wife, nor as far as Krystyna knew, did he have a girlfriend, but he was devoted to his sister Susan who was married with a couple of children and also lived in Brighton. There was a rather public pay phone by the office door and he would sometimes spend several minutes talking with Susan about his travels, and when he would be back. Krystyna thought he was a very nice man, and once in a while invited him home for a meal with her husband.

Deborah Troutmann was very drunk. She lay on her back in her bed with her cheek rubbing quite hard against the labouring, bearded face of the foreign student, straining to reach his climax. Afterwards they slept a bit until waking, cold, from their evaporated sweat. He went back to his room to sleep until the alarm at six in the morning. She struggled to the bathroom to wash herself. Debbie always liked to feel clean. Having cleaned her teeth she swallowed two of the little blue pills Gennadi had given her as payment for his pleasure, and made it back to bed before the Valium took her into a very deep sleep. She knew she would be dreamy in the morning, but reckoned that the small white dexamphetamine would soon correct that. 'Oh God,' she thought to herself as oblivion came, 'I must stop this or I shall be in trouble.'

There were others, and not all as considerate as Gennadi.

18

1981 Tetbury 2

Just before Christmas 1980 Catherine acquired her small shop in Church Street Kensington. She had enough capital to stock it with a small quantity of exquisite antique jewellery, partly from her own family resources, partly from a willing husband, and partly from the bank. The tenancy on the property gave her freedom to fit it out in a lush manner. To aid the impression of expensive luxury, she installed a door which would only open when a release was pressed from within.

In no time at all the neighbouring shops were telling their customers that one needed to talk in telephone numbers in order to ring the bell for admission, an attribute which added both to the mystique and to the prices she felt able to charge. There was a small apartment over the shop, which she fitted out for her use, and for anyone with whom she chose to share it. She employed a highly experienced older lady, an expert in the business, to share the work, but who was not allowed upstairs.

News of her new venture spread quickly through her extensive network, and so she found herself in London more often than she was at home in Gloucester, which suited George admirably. He did not need to explain his own movements quite as carefully.

It was during the last week of July 1981 that Deborah had a whole week off and came home to stay. She wanted to renew her acquaintance with her own horse and to have a rest.

She was feeling terrible. It was time to dry out she thought. But in fact she felt steadily worse, and was particularly nauseous before mealtimes. Catherine, who was home at the time, thought that she might have a urinary infection, since she was getting up at night a couple of times. Eventually she suggested a visit to the Cirencester surgery.

The family was registered with Dr Crossman, though Debbie herself was newly attached to the practice in Tetbury, so the family firm treated her as a Temporary Resident under the NHS.

Dr Crossman was fully booked that Wednesday July 29th so she arranged to see the lady doctor, Dr Bellini. Having told her story, Debbie was firmly asked if she might be pregnant, a possibility she initially denied. She said she had always had irregular periods and had not taken any notice of being without for a couple of months or more. But, having admitted that it might indeed be possible, she accepted a laboratory bottle and documents that requested a pregnancy test to be performed on the first urine specimen passed the next morning. Debbie did not tell her mother about the test, but duly did send it in on July 30th. She was told that the result would be back in a couple of days and that she would be told the answer if she rang in. The test result, arriving at the surgery in the Saturday mail, was positive. It was clipped to her temporary record card, ready for her to ring.

'But you knew you were pregnant Debbie', said Maria Bellini when they next met. It was the week before Christmas 1981 over four months later. Deborah Troutmann sat in Dr Bellini's office hand in hand with a handsome young man whom she had introduced as Robin McDougall, her fiancé.

'You came in several months ago and I organised the test for you. It was positive. I knew you were only seeing me because you were home on holiday, and naturally assumed that you had collected the result and were seeing your doctor in Tetbury.'

'I didn't know that, Doctor.' said Debbie. 'I did not get a call from you, and when I called here nobody seemed to know.'

'The standard procedure is that we ask people to ring in for their test results. We have perhaps a hundred results a day of one sort or another, and could not possibly ring them all. We only ring a patient with dangerously abnormal results. In any case Debbie, would you really have wanted me to telephone that result to your home? I would not wish to navigate around your mother if she had answered the phone, and you had probably gone back to the farm by then anyway. That is why it was clear that you should make the contact with us, not the other way around. I am truly sorry you did not do that. Anyway, let's put that on one side; that obvious lump in your belly is a baby, so we had better organise your proper care.' Maria reached for her pen to make the needful arrangements for scans and blood tests.

'Can I have an abortion please?'

Maria's hand halted its reach for the forms. There was a long pause whilst Maria collected her thoughts.

'No Debbie, I think not. By my calculation you are 26 weeks now. The only legal grounds for termination at this late stage would be grave concern about the mother's health or a grossly abnormal baby. We would not find anyone prepared to terminate you at this late stage unless there was something of that nature. I'm afraid you are going to have your baby, like it or not. I think you must tell your parents now. Your baby is due in late March next year. Do you want us to look after you here, or will you see the Tetbury doctors?'

'We will see my family doctor in Tetbury. I think that will be easier.' said Robin, suddenly asserting himself.

They left, Debbie clutching Robin's hand firmly, leaving Maria feeling a little uncomfortable without quite knowing why.

Predictably, all four parents were less than pleased. George scratched his neck in irritation, with a strange sense that this had been utterly predictable. Catherine gave Debbie an unusually empathetic hug but looked hard at Robin in an unsmiling manner. Both said that Debbie was welcome to come home once she could no longer work. They would, if need be, look after her over the confinement and afterwards.

It was George who asked if they had any plans to set up home together. Robin replied that they had not discussed the matter yet, but that he felt sure a cottage could be found for them on the farm. Nobody discussed what was going to happen to the baby, at least not at that first meeting.

The McDougalls were even less relaxed than the Troutmann parents. Elizabeth burst into tears and sat slumped in a chair with her head down and a handkerchief dabbing her eyes, saying little. Mark was straight backed and bristly in his most military manner, something only seen when he felt truly upset. Here was his only son, in whom he had placed great expectation, getting a teenager pregnant on their own farm. This was seriously at odds with the clean cut, decent living image Mark always worked hard to promote.

Robin was defiant, saying he would stand by his girl; that he would look after her, and hope eventually to marry her. He asked his father for the next available cottage letting. Mark nodded in reluctant acceptance.

And so Debbie went back to work almost as if nothing had changed, except that there were no more visits from Gennadi or the others. She managed to stay off the drink and cut the drugs down to an occasional spliff.

William Mason was one of the first to notice her bump. He understood the apparent situation and was very considerate to Debbie, carrying piles of work for her, helping her with her overcoat in the cold of the winter, and generally trying to make her feel good about herself. They became friends.

The same could not be said of Krystyna. After several weeks of restless nights and curtain lectures with her husband, she quietly slipped into Major Mark's office one day, carefully shutting the door, and sat to tell him of her suspicions. 'Major, I must tell you I am not happy about Debbie and Robin.'

'Nor am I Krystyna. Stupid young scamps. Embarrassing for all of us.'

'No, Major, it is not that which worries me.'

'What is it then?'

'I am very fond of Master Robin and would not want him trapped into marriage over a child that may not be his.'

Mark stared at her for a long time. 'Do you have any grounds for making that remark, or is it just your dislike of the girl showing?' he demanded.

So she told him of the days of trembles and irritable fatigue, of the smell of cannabis, and of the not so discreet romps in Debbie's room. He thanked her quietly and she left the room to her own office.

Mark sat staring at the ceiling until the phone brought him back to the business of the day.

Catherine did discuss adoption with Debbie, but the thought was rejected out of hand. Debbie was determined now to keep her baby. When asked what the difference was between termination and adoption and why the one was acceptable but the other not, she replied only that getting rid of a baby was not the same as giving it to someone else. She would or could not elaborate beyond that enigmatic statement.

No cottage was available on the estate, and Robin was surprised to sense that his normally very supportive parents seemed in no hurry to find one for the fledgling family. Neither was Debbie invited to move into the family home, though Robin hinted several times that this would be the civil thing to do. There was space after all, and Debbie could share his room. Elizabeth would have none of it.

'When in Rome do as Rome does' was her motto, so she insisted that the young lived by the same standards as she and Mark espoused. There would be no sharing of rooms in her house outside marriage.

At the beginning of February, some six weeks before the baby, Debbie moved back home to South Cerney. The village talked among themselves about her pregnant state, but some knew of her previous behaviour at school, and so nobody was particularly surprised.

During this time Robin saw less of her and began to question in his own mind what was right for their future together. He realised that there were big differences of outlook between them and that Debbie was completely self centred. He could not really envisage her as mistress of the estate at Tetbury once his parents had passed on, and worst of all, although he lusted for her hungrily, he was not sure he loved her. Nonetheless he had got her pregnant and must do the right thing, however much doubt he might harbour about it. He had made his bed and he would honour his responsibilities. He must look after his child and that child's mother. That was his inescapable responsibility.

To that end he challenged his father about the estate cottage once more, hoping to extract a promise of support for when Debbie had produced the baby. They hoped to set up home together on the farm and to have an early wedding. Or at least, Robin realised suddenly, that was what Debbie wished for. She went on and on about it. She was even planning the ceremony and choosing furnishings in her mind.

Father and son were walking the farm checking on crop readiness. Just as he swung a leg over a stile Mark stunned him by saying 'Yes, of course Robin, you shall have Ivy Cottage. It needs a bit of work, but would be just right for a young family. I shall get it done just as soon as we know this baby is actually yours.'

Robin stared in disbelief at his. 'Mine. Of course it's mine. Who else's could it possibly be?'

'Well, I do not want to blacken Debbie, or to make any accusations,' said Mark, 'but you must be aware that very large sums are at stake here. This child, if it a boy, will be the first son of the first son, and will inherit all of this land one day.'

He stood where they were at the highest point of his land and gestured around him. All that could be seen and more, much more, belonged to Major Mark McDougall.

Robin's face was grim. 'There is something more, isn't there Dad, something you are not saying? I know there is. I have felt it and seen it in Krystyna's eye and in some of the other staff, even one or two of the drivers.'

'Well, let me be content with observing that some people on the estate suspect that you were not the only bee at that particular flower. Some of the young men in the accommodation block have been seen to be very friendly with her. I would just like to be sure that the child I would be welcoming into our family is indeed of our family. Is that too much to ask in the circumstances?'

It was of course too much to ask, thought Robin, just because it revealed a lack of trust in his potential daughter-in-law, a lack which did not bode well for future relationships, whatever the answer to the current question. They strode on in silence for a while before Robin asked if a formal paternity test was being requested.

'Yes, it is,' answered Mark, 'although I doubt if I have any legal right to demand it. You certainly do have that right though, and your mother and I must ask you to exercise that right for all of our sakes.'

'Very well. I understand.' said Robin.

Ruth Kathleen Troutmann was born in Cirencester, just as her mother had been, on March 7th 1982. The confinement was completely normal.

Subsequent tests proved that Robin McDougall was not the father. He did not say goodbye.

George went into the worst rage for years and demanded of his daughter the names of all of the potential fathers. She got it right at the fifth attempt. Several young men returned home to the East unexpectedly early that season. Among them was Anatole Gennadi.

19

1982 William Mason

There was just one person at Tetbury who was upset on Deborah's behalf. She did not have any sympathy from the rest. William, the loner lorry driver, had got on particularly well with her from the beginning, and indeed the feeling was mutual. Perhaps it was that William felt a kindred spirit for Deborah's undercurrent of inadequacy, the girl who had never quite matched her parental expectations, since he had experienced similar problems, though for different reasons and with a very different outcome.

On the pretext of returning some of her stuff to her he found his way to South Cerney one afternoon, parked his lorry in a long lay-by and walked to the house, quite uninvited and unexpected.

Deborah, though, was not really in the mood, or ready to receive visitors. She was in fact quite severely depressed. But she was very touched that he should have bothered to come, so she popped Ruth into her cot, squirted a little scent over herself to hide the smell of baby powder and breast milk, and welcomed him warmly.

William, being quite used to his sister Susan's offspring was soon billing and cooing over the baby, picking her up and inspecting her as if to the manner born. Debbie found herself thoroughly at ease with him, and recalled that it had always been so. That afternoon she invited him to stay for some tea, and did not bother to be too modest when Ruth required another spell of feeding.

Both William and Debbie would later describe their relationship as being comfortable, a characteristic that was immediately apparent to Debbie's family as they joined them later. In a household full of anguish and anger, with a baby that yelled more than most, and a sleep deprived teenage mother, William represented a delightful island of calm assurance which led to all of the Troutmann family pressing him for further visits.

Before long he was calling whenever he was in the area, sometimes driving out of his way to do so. For some time he was the only younger face that Debbie saw, so naturally, he grew in importance for her.

Black Cat received notably less attention than had been the case since Debbie had returned from Tetbury. Her need of him reduced as William's importance waxed greater.

William came from a family of smallholders, both sets of grandparents running small acreage fruit producing farms in Sussex, not far from one another. They had never made much money but they were happy with their world, especially when their newly wedded offspring decided to run a greengrocery in Brighton. Susan and William (he never liked to be called Bill) were born there, and Susan, after leaving school, had stayed to help her parents run the shop. The parents were into folk music, and played in pubs and clubs throughout the area. They had a tinny old piano which William came to love.

But William was painfully shy as a boy and had great trouble mixing with his peers. He was bullied at school, being teased mercilessly because he would run for refuge to his sister Susan. His problem was made worse because he was academically not quite able to keep up with the other children, so that, although he had a good pair of hands, was very sensible and practical, he was always the butt of the teacher's cruel jokes, and sat out of harm's way at the back of the class.

Fortunately, being poor at writing and not very special at arithmetic did not prevent him in any way from being a good driver. William was an expert. He could reverse his enormous truck onto a sixpence and loved his life on the road. He was enormously strong and had no trouble, if need be, in loading and unloading his vehicle. His family, several generations of them, had stumped up for his wagon. Susan, his housewife sister, acted as his manager, taking his orders, planning his routes, and managing his money, whilst William spent his life driving.

But that existence did not encourage much of a social life, nor provide a secure base from which to live, so William had perforce become something of a loner, though, unlike many other loners, William was not hostile towards other human beings, just shy of them. In Debbie, he felt that he had found someone who was not judgemental, who took him for what he was, a kind, sensitive, loving human being. For her part she was grateful that he had arrived in her life just as she most needed support. He was a strong masculine presence, but one that she knew she could easily control.

Quite often, when William arrived, Catherine and George were both out at their businesses or involved in some leisure activity, so he and Debbie soon found themselves with plenty of time together. Inevitably they became lovers, which was a new experience for William. In fact he was not at all sure how it came about. She could have told him, if he had asked. He loved being taught just how to please her, and she loved the return to what she did best - sex.

But Debbie was getting restless. Whilst at home she had too many hours alone, too many hours to think about the fortune which had escaped her, too many hours to consider her bad decisions. She did as little as possible to service baby Ruth's needs. Indeed Ruth had become an encumbrance. Her father, George, had a very large cellar and had no idea what was in it. Debbie became a closet drinker. Initially it was just a glass or two of sweet sherry, but before long she was regularly drinking by mid morning, and by the time the family came home, she was desperately eating peppermints to hide the smell on her breath. Fortunately they were not a demonstrative family, so there was little in the way of kissing between parents and daughter, or discovery would surely have come about.

She looked forward to William's visits, mostly as a diversion, but she had already begun to perceive that he might offer a way forward for her. When he talked to her of his home and his family she always expressed great interest.

In October, William told her he had bought a large mobile home on a beautiful site near Brighton. She did not need to be told that this was his way of inviting her to live with him.

The lack of a period again and the return of the nausea told her it was time to accept. She used these events to browbeat her mother into accepting the arrangement. George was furious that his daughter should have fallen so low as to live in a mobile home. He knew that within a few weeks his daughter would be distraught with claustrophobia because of her surroundings, having always had the luxury of space and large grounds. He was overruled as usual.

George noted that Black Cat was safely in a basket in the back seat of William's car as they drove away from South Cerney.

20

1983 The Dinner Party

The house at Cerney was at its best that evening. The sitting room log fire blazed warmly and was prettily reflecting its flames in all of the brass and copper hung on the walls and in the glass display cabinets. The house was infused with the wonderful smell of apple smoke. The Hi-Fi had been quietly playing standards, including Elvis Presley's 'Can't help falling in Love', and Duran Duran's Synthpop hit 'Planet Earth', as well as some Louis Armstrong and Ella Fitzgerald. The dinner had been a triumph, a whole poached salmon washed down with a 1976 Mersault, and a light syllabub to finish.

The company was chatting over coffee and brandy. The guests were old friends, Jim and Gillian Marks from the village, business associate, Christopher and June Martins, and the new young partner in the local law firm, Graham Sidebottom with his wife Marcia. They were from Swindon.

The men seemed to be having their own conversation so Gillian took the opportunity to ask Catherine how Deborah and baby Ruth were getting on, now that they had moved away from home. Catherine, determined not to let the side down, declared that they were fine and that Deborah's boyfriend seemed great. His job being in Brighton, they had decided to move there to be with him. She did not reveal that Deborah was pregnant again and that this had triggered the move. 'It must have been a difficult time for you dear', said Gillian, 'what with an unexpected pregnancy and then keeping both Debbie and her baby here all that time.'

'Well, you are right, it has not been easy in any way. George hardly came home. Debbie was very depressed after the birth, so I had a lot of caring to do and that meant giving up a lot of my own interests. But we did not have any choice, really, Gillian. You see she did not have any money except a bit of state benefit, and Ruth's father just disappeared, so she has not been getting anything from him, neither money nor support. Actually we feel very angry about that and think the government should chase these lads and force them to pay for their pleasures. We have lost out a lot, both in money and inconvenience, because we have had to support our daughter and grandchild in order to give them some decent place to live. Debbie has not been able to contribute much towards it. She could not get a job, and Ruth is quite a handful, so George and I have been paying.' Catherine sounded quite petulant, her more strident tone intruding on the men's talk, so she suddenly had the attention of everyone present. George briefly wondered what inconvenience, if any, his self centred wife had experienced. As he recalled he did all the paying, as well as all the fetching and carrying. Furthermore it looked as if he would be going on paying for some time yet.

'I totally agree with you Catherine.' said Christopher. 'Your husband here has been looking very down at heel recently, haven't you George?' he joked, everyone knowing that George was making a fortune.

'But that is not the point is it?' said Jim, 'George and Catherine happen to be comfortable and well able to afford to help Debbie, but what if they were not in that position, what would happen then?'

'I agree that the government should chase them, the lads I mean,' said George. 'Not everyone is in our position and I think that real hardship must sometimes occur but, as the father of a single mother, I must state that my family would always have thought it their responsibility to look after their own. It should not be the state's job. Why should you, as tax payers, at your expense, keep my daughter and her baby in a situation which she courted with her eyes wide open? That cannot be right, surely. Having said that, I believe it is quite wrong that a boy can make a girl pregnant and walk away as if it is nothing to do with him. I have many sins in this world, but I am always prepared to pay for them.'

'You'll be telling us next that Dads should 'Lock up your Daughters', George.' said Jim. 'That would cause a stir, even though we have all been to see the musical.' He smiled at his attempt to lighten the tone of the conversation.

'But is it so unreasonable a thing to ask?' retorted George. 'After all, having a nubile young woman about the place and the honey pot effect that has on the boys, has been a big issue since the beginning of time, especially for fathers. In fact I have wondered often this last couple of years if all this would have happened had Deborah been living under our roof instead of unsupervised out there in the world at such a young age. I sometimes feel guilty about that.'

'Well, I think someone should lobby the politicians,' said Marcia. 'Perhaps one day a law will come to oblige each of the parents to take responsibility. Why should it always be the girls who pay the price? It always has appeared to me that if a teenage girl allows her knickers to be taken off, she risks a totally different life with a completely altered future. That is a big risk to take, and a big price to pay for a few minutes of lust, is it not?'

'But that is the whole point Marcia,' said June. She looked deprecatingly at Catherine as if apologising for what she was about to say. 'If you will forgive me folks, I would like to say that pregnancy is completely unnecessary nowadays, unless one actively seeks it. There is, after all, something called The Pill which, despite rumours to the contrary, is both safe and pretty well completely effective. I only wish it had been about in my time. In short, is it not now the case that unplanned pregnancy is irresponsible? Sorry, Catherine.'

'Then why do we have the highest teenage pregnancy rate in Europe? Why do boys and girls have sex as young as twelve years of age?' asked Jim rhetorically, his voice rising in pitch and intensity with each point he made.

'Well, I can tell you. It is because we live in an age of instant gratification, encouraged by Automatic Telling Machines, the loss of any sort of religious observance, the influence of mass communication, from which children cannot be protected, and most of all there has come about the abdication of authority by every adult they meet, which includes teachers, police and parents. We are all ridiculously afraid to tell off or punish young people who remain legally in our care. It is madness.'

Gillian leant over and gently restrained Jim with a hand on his arm. She knew he was climbing on one of his hobby horses and did not want to upset Catherine any further. Actually Jim was quite a bit older than the others and had very strong, probably perfectly justified, feelings about the 'lunatic liberals' in the higher reaches of the education world who, from their Ivory Towers, had overseen a revolution in teaching in the late 1950s and early 1960s. From that point teachers encouraged, rather than obliged children to learn, and a whole generation was spawned, for whom the word discipline had a negative connotation, instead of the positive and encouraging one their parents would have understood. Gillian knew that, in Jim's mind, Deborah was a product of that system and, for all her faults, Catherine was a victim also. George had been the only restraint in Deborah's life and his wife had opposed him every inch of the way, having been taken in by this educational nonsense. In the process, George had in some ways been driven out of his own house and into his business as an escape.

'You all make good points, but it is not the whole story.' said June, 'I have some experience of this at school and believe that most young women today, once they have become sexually active, do go on the pill in a responsible manner. Unwanted pregnancy is not so very common in 20 year olds and over, because they have come to terms with the issues and have grabbed responsibility for their destiny. They are the truly modern women; in control, and becoming more and more confident both in themselves, and their place in the world in which they live. Actually they frighten me, and I am female. God knows how they must frighten young men.' She smiled, looking at the men in the room as if gauging their imaginings on the prospect of young female predators; but, not getting any response, continued with her theme. 'But it is not those people we are concerned with here, is it? We are bothered by the 'tweenies', those who are hormonally blooming but have not the experience or wisdom to handle it. We're talking about the people who have not yet fully grasped the law of consequences, who do not properly connect today's experience, enjoyable or not, with next year's responsibility. Those are the young people who miss out. As you all know, GPs, even now, are attacked by parents for giving their underage daughters The Pill, and those are the switched on, thoughtful, girls. There are still a large number of young, relatively innocent, ingenuous 15 year olds you know, who would curl up and die rather than tell their GP that they are having sex. It takes a pretty courageous young woman of school age to go and ask for contraception. Some behave like ostriches and some of those get caught. The problem comes down to a gap between the acquisition of reproductive drive and peer pressure on the one hand, and emotional maturity on the other. Lack of adult control from school, or from parents, also plays a part, as probably does the loss in our culture of any sense of shame. God knows most of us diced a bit when we were young, but fear of the shame we would bring kept most of us in line, just.'

'So you would lock up your daughter.' said Jim, laughing at the idea of his wife doing any such thing to their daughter, now well and truly grown up and gone.

'Yes, I think so, not literally of course, but figuratively speaking, I would. I would try to keep her focussed on other matters, and would encourage the best communication, so that, hopefully, I got enough early warning of an important relationship to suggest protection before it was too late. And, I do still, if you remember that far back Jim, believe that, in perfection, one should not open one's presents before one's birthday.'

'Thank God we were not entirely perfect,' muttered Jim.

'Well, you know, we were almost so, certainly in comparison with today,' smiled June.

'It was that bloody doctor. She is the one to blame,' interrupted Catherine moodily from the edge of the company. 'If she had behaved properly, Deborah would have had a termination, but she never had a chance to.'

Everyone looked at Catherine for what seemed a long while. She just stared moodily into the fire. The joy of the evening had evaporated just like the brandy off the Christmas pudding and everyone felt flat. Gillian thought her friend was looking tired and very depressed. Of course she did not know the current situation; another baby, another man, no marriage, no security. All of these thoughts were coursing through Catherine's mind and her face reflected the solemnity of them.

The party broke up soon after, but as they took their leave Graham Sidebottom took Catherine to one side and asked just how old Ruth was. On learning that she was eight months old he suggested that Catherine should come to talk with him in his office, and that she should not delay. When she looked surprised he whispered that medical negligence was a professional interest of his, but that if a complaint was to be made it should be done within a year or the court could deny it a hearing.

As they shut the front door George returned to the fire to drink another brandy. He had already had several, though he did not seem in any way impaired.

'I wish you had not started all that,' he said. 'These things are private matters, not for public debate.'

'Oh, come off it,' she replied, 'This is not a public debate, just a caring conversation between friends, and interestingly some good has come from it?'

'What good?' he demanded.

'Well, Graham Sidebottom wants us to go and see him in his office. He clearly thinks we may have a case against Dr Bellini, and evidently it is his speciality.'

George, turning in his seat towards her and waving his glass in emphasis, said intently. 'Do not go there, woman! Dr Bellini did not make our daughter pregnant. It was not her who stupidly did not persist until the result was known. It was not her who kept quiet until more than half way through. It was Debbie herself who did all of that. I will not have you pursue a thoroughly decent person as well as a fine doctor. Apart from anything else it would be bound to come out in the press and then where would we be in our community? You know perfectly well how they would react. All the goodwill I have worked for over the past 20 odd years would disappear. Just, do not do it. I shall certainly not pay for it.'

His anger at his daughter and her behaviour was laid bare for all to see. If challenged about his own behaviour, and made to examine how he differed from Debbie, he would have declared that, in his mind, discretion is all. It does, of course, matter what you do in life, and he was not proud of his behaviour with Elaine and others; but to George it mattered even more what you are seen to do, because, to be seen to behave badly causes social uproar and disruption. Social disruption in George's book was part way to anarchy. That is why he would remain tied to a wife for whom he now cared little, and certainly did not love. Debbie had failed that discretion test conspicuously, and George was cross with her. He realised at that moment that this was why, until now, he had been happy to pay for everything, but not able to get too personally involved. He was still angry with her. He was prepared to go on with some level of support for her, even though she had gone off to live with this new man, who seemed decent enough, but he was not going to spend money attacking Dr Bellini. Also, in his heart, he suspected that Debbie had darker motives all along. He knew his daughter to be a manipulator, and did not believe Catherine's version of the innocent little girl who got caught.

'Then don't!' snarled Catherine. 'I shall take full responsibility, and if it costs money I have a little of my own. I must have justice for my daughter even if you do not. I shall make an appointment go to see Graham tomorrow.'

'Catherine, we have already been as far as I am prepared to go and we did not like what we found then, did we? When the first boy, what was his name? Robin? refused to accept responsibility we asked for paternity testing. It took Deborah five suggestions and five tests before she got it right!!! How do you feel about having that paraded in court? Do you have no sense of shame, woman?' He was shouting by now, 'Have you no shame?' he repeated.

'Difficulties with local folk must be avoided, especially now'. He went on. 'Mrs Thatcher has been Union bashing, inflation is very high, small businesses are going bust, and industrial production last year fell so much, that roads and houses are not being built as they were. Our gravel is still required but not on the scale of previous years. We have done very well for twenty years in a period of national reconstruction, but our order books have shrunk by a quarter this year, and I have today decided to lay some of the men off. That will not be popular in the villages around here and some fingers will be pointed in our direction. I do not want to make that worse, through a row with a popular local doctor, especially my own doctor, whom I regard highly.'

She just looked at him scornfully, then turned and stormed out of the room, leaving him staring morosely into the fire, smoking a last cigar before going up to his little single bed in the attic.

21

1983 The Case Begins

It was about a week later that Catherine and Deborah Troutmann sat in Graham Sidebottom's comfortable office in Commercial Road, Swindon. Clarksons were an old established firm and Catherine felt at home with her surroundings. Graham Sidebottom was the newest of their partners, but Catherine knew that George thought well of him, which is why he was at dinner with them.

The same comfort did not extend to Deborah, who sat perched on the edge of her chair looking hard at the floor. She had come up from Brighton the day before and mother and daughter had spent the evening preparing what they had to say at this interview. Debbie was not at all happy, but she knew she had no choice but to go through with it.

Graham could not help noticing the expansion of Deborah's waistline and thought she was about half way into a new baby. Well, that explains why she has moved in with the boyfriend, he thought.

He turned to face the mother more squarely. 'Firstly,' he said 'I need to be sure that you understand the law as it applies here. Medical negligence comes under the heading of the law of Tort. In order for a claim to succeed, it is first necessary to demonstrate that an individual has a legal responsibility towards another, secondly that the individual concerned failed to carry out that responsibility, in so doing failing the test of a reasonable standard of care, and thirdly that the second individual suffered injury. That phrase 'reasonable standard of care' is one you will hear over and over if we pursue this case. It follows that the law cannot apply unless there is some form of injury. It is not enough to claim that a doctor should or should not have taken this or that course of action, unless you can show that, from that action, damage of some sort actually did occur.'

'The phrase 'reasonable standard of care' means that any practitioner, be he a doctor, dentist, builder, or even lawyer, (he smiled at this) is not required to be the ultimate expert on every subject, making decisions based upon the latest esoteric research, but is expected to operate at a level of competency which matches good standards in his peer group. This gives rise, in tort cases, to conflicting witnesses declaring support for, or condemnation of, the action under scrutiny. It happens that in medical practice it is the case that two perfectly sensible doctors might take differing views of the same situation, and this leads to confrontation in court.'

'You need also to be clear that a genuine accident is not a source of claim. If a surgeon is struck by a piece of debris in an earthquake, and cuts a nerve as a result, the patient could not hope to succeed in a claim against the surgeon.'

'The person who is reputed to have suffered the injury is called the Plaintiff, and the person accused of inflicting the injury, or committing the tortious act is known as the Defendant.'

'In your case, Deborah, it was your mother's remark, blaming your GP for not giving you a termination, or an opportunity for a termination, which made me think there may well be a case of negligence here. Would you like to talk me through exactly what happened to you at each step of the way, please.'

For almost an hour they went through the story, from Debbie's weekend at home being sick to the arrival of little Ruth. They discussed the paternity issue in all its details, which, Graham noted, did not seem to disturb Deborah or even her mother at all.

Towards the end Catherine asked 'At the start you said it was necessary to have damage as well as a failure of care. I suppose little Ruth is the damage in our case.'

'Not really', said Graham, 'or at least, not in my eyes. The doctor certainly was in a legally responsible position, and is therefore required to act with a reasonable standard of care, but she was not the cause of Ruth. She certainly did not make Debbie pregnant.' he said, smiling wryly. 'But she did, by failing to inform Debbie of her pregnancy, deprive her of the chance of a termination. Debbie was denied the crucial choice, which should have been hers to make. By failing to give her that opportunity, Dr Bellini created a social and financial state which is going to have an effect for the whole of Debbie's and Ruth's lives. There are costs involved to you all, which would not have been the case had the doctor operated the law properly. That is what we shall be attacking, not the existence of the pregnancy itself.'

'I must warn you that there will be a second prong to my attack, which will concern the ordinary office standards of the practice, which I think fell below normal acceptable levels. That means that there will be an involvement of staff and possibly the senior partner.

If you are you still patients there I would advise you to change your doctor, because the whole relationship will inevitably become untenable.'

'George and I are registered with Dan Crossman, although George often sees Dr Bellini and I suspect quietly fancies her,' said Catherine. 'George will not like this one bit, but I will fix it, don't worry. Debbie was, of course, not living at home at the time, and has only been at the practice briefly as a temporary patient. When she came home to have the baby she registered with another practice, because she was so cross. Now of course she is in Brighton.'

'I assume Catherine that you and George are bringing this case, and must warn you that it will not be a cheap exercise. If the doctor denies responsibility, and the case drags on for a long time before coming to court, it will be very expensive indeed. Should you lose, the court might awards costs to the other side, which would mean that you have the whole bill for both sides to pay. You could be talking of many thousands of pounds.'

'Well, Graham,' said Catherine, 'I must confess that George is hostile to this whole thing and will not fund it. We have quarrelled about it, in fact. I have funded today's consultation, and could do so up to a few thousands, but I am not rich enough to do it all by myself. In any event, the whole complaint comes from you Debbie, doesn't it? She said, gesturing to her daughter, who did not respond. 'Debbie has no money of her own, and is in fact still needing a bit of help just to get by. Can you tell us about Legal Aid? Does it cover this sort of thing, and would she qualify?'

Graham sat back in his chair locking his fingers behind his head. He had not anticipated this. Knowing that George was making a packet, he had assumed that this would be a lucrative, privately funded, fishing trip, not one on the bread rations of legal aid. He considered his options for a moment, but then mentally shrugged in acceptance. He had encouraged the whole thing, so now he had to go on with it.

'We shall have to apply for legal aid, but I would expect that to be granted. It does of course mean, Catherine, that from this moment you cease to be the prime mover and that we shall be dealing directly with Debbie. Since she is nineteen now she is perfectly able to take control of her own destiny.' He noted that Catherine was a little crestfallen at this, but that Debbie seemed to sit a little more upright, as if more self-assured.

'We shall of course be asking the doctors, all of them, to send us their records, though we shall have especial interest in the Bellini practice. We examine those carefully, matching them with your story. If all is as we think we shall instruct counsel and a writ will be issued through the court, which will be the High Court in The Strand, London.'

'The application for records will go out from here within a few days, and of course that will alert the practice to a possible law suit. You would be advised to make the change in your registration before those papers arrive.'

He stood to indicate the end of the interview, shook them both by the hand, but rather pointedly said to Debbie that she would be hearing from them before long.

A few days later, Graham received a request to take his coffee with Matt Clarkson the senior partner. As the two men sipped their drinks Matt quietly moved the conversation to the purpose of the exchange. He explained that he had noticed some papers in the secretarial basket about the Troutmann girl, whom he regarded as a little tart, spoiled rotten by her parents. There had been some problems at school, he recalled, which led to her leaving early. 'Am I to understand Graham that you are encouraging a claim against the GP concerning the baby?'

'Yes Matt, that is the case. I think she should have been given the chance to have an abortion and something went wrong in the practice which meant that she never had that chance.'

'Hmm,' Matt sipped, staring out over the top of his glasses, attempting to avoid being judgemental, but not entirely succeeding. 'Are you too far along to drop the whole thing?'

Graham was astonished at this turn of events. 'Well, it would be very difficult now. I have actively encouraged the action, have agreed to get Legal Aid and have outlined the basis of the attack on Dr Bellini and her practice. To drop it now would be very professionally embarrassing for me, and perhaps for the firm as well.'

'That is a great pity Graham. I very much hope you will not be even more embarrassed at the end of the day.'

'Are you telling me to pull out then and if so why on earth do you want me to do that? Are you friends with Dr Bellini or something?' asked Graham.

Matt tapped the side of his nose 'This tells me all is not as it seems. I doubt I would have taken this case, and would probably have told her that she has made her bed and she must lie on it. Oh, and yes, I am friends, not with Maria Bellini, but with Dan Crossman her senior partner. He has once or twice quietly offered this firm advice in medical issues, and I have learned to trust his judgement. For example he advised me a couple of years ago about the rights and wrongs of general anaesthetics in dental surgeries, advice which was completely in line with good practice thinking. Now dentists do not give general anaesthetics in their own premises. It is always done in hospital. That came about because of reports about anaesthetic deaths, where dentists had neither the proper resuscitation system, nor the needful skills. But that is not why I am unhappy about this case. Dan and Maria are big enough people in my judgement to cope with this, and if I felt right about it I would have taken the case despite my affection for Dan. No, my problem is the girl. I think she is a mischief maker and I would not have any trust.'

Graham observed the older man, thinking how very different they were from each other. Matt, wrinkled and wise, had always felt, indeed had been taught by his mentors all those years ago that Law needed to be tempered by judgement; his judgement, not anyone else's, whereas to Graham the practice of Law was simply about exercising the letter of the law, without any sense of right or wrong, or of personal responsibility. That is what he was here for; to make as good a living as he properly could, exercising the law as it stands, not overlaid by any sense of morality or emotion. He had no sense of community as such, and certainly no sympathy or understanding of Matt's paternalistic view, making judgement calls depending on his perception of a person's moral worth. Although they would never actually say so, each despised the other's creed. Both knew that the world had changed.

22

1983 The Writ Arrives

The weather was glorious, the spring flowers lining the lanes as Maria drove to work in her small convertible. She loved to have the top down and her hair blowing in the wind. She looked so radiant, so very elegant, so full of Italian chic that those who saw her could not help smiling. She was in good time and had a moment to greet the reception staff and her secretary whom she shared with Dr Dan, before seeing her first patient. She was excitedly explaining that she and Michael had booked dinner that night at the Wild Duck in Ewen to begin the extended celebration of his big birthday. It seemed inconceivable to her that her husband would be 50 tomorrow. With the staff's teasing remarks she strode smiling to her surgery.

Today her first patient was Captain Smythe RN, a wonderful old sailor of about eighty, who was actually Dan's patient, but he had taken, surreptitiously, to passing Dan's door and seeing Maria for his blood pressure and heart check. He always liked to be first in the day, probably because that way he never had to wait long. Today he bore with him a parcel which he placed diffidently on her desk prior to removing his coat and rolling his sleeve up.

As he took his leave at the end of the interview he said 'Dr Bellini (he called her Maria in his mind, but would never address her with such familiarity), I have just finished my memoirs. There are notes about the War at Sea, especially in the East around the time of the fall of Singapore and the sinking of the 'Prince of Wales'. I should be delighted if you would read them, and would like to invite your suggestions for any improvements.'

Maria considered the question. She had no interest in naval warfare, nor even especially in Memoirs, but she was fond of the old man, and recognized that this was a very special intimacy for him to offer. 'I shall be honoured and delighted, Captain,' she said, picking them up from the desk surface and solemnly placing them with her own possessions. 'I shall have them here for you when you come for your next appointment, if that is acceptable to you.'

And so the morning passed in pleasantries and without any major crisis. There was the usual small gathering of ardent feminists who flocked to the lady doctor, but Maria had long ago noted that the happily married, or personally secure women, still queued long outside 'Dr Dan's' door, and that her own clientele was mostly older men, very young girls with problems they thought too embarrassing to discuss with a male doctor, and a small, irritating, group of frequent attendees, who always seemed to have something to complain about. It had long ago occurred to her that the other partners had been delighted to lose their 'heartsink' patients to her more gentle care. In fact she and Dan had joked about it, especially since it was so different from what Dan had imagined would come about once Maria was established.

It was her habit to read the morning's mail over the coffee break that she took from ten thirty till eleven each morning. Quite apart from allowing a little 'catch up' time for any overrun on the first two hours of the day, it was a little break from seeing patients. Reading the post sometimes took the half hour until the next appointment, but usually there was a moment to collect her thoughts, and to see who and why people needed house calls. The practice being quite large, some 200 square miles, some calls might be almost ten miles away and therefore planning a sensible route might save a lot of time and fuel. The trick was to marry those considerations with the overriding need to see the acutely ill, who might need hospital admission as soon as possible.

On this day however Maria sat at her desk utterly still and expressionless for a long time, a cold chill gripping her heart, and a tear slowly descending her face. The coffee was ignored.

In her hand was a large brown envelope marked private and personal, which the staff had not opened. Within was a parchment coloured document bound with pink ribbon. It was a writ accusing her of professional negligence in the matter of Deborah Troutmann and her pregnancy. The writ accused not only Maria but the whole practice of failing to give Deborah the result of her pregnancy test, thereby denying her the opportunity to terminate her pregnancy, an opportunity which according to the document, was her right by law.

She sat there turning the events of the case over in her mind. She found the argument totally convincing and concluded that she was guilty as charged. All that she had worked for all these years came to nought in her mind. She had been labelled that most despicable of creatures, an incompetent and even worse, an uncaring doctor. She must tell someone, immediately, but whom and how? Fearful that she would not keep her composure Maria rose and took the offending document to show Dan, who too was sorting the remainder of his day and signing repeat prescriptions. He greeted her with his usual courtesy, waved her to a seat, noting her stricken expression and accepted the envelope wordlessly proffered. He read the paper carefully, sat back in his chair and surveyed Maria with concern, thinking this would be a very tough time for his soft-centred colleague. 'Do you notice that I am accused also?' he said.

'No, how could that be? You never saw her.'

'True, but the writ accuses the practice of being neglectful as well as yourself. They are criticising practice procedures, and as the head of the firm that will involve me.'

Maria lifted a little at this, feeling that at least she would be sharing the road ahead. Dan asked with whom she had taken out professional indemnity insurance. It transpired that they were both in the care of the Medical Defence Union. Dan undertook to contact them at the end of the session. Then, without looking up from the document, he said 'The bastards! Do you see who is behind this?'

'No, I hadn't registered that.'

'Well, the headed paper on the covering letter is Clarksons of Swindon. I know Matt Clarkson well. In fact, I played golf with him a couple of weeks ago. It is a very good firm, not one that normally goes in for ambulance chasing, or encouraging frivolous actions. Clearly Matt does not see this as the scam we believe it to be. I wonder why they have taken it on and how far they will run with it. I also wonder if Matt knows about this. It is not signed by him, but someone I don't know. Matt is a fine man who would, I reckon, show the door to someone he considered to be trying it on. He has not done so and I find that quite alarming.'

They sat in silent misery together, thoughts intermingling in a jumble of fragments, little mental snapshots about who said what, to whom and when; mental images of the newspaper headlines to come; despair at the loss of standing and reputation so hard won. Dan was particularly hurt to be attacked by a legal firm he respected and admired. Strangely that counted a lot with him.

Eventually Dan shifted in his chair, looked at his watch and commented that they were late starting the second part of the morning. He stood, pulled her to her feet, and gave her a brief but warm hug before gently steering her to the door. Later Maria confessed that she had very little recollection of the interviews later that morning, and hoped she did not compound one supposed crime with another.

It was Dan who rang the Defence Union in their Henrietta Street Offices in London. He was connected immediately to the secretary, a distinguished doctor, who listened carefully and with some sympathy. Dan was advised to furbish them with all of the records concerned and to reply to Miss Troutmann's lawyers that he had put the matter in the hands of the MDU, who would consider how to proceed. Dan was told that there would almost certainly be conferences in London and that both he and Maria would be required to attend. As he replaced the phone he felt that they were in very good professional hands.

Later that day Dan called a general meeting of the partners and staff to tell them what had happened. Maria, being part time, had gone home by then, which was deliberate on Dan's part, since he perceived that she would cry her way through it all. Everyone was appalled that their very own Maria, the most charming, competent and conscientious one of their number, could possibly be accused of medical negligence. Dan asked that all of the records be got out and put on his desk. He would personally interview everyone concerned to piece together exactly what had happened. Everyone realized that memories of events two years previously, which had not seemed all that important at the time, might be difficult to garner and might be unreliable. The meeting broke up with a very subdued staff returning to their desks. At least one of them remarked that is was a rotten birthday present for Michael too.

23

1986 Kevin

'Oh God!' she thought.' Not again, please, not again!' She wretched into the lavatory pan for the umpteenth time that day and eventually slumped on the bed doing her sums in her head.

Perhaps a joint would help her calm down and make her less nauseated. She knew she was using more of them these days, but did not seem able to resist anymore, not that she wanted to really. She noticed that her hands were shaking, and realised that she had not had a drink since morning. He had been furious when he found so many empties, and had begged her to stop.

'Stop? Stop what? Stop living! You stupid, ignorant man.' She ranted to herself, replaying their argument to herself. She knew that she would never stop. Her problem was not stopping; it was continuing, or rather, finding the means to continue. William was very generous with the housekeeping, and was always begging her to eat more and keep more food in for the children, but booze and cannabis ran away with the money so there was less with which to eat. She sometimes felt guilty about that, but not very often. She would have to find some way of getting more money. She wished the wretched lawyers would get on with it. She must have more money, somehow, anyhow. 'It doesn't matter much how! Just get more money!' she thought.

And now, just as she was getting over the last one, there was this 'thing' in her belly again, this parasite that he had placed there. It was time for some sherry.

Late that Friday evening in May 1986 William arrived home from a particularly tiring journey. He was jaded and looking forward to some supper and a quiet relaxation in front of the television. The house was silent and dark. He went to the kitchen and immediately saw a note in Susan's hand, which said. 'Debbie obviously not well, so I have taken the babes home with me. Please ring me.'

William knew what that meant and went directly to the bedroom. There he found Debbie almost unrousable. The smell of her vomit, and the loss of self worth appalled him. He wondered, not for the first time, how he had got himself into this marriage. Later she told him she thought she was pregnant again. They stared speechless at one another, both feeling trapped; he, because of her behaviour, she, because she was pregnant again for the third time in 5 years.

William tried his best to make things work for them. He rearranged his work schedule so that he had fewer nights away and was home more often to care for his wife and children. He took to entertaining Ruth and Bridget as much as he could so that Debbie was less tired. He shopped, and often cooked as well. He drew the line at doing the laundry.

Ruth was four, and was remarkably mature, almost old for her age. William realised that she had needed to do more than perhaps she should have done for herself, and so was losing out a bit on her childhood. She was quite independent, dressing and washing herself. She could tie her shoelaces, and deal with the most difficult of buttons. William was beginning to realise that she was very bright, and not for the first time wondered about her biological father. Who was he? What was he doing now? Where was he?

Ruth loved Bridget and took a great part in her care, often feeding her at the table, and taking her for explorations around the garden. She loved her Daddy and her Auntie Susan, but was often very solemn when dealing with her mother. William noticed that Ruth cuddled him more enthusiastically than she did Debbie.

Sometimes William would sit at the old piano, with the ivories falling off the keys and an ominous jangle at the bass end. He would play the tunes his grandparents and parents had taught him. He was not a real pianist but he knew his way around, and began to show Ruth how it all worked. He became quite excited one day when he hummed and played an old song only to find that Ruth sang it back to him absolutely in tune. Encouraged by this he made these little explorations their own speciality, something both would look forward to. Sometimes she sat, looking very waif like, on the piano stool and pretended to play.

Debbie seemed rather better as the pregnancy progressed. Ruth started school in the September. William had the impression that Debbie was drinking less and the smell, which he thought was of cannabis, was not noticeable very often. There were no complications when baby Kevin arrived just before Christmas. William was very proud. He had a son. Debbie was just pleased it was over.

But William was worried. He knew that Debbie had a problem with the drink, and probably with soft drugs too, and was concerned to note that little Ruth, only just at primary school was acting as carer for the babies, much too often and with too much responsibility. He arranged that sister Susan would call at least once a day, and was most careful to ensure that Ruth was not expected to come home tired from school and be obliged to look after the youngsters, even though she never complained about doing so. If Deborah had been drinking, which to be fair was only a couple of days in a week, William knew that she would be getting past caring by teatime. It seemed to him that she was able to resist most days, but that, if she once started, she could not stop until she reached oblivion. Then she would sleep for many hours and be worth little the next day. He also understood that she never drank on the days she went back to Cerney to see her mother, or for her legal appointments. It was as if, when she needed to be smart and in good form, without any interruption she was quite capable of being so. William doubted if Catherine had any real notion of the severity of her daughter's problem.

There was a limit as to how much time William himself could be at home without jeopardising his earning and the whole family's security. Try as he certainly did to be at home as much as possible, he was inevitably missing sometimes when Debbie had a bad day. Susan was a tower of strength and did all she could to help, but she had a job, a husband and a family of her own. She could not be a full time nanny to William and Debbie's children. Ruth therefore made tea for them all, often changed Kevin's nappies, and always supervised Bridget's bedtime bath. When Kevin was a little older and could sit up properly the two little girls would between them get him into the bath too, and would both share it with him. These were perhaps the happiest moments of Ruth's day.

24

1990 The High Court 1

Dan elected to stay in the Strand Palace Hotel. It was not too expensive and was a few hundred paces only from the High Court, more correctly entitled The Royal Courts of Justice. The building was a magnificent grey stone Victorian edifice with an imposing porch, familiar to many who watch films or television. The media gather like vultures on the pavement outside, to photograph celebrities attempting, usually in vain, to defend their privacy or pocket, through the law. The late evening news programmes commonly featured interviews of Plaintiffs or Defendants in some 'cause célèbre' or other.

Dan arrived very early and had to wait in the street for the doors to be opened. It was a fine morning and despite his anxiety he found himself half enjoying the buzz as people gathered for the day's hearings. There were several easily recognisable faces amongst them. He noticed a couple of sandwich shops and cafés on the other side of the road, one of which, he thought would make a good meeting place for his staff over the next two weeks of the hearing. He had taken two weeks away from the practice so that there was some continuity of presence throughout the trial, but everyone else would come and go as they were required to give evidence. Clearly they could not shut up shop and neglect their patients for two weeks. As it was they were faced with the expenses involved in bringing all their people to London, often staying at least one night in a hotel. They had decided to get a locum in to help out since at least two partners would be missing most of the time. Win or lose the whole exercise was going to be expensive.

Behind the famous porch lay an imposing hall, not open to the media, in which persons with business in the many court rooms forgathered. There were some benches, not many Dan noted, and a small cafe. The courtrooms themselves, quite a number of them, were arranged around the periphery of the hall on several levels. He read the notice board, which gave details of the cases currently being heard. The High Court was, he realised, a very busy place with many important trials conducted simultaneously.

Dan had never had reason to be in a place like this before and because of the knot of anxiety he felt for himself, and Maria, he had done some 'homework' on what might happen. Proceedings were normally open to the public unless the judge directed otherwise. This would happen if evidence of a particularly sensitive nature was to be heard. The Central Criminal Court, known as The Old Bailey, about half a mile away, was unrelated. The law courts heard and decided in civil cases. Medical negligence cases were tried in the Queen's Bench Division.

Crossing back from the sandwich shop he had chosen as their meeting place, Dan spotted Michael and Maria O'Leary getting out of a taxi and went to greet them. Michael was very much in control of things, smartly presented, calm and assured as one would expect an Oxford surgeon to be, but Maria looked awful. She was puckered in anxiety, walking with her head down as if hiding from the world. She had visibly aged in the past year or two. It struck Dan, not for the first time, that this business was extracting a heavy toll on her, and that the monstrous eight year delay waiting for the hearing had damaged her life quite seriously. The two men walked on either side of her, trying to look nonchalant just in case a press photographer thought them worth a picture.

Inside the building Maria and Michael were somewhat overawed by the sheer size of the place and Maria seemed to shrink further. Dan was glad he had come early and located which court room they should attend. The court room looked just like any other. There was a raised area at the front where the judge would sit after entering through a heavy door in a panelled wall. In front of that there were desks for court officials recording the proceedings, and then, facing the bench were rows of seats; the first row having desks but each of the rows having a flat shelf rather like that found in a pew, only deeper. This was clearly so that all concerned could look at their papers easily and tidily. To the side of the court on the judges left was the raised dais with a lectern and rails which was the witness box. There was no dock and no jury. All those concerned with the Plaintiff assembled on the Judge's right and those concerned with the Defendant on his left.

Just before proceedings were due to start Dan noticed Matt Clarkson, his erstwhile lawyer pal whose firm was bringing the case on behalf of Debbie Troutmann. Matt was talking earnestly with a robed and wigged barrister and with a younger suited man whom Dan thought was his young partner Sidebottom. Unable to restrain himself Dan crossed to Matt, shook him by the hand and said, looking him directly in the eye. 'I am truly surprised at the company you keep these days Matt.'

'No more surprised than I am Dan. I am sorry, but even lawyers must eat you know.' Matt replied, looking wryly at his clients, who were just out of earshot. There was a young woman, smartly dressed, in animated conversation with a tall, slim, lady with short hair and a grim expression. Dan recognised her as the mother, Mrs Troutmann from when she was a patient of his. They ignored one another. There was no sign of Mr Troutmann.

No sooner had Dan regained his seat when a gavel was struck loudly and a court official invited everyone to stand for Mr Justice Williamson. Judge Williamson entered through the panelled door, bowed to the assembly and sat at his desk.

Everyone sat again as he shuffled a few papers, took out an expensive looking fountain pen and then looked up smilingly to the court. 'We are here to examine an accusation of negligence brought by a young woman, Mrs Mason née Troutmann against her family doctor, Dr Bellini, and the doctor's practice as a whole. The case relates to the management of a pregnancy. The Plaintiff asserts that because of the doctor's failure in her duty of care and the practice's failure in its procedures she was denied the opportunity to seek a termination within the legal limits of such a procedure. She is claiming for maintenance of the child concerned until that child reaches 25 years of age. I shall hear argument from both Plaintiff and Defendant and their legal teams, as well as taking evidence from expert witnesses on both sides. It is important that all parties note that this is a civil court, not a criminal court. Nobody faces a criminal charge. Nobody is at risk of losing their liberty. May we begin please? Mr Smart.'

Dan was immediately struck by the judge's gentle calming management of proceedings. He was, and remained throughout the hearing, a benign, almost avuncular figure, though he probably would not like that description. The effect was to put people at their ease, at least as far as was possible in the stressful nature of a cross examination. It also had the effect of making those examinations civilised, without any of the theatricals associated with the world of film or theatre. Of course civility and sensitivity in no way lessened the rapier like precision of the enquiries everyone faced in the two weeks of the trial.

That first day was concerned with Mr Smart presenting the facts of the case, rather than making overt attempt to portray cause and effect. He started by outlining the law on abortion. 'My lord, it would seem appropriate to spend a few moments defining the law on this matter. Until fairly recently abortion was illegal here as in most other countries, but in 1938 Alec Bourne, a highly respected Gynaecologist, from St Mary's Hospital, here in London terminated the pregnancy of a fourteen year old girl who had been raped by five soldiers in

St James' Park. This was before any state medical care system of course and Mr Bourne did not charge the girl or her family for his help. He then reported his actions to the authorities and was duly charged with being an illegal abortionist. After much argument he was found not guilty on the basis of a higher responsibility to the psychiatric health of his patient. The case brought about an increase in debate on the subject which led eventually to Mr David Steel MP bringing a private members bill before Parliament in 1967. The Abortion Act was passed on a free vote and became law in March 1968. It allows a woman legally to seek an abortion from an appropriately qualified medical practitioner until 28 weeks of gestation, which was regarded as the onset of viability, that is, when a baby might sustain life outside its mother. That Act remains in force today**.

'If the Court will indulge me a moment it is of interest to compare our situation in Britain with that in America. There, in 1973, the case of Roe v Wade reached the Supreme Court. A woman, Norma McCorvey, alias Jane Roe, had failed to find anyone willing to terminate her pregnancy. She had even knocked on the door of an illegal clinic, only to find it had been closed by the police. She applied for an abortion and was opposed by Henry Wade, the District Attorney for Dallas County. After much contradiction and controversy the case reached the Supreme Court, where the controversy continued. Eventually Justice Mr Henry Blackman read a judgement supported by seven of the nine Supreme Court Judges supporting the right of a woman to terminate her pregnancy, until the point at which that pregnancy was deemed to be viable. They also made provision for exceptions in the event of severe risk to the mother or severe disability in the foetus, though that was never precisely defined.'

** *please see appendix on page 306 for notes on changes to the law concerning abortion in the UK.*

'There are two prime differences between the American and the British position. The legal difference is that the American Supreme Court did not precisely determine the age of viability, whereas the British did attempt to do that, drawing the line at 28 weeks. The other difference is not a legal one but is a social matter. In Britain there are few voices speaking out on the matter of abortion and it certainly is not a party political issue. In America, however it was and remains a socially and politically divisive issue which had even led to the murder of doctors running abortion clinics. The nation divides itself into the Pro Life movement, which is largely Republican, and the Pro Choice Group which is largely Democrat, though of course those divisions are not universal. Here we have none of that, but of course doctors may refuse their help on the ground of conscience. You will hear more of that later, since it might be relevant in this case.'

'You will see in the papers related to this hearing that Deborah Troutmann, as she was then, was twenty six weeks pregnant when she returned to her doctor. She was declined an abortion. We contend that that, in itself was outside the law, depriving my client of her rights under the law.'

Having carefully explained to the court that it was Deborah bringing the case, not her parents, and that therefore the action was being financed through public funds, he called her to the witness stand. She stood there, soberly dressed, looking very demure. She answered all of the questions clearly and concisely. She was a good witness. He took her step by step through the job she had away from home, her visit to her mother when she was not well, how that had led to her visit to Dr Bellini rather than her own doctor in Tetbury. He made her describe the interview with Dr Bellini, which she did, truthfully describing how Maria had suspected pregnancy and offered to test her. She said she had tried to get the result from the doctor by phone when she had returned to Tetbury, but that nobody seemed to know anything about the test. She stated that she assumed that the doctor would tell her if it was positive. She assured the court that she herself did not really think she was pregnant because she thought herself infertile, and had always had infrequent irregular periods. She described the second interview to which she had brought her boyfriend and the upset she had experienced on learning that she was indeed pregnant, and was told that it was too late for a termination. She explained that the birth was normal, that she had later married a different man and now lived in Brighton with her husband and their two children, making a household of five. No, she was not formally employed, the children being too much of a handful.

When Mr Smart had finished with Deborah he completed his initial statement by indicating that although Maria had rightly suggested a pregnancy as the cause of Debbie's nausea and had indeed sought to ascertain that to be the case, she had negligently failed to inform her patient of the result of that test. He claimed that this failure was a failure of Maria's duty of care, and fell below the normal standards of a responsible doctor. It was not sufficient in his eyes to make the test available for the patient. Rather it is the doctor's role to be proactive in informing the patient of the result.

He went on to extract from Debbie how she had tried on several occasions to obtain the result from reception staff on the phone from her work at Tetbury, but had failed to get any satisfaction. She said that nobody had offered to look for the result and ring her back with it, even though she was desperate to find it. Mr Smart indicated that in his opinion this constituted a clear breach of best practice on the part of the partnership itself.

Mr Peter Tregelles QC for the Defendant was tall and cadaverous, with a very bass voice which resonated around the court room even when he was speaking quite quietly. He took on the questioning of Debbie after the lunch break. He checked a few minor points to corroborate the morning's exchanges, and seemed completely content with her answers, when suddenly he asked 'What is your daughter's name?'

'She's called Ruth.'

'Is she a normal child, healthy and bright?'

'Yes.'

'Is she happy?'

'I believe so.'

'Who is Robin McDougall?'

There was a pause in which Deborah looked at the judge for protection, and, none being forthcoming, she answered 'He was my boyfriend.'

'Your boyfriend at the time of the pregnancy in question?'

'Yes.'

'What did he do for a living?'

'He worked on the farm in Tetbury.'

'Is that Major Mark McDougall's Fruit and Vegetable Farm?'

'Yes.'

'And is Robin, Major McDougall's son?'

'Yes.'

'His only child?'

'Yes.'

'So he will eventually own the farm?'

'I suppose so.'

Tregelles shuffled some papers as if looking for something. 'And you thought that he was Ruth's father?'

'Yes I did.'

'But in fact he was not the father, was he?'

'No, he wasn't.'

'Did you or your family attempt to identify Ruth's father?'

'Yes we did.'

'How many men were subjected to paternity tests?'

'Five.'

'So your fifth suggestion turned out to be correct?'

'That is so.'

'And, if it had not been correct, might you have gone on to more tests?'

The Judge intruded 'That is enough Mr Tregelles. You have made your point. There is no need to pursue it further.'

'Thank you My Lord.'

'Mrs Mason, what has happened to the father of your child?'

'I do not know. He disappeared. He was from Eastern Europe and went home.'

'And so your child has no father supporting her?'

'No.'

'And you therefore think your doctor ought to do so?'

'Objection!' snapped Mr Smart.

'My Lord,' said Tregelles. 'Maintenance of a child for twenty five years including compensation for the mother's loss of earnings is part of the case. I wish to establish whether this mother would be likely to be earning, even without this child since she has two other, younger ones.'

The Court sat riveted throughout this cross examination. The public revelations of this girl's amorous adventures were astounding to most people present. She however seemed completely undisturbed.

Tregelles opted not to ask about Debbie's school history, or about her current domestic situation other than to establish that she was married with children. William was not mentioned except as the current husband. He was however sitting in the back of the courtroom, his face mask like and inscrutable. Ruth, now eight, was at school of course, and would be cared for by his sister Susan until Debbie and William returned.

Debbie's cross examination took all day, the first of ten. She left the court, white and tired, but had not broken down and wept at any time. Dan thought it had been a courageous performance. Matt Clarkson thought it was not courage, just brazen shamelessness.

That evening William and Debbie drove home in silence. She was exhausted and he was very pensive. Eventually he said 'Why have you never told me?'

'Told you what?'

'About the others, those other guys you slept with. I thought it was just Robin.'

'You mean to say your little Polish busybody Krystyna never told you? I find that hard to believe. She told Robin, didn't she, the bloody little creep. She is the reason we are here today. She stuck her nose in my business. Why don't you blame her for all of this, not me?'

'No, she is not to blame Debbie. She was employed by Major McDougall and is loyal to him and his family. She could not stand by and see Robin entering a marriage because of a pregnancy which might not be his, could she? But then, after today I realise that you would never understand that, would you? You! Who are quite prepared to tell the world that your eight year old should have been aborted could not possibly understand Krystyna's motives!' William drove on in angry silence, jaws clenched, ashamed, and dejected. Debbie just stared out of the side window, engrossed in her thoughts.

25

1990 The High Court 2

The next day Maria Bellini spent all day in the witness box. The hearing went perfectly smoothly until Mr Smart for the Plaintiff suddenly asked 'Tell me Dr Bellini, how many women do you refer for termination of pregnancy?'

'Well, I am not sure. From memory I cannot recall ever doing so.'

'Are you telling me that Deborah Mason, had she returned to you with a positive test would have been your first case requesting a termination?'

'Oh, no. You misunderstand. Of course I see women who request a termination from time to time, but you asked if I refer them for the purpose. I said truthfully that I do not recall ever having done so.'

'Please explain to the court what you mean by that Doctor.'

'Well, I do not do Obstetrics and ask one of my partners to take responsibility for all of my pregnant patients.'

'Do you mean to tell the court that you are the woman doctor in this practice, and yet you do not deal with female issues?'

'Yes, of course I deal with female issues, as you put it, but not Obstetrics. My partners have much more experience of Obstetrics. In fact they have their own Obstetric beds in the hospital.'

'But, to press you a little, you do not deal with abortion?'

'No, I do not.'

'Dr Bellini, might I be correct in surmising that, with your Italian name, you are a Catholic?'

'Yes, Mr Smart I am.'

'So how does that affect your decision making when it comes to abortion?'

'Well, I do not like abortion, and will not, myself, get involved; but if one of my patients requests one then I invite them to see a colleague to discuss the matter. Usually, as I have said, they are already seeing my partner who deals with pregnancy. I try to remain completely neutral.'

'Might that aversion to abortion have influenced your behaviour in this case?'

'Of course not. The matter had not been discussed in those terms until it was too late legally, and in our previous appointment I had no means of knowing that it would do so.'

'I put it to you Dr Bellini that you might have failed to inform the patient because of your religious standing, knowing that inaction might save you the moral dilemma.'

'I am not clairvoyant, Mr Smart. I could not know that she might request an abortion. I behaved exactly in the standard way that all doctors of my acquaintance would behave. I organised the test, and as far as I am concerned the result was available to her as promised.'

Dan was concerned that religion had been introduced into the case. It had long been accepted that, although abortion is legal, it is not incumbent upon the practitioner to offer that service. The state allowed for doctors to sidestep the issue as a matter of conscience, as long as the patient's freedom of choice was respected. In his practice Maria's Catholicism had never been an issue. Other partners would quietly step in to save any collision, as and when needed to do so. He had no idea why Smart had introduced it. To Dan it was a complete irrelevancy, though he supposed the court might as well hear it, if only for the sake of completeness and to dismiss it.

'Dr Bellini, you sit in your morning surgery and are faced with a young girl who presents not as being pregnant, but as being nauseous. In short, someone to whom pregnancy did not seem likely and who had apparently not considered the possibility until you raised it.' He paused for effect. 'Does that not tell you that she was naive?'

'Yes, I suppose it could imply that.'

'Then that understanding increases your pastoral responsibility, does it not?'

'I think I offer a high level of pastoral responsibility as a normality, Mr Smart.'

'I am sure you do Dr Bellini.' He smiled benignly. 'But I am not talking about your normal behaviour. I am talking about this individual case. Is it not the case that you did not function with your normal level of pastoral care in the matter of Deborah Mason? Could it be, for example, that since she was a Temporary Resident, you did not feel your usual sense of obligation, or at least not as acutely as usual?'

'I do not think that is true.' Maria's voice told Dan that she was wilting a little with this line of questioning. She was fine when dealing with fact, but seemed less comfortable when asked about reasons, and instincts. Dan could feel self-doubt in her answers and thought that maybe the courtroom in general might feel the same. His mind slipped into a reflective mood, examining the thought that, in this atmosphere, how something is said might weigh at least as heavily as what is said. Then he realised with a start that evidence read later would not communicate the subtlety of nuance contained in the live exchanges of a cross examination. He understood at that moment that Court Records must by definition be deficient in that sense.

'So, Dr Bellini I must take you to the matter of the laboratory result. Please tell us exactly what happens to results in your practice.'

'Well, they come to us in three ways, by phone by post or by courier. The laboratory will ring through any results which are well beyond acceptable margins, and which might represent a risk to life. The obvious illustration would be someone on Warfarin whose clotting ratio was much too high, putting them at risk to a big bleed. Routine results, especially from laboratories that are not in our local hospital would come by ordinary mail. All other results come through a daily courier delivery.'

'And what happens to those results when they arrive?'

'The result forms are sorted by the staff into wire baskets, one for each doctor. The doctor reads them, usually over the mid-morning coffee break, or at the end of the surgery, and initials the form to indicate it has been read. Results that require action would have a remark added instructing staff what to do, otherwise a simple F for file would be added. Some results, which the doctor felt need action on his or her part, would be retained on the doctor's desk to be dealt with at an appropriate moment. Usually those results involved the doctor ringing the patient with information, or asking the laboratory for clarification, or very occasionally asking a specialist how to react.'

'And which category do pregnancy tests fall into?'

'Well they are just marked F for 'file', so that they are ready for the patient to ring in for the result.'

'And would there be any exceptions to that procedure?'

'Well, I suppose one can picture a pregnancy test which is positive in someone who has been trying for a very long time, maybe with medical assistance. I think one would be likely to ring that result through as a matter of shared excitement.'

'Any other exceptions, Doctor?'

'Perhaps a pregnancy in a minor would require different and delicate handling. I would feel the need to ring a parent in those circumstances.'

'But Deborah was not, in your mind, a minor?'

'Of course not. She was a sexually active adult woman, working and living away from home. She was almost eighteen at the time. We would not consider her to be a minor, nor would we feel any obligation to talk with parents. In fact it would be unlawful to do so. Also as a matter of practicality it might be difficult to reach her by phone.'

'Mr Smart.' she said with slight asperity, 'I think it is crucial to realise that pregnancy is not a disease, but is a normal consequence of healthy adult behaviour. We do not regard it as a medical emergency, except in very special circumstances.'

Dan noticed the judge smiling at this outburst and writing a copious note with his beautiful pen.

Smart looked down at his papers, allowing a lengthy pause to develop. 'Now I should like to turn to the behaviour of your staff, Dr Bellini. Deborah has stated that she rang on a number of occasions without success. How do you respond to that observation?'

'I find it truly remarkable. We know the result came in from the laboratory because I knew the answer. It would therefore have been in the reception area, filed with her card ready for her to enquire. I can think of no good reason why the staff members were unable to help her. They all deny ever having taken a call from her.'

'Is your staff generally reliable?'

'Yes, we are fortunate in having a number of part timers, most of whom have been in post for a decade or more and know the job inside out and backwards.'

'We shall have a chance to ascertain that for ourselves later,' said Smart, 'but I wish to know your opinion. Would your staff have just brushed an enquiry aside?'

'I do not believe that would happen. I can envisage somebody, with a patient on the phone, and unable to find an expected laboratory result, stating that it seemed not to have arrived; but then, if the expected time was well overdue, I would expect that same member of staff to take it upon herself to find out what had gone wrong. Was the result on the doctor's desk, or stuck in the lab, or even lost in the post? One would not leave such a query unanswered.'

'Would that, quite rosy, appreciation be uniform throughout your staff, doctor?'

'Yes, I think so. All of the girls are thinking, experienced people who well know the importance of these tests. I do not believe a request would have been fobbed off.'

Another long shuffle of papers followed. 'Lastly then Doctor Bellini, would you like to tell the court about Temporary Residents? Deborah was one, was she not?'

'Yes she was. A patient is asked to register with their local practice, regarding the place of longest residence as their local address. University students for example register with a GP at their university and then if they need attention at other times they sometimes see their long established GP, as a temporary resident. This is because, albeit marginally, they are longer at University than at home. The point is that the full NHS record lies with the registered doctor and is the lifetime repository for every individual's medical record. After some three months as a temporary resident, the notes taken during that time, which are usually contained on a simple form, find their way through the system to the master set of notes. This is done because the patient fills in a form stating who holds their records. That is part of the Temporary Resident record and cannot readily become detached.'

'So in your practice this young woman would have had a temporary card?'

'Yes, and those cards are kept in a filing box right next to the reception hatch for ease of access. The form would be there, as would the laboratory report, normally clipped together.'

'So there would be no excuse for not finding it, if it was indeed, as you say, clipped together?'

'No excuse at all.'

The day ended without any more dramatic events. Dan took Michael and Maria out to supper quietly before they slipped up to Primrose Hill to stay overnight with Maria's parents. Enrico, now eighty five, was a pale shadow of his former self. Crippled with Parkinson's disease and very forgetful, he had reached that stage in elderly existence in which one is oblivious to one's surroundings, sometimes hazardously so. He had a tendency to 'freeze' in the middle of doing things like crossing the road. Twice in recent months he had got out of a car on the road side and just stood wedging the door wide open, to take in his surroundings, ignoring the swerving, alarmed drivers as they passed. Sometimes he was so rigid and ill co-ordinated that he needed help to dress or undress. Maria, observing sadly at first hand the slow disintegration of her Papa, who she loved so deeply, was forcibly reminded of the old name for the disease, *Paralysis Agitans*. Rosanna, in contrast was mentally and, indeed, physically as sharp as ever. She had needed a bypass operation a couple of years previously and was busy, correctly, telling everyone that she was absolutely fine now she had had her 're-bore'. Enrico and Rosanna still sat in front of the TV, holding hands, and still went to church in Clerkenwell every Sunday morning. But they had passed on the management of the business several years previously, after working for over fifty years in the restaurant business. They were among the most loved residents of Primrose Hill.

Maria worried that the wrong result from this awful case would kill her father. She had not perceived that her parents' positive exterior was a front to support her, and that their private anguish was not shown to anyone.

26

1990 High Court 3

Dan woke very early next day, had a long shower, not too hot, a very careful shave, not using a new blade for fear of cutting himself, dressed in a smart suit, a Jermyn Street tie and shirt, and went down to a leisurely breakfast in his hotel, over which he pretended unsuccessfully to read The Times. It was not that he had stage fright, nor even that he felt especially nervous, though of course he was not without apprehension. 'No.' He thought in surprise. 'I am more excited than nervous.'

He had never given evidence in a major hearing before and knew from what he had seen already that he would be subjected to a searching time in the court room. It would be polite, almost respectful, but nonetheless searching. Any weakness in his presentation would be exposed clearly and concisely for all to see.

He strolled along to the Law Courts, or rather to the little sandwich bar opposite where he had arranged to meet Maria and Michael, who were staying up in town for another day, just to hear how Dan fared. Dan appreciated their presence. They were already there and greeted him warmly, Maria in particular, thanking him for the support he offered to her, and to the staff in general. After a cup of coffee together they went into the High Court building.

Mr Tregelles and the MDU secretary were waiting outside the courtroom and took Dan on one side to brief him. Tregelles was most insistent that he must not evade answers and must tell the truth. 'Do not tell even the smallest white lie Dan.' He said in his sepulchral whisper, which seemed to echo around the corridor. 'Just answer the questions in a straightforward manner, because, believe you me, Smart is indeed smart, and will smell the slightest avoidance or deviation, and have you on a spit roasting over his fire in no time. You have nothing to hide as far as we know, so just give it straight.'

Dan was called to the stand as soon as the judge had opened proceedings. He spent the whole morning dealing with the facts of the case as were known to him. Much of the questioning was repetition of the previous day with Maria and was easy.

The lunch break came and he still felt as fresh as when he arrived. Mr Smart had been totally benign.

It was after lunch that the first difficulty arose. 'Dr Crossman, would you mind telling the court what happened to the Temporary Resident Record.' Mr Smart's tone had altered fractionally, carrying with it a predatory edge.

'I do not know what happened to it. At the end of the period of temporary residency, three months, it should have been returned to the government and then forwarded to the patient's proper doctor, but we checked with Dr Prossor in Tetbury who tells us that no record ever arrived. Therefore Deborah's pregnancy test result was not known to him. Even if he had thought it appropriate, he would therefore have had no cause to contact her. We have no idea what happened to it.'

'Is there any chance that is was 'lost' on purpose by someone in your own practice who knew that there was trouble brewing?'

'I cannot believe that any of my staff would do that. The record was material evidence of the appointment and the test with the result. It would have been very wrong to have destroyed it. In any event there would be no merit in so doing. The evidence contained in that form is not contested. Both sides are in agreement about the facts.'

'Not quite true doctor. There is the little matter of your staff not being able to tell my client her result. What if it was not in reception with the staff at all, but was, shall we say, in Dr Bellini's work case, or worse in her waste paper basket, or even on your desk or waste paper basket?'

'I have no comment to make other than what I have said. The absence of the form is a mystery to me as much as to you Mr Smart. I can only say that it was in nobody's interest to destroy or lose it, and to suggest that this is what happened is, frankly, unworthy.'

'Stoutly defended, doctor.' Smart smiled thinly. 'But, just before we leave that issue I believe that the government pays a small sum for doctors looking after temporary residents. Is that so?'

'Yes, it is, and, anticipating your next question, we have tried to ascertain whether we were paid for this record. I must confess that we have failed. The sums concerned are quite small in our practice since we are not a large tourist area, and I must confess we had never set up a checking system to ensure that we were accurately paid for every temporary resident form submitted. One of the benefits of this case is that we have now set up such a system, but it was not in operation at the time. The health authority was not able to help us either.'

'My last question to you concerns the procedure for dealing with post in the absence of a partner. Dr Bellini for example was not full time. If post came for her when she was not present how would it be dealt with?'

'The staff would open the post as usual, putting private mail unopened ready for the return of the absentee. All official post would be placed in the absentee's basket, which would be delivered as an extra to a working partner. That partner would read and mark as read all of the absentee's post. He or she would also take action if it was thought to be appropriate. The whole basket would be on the absent partner's desk ready for his or her next attendance, so the absent partner eventually reads all the post which concerns them.'

'We know that the test went off in the middle of the week. When would you expect the result to be in?'

'Probably on Friday morning, but possibly not until the Saturday.'

'Does Dr Bellini work on Saturdays?'

'No'

'Then who would have seen the post that Saturday.'

'Our records show that I was the duty doctor that Saturday morning.'

'Do you remember seeing it?'

'No I do not, but it was eight years ago. I would not expect to remember a common result so long ago.'

'Let me take you back to the arrival of the test result, doctor. Do you think Dr Bellini had an obligation to contact her patient on learning that she was pregnant?'

'I do not think she had any such obligation in law, or even in normal practice. Pregnancy is not a disease. It is a normal condition for womankind. The patient was over the age of consent, was living an independent adult existence and knew that the doctor suspected her to be pregnant. She had been advised to ascertain the result. The ultimate responsibility was clearly hers to take, not the doctor's. Also I would like to point out that, in the eight years this case has taken to come to court, practice has changed. Nowadays we do very few tests indeed. The girls simply go and buy an inexpensive home testing kit from the pharmacy. We only see the ones who are already positive. In other words the women themselves regard it as a social situation not a medical one.'

At this point the judge interjected to ask Dan, 'Doctor, just for my interest, as the older, more traditional doctor in the practice, would you have made that call, had you been the responsible doctor?'

Dan paused for quite a long time and then looked up at the judge, facing him directly and said. 'I think I probably would have felt a need to communicate with her. I would not have told her mother, or even caused domestic eyebrows to be raised, but I would, I think, have looked for some excuse to speak with her, not as a matter of law, or best practice even, but simply because that is the way I am, old fashioned and, perhaps, too paternalistic.'

His Lordship smiled at Dan warmly and nodded in total understanding.

Tregelles then had an hour or so checking various points with Dan before he finished the day by asking, completely out of the blue. 'And what, doctor, do you really think of this case?'

'I am very sad that an apparently responsible firm of lawyers saw fit to support it. As far as I am concerned it is a complete nonsense.'

'Why do you think that doctor?'

'Well, I believe it has all the hallmarks of a deliberately concealed pregnancy.'

'What makes you say that?'

'I have been a family doctor for over 30 years. I have seen many hundreds of pregnant women. I am yet to see one who, having had the question of pregnancy raised by a doctor would rest until she is certain of the answer. A normal woman would have pursued the result, and if, for whatever reason, she failed to get it through to the surgery, she would have arranged another test with her own doctor immediately. She would not, indeed could not, rest until she knew the answer. This woman did not apparently do that. She continued without periods for several further months without challenging the situation, and then reappeared at a time just too late to have a termination. One must ask why? The only answer that makes sense to me is that she wanted the pregnancy to continue.'

There was a major shuffling of papers and an outbreak of coughing in the court at this. The judge, allowed the court to settle, before he called an end to the day's proceedings, saying that the next day would concern itself with character witnesses on behalf of the Plaintiff, and with appearances by the practice staff.

Dan had a cup of coffee and a Chelsea bun with Michael and Maria. They had decided to go home and not return until the last day. It was obvious to Dan that Michael was protecting his wife, and he approved. Maria was clearly in emotional difficulty with the whole thing now. She was just fifty five, but suddenly looked a lot older.

Dan himself bought the London Evening Standard and read all about the case, which was getting quite a lot of prominence, He noted grimly that the reporter seemed biased towards the Plaintiff, but recalled that always seemed to be the situation. Newspapers take great pleasure in attacking professional people, especially doctors. He looked at what was on in the London Theatres, seeking a comedy to lighten his mood, but, apart from the musicals, which were all sold out, could only find sick humour, sex or tragedy. He went to a film instead.

27

1990 The High Court 4 – Ruth

Aunt Susan's breakfasts were Ruth's favourite. She had chocolate chips cereals, a properly boiled egg with toast 'soldiers' and fresh orange juice with bits in. Nothing like that happened when she was at home. Ruth went off to school that third day of the trial skipping with joy and energy. Every day at school was good. Miss Matson, her teacher, laughed a lot and made the classes very interesting. Ruth found the work very easy and so enjoyed it. She had no idea that other children less able were jealous of her obvious brightness.

Today, however, was different. When she arrived, only just in time for assembly, she heard others sniggering and looking at her across the room. She had an uncomfortable feeling that they had been talking about her and that there was a joke at her expense. Miss Matson seemed especially kind that morning, not even telling her off for watching a bird on the windowsill when she should have been listening.

It all came out in the playground mid morning. Ruth suddenly found herself surrounded by a ring of children all linking arms and jeering her in a parody of their 'Ring a ring o' roses' game. 'Mummy wants to kill you! Mummy wants to kill you! Ruth's Mum wants her dead! Ruth's Mum wants her dead!' The rhythm of the chant went on and on, the children getting more and more strident. Ruth just stood in the middle, totally without understanding, but realising that she was the butt of their jeering and she did not like it. Eventually she covered her ears with her hands, sank to her haunches and burst into tears.

After what seemed a long time a teacher came over and broke the whole thing up. She took Ruth gently by the arm and steered her, weeping, back into the school and to the headmistress's office, sitting her down on the large leather Chesterfield, so deep seated that Ruth's feet didn't touch the ground.

The headmistress was reading the morning paper, with Miss Matson leaning over her to read the same article. Both were looking shocked. Eventually the headmistress looked up at Ruth and Miss Matson came to sit on the Chesterfield beside her. 'Have you read the newspapers today, Ruth?'

'No Miss Grieg. We don't have them at home.'

'Do you know where your Mother has been?'

'She's in London. She goes sometimes, but it's been longer this time. Is something wrong? Has something happened to my Mummy?'

The headmistress was silent for a moment, looking at this little girl, trying to decide how to respond. She nodded as if having solved a problem. 'Yes, in a way Ruth, something really awful has happened. It seems your mother has been seeking money from a doctor because she is unhappy about her care when she was expecting you.'

'Why? We are all right. Mummy wasn't ill, and I was born, wasn't I? Why is she upset with the doctor?'

'I'm afraid it seems that she did not want a baby, and blames the doctor for not helping her to stop it. It is all over the morning papers. We think that some of the children probably heard about it over breakfast from their parents. That is why they were chanting at you. I am very sorry Ruth. Maybe we could have done something to prevent this.' Miss Grieg paused thoughtfully. 'Is Mummy home yet?'

'No, she'll be back this evening. I've been staying with Auntie Susan.'

'I think it would be best if you do not go back to class today, Ruth. I shall ring your Auntie Susan and tell her what has happened. Perhaps she will collect you and take her to her home. We will talk to the children so that you do not have to worry about this again.'

Susan came for her, and took her to the shop, because she was working that day. Ruth spent the day helping to put vegetables in brown paper bags; haunted by her classmates cruel version of 'ring a ring o' roses' playing in a loop in her mind.

William and Deborah arrived home about seven that evening, collecting the children from Susan's house on the way. Susan was very cool towards them, especially towards Deborah. William, as he picked up the children's case whispered 'What's the matter Susan?'

'She knows all about it, that's the matter. This little eight year old knows that her Mummy did not want her, and is so angry she takes her doctor to court. She had to endure a mass mocking from children at school. Children can be very cruel you know, and this, in my opinion, comes pretty high up the list of cruelty. How would you be if you were in her shoes? Come to that, how do you think I feel about it?'

'I'm so sorry Susan. I'm so sorry.' William's expression hardened still further as he strode to the car with the case. When they got home he took Ruth by the hand and sat with her on the sofa, demanding that his wife sat with them. Ruth was more upset than he had ever seen her. 'I think you owe your daughter an explanation,' he growled.

'But no. No I can't!'

'Yes, you damn well can, and you will if you wish to remain in my house this evening. There has been terrible harm here, which you, and only you, can help. Do it woman!!!'

Debbie sat with a steely resentment and eyes glinting with anger. 'I have only tried my best to get the support that was due to me and to Ruth. That pregnancy was not planned. It altered my life for ever. I was not able to have a proper career. My boyfriend deserted me. What would you have done, you pompous little man?' She spoke very quietly but with such intensity she might as well have shouted.

'I do not think I would have tried to blame somebody else for my own deeds.'

'She is the so called professional, isn't she? She is the one who was in control, wasn't she? She could have prevented this problem, couldn't she!!? Of course she could. It is all her doing. She must be made to pay!' Deborah thumped the arm of the sofa rhythmically in time with each angry point made.

'Am I not paying enough then? Do I not support you properly? I took you and your baby on willingly and happily, but now you seem to be telling me that my efforts are not good enough for you. I'm sorry if I no longer please you.' William spoke quietly and sadly.

Neither adult noticed that Ruth had stopped snivelling after William's remark, and sat staring wide eyed at her mother. 'So Daddy is not my Daddy!'

William and Debbie froze in horror that their conversation had been so revealing. William was the first to react. He put his arm around Ruth's shoulder lovingly. He knew there was no choice but to tell the truth. 'Not really Ruth.' William said. 'But I feel like your Daddy, and I've always tried to be your Daddy. I love you very much. Until today you wouldn't have known that I wasn't your real Daddy, would you?'

'But, if you are not my real Daddy, who is? What happened to him?'

William looked to Deborah to provide the answer. 'Yes, I'd also like to know about that Debbie. You'd kept me out of all of this until the hearing. I just thought you'd been abandoned, but it is more than that isn't it? He wasn't named in Court and you've never told me. He wasn't your boyfriend, this Robin, you'd expected to marry. Who was he?'

Debbie stared down at her hands, and took a deep breath. 'Do you remember the foreign boy who used to play the piano with you in Tetbury? He used to sing folk songs too. Everyone listened to him.'

'How could I forget? He was brilliant. He was a music student wasn't he? We got on very well. But he disappeared quite suddenly, didn't he? Oh! I see it all!! You made him take a test, and he got scared and went home before he could be fingered for it.'

'Yes, that was him, the bastard. Your little friend Krystyna let him off his contract and arranged his transport back East before we could talk with him. He went the day after the test was taken, before we knew the answer. Nobody knew he had gone till afterwards. We couldn't trace him.'

William could see it all in his mind; Robin, and his father, indignant and relieved all at once. The young musician, frightened; the calm, efficient manager, Krystyna, with her finger on the pulse, solving everything; the boy escapes back home; the McDougall establishment is clean, and free to pretend that nothing has happened. 'I bet she got a rise,' thought William. 'So you turned on your doctor because someone had to pay?' he demanded.

'Yes, exactly; someone has to pay, and that someone is not going to be me, nor even you.'

'I wouldn't be too sure of that if I were you, Debbie.'

Ruth soon went upstairs to get ready for bed. William read a little to her, just to make things seem more normal. Debbie opened a new bottle of sherry. Things were not good at any time between Ruth and her mother, but after this day they got much worse.

28

1990 The High Court 5

Days four and five in court did not produce anything unexpected. Deborah did very well in her character references, mostly from Daddy's business acquaintances and from village friends. Dan thought it strange that nobody from her place of work had been called, but then he realised that Debbie would not be the most popular person on that campus. Those that gave evidence spoke of her equestrian skills, her domestic charm, and the willingness with which she helped other residents in Cerney. By the time Mr Smart had finished Deborah Mason was made to appear a guardian angel of all that was good in life.

Similarly several eminent medical persons and a couple of well-chosen patients were called upon to testify that Maria Bellini was not only a delightful human being but a most competent and a most caring medical practitioner. Dan thought all this was a bit of a waste of time. Anyone could see that Deborah had been well brought up and was capable of presenting herself properly, and a few minutes in Maria's company would convince a normal person that she was something of a star.

He reflected that none of the evidence and little of the cross examination had been intended to suggest otherwise. It was not Maria's competence in general which was under attack, rather it was her judgement in one tiny incident. Dan knew that in Maria's mind her whole working life and her credibility hinged upon this case. Suddenly the enormity of it all staggered him. How can a person's real worth be judged on such a small thing? Just one hundredth of one day's judgement calls, in a whole lifetime of work had led to eight years of misery. Thousands of hours in preparation by all concerned, much expense, the whole force of the High Court being concentrated for all of the trial, the stress and distress for those involved, all pivoted on one small decision or omission, or mishap, call it what you will.

The monumental unfairness of it all engulfed him. Anger rose like some volcanic miasma within and would have spilled out in some sort of uncontrolled and uncontainable outcry but for the inhibiting nature of the quiet formality around him. Suddenly he understood one of the reasons, maybe the main reason for the trappings of a law court, the wigs, the gowns the formal speech and the deference. It was to constrain the behaviour of those engaged in the exercise, to rid the experience of naked emotional expression in favour of the cool intellectual rigour of the mind. He knew then that the practised civilities of the main players, the barristers, and the judge were all to serve the prime interest of reaching an intellectual, unemotional decision. The Law must be upheld. Emotion was deliberately eliminated.

The cynic in Dan accepted without question that every human being who makes decisions sometimes makes bad ones. It is simply not possible to go through life without error. He was quite painfully aware that he himself had made a number of bad calls, but had never been lambasted in a court room about them. 'So it is all a lottery?' He thought. 'Maria is like a rabbit caught in a headlight, and might well be mown down in the process.'

Bitterly he mused that the Plaintiff would not survive the scrutiny for five minutes were the tables to be turned. But then perhaps an expectation of perfection was now regarded by the public as a right. Perhaps the old attitude that one was simply required to 'do one's best' no longer sufficed. What if one's best fell short of perfection? Is perfection demanded? Is it a right that the consumer has at all times? Dan felt that, if the answer to these questions was in the affirmative, then professional advisors, doctors mainly, but lawyers, teachers and others would become increasingly reluctant to offer advice, would never make judgement calls, and would simply tick pre-determined boxes. They would certainly join the political classes in never admitting error. This, Dan felt would be the end of what he understood to be professionalism. A professional is surely someone trained and licensed to make judgements. How dare an untrained, ill advised, politically motivated, society challenge that view? But challenge there certainly was. Dan felt an era slipping quietly away without many folk being aware of its demise. 'It is all part of the end of deference, the falling away of respect,' he mourned within himself.

Society was no longer operated by a professional elite, but by the masses. He recalled that in some countries people like himself had been stood against a wall and shot, just for being decision makers, and therefore a threat to the proletariat. As far as he could recall, all of the new regimes in those countries had eventually failed. All societies need decision makers and they might just as well be properly trained and competent. He knew himself to be an old fashioned man, not entirely in step with modernism, but he thoroughly resented the mass confusion between elitism and exclusivity. To him, elitism was simply a measure of excellence, something to be strived for, whether one was a brain surgeon or a member of the Arsenal football team. The only criterion was one of competence, not social class or money. As such, to be elite was only exclusive in the sense that not everyone possesses the ability to play football for Arsenal, or to work as a brain surgeon in the Mayo Clinic. We should, he believed, do our very best to create an equality of opportunity, through education of all sorts, but that is emphatically not the same as believing that we are all of equal ability. We manifestly are not.

But of course to be elite in the sense he understood was to accept special responsibility for conduct. That is why the General Medial Council and the Law Society took such a poor view of members falling below normal standards of behaviour. Criminal acts of a non-medical nature might well lead to a doctor losing his licence to practice medicine, quite apart from any punishment in the criminal courts.

All this scrutiny was about whether Dr Maria Bellini had behaved properly on one tiny occasion, not whether she is generally unworthy of the trust placed in her. Maria's inflation of the importance of the matter was, in one sense, arrogance on her part, an arrogance shared by many professional people who need a great sense of self-worth to function properly and who find difficulty in dealing with criticism. 'How dare one expect to be perfect!' He thought. But he knew that they all did expect exactly that. There was the problem.

Suddenly he was roused from his reverie when hearing that his principal receptionist was being called to the stand. He must have missed some of the evidence in his day dream. The reception staff, called rather monotonously one after the other, all stood up well to interrogation. With minor variations they all accurately related the established procedures that had been in force at the time. They all denied ever receiving a phone call from Deborah Mason. Two of them, who both lived near the Troutmann family home recalled seeing the test result. The judge interjected again to compliment the practice on having such a stable work force of sensible people.

The trial recessed for the weekend quite early on Friday afternoon because the judge did not want to start the potentially controversial evidence from the experts on both sides, and then break off in the middle.

Judge Williamson informed The Court that they could expect a ruling at the end of the trial. Rather than the expected 'reserved judgement', at special hearing often a month later where his considered judgement to the evidence would be read. He stated that there would be a day of rest after the expert witnesses and that he expected the closing arguments would allow him to make his judgment on the Friday, concluding the hearing within the two weeks allotted time scale.

Dan returned to Cirencester and to his wife Judy for the weekend. Judy, who had been a teacher until their children arrived, but who had not been gainfully employed since, was not in any way medical. Dan liked it that way. To go home at night or for the weekend was like stepping into another world, a world of gardening and fishing, with an interest in good food and wine and old friends, of whom there were many. Dan found it very therapeutic. He spent some time on the phone with Paul and Linda, the other partner in the firm and his wife to update them on his impression of the case. He also rang each member of the staff to thank them, but he did not disturb Michael and Maria.

Bright and early on Monday morning he was back at the Law Courts ready for the second week. Dan had arranged that Maria would return to court for the arguments and the summing up. Expert witnesses for both sides in the case had attended meetings with the legal teams on each side and had prepared agreed statements which were available to both sides before the trial, and which formed the basis for cross examination. This principle had of course been true for all of the witnesses as well as the Plaintiff and Defendant. The careful arguments in those preparation meetings in the Inner Temple were designed to establish the fixed position of both sides of the case, and led to the publication of the trial papers. However, questioning sometimes strayed beyond those statements, and so surprises occasionally occurred.

The expert witness for the Plaintiff turned out to be a rather boffin like General Practitioner, Dr Bentall, from Surrey. He had served on some national committees concerning standards of practice, and was clearly committed to the notion that doctors should automatically tell their patients all of the results of all of the tests as they become available. He did not seem to have any notion of how that might be achieved, and became very confused in the face of Mr Tregelles's probing cross examination.

Suddenly Dr Bentall turned to the judge and declared that he wished to withdraw from his position as an expert witness.

There was a gasp from the court and the judge fixed him with a particularly withering inquisitorial look. 'And why should you wish to take this step Dr Bentall? Has anything occurred here to upset you? Has Counsel been too aggressive for you?'

'No my Lord, it is none of those things. It is that I have changed my mind. I do not think that my argument is sustainable.'

'Then you are excused Dr Bentall. Thank you for coming.'

Dr Bentall stood down and left the room hurriedly, avoiding the stares of Mr Smart's team of lawyers. Dan could not hide his grin until he received a sharp kick from his neighbour, the Defence Union secretary.

The Defence Union had found a number of eminent people willing to give evidence that they thought Bellini's behaviour perfectly reasonable. Three had been selected to give evidence. One was the past president of the Royal College of General Practitioners, another was a distinguished lady Obstetrician and the third a prominent campaigner for patients' rights.

Mr Tregelles treated the lady Gynaecologist to a rare smile, glanced at his notes, and said, 'Now Miss Jocelyn, would you please tell the court what the latest gestation time for a legal abortion is.'

'Thank you.' She turned towards the judge 'My Lord, since 1967 the Law states 28 weeks, but, in the professional mind, the import and intention of the Act was that abortion is legal until the moment of viability. As technology has improved, low birth weight, premature babies have been surviving in much greater numbers. As that process has gone on the consensus has been that 28 weeks is too late. Now, 26 weeks is regarded as the latest date, and many professionals think that is still too late, and that the date should come back to twenty four weeks. I can see in the future that there will be further downward pressure. In this respect most professionals here think the American ruling is more appropriate because it leaves the door open for judgement on the question of viability.'

'So, what are you saying about Dr Bellini's assertion to Mrs Mason that she was too late at twenty six weeks.'

'I would say that the decision was absolutely correct. Nobody in this country would abort a twenty six week pregnancy now, except in the face of extreme maternal risk or foetal abnormality. Neither of those factors was present here.'

'Thank you Miss Jocelyn.'

All three experts gave accomplished and unequivocal evidence of an impressive nature, but the one that Dan cherished most was the Patients' Campaigner, whose public utterances had often been very hostile to medical people, but who was clearly of the opinion that Deborah Mason had been properly cared for by all concerned. Mr Smart was unable to shake any of these witnesses from their previously declared statements.

When Mr Tregelles was examining the Patients' Campaigner, he suddenly asked. 'Mr Grimwade, would you please bring all your experience of doctor/ patient relationships to bear in offering the court a general comment about this case.'

'Why certainly Sir. I spend my time trying to improve the service that patients receive in this country. The medical profession and government are very traditional in their stance, and it is difficult to bring about change. In my attempts to do so, I am aware that I am often seen as being hostile to the establishment. I welcome this opportunity to declare that this is a wrong impression. I have, in my role, gradually come to understand that the vast majority of professional people carry out their tasks with a truly remarkable degree of dedication, often sacrificing self interest in the cause of public service. In this case it seems to me that a perfectly sound General Medical Practitioner has been targeted by a young woman seeking retribution for her own failings. In my opinion a doctor is a personal advisor not a controlling parent.'

'Thank you, Mr Grimwade.'

'If I may Sir, I would like to make one further comment, which though not specific to this case, is a general concern for all those who care about justice. My concern is that certain groups in our society, notably teachers and doctors, are very vulnerable to frivolous complaint and seem unable to protect themselves except through the long process of law such as this case represents. The very length of that process is punishment for a guilty person, is cruelty to an innocent one. I believe that lawyers should exercise careful thought about concepts of right and wrong before embarking upon such a case. There is, as far as I am aware, no law which states that a lawyer is obliged to take a case.'

There was a long pause in the courtroom while Grimwade's observations were digested. Dan thought that Matt Clarkson might have something to say to young Sidebottom about that.

Wednesday was, as promised by the judge, a day of rest and Thursday was taken up with technical discussions about the Legal Aid system and financial matters between the lawyers. On Friday Maria came to Court. She sat between Mike, her loyal husband, and Dan her supportive partner, to learn her fate. They had spent much of the past couple of weeks in this configuration.

Both counsel gave lengthy and erudite closing speeches, in which the listener found himself swayed first one way and then the other. There was a break for lunch and when the court reassembled Dan noticed that there were no spare seats. The press seemed to be present in force and everyone who had an interest in the case had returned. He noticed the expert witnesses had all re-attended, which he knew was above the call of duty and reflected their interest in the outcome.

All stood as Judge Williamson entered. He smiled and bowed to the assembly and then sat for a few moments to allow everyone to settle before offering his judgement. 'We have listened with care and considerable interest to the issues raised in this case. To my mind the principle matter to be decided was whether a medical practitioner has the responsibility to communicate laboratory results to his or her patient, and if this is found to be generally but not totally the case, what would the exceptions be.

'I find that I agree with all of the expert witnesses that the practitioner does indeed have a responsibility to communicate results which have a significant implication for the patient's health, or for their medical management. However, I accept that many results that come to a practitioner on a daily basis are neither health threatening, nor do they carry any therapeutic significance. In fact the majority of laboratory results come under this heading. I find that it is the responsibility of the practitioner to make results available to the patient on request, but that it is simply impracticable and unnecessary to contact patients with normal or expected laboratory test results, of which there are very many every day.

'Turning to the question of pregnancy tests, I consider that, to some extent, the protocol is turned on its head. Pregnancy is a normal function of womankind, is not a disease and for most people carries little or no risk. Indeed, as has been said in this hearing, nowadays women test themselves with a simple home kit. I therefore do not think it is the practitioner's responsibility to communicate results personally, and that it suffices to make results available. Indeed it could be argued that a practitioner might decline to spend the government's money on a test and require the patient to organise her own. But I believe there are exceptions to this general rule. They would be medical exceptions if the patient's life was at risk from pregnancy, or social exceptions if the patient was considered to be at risk because of immaturity or mental health. Neither exception applied here. The evidence is clear that this young woman was living independently away from home, managing her own life. Indeed, on an age basis only, she was well above the age of consent and did not require, nor expect adult supervision.

'Turning to the matter of the behaviour of the practice staff and the availability of the result, I was initially disturbed by the absence of the record, thinking that this may reflect a sloppily run business, but I am reassured that this is not the case. I was impressed by the soundness and clarity of the staff evidence, and accept that none of them recall any attempt to learn the result on the part of Mrs Mason.

'The question of abortion being possible at the time of the second attendance arrested me also. I am grateful for Mr Smart's explanation of the evolution of the Abortion Law and the comparison with American law. I accept that the law is perceived to be out of date in its timing and am drawn entirely to the concept that date of viability is the deciding factor. In our modern times it seems that this is earlier that twenty eight weeks and that Dr Bellini's judgement that nobody would be prepared to operate is correct.

'For all of these reasons I find in favour of the Defendants, Dr Bellini and her Practice.

'A strange feature of this case is the remarkable lack of apparent curiosity about her own body and its behaviour that this young woman demonstrated for almost five months. I make no further comment about that, except to state that I found Dr Crossman's assertion that no normal woman would rest until she was certain of the result of her pregnancy test compelling. I also recommend Mr Grimwade's observations about the vulnerability of certain professionals in our litigation culture.

'I therefore award costs against the Plaintiff. Thank you all for your clear and honest representation.' He stood, bowed and left the room.

There was a moment of utter silence. Maria sat, head bowed as if in prayer, before turning to Michael and to Dan planting a big kiss on each of them. Then they all turned to their advisory team with Maria hugging each of them and the men shaking hands warmly. There was a general buzz of approval in the Court, some laughter and even some tears. The release of tension was amazing. Dan noticed Deborah's mother leaving very quickly, as if trying to be invisible. Matt Clarkson winked at Dan from afar. And so they returned to Cirencester that Friday evening, and had a big party with the others who worked in the practice and all their spouses too. Maria had a month off, two weeks holiday and two weeks compassionate leave. Dan was behind his desk as usual on Monday.

29

1991 Brighton 1

Ruth fell asleep in class one morning, a very minor event, but one that Miss Matson noted, particularly in view of the ugliness a few months previously. It was highly unusual for a pupil to fall asleep in her classes. Nothing was said, but Miss Matson made a mental note to keep a wary eye on this child. She thought Ruth looked thin and a bit hollow eyed, lacking the robust health she used to show.

William too, was concerned, not just for Ruth but for all of the children. His wife was clearly becoming less and less interested in the family wellbeing. When he arrived home from work he found himself needing to set to and do most of the housework. Debbie was quite often out, the children would be alone and there would be no supper ready for any of them. They would usually be sitting in front of the TV completely absorbed in Blue Peter. William invested in a VCR and a load of children's tapes to go with it. When Debbie returned, sometimes in the evening, once or twice late in the night, she had a dreamy quality about her and he could not get any proper answers from her about where she had been.

He began so suspect she had a lover. Certainly she was not interested in him physically, not even as a person. Their conversations became steadily more remote and confined to the sharing of essential information. She never for example asked him how he was, how far he had driven that day, or indeed what towns he had visited.

In fact William was struggling. He knew he could not trust Debbie with the care of the children any more, and was very aware that sister Susan, willing though she was, had her own life, her own family and a job, as well as looking after William's business affairs for him. He had never been any good at that. His parents had no spare energy. He knew that by the time they finished in the shop they were very tired, and, after all, they were no longer young.

There was really no alternative. William needed to be home as much as possible, so he shortened his routes, seldom stayed away at night, and suffered a significant loss of income as a result. Also he was very tired. The job was heavy enough, but instead of coming home to an orderly house, he had to set about the shopping, the cleaning, and most of the cooking. Ruth was a great help and even the youngsters learned to help wash dishes and make their beds, but it was often after ten at night before his chores for the day were done.

William and Debbie had little to say to one another. They shared the same bed, simply because there was no other bed in the house, but they lay back to back, each holding the mattress piping to prevent accidentally rolling over into one another in the night. She spent much longer in bed that he, certainly rising a lot later. Her breath was foetid with alcohol fumes and although William enjoyed an occasional pint, he found the proximity of the reek very distasteful. Like many working men, used to getting dirty in their jobs, William was a fastidious person when it came to his own cleanliness. He hated the smell of an unwashed body, so different from one that was just hot and sweaty. William was always up and gone early in the morning. Ruth provided breakfast for herself and the two younger children, before Susan collected them for school each day.

Increasingly Deborah might as well not be there. When she was at home she was very unpredictable, sometimes emotional and demonstrative, but mostly angry and irritable. On several occasions she hit Ruth for trivial reasons. Debbie's anger was rarely directed at Bridget or Kevin, and Ruth acted as protector to her younger siblings on the odd occasion it did.

One day at school Ruth's skirt rode high on her thigh revealing a hand print sized bruise, just below her knickers elastic. Miss Matson, having experience of such things, gently asked if she may see the bruise and was reluctantly shown it in its full glory. 'Ruth, how did you get this bruise?' she asked.

'I think I bumped into something.'

'I see. It doesn't look like that sort of bruise. Are you sure nobody hit you?'

'No Miss Matson, I'm not sure.'

'Who might have hit you then Ruth?'

'Well, sometimes Mummy gets angry with me.'

'Why was she angry Ruth?'

'Ummm, maybe it was because I forgot to feed the cat.'

Miss Matson and Miss Grieg spoke together about this small exchange later that day, and decided to have a quiet word with Social Services.

It was not long after this that William opened the bathroom cabinet and Debbie's own wash bag fell out onto the floor. The flap jarred open on landing and some contents spilled out. As he gathered them together William was puzzled to find a cigarette lighter, an old toilet roll end and some aluminium foil. He had no notion of what all this was for, but something in his mind was unhappy, so he asked a pal what activity might bring those objects together. He was told solemnly, the most likely thing was heroin.

30

1991 Brighton 2

Ruth was beside herself. Her mother would not wake up. She was lying on the sofa, her clothes in a tangle, an empty bottle of Vodka on the floor beside her. She was snoring loudly.

Susan had brought them all home from school but, partly because she did not want to meet Debbie, and partly because she had to get back to the shop, she just dropped the children outside and drove off. They had come inside, found their mother on the sofa, and stood staring crestfallen at her. Ruth knew all about Debbie's problem by now, but was frightened because it used to be only occasionally that Debbie was dead drunk, but now it was becoming rather more frequent. She would seem to be all right for a few days, and then she would start drinking again. Ruth knew that once she started she would not stop until she was not able to function at all. In some ways it was easier for the children when she was very far gone. She was less irritable and the awful shouting which usually ended in smacks would come less often.

They hung their coats up in the hallway and turned the television on. Bridget went upstairs to visit the bathroom. In her hurry not to miss the programme and to rejoin the other two she fell down the stairs and lay at the bottom, unconscious, with a red burn from the carpet on her cheek.

Ruth, on hearing the fall and the absence of her sister's wail rushed to investigate. She and Kevin looked aghast at Bridget.

Ruth instructed Kevin to stay and hold Bridget's hand, while she ran to Debbie. Desperately Ruth shook her mother again and again 'Mummy, Mummy. Wake up! Bridget's had an accident, Oh Please Wake Up!!' Her voice rose to a high pitch of anguish, and the tears rolled down her cheeks, but there was no response. Ruth stopped shaking Debbie, and ran to the telephone. She knew that the Emergency number was 999, so she dialled. It was answered immediately. 'My sister's fallen downstairs and I can't wake her. My Mummy won't wake up either. Please send an ambulance!'

When William arrived home an hour later he found Kevin in the care of an elderly neighbour, Debbie was still unrousable, and there was no sign of Ruth or Bridget. The neighbour said they had gone to the hospital in an ambulance because Bridget had fallen downstairs.

William raced to the Accident Unit and there found his children, Ruth, very solemn and unhappy, and Bridget, now conscious but with a very red cheek, obviously still very shaky. The young casualty doctor told him that they thought Bridget would be fine but that she would be kept overnight to be sure as was the protocol for all head injuries.

But the doctor did not finish there. He looked hard at William and asked a lot of questions about the supervision of the children. In particular he wanted to know how it was that a nine year old girl had made the call to the ambulance.

William muttered something bland and defensive, but being a straight forward, honest man he could not hide the truth that, although he had still been at work, his wife had been present but was incapable at the time through alcohol.

Quite soon there was an investigation by Social Services. They had already filed a message from the school expressing concern about Ruth. As a result of which the children were placed on the 'At Risk Register'. This meant that Social Services visited unannounced from time to time and that there were periodic case conferences between all the interested parties. In a sense the register was a sort of Probation. The eyes of officialdom were upon them and any serious shortcomings would lead to removal of the children into care.

All went well for a few weeks. Deborah remained sober most of the time. Then one day there was a call to Social Services from the school. Miss Grieg reported that Ruth had another couple of big bruises on her legs, and that one arm had finger mark bruises where it had been tightly grasped. Ruth would offer no explanation for the bruises.

They decided that they could no longer properly leave the children in Deborah's care. Formal proceedings were put in place to remove the children into the care of the Local Authority, in essence replacing the natural parents with the State.

A very distressed William pleaded with Susan to help with his children. He knew he could not cope with three children and do his job, but hated the idea of them being in the care of the Local Authority, which he regarded as a shameful thing. Eventually, Susan agreed to take the two younger children who were William's, although it would be a severe squeeze in her household space. She refused to take Ruth, who was not William's child. She did not come to that conclusion easily or lightly, but just as a matter of practicality. The authorities agreed to this arrangement, so William very reluctantly agreed that Ruth should stay at a children's home, called Ryelands House.

After the children had gone from the house there seemed no reason to pretend that the marriage still existed. Deborah was drinking more and more heavily, was out more often than at home, and William felt sure she was using drugs as well. He remembered the foil and the cigarette lighter, which seemed to have disappeared somehow. Whenever he challenged her she dismissed him scornfully. In fact she always dismissed him, unkindly mocking his illiteracy, and giving no credit whatsoever for his stability and worth. William felt that everything he had worked for was slipping away from him. His business had not been going well as his household disintegrated, simply because he had been obliged to decline the long haul overnight work, which was so much more lucrative.

Also, he wondered how Debbie was able to buy all this alcohol. The housekeeping he provided was more than adequate, but not sufficient to buy litre bottles of spirits at the rate she was doing.

One day, just a couple of months after the children had gone into care, he came home a bit early, tired and dispirited, to find Debbie rather hurriedly saying farewell to a man he did not recognise. Somehow he had the impression that the sound of his car going into the garage had disturbed them. 'Who was that, Debbie?' he asked.

'Oh, just a friend, nobody you know.'

As he took his shower he could not prevent himself repeating the question. 'Who was that Deborah? What's his name? What did he want?'

'He was here to see me.'

'Answer the question. What was his name and what did he want?

'It's none of your business William. He was here to see me, that's all.'

He came out of the bathroom and reached to get a clean pair of underpants from his dressing table. It was then that he noticed the rumpled bed, and the unmistakable smell of sex. Suddenly everything made sense. He stood staring at her, naked after his shower, and slowly absorbed all the evidence he had ignored for months. The pieces fell into place, the secretive responses to his questions, the staying out late without explanation, the big mood swings and the clothes which were more revealing than they used to be. 'So that is how you pay for the booze isn't it! By selling your body!'

'What if I do? What has it got to do with you?' She faced him defiantly.

'Because I am your husband, and you are my wife, you filthy whore!'

William strode across the room grabbing her and fully intending to hit her, but she was very slightly dressed with no underclothes and he was a naked full blooded man, and somehow the intended violent blow turned rapidly into violent sex, such as he had never previously experienced. He threw her on the bed and roughly thrust himself inside her, saying 'I am your husband. Do you understand? I am your husband!!!.'

She lay unmoving beneath him, just looking at him with hard eyes, and then, as he climaxed, a huge climax that seemed to engulf him, she spat in his face.

William slid off her and lay, sobbing, face into a pillow, distraught at his own behaviour, the violence that he had not known lay within him, and the humiliation over the way it had expressed itself. All violence was dissipated and replaced by overwhelming shame and regret. He stayed that night on the sofa downstairs, but in the morning before he left to drive out to the lorry park he went to the bedroom and roused her. 'I want you out of this house. My house. It's over.'

To his surprise she laughed at him and said she had been planning to do just that. When he got home that evening she had gone. Her wardrobe was empty and one or two of her precious possessions were missing. Suddenly the house which had seemed so right with five of them was as quiet as the grave. William surprised himself by ringing his sister Susan to tell her what had happened, and realised that his voice was quite upbeat and that there was a lightness in his heart which had not been there for a long time. There was a sense of release.

Deborah found a bedsit in a rundown Victorian street, and moved there without complaint. She was good at her new role and quite enjoyed it. She would sit on a bar stool in a friendly hotel with an eye for likely customers. Sometimes the knowing barman would fix a meeting in return for a small backhander. Often she would go with her client to his hotel room. Sometimes she would take him home to her bedsit. She made more than enough money to keep her in clothes, pay the rent, and feed both of her addictions. She sometimes forgot to eat, but she never forgot to drink.

One night walking home from a hotel, she came across an injured kitten who appeared to have no home. The animal was unable to walk properly and Debbie thought it might have a broken leg. She took it home with her and attended the veterinary surgery the next morning to have the leg fixed. The vet was surprised that she did not want to have the cat put down, but to have it mended to become her pet. He was a ginger tom, whom she named Tiger.

One day an older woman came into the bar and sat next to her. She engaged Debbie in conversation and the two women got on very well. They had both experienced good educations and both had some social polish. The older woman, Lois, was very expensively groomed and dressed. She invited Deborah to join her for dinner, saying that she would pay.

They enjoyed the dinner, the conversation and the wine. Afterwards Lois asked Debbie to her suite, and, once there, retreated to the bathroom, emerging shortly in an exquisite dressing gown and nothing else. She reached down to Debbie and guided her to the enormous king sized bed. 'I like beautiful young women Debbie.' Lois said, 'Will you entertain me please?'

They made love in a slow, very gentle, tactile manner, kissing all over, and sucking ear lobes even toes. Debbie found it more erotic than anything she had known before. Afterwards Lois gently encouraged her to dress and leave, but tucked some notes in Debbie's bra as she left. She said that she would be back in a week. Later Debbie counted £200. She would certainly return.

William changed the locks on his home. After a few months he thought the house too big for his needs so he moved slightly smaller modern one that was easily maintained. This, he felt, was another stage in his new start. He visited Ruth from time to time, taking her out to tea, but he did not bring her home. The other two he looked after every day that he was not working. He began to feel better.

31

1992 Sheila Green

It was always harrowing for Sheila to visit Ryelands House. Married, mostly very happily, and with her own children successfully flown the nest, she found this part of her role particularly upsetting. There was nothing wrong with Ryelands itself. The staff were warm and caring, offering the children in their care as much as was possible in the context of a Local Authority Children's Home. No, she had no complaints about that; it was just that she wished there to be no need for Ryelands, nor for many similar places in the land.

How could a child so traumatised by life, that the department felt they could no longer allow a domestic situation to continue, find real love and affection in an environment that could never replace a sense of Mummy and Daddy? How could a primary school child thrive in a household in which the staff members are not allowed to offer a cuddle?

Sheila felt strongly that hugs and cuddles are amongst the most important human activities, and lead to more complete human beings. She never turned away when a youngster held arms up to her, or wrapped themselves around her voluminous skirts. She would pick up the little ones and prop them on a hip whilst she spoke with grown up people; and the older children, too heavy to carry, she would hold by the hand, a hand that often also held a sweetie.

Consequently when she arrived for her weekly visit she became a magnet for children, who gathered around her vying with each other for her attention. She knew that others would think she was leaving herself vulnerable to accusations, but she refused to allow this 'silly PC nonsense', as she labelled it, to intrude upon her primary role in life, which was to love and support children; helping them into better environments than they had perhaps ever known.

Sheila was the Social Worker responsible for Fostering in East Sussex. She was the Real Thing, an intelligent, wise, caring motherly figure in middle life. The home superintendent, herself very experienced, had come to regard Sheila Green as very special, so it was something of a surprise when Sheila admitted to sleepless nights about the Mason girl.

The ten year old had been taken into care by the courts. Her mother was a hopeless, alcoholic, heroin addict, who paid for her addictions by whoring. She had become dangerously irresponsible, neglecting her children, and even actively ill-treating them. Ruth Mason had in effect been the carer for the two younger children who had a different father from herself. All three children became the subject of a court order, but William Mason, a decent man, the father of the younger two, had managed to arrange for his sister to take on his own children but, try though Sheila knew he had, he had not been able to persuade his sister to take all three. The sister, who was a working mother with children of her own, had insisted she did not have room and that, in any event, this child was not her responsibility. William had no choice to comply because he must continue to work, and could not be home to care for his family. He certainly could no longer rely on his wife to undertake anything. His relationship with her having finally broken down, he had sadly moved her out of the home. The wife had found herself a poor backstreet bedsit in which to live her miserable life. William had told Sheila that his wife, Deborah, utterly rejected him, was usually completely drunk by teatime, and was now regularly using heroin. She had started, he knew by smoking it, but was now injecting. He felt dejected and defeated, but determined to try to rescue his own children, and to see that Ruth, to whom he had been Daddy, was properly cared for. He applauded the court decision. Sheila thought he was a simple man of great principles, caught in a situation beyond his control

William brought a sullen, emaciated, pale and withdrawn Ruth to Ryelands House, and had left quickly, a streak down his right cheek, his ten year attempt to bring order to his wife and her daughters' lives a complete failure.

Yet, Sheila thought, but not totally so. This little girl was clearly intelligent, and had sustained her younger half siblings for years, at times almost by herself. She had good manners, almost old fashioned in her polite speech. Sheila knew that her mother had been quite well brought up and educated. In addition Sheila had found a book of simple piano pieces and a hymn book in Ruth's luggage. There was a keyboard in Ryelands House and the staff sometimes found her perched on the stool playing the pieces from her book, and occasionally picking out a tune she had heard on the radio. They thought that maybe this had been how she consoled herself in her previous life.

All this gave Sheila food for thought. Part of her job was to distribute the children from Ryelands to foster parents. Sometimes fostering is short term, the parents retaining control of the child, but clearly in Ruth's case she would need to find long term foster parents. One of her skills was to try to fit like with like. Because Ruth had been formally committed into care by the Court she was the responsibility of Social Services, not of her parents.

Sheila had looked at her list of potential foster parents and did not see anyone that she felt fitted exactly, though there were a number of excellent candidates. It was her habit never to rush these things. Mistakes do occur and she knew the importance of being right from the beginning.

A couple of evenings previous to this visit she had taken a phone call from her childhood friend Rachel Plowman, inviting Sheila and her husband David to the Plowman's thirtieth wedding anniversary party. Sheila had been Rachel's bridesmaid all those years ago. The exchange had left Sheila musing about the Plowmans. They seemed to live such a satisfactory life. Ian was a very successful rural GP, happy and fulfilled in his work, playing the piano for a number of instrumentalists, and accompanying choir practices in the local choral society. Rachel played her cello in a fine amateur orchestra in Exeter, and spent her day as head of music in one of the city's schools. Their one sadness was that they had no children. Sheila knew they had undergone all of the tests and tried everything they could think of, but in the end no child had arrived.

She had woken this morning with the idea in her mind that perhaps, just perhaps, she might join Ian and Rachel Plowman with Ruth Mason. As the day progressed the thought grew ever more pressing until it was no longer a thought, but an excitement which she must explore.

'Ruth, have you ever been to Devon?'

'No Miss Green, Dad was always very busy and my Mum never took us anywhere.'

'Well, I have some friends from Devon, and if you like I will try to introduce you. How do you feel about that?'

'OK,' said Ruth, unsmiling.

That very evening Sheila telephoned Rachel in Cullompton and after talking polite nothings for a few minutes asked 'Rachel, darling, have you ever thought of fostering?'

There was a long silence after which Rachel replied in a much lower, rather defensive tone, 'Why do you ask?'

'Well, I have a ten year old here who needs a home and I think in intellectual and talent terms she is exactly like the child you might have had.'

'Oh my God Sheila! I wish you hadn't opened that can of worms. In fact how dare you do that to us after all these years? We've come to terms with the fact that it is not going to happen.'

'I dare because I love you both very much, and because I have a child here who needs what you have to offer, and who I suspect might bring you emotional riches beyond your dreams. I would love you both to come up this weekend, stay with David and me, and I shall take you to meet her. I have not suggested that you will foster her, but she knows I have friends in Devon I wish her to meet.'

'I shall talk to Ian, and think about it. We'll ring you back.'

The phone was rather precipitately replaced and both ladies, almost two hundred miles apart, sat staring at it for a while.

When Ian came home that evening he found Rachel in quite a state of agitation. She poured him a large gin, and told him about the phone call. To Rachel's surprise Ian was in no way hostile to the notion. He said that they had got by on spaniels for some years, and he was open to a challenge greater than a spaniel's brain, which he had always reckoned was like living with a two year old child, but in perpetuity. In any event they were currently without a dog.

'But surely we are too old?' she said.

'No, I do not think so,' Ian said. 'I think the cut-off point is normally sixty, but I'm not sure. Surely Sheila would not have stirred this pot if we are too old. She knows the law of course.'

'No, I suppose she would not have done that.'

'Your work fits perfectly well with having a ten year old. You are more or less working school hours, so there would be no long periods of being left alone. You have school holidays as a teacher. I think teaching is the perfect occupation for mothers, don't you? I vote we go and meet her, as Sheila suggests.'

The following Saturday morning Dr and Mrs Ian Plowman drove from Devon to Brighton, a very long drive, ostensibly to meet their old friends, but in reality to vet a ten year old potential foster child. Ian was pleased she was ten, which he regarded as a more appropriate age than a new born would be for a couple of middle aged 'squares'.

On the Sunday morning they all went to Ryelands for coffee. Sheila and David, having introduced Ian and Rachel to several of the children and staff, quietly eased all but Ruth out of the room, shutting the door behind them. If Ruth noticed she made no comment. For about half an hour they chatted about all sorts of things. Both of the adults were adept at interviews, and managed to make this one appear to be a normal conversation, but nonetheless they soon knew that Ruth loved her Dad and her young half brother and sister very much, especially Kevin who obviously gave her a hard time. But she had a strange attitude to her mother. She clearly found it hard to forgive her behaviour, yet took a view very like an older sister, explaining and almost excusing her. Deborah had clearly become more child than mother to Ruth. In particular Ruth was very realistic about her mother, even revealing that she knew about Mum's men friends who would come for quite short times, and be taken to Mum's room. Ruth meanwhile was told to look after the babes. Ruth obviously knew this was not normal behaviour. The Plowmans guessed she knew more than she was saying.

She even let them know that she sometimes cleaned up after her mother had been drinking too much and that occasionally she had to destroy needles to keep them away from the babies. It was not uncommon for her to put her mother to bed. Rachel wanted to pick her up and hug her, because she looked so waif -like. But she didn't, feeling that this girl might be very untrusting and not yet ready for hugs. But, they both were strongly aware that she was worldly wise to an amazing degree.

Ian asked her about music and Ruth smiled for the first time, jumping to her feet, taking them to the piano, and asking 'Do you play?'

'Well, yes Ruth I play a lot.'

'Will you play with me?' The little 'mother' had taken control, as Rachel guessed she might have done often before. She sat Ian at the piano beside her and treated him as if he was a child having his first lesson. Rachel could not help but smile at the restraint her husband showed. In no time they were both playing together, Ruth coming to understand that Ian was very good indeed. Smiles replaced inhibition, and eventually there came some laughter, which brought a very happy Sheila and David back into the room.

'We enjoyed meeting you,' said Rachel, rather formally at the end of the visit 'Would you like to come to us and stay for as long as you want, maybe for a long time?'

'Yes please!

'Would I see Daddy and Bridget and Kevin?'

'I expect that could be arranged sometimes, but not very often. It is a very long way.'

'Do I come now?' She was suddenly keen to be on her way.

'No, not quite now,' laughed Sheila. 'Forms must be found and filled in and there are all sorts of permissions to arrange, but I think it will only take a couple of weeks.'

And so Ruth Mason was fostered with Ian and Rachel Plowman of Cullompton.

32

1993 A New Challenge

Uffculme was very different from anything that Ruth had experienced before. The large village, almost a town, spread itself over the low hills in a manner apparently quite random. There was some industry, a branch of the cloth business in nearby Wellington and, of all unlikely things, a fireworks factory. But the village somehow retained a sense of its agricultural roots, sitting as it did in some of the finest farming country in the land.

Increasingly Uffculme had been occupied by commuters from Exeter. The motorway, passing just a couple of miles away, reduced the journey time to about twenty minutes. In so doing it made the village an attractive option for many who worked in the city. Indeed this easy commute was central to the Plowman's decision to live in Uffculme, since Rachel could easily manage her job in Exeter.

There had been a considerable amount of new housing built since the motorway arrived. One effect of all this during the 1970s and 1980s was to increase the demands upon the school, which responded to its new role magnificently, acquiring a reputation for good education far beyond the village confines. It was here that Ian and Rachel enrolled their foster child Ruth Mason. The decision was not difficult since Ian himself had started there as a child. The school was about a mile from the Plowman home, but such was the nature of the community that even as a stranger aged eleven, Ruth was soon allowed to make her own way, on foot.

Ruth was compliant, polite, perhaps much too polite Ian thought, but she seldom laughed or smiled. She ate well and became physically tougher with a more active lifestyle, but she was quite withdrawn. Ian and Rachel thought she was missing her siblings and William very much. They felt that she was on loan to them, but no more than that. She woke very early in the morning and used to read for a long time before the alarm raised the household. Her choice of books was seldom fiction, but most often modern history or natural sciences. She became especially interested in biology and chemistry.

Ruth seldom offered opinions, preferring to observe and absorb the conversation, but not take part. This made her rather silent in the house, silent that is except when her foster parents were practising their music. Then she was all attention and wanted to join in. Perhaps her happiest moments were when playing duets with Ian. Curiously she came to dominate this activity, choosing what to play and when to play it, even telling Ian off for a very occasional wrong note. This became a routine activity for the hour before bedtime, whenever Ian was home from work in time. One of the very first things Rachel and Ian did when Ruth arrived was to arrange piano lessons with an excellent teacher. She was very diligent at this, practising for long periods, determined to play properly whatever she was studying. They could hear the increasing competence and maturity in her playing every week that passed. If she found a phrase especially difficult, she would play it over and over again until the Plowmans wished she would stop. But she always got it right in the end. She was also fastidious about her person, taking a shower twice a day and seldom appearing in any way dishevelled.

One day Ian returned home after the evening surgery to find Ruth had gone to bed and Rachel was clearly upset. Thinking that the two had had some disagreement he was surprised to learn that no such thing had happened, rather it was the lack of emotion in Ruth which had upset his wife. Rachel said it was like being given a lollipop and then being told that you can only have half of it. In some ways it was worse than having no lollipop at all.

The same situation applied at school. Ruth was diligent in class, never failing, but not shining either. Her teachers observed that she was very precise but was perhaps reluctant to be seen as different, so she made herself as invisible as possible. She did not contribute verbally, and they found it impossible to guess what she was thinking. She was a very private little girl. Of course they had no notion that she had seen and heard many things that would not have made for good school talk.

Soon Ian realised that Ruth needed greater freedom. There were signs of some relationships beginning with some of the local children who figured in the supper time conversation. He understood that a solitary home with late middle aged people whom she hardly knew, was not good enough, and that something had to change. That something took the form of a bicycle.

The bicycle was a thing of beauty to Ruth. Her very urban upbringing had not encouraged bicycles, and in any case neither William nor even Debbie would have been happy for her to cycle alone, so she had never learned to ride.

Ian and Rachel spent many an hour up on the disused aerodrome nearby, firstly walking alongside whilst holding the back of Ruth's wobbling saddle to stabilize her, then, as her balance improved, slowly cycling alongside. But, Ruth was a quick learner and soon mastered the art well enough, though in truth she never became quite as skilled as her peers, and never quite understood the need to lean into corners. But the bike emancipated Ruth. She knew that her loneliness was a big problem, there being no siblings in the house. Also she needed easy access to her school. She was beginning to make a few new school friends. Two of these were Jack and Sarah Wilson, whose parents were tenant farmers with a dairy herd close to the village. It was a steep climb from the Plowman house up to the farm but there was always the joy of the free wheel almost all of the way home.

Jack and Sarah's Dad liked them to get involved with the farm, so soon Ruth too was becoming informed about farm animals and their ways, but although that interested her, she was more excited by the plants that grew in the hedgerows and in the grasses that the cows ate. She found it amazing that these huge creatures lived entirely on green grass. She wondered how they could possibly get enough fuel from such a little thing. Jim Wilson told her that, whereas she only needed to eat for an hour or so each day, the cows needed to eat for most of the time in order to get sufficient nutrition to look as fit and sleek as his cows did. He told her that his herd was famous, very largely because his farm enjoyed the right mix of sunshine and rain for the grass to grow very well. The effect on the cows could easily be seen. That simple piece of biology, witnessed at first hand, impressed the young Ruth and increased her interest in biology and biochemistry, which significantly fashioned her academic career.

Rachel and Ian both worked hard, and had over the years acquired quite a lot of commitments in the community. They earned quite well without ever being rich and had spent a long period of productive living without the cost of children and all that stems from that. They did not have expensive hobbies or a second home, but they did employ a gardener and his wife part time to look after the house and garden. Mrs Pyne was quite prepared to alter her hours so that instead of coming in the mornings she worked the Plowman house in the afternoons. This meant that in those early years, before Rachel was content for Ruth to be alone, there was somebody home when she returned from school to cover that hour or two before Rachel herself arrived.

Mrs Pyne knew a thing or two about hungry youngsters and so, on getting home from school, Ruth would, as often as not, sit in the kitchen watching her iron the clothes, whilst tucking into a cup of tea and a bun or a buttered crumpet. The two got along very well, perhaps because Mrs Pyne reminded Ruth of Auntie Susan. And so it was that Mrs Pyne learned more of Ruth's difficult early life and the things she had witnessed, than Rachel did.

Meanwhile Ian and Rachel were getting more concerned about Ruth's withdrawn state. She was still sitting silently at the meal table most of the time. She seldom asked for anything, and seemed unhealthily detached. They noticed early budding breasts and an increasing preoccupation with self.

Christmas was particularly disconcerting in that Ruth tended to look in on the festivities as if from the outside. She did not want anything for Christmas she said, though they ignored that, and she did not want to go carol singing with Rachel.

One day Ruth returned from school flushed and upset, going immediately to her room without greeting Mrs Pyne. Shortly afterwards Mrs Pyne was alarmed to hear loud crashes and shouts from the room, and went to investigate. Ruth was in the middle of the floor whirling her school satchel around her head crashing it into furniture, bookcases and lamps and shouting, 'Damn. Damn. Damn. Why me? Why me? Why me?' at the top of her voice. On seeing Mrs Pyne Ruth stopped her whirling and shouting and a moment later was in Mrs Pyne's arms, crying pitifully. It was as if all of the hurts she had endured for all of those years had burst to the surface. Order was more or less restored by the time Rachel returned, but Mrs Pyne did make sure Rachel knew what had happened.

Rachel and Ian discussed the situation at length before turning their lights out that night. Ian concluded that their charge was really quite depressed and needed some help, but what help would be best? Then he had an idea.

On Ruth's twelfth birthday in March 1994 they all got into Ian's car and drove towards Exmoor. There was an old coaching inn on the approaches and the remains of a winding house for a cable railway that used to take iron ore down from the Brendon Hills to Watchet on the Bristol Channel. Just close to there lies a Georgian farm house which was their destination. Ian's premonition proved correct for Ruth became truly excited by the six tiny puppies that they had come to see.

Her eyes shone with delight when she was invited to choose one to take home. She chose the curious one, believing him to be intelligent, and so became the proud owner of a real Springer Spaniel; not one of the curly show dogs, but one with a smoother coat and slender, muscular body, the true 'gun dog' Spaniel. Of course Sam would never be used to hunt, or shoot but would become her friend and faithful companion for the remainder of his life.

She sat in the car holding this wriggling little eight week old scrap of fur, and was licked all the way home. The bonding began at once. Ian smiled into the rear mirror thinking that this would be better than anti depressive pills. He was right.

Uffculme School was keen on its music and so Ruth soon became a member of the school choir. She sang a piping soprano and the adults who heard her began to whisper amongst themselves that this girl was making a very special sound. After a while she was given bits of solo to do, which because of her long experience at the piano posed absolutely no problem. In one concert at age just 14, she sang 'I know that my Redeemer Liveth', from Handel's Messiah very well indeed, without realising how difficult most singers find it.

Perhaps because of her music, which involved others, and because of her love of the puppy, Sam, she began to emerge from her depressive phase and to show warmth and humour towards other people. Having negotiated puberty without any crises, (after all her childhood was full of things biological, she played on a farm, and her foster father was a family doctor), she became a confident, aware and attractive teenager. But all this happened almost without her realising it. Certainly she made no play of her burgeoning womanhood. Her auburn hair and green eyes with her slightly Slavic face, made her very conspicuous, especially as she became tall and willowy. Heads began to turn as she passed by.

Academically she surprised everyone, including herself. At the school summer celebrations in 1996 she carried off several prizes. Ian and Rachel began to bask in her company and proudly introduced her to their long standing friends.

Jack and Sarah continued to be her school chums, though Sarah, being an unusually buxom, red cheeked fourteen year old quietly envied Ruth's elegance, and Jack, who was sprouting a prodigious amount of hair as well as a very bass voice, suddenly became bashful and tongue tied when Ruth rolled off a hay rick when they were all skylarking, landing almost in his lap.

Ruth sat up, pushing him away with a laugh, but suddenly paused and looked hard and closely at him, the laughter choked off for the moment. 'I like you Jack Wilson.' She said in a low voice. 'I like you a lot.'

With that she got up, brushed bits of straw from her clothes and fetched her bicycle. She felt a strange confusion as she rode home, but knew that suddenly things had changed. Childhood was over.

33

1994 August Bank Holiday Weekend

The Royal Sussex County Hospital, Brighton casualty department, was very busy that summer Saturday evening. The access to Accident and Emergency was around the corner from the main Barry Building, but this did not seem to deter the stream of customers. The waiting area was packed tight, almost exclusively with youngsters. The air was full of the smell of alcohol and sweat, mixed with blood, some anger and a lot of fear. The weather had been good, so lots of young singles had come down to the sea from London, many of them without anywhere to stay, and often without any warm clothing or even a toothbrush. It was reminiscent of the famous 'Mods and Rockers' weekends of thirty years previously, though without the Vespas and Lambrettas that used to dominate the town in those days.

They crowded the resort's clubs and bars, drinking and using recreational drugs in the urgent pursuit of an oblivion which, in their world, they considered to be happiness. Jon Garside, the young casualty surgeon in charge of the unit, had never been able to understand the need to drink so quickly and copiously as to become completely out of one's mind. A more traditional man, he had always considered alcohol a social lubricant to be used sensibly. To him drunkenness was a misjudgement of dose, to be paid for by a bad head and inefficiency next day. It was an enjoyment to him at dinners or drinks parties, and indeed he almost always had a late night malt, but it was one always to be used with care, and if that proved impossible to be avoided altogether. To use it specifically to become quickly mindless, and a social embarrassment, or worse, was beyond his comprehension. But then, he knew, as these young people apparently did not know, that alcohol in itself caused more demand on health resources than anything else, and was a great nuisance to hospitals. When admixed with drugs, particularly with amphetamines or crack cocaine, it created in the consumer a volatile powder keg, often exploding into unpredictable mindless violence for no apparent reason. Of course the testosterone laden lads were the main problem, but the modern girls were catching them up fast.

Most of the so called recreational drugs had been about since early times, and had indeed in the past been available over the counter. Tincture of Laudanum, a heroin variant had figured largely in Conan Doyle's Sherlock Holmes stories, and much of the world's finest art, even poetry, had been produced when under the influence of narcotics, but their use had been relatively confined to the very poorest slums and to the arty sets in such places as Bloomsbury, and of course to the intellectually and exploratory exotica of the university campus. Very little had impinged upon ordinary life until the late 1950s, but their use was spreading like wildfire. Jon knew that about a third of young men and women regularly used cannabis and that heroin was a big problem, especially in urban communities. Amphetamine and cocaine usage was increasing alarmingly. Jon dealt with the consequences.

The town's prostitutes were doing a good trade. In fact they were hardly able to cope with the demand upon them. However, sex was so freely available without charge, that one might be tempted to enquire how they found enough clients to pay the bills. But find them they certainly did, and they paid their bills, often not just the groceries and the rent, but their own supply of drugs as well. Some were dealers.

It was usually around about midnight that the fights started and the police became very busy. Mostly they were simple fist fights leading to nothing more serious than bumps and bruises, but in the past few years the young lads had increasingly taken to secreting a knife about their persons in the mistaken belief that it would make them safer. Repairing slash and stab wounds was now a regular feature of the Casualty Surgeon's work and his department had become so overwhelmed with cursing, violent, obscene and dangerous young people of both genders, that a permanent police presence within the department had become necessary. There had been one death and several near misses already this weekend. Jon's young registrar, not so very much older than his clients, looked excessively world weary, as well he might. He had been on duty for close to 36 hours and had seen more than he wanted of the sordidness of human beings. He had been sworn at, punched and spat upon already this evening.

But even he was appalled when he finished his examination of the latest piece of debris to be brought in from the beach tonight. It was on the beach that many, exhausted by their excesses, gathered at the day's end, to crumple on the ground and hopefully sleep until morning. A passing constable had thought this one did not look good, and had summoned an ambulance.

The registrar stood straight, not quite able to restrain himself from wrinkling his nose at the woman on his couch. She was not as young as the usual brawlers, probably around 30, and her purse had a local address, so she was most likely to be one of the whores. 'We shall have to admit her, nurse.' He said. 'She is obviously unconscious, but I'm sure it is more than being very drunk. Young women are seldom drunk enough to foul and wet themselves like this, and this smell is not of recent fouling but of long term poor hygiene and a lot of infection too. What you smell mostly is pus. Remember that smell nurse. It is important that you do.

'I reckon she is not much more than 6 stones and her skin suggests to me that she has lost a lot of weight. Just look at those rotten teeth. They are the result of all sorts of neglect.

You won't see teeth like that on any woman with personal pride. You and I have just counted 68 injection sites, several of which are actively infected now. This one in the right groin is a major problem. She is also feverish so I think a big part of her problem is a septicaemia from dirty needles.' He scribbled his observation on the casualty records and moved to the phone, seeking a bed from his ward colleague.

The nurse was even younger and new to this scene. 'I've never seen anything like this before,' she said. 'What are her chances of survival?'

'Well,' he replied, 'we might be able to get her back on her feet in a few days, and deal with the infection, but not her liver disease, or her chronic anaemia and malnutrition, nor her underlying addiction. All that would take time and persistence. Usually this type of person cannot cope with the disciplines of a hospital ward, and so they discharge themselves as soon as they think they can manage.'

'So she just goes out and starts all over again?' said the nurse, aghast.

'That's about it,' he replied. 'Unless the psychiatrists can legally detain her against her will on an order, I give her six months at the most.'

Deborah woke in the ward the following afternoon. She lay there staring out of the window at the sea and said nothing. Her head felt terrible and she hurt everywhere. She was already worrying about her next fix. There was a drip in the back of her left hand. She managed a wry smile to herself that they had managed to find a vein. She was finding it ever more difficult.

The next thing she noted was that she smelled clean. Her clothes were gone and all she had on was a hospital gown, but someone had given her a bed bath and even in her heavy state she recognised the smell of soap and enjoyed the sensation.

After a while she noticed a jug of water and a tumbler on her bed side locker and managed to reach it. Her thirst was worse than it had ever been before. Her movement attracted the staff nurse who came over to her bedside with a clip board and asked her too many questions. Not long after a white coated young woman doctor came with a file, introduced herself as Dr Robinson and sat down to ask the same questions all over again. Debbie would get used to this, at one time counting five people in a day asking her the same questions, each person with their own clipboard. She did wonder about the awful waste of professional time. She wondered why they did not all use the first 'master' edition. Then there was a physical examination associated with a certain amount of 'tutting' and frowning. Deborah knew this was because of her many abscesses, but was still very muddled and in any case was beyond caring, having nothing left to conceal. Later she tried to eat a little supper but promptly vomited and so did not persist. The nurses said she was very dehydrated and must drink in addition to the drip.

Several days passed during which she endured the most appalling episodes of jitteriness and cravings associated with bizarre images of babies and of her husband, who appeared dressed, she thought, in a judge's gown and wig. She thought she was going mad and became increasingly desperate to get out of the hospital and back to her bedsit. Squalid and mean though it was, it was nonetheless home for her. She had not seen her parents for a year since that last awful row, when Mum had caught her stealing from her purse. She knew that some of her regular clients would be wondering where she was, and she would miss the money. She had been dealing in drugs as well as consuming them and began to worry that her suppliers would find an alternative dealer. Nobody knew where she was.

About a week later, the drip was gone, the intravenous antibiotics finished and she felt considerably better. Well enough to sit out and dress in her laundered clothes, though the dressing on her right groin was not comfortable and showed through her flimsy dress. She was told that her liver was in poor shape but not totally failing, that her blood count was very poor because of malnutrition and infection, and that she had had a near death experience from a cocktail of drugs and alcohol. It certainly felt like it.

The Psychiatrist came and spent a long time with her, enquiring deeply about her family, her own life and her circumstances. His report showed that, although she was quite physically sick and mentally disturbed both as an addict and from depression, she was neither suicidal nor homicidal, and therefore could not legally be detained against her will. He offered to transfer her to the Psychiatric Unit for voluntary treatment of her addictions, and when she refused he settled for an Outpatient appointment, though he well understood that she would not keep it.

The next morning Deborah took her own discharge from the hospital against advice and tottered home to her bedsit, pausing to visit her dealer on the way. Having serviced him enough to satisfy his own idiosyncratic sexual appetite she went home with her reward, sufficient to last a couple of days at least. She realised he had not used a condom. They had told her in the hospital that she was HIV positive, one of half a million people in Europe in 1993 to be so. She smiled to herself at the implication of what she had done.

34

1995 Dark Alley

Dick Trevelyan had been doing this round for about ten years, delivering milk to the doorsteps of Brighton. He had started his working life as a salesman in an insurance company, paid almost entirely on commission. When business was especially good, as it had been in the 1980s, he did well, marrying, buying a house and fathering two lovely children.

Marjory had always been keen to live on the south coast so, when a colleague retired, Dick managed to persuade the company to give him the Brighton patch. The whole family moved down from London, buying a pleasant house just outside of town. The children were very happy at school, and Marjory had a small business, running dinner parties and other events for wealthy Brighton residents who preferred not to manage their own catering.

After a few years however, dreadful sleeplessness and irritability led Dick to the family doctor, who discovered he had extremely high blood pressure. This proved to be very resistant to management with medication, and so Dick was advised that the seventy hour a week job, depending utterly on his sales successes to pay the mortgage, would shorten his life significantly.

Much to his friends' amused surprise he took the advice, resigned his job and went to work for a small family owned dairy, working as their milkman. On six days a week in all types of weather Dick rose at three in the morning and spent the night hours delivering milk to the doorsteps of the citizens of Brighton. He was home, finished, by ten thirty in the morning. He would never earn as much as his previous job, but the money was steady, regular, and just sufficient. He became bodily fit and his blood pressure settled to almost normal levels with minimal medication. Most importantly his family were delighted to have a cheerful and loving husband and father again. After all, his strange working hours meant that he was at home during most of the others' waking day.

The job took him through the streets of the old town, where he became accustomed to the smells and noises of the night. Garbage bags and bins were normal obstacles for him, as was the occasional shop doorway drunk.

That icy cold February Friday night was in no way different, until he stopped his milk float at the end of one alley, not far from The Lanes, and walked with his crate of milk bottles through to the little houses beyond the narrow passageway. He stopped suddenly, almost unconsciously, in the narrowest part of the passage, recognising that one dark bundle was not a collection of garbage but was something different. Dick always carried a small torch since his work took him away from reassuring street lights. He turned his light onto the shape and saw that it was a human being, who appeared to be dead. He hurried to the nearest public phone box to ring the police.

The discovery of this body was investigated by the Office of Coroner; one of the oldest in the land, its name stemming from the title 'Crowner', meaning the local representative of the monarch of the time. In the ages of absolute rule by Kings, before Parliamentary law superseded much of the Crown's power, the Crowner was a very significant figure dispensing justice in his region. In modern Britain, the Coroner's role had diminished to one of enquiring into treasure trove, and more commonly, into deaths that occurred in a manner which did not allow a doctor properly to issue a death certificate. This of course included all violent or unnatural deaths and also those that were totally unexpected and not preceded by medical care.

In America the Coroner, often called the Medical Examiner, was a Forensic Pathologist, but in Britain he or she was part of the Judiciary, operating a Coroner's Court where the hearings were called Inquests. Usually Coroners were lawyers, though occasionally they were medically or even doubly, qualified. In his own Court the Coroner wielded considerable power, being free to operate without a jury, and to bring verdicts, some of which had far reaching consequences.

The Coroner had his own staff including a Coroner's Officer, who in this case was a mature, sensible and empathetic policeman, capable of managing the trauma of bereaved families with tact and care.

Just after breakfast that Saturday morning William, not working that day, was chatting with Susan whilst keeping a careful eye on Bridget and Kevin, who were busy teasing the cat. He felt more at ease with the world than for years. Susan had proved a wonderful surrogate Mum for the children, who had blossomed under her care and love. William could go about his business, not worrying about whether his children were being properly fed and supervised. He regularly collected the children from Susan on Saturday mornings, spending the weekend with them in his small home, but returning them to her at bedtime on Sunday. Susan usually gave him breakfast on Saturday, so they could catch up with each other's news. The formula worked well, allowing both parts of Susan's extended family to have some prime time together.

William was very conscious that whatever had happened, however angry and let down he felt, he still had some feelings for Debbie. No matter what she had become, she was nonetheless Bridget and Kevin's mother. So he arranged that some occasional contact with Debbie still happened, usually with him inviting her to a meal or to watch one of the children's activities. He had therefore witnessed her decline at first hand, and had tried his best to change her course. His attempts usually ended in angry exchanges and with her stomping away from the room. He never brought her to Susan's home. Neither Susan nor her husband would welcome it.

This morning however, they were interrupted by the arrival of a police car driven by a grey haired Sergeant who asked if he could have a private word with William. He explained that a woman had been found dead in the street that night, and that from the purse in her pocket she seemed to be Deborah Mason. A visit to her bedsit and a rummage in drawers there had led them to his name and address. A neighbour of William seeing the official car, had advised the sergeant where William might be found.

He was very apologetic for intruding upon the gentle domestic scene but needed William's help. 'I'm sorry to disturb you sir, but could you please confirm that Deborah Mason is your wife. We'll also need you to identify her in the mortuary.' He went on to say that the police required a statement about Deborah, their marriage, their current relationship and an explanation of William's whereabouts the previous evening. The sergeant also gently enquired as to what he should do with the half a dozen cats found in Debbie's flat.

As the sergeant spoke, Susan, who had understood that there was something far wrong, came to William as he sat at the kitchen table, and rested her hand upon his shoulder. William's head sagged and a great wave of sadness came over him. He had perceived this moment might come as he witnessed Debbie's gradual decline, but knowing something does not make it easier to bear when it happens. He realised that, despite everything, he was not immune to Debbie's fate and found it very distressing. He went with the sergeant to the mortuary, confirming that the body was indeed Deborah, and then spent a couple of hours in the police station giving statements. He hid nothing, admitting that he knew that she had become a prostitute, living off the streets to fund her substance abuse, which, as far as he knew was of alcohol and heroin.

Later he rang the Troutmann household in Cerney. The phone was answered by a woman unknown to William who summoned George to speak with him. George listened to what he told him without any interruption, and then, after a long silence, said 'What a terrible waste, William, and thank you for trying so hard. You have been to hell and back. I want you to know that I admire you greatly for the way you have managed yourself. I am truly sorry that, as Debbie's father, I have not been more supportive, something I shall regret for the rest of my life.

There is likely to be an Inquest of course. Please let me know when it is. I shall be there.' The phone went dead. Only then did William realise that Catherine, Debbie's mother, had not been mentioned at all.

The Clerk called the Court to order and the Coroner entered. He was a kindly looking man, with a florid complexion, who put everyone at ease with his quiet, gentle manner and obvious professionalism. After a brief explanation of the circumstances of the hearing and establishment of identity, those who were considered to have knowledge relating to the death concerned were called to give witness. The first was Dick Trevelyan, the milkman, who explained carefully the circumstances of his discovery, and the attitude in which the body was lying. He made clear that it was a bitterly cold night, so cold in fact that he himself was affected by it, despite generating heat by working and despite being well dressed. He indicated that he had not moved her in any way, just established that she seemed to be dead before he summoned the police.

The Coroner's Officer corroborated Dick's testimony saying that they had removed her to the mortuary once the Forensic Team had competed their onsite investigation, and that he had then sought and identified Deborah's husband William.

The East Sussex County Hospital Pathologist, who had performed the autopsy, gave very precise information, saying that there was no indication of violence or assault. Her clothes were all in place, though she was inadequately dressed for a bitterly cold winter night. She appeared to be in poor health with signs of malnutrition and multiple injection sites, some of which were infected. She was anaemic and was HIV positive. There were signs of cirrhosis and some chronic pancreatitis but there were no bodily diseases likely to cause a sudden collapse. In particular there was no significant heart disease. However her lungs were congested and her blood showed very high levels of both alcohol and narcotics, suggesting that the cause of death was hypothermia, associated with an overdose of drugs and alcohol. He explained to the hearing that morphine and its related drugs suppress the respiratory centre in the brain, so breathing is slowed and subdued. In extreme circumstances this is sufficient to be fatal. He concluded that she had been unable to reach home in her drugged and inebriated state, and had died in the street, where she lay, of respiratory suppression, due to narcotics and of exposure due to the cold weather and inadequate clothing. Foul play was not suspected.

William was called upon to give a brief description of her lifestyle and of her descent into addiction.

George Troutmann, and Shelia Green, Ruth's Social Worker were present. Nobody had told Ruth, or the Plowmans of Debbie's demise. The Coroner brought a verdict of Death Due to Drug Dependence and released the body to the family for disposal.

A few days later William received a request from Sheila to meet and discuss his step daughter Ruth. Ruth had not been involved in any way over the Inquest, but Sheila felt that she must be informed of her mother's death and given the opportunity to consider coming up from Devon for the funeral. William agreed. Ruth was now twelve and should be treated as such. Since Ruth was fostered and was officially the responsibility of Social Services, it was left for Sheila to contact the Plowman family in Devon.

Shelia noted that there was no report of the inquest in The Albion, Brighton's local newspaper. When she mentioned her surprise at this to a doctor friend, she was told that such drug related incidents were now so commonplace as not to be newsworthy.

The funeral service for Deborah Mason, née Troutmann aged 31 and 3 months was held in Woodvale Crematorium, Lewes Road, Brighton, on Tuesday March 7th 1995. William Mason, his sister Susan, their parents, Bridget and Kevin Mason, and Sheila Green were the only Brighton folk present. No friend or acquaintance of Debbie from the town came. Nobody commented that it was Ruth's thirteenth birthday.

George Troutmann however did come in his shiny Rolls Royce. His companion was a young woman whom he introduced as Barbara. She was a curvaceous blonde who exhibited a remarkably motherly and possessive attitude to George, who was clearly upset by the occasion. George did not elaborate upon their relationship. Catherine Troutmann, Debbie's mother, was nowhere to be seen. George and Barbara did not stay for the funeral meal, though George did quietly slip an envelope containing cash to the funeral director before he left. William only discovered this, when he enquired as to why he had not received a bill.

The Plowman family and Ruth did not come because Ruth had chickenpox. Ruth had a long tearful phone call with William whom she loved dearly, in which she said that she had settled well in Devon, and that she was enjoying her new school, but she missed William, Bridget and Kevin. Thus, by chance Ian and Rachel Plowman never met George, Ruth's grandfather, with whom there was never any contact. They did not even know his name.

Later that year William took Bridget and Kevin on holiday to Cornwall and on the way back they had tea with the Plowman family in Uffculme. The Plowmans, in common with many of their neighbours, were quite used to old friends and acquaintances having a break in their long journey back from their holidays. Ruth was delighted to see them all, but having showed them her lovely room with its view over the surrounding countryside and toured the garden, encouraging the children to feed and play with the Koi in the garden pond, she then sat with her step father William on an old wrought iron garden seat, and stared solemnly at him. Ruth thought William looked so much better, almost a young man again. Obviously his relationship with his children was great and he spoke very warmly of Susan and her husband, to whom he was rightly very grateful.

She learned that her mother's death had not really been a surprise, and that after the funeral there had been no further contact with Debbie's parents. Indeed William confessed that he had heard nothing from Catherine for a long time, but had concluded that she and George had finally parted. He thought it likely that Catherine was now entirely London based, and not in contact; also that George's blonde companion at the funeral was living in Cerney with the old man, who must now be of retirement age.

Ruth silently absorbed this news before looking up at him and saying, 'Sometimes I feel quite alone. You see, as you have made clear, my real grandparents do not want to know me, my mother is dead. I have a lovely step father, and wonderful foster parents, but no real father. That leaves me with no sense of history, or of belonging. Sometimes that makes me very sad. Do you know who he was?'

She looked at him with a determined challenge in her eyes, taking him by surprise with its intensity. William reached for her hand and sat there, seemingly seeking divine guidance as to how he should answer her. Of course she was right to be curious. All normal people want to know their parentage, and probably have a right to know. 'Your mother was working at a fruit farm at Tetbury, when she became pregnant with you.' He said finally. 'That is how I first met her. I used to collect the produce in my truck and sometimes stayed over. It is a very big concern, with a proper sleeping block and canteen for the labour. Lots of the workers were Eastern European, boys mostly, but some of them were girls. They are good workers and reliable and so are very popular with the owners. As a matter of fact I still go there occasionally. The old man has given the farm over to his son now, the same son that Debbie hoped to marry. I sometimes wonder what difference it would have made to her if that had happened as she planned.'

'But who was he? I might want to meet him. Do you know his name?'

'No sweetie, I don't know who he was.' He sat quietly for a long time, still holding her hand, before adding. 'Be careful Ruth. I understand where your thoughts are taking you, and why; but always remember that this man deserted his young lover and disappeared rather than take responsibility. I fear he would be very unlikely to want to know you now.'

'Yes, but if he knew that he would always be second best to the farmer's son, he would not want to be tied to her, would he? Also it might have been very complicated having a pregnant English girlfriend if you were a student from the East. I can understand why he disappeared.'

'Well Ruth I am not sure if that is a good argument. After all somebody did take her, knowing he was always going to be second best.'

She looked at him lovingly and, smiling, said 'Yes, somebody did. But not everyone is wonderful like you Daddy William.'

35

1998 March

One Saturday Ian, Rachel, and Ruth sat in a restaurant in Exeter, enjoying a celebratory meal. They had been to the matinée of a show in the Northcott Theatre to celebrate Ruth's sixteenth birthday. The show had been a delight, and the mood was one of hilarity.

Ian was thrilled to note how close his wife and daughter were becoming, sharing an outrageous sense of humour. He knew that this was often at his expense, but did not mind one scrap. This afternoon he had almost had to restrain them because their laughter was in danger of disturbing folk at nearby tables.

Rachel seemed to have lost years as Ruth increasingly gained poise and competence, so that they behaved more like two sisters than like mother and daughter. 'So now, Ruth, now that you are legally able to do many things that, until today were forbidden, how do you feel about growing up?' she asked.

All of a sudden Ruth's smile disappeared and she became serious. She took a deep breath and said. 'Ian and Rachel, you are not my parents in the eyes of the law because I am still fostered with you. My biological mother is dead, and my father has always been unknown to me. He was, we believe a foreign student who was one of Mum's men friends. I have been thinking a long time about what I wanted to happen when the Social Services released me from their care. You are my family now and have been for several years. I have come to love you both dearly and I have decided that if you agree we might all give each other the best present possible.

'I would like you two wonderful people to have a daughter, and I would like proper parents. So my wish is that Ian and Rachel Plowman consent to formally adopt me and become my real Mum and Dad.'

Ian and Rachel stared at each other and, as if synchronised, looked back to Ruth. Rachel leapt to her feet and gave Ruth a long hard hug, joined almost immediately by Ian. Neither could articulate wonderful things they felt, until all of a sudden they all became aware that other diners must have overheard the request and the whole room was full of clapping smiling people. Ruth blushed prettily, smiled at everyone and said 'Thank you. I guess that is settled then.' and returned to her tea and cream cake.

Shortly afterwards they invited Sheila and David Green for the weekend without telling them the reason. There was a drinks party that evening attended by lots of their local friends, some family from Plymouth and school friends of Ruth, including the Wilsons. When everyone had arrived, a glass or two had been consumed, and the conversation was very lively Ian stood on a small table and called for silence. 'My friends, most of you know that, recently, Ruth celebrated her sixteenth birthday. Indeed some of you might be thinking that this gathering is to mark that event, and to some degree it is. But, being sixteen gave Ruth some freedoms she had not previously enjoyed. For the first time she is legally able to take the control of her destiny into her own hands. At the very first opportunity she has exercised one of those freedoms.'

He paused in order to get control of the tremble in his voice before continuing. 'My friends, Rachel and I are proud to announce that Ruth, on her sixteenth birthday, invited us to formally adopt her as our daughter. You will all know that she is much loved, and admired so it felt like a great privilege to be invited to become a Mum and Dad properly. Children do not normally get to choose their parents. Ruth has had that luxury, if luxury it is, and has lost no time in determining what she wishes to do. So Rachel and I have just acquired our first daughter, a bit late in life, I might hear some of my more outspoken friends claim, but better late than never.'

He jumped off the table crossed to where Ruth was standing in the middle of her school friends and brought her to the centre of the room. 'Ladies and Gentlemen I present you with our new daughter who from now on will cease to be Ruth Mason but will be Ruth Plowman, the young woman who has made Rachel and me immensely proud and happy.

Please raise your glasses — To Ruth Plowman.'

They all cheered and drank the toast, even the Plymouth Methodists. The delighted company descended upon Ruth to hug and kiss her, but after a suitable lull Ian returned to his table top and demanded silence once more. 'There is one other matter of great importance to bring to your attention. We all go through our working and our domestic lives doing what we have to do; some of it good and some not so good, but it would be fair to think that everyone here would always be doing their best, even if we sometimes lose sleep and fear that our best is not good enough.'

'But, once in a while, quite rarely for most ordinary mortals, there comes a truly life altering decision, a turn right or turn left moment, which is going to change things for ever. When those moments come we must all pray that he or she concerned has the necessary knowledge wisdom and foresight to make a good judgement call.'

'Such a moment came in our lives in 1992. Rachel and I were shaken out of our dull, middle aged, comfortable complacency by our bridesmaid, Sheila Green, who with great skill, and tact allied to instinct, a good deal of lateral thinking, and at no small risk to our cordial relationship, suggested that we foster a ten year old on a long term basis. Sheila was, and still is, the children's officer for West Sussex and in that capacity quite commonly oversees placements into foster families of children in care, probably more commonly than she would wish. On this particular occasion she noted a musical talent in the child concerned and so contacted her long standing friends the Plowmans whom she knew to be childless, and likely to remain so. We had not expressed an interest in fostering, did not live within Sheila's catchment area, were at the top end of the permissible age range, and might have been hostile to her for upsetting our equilibrium with such a suggestion. Yet she went ahead with it, and in so doing set in train a sequence of events which have led us all to the party this evening. This was the ultimate exercise in judgement, in good judgement and in belief in all that she stood for.'

'Sheila and her husband David are here this evening having been induced to visit for the weekend without any clue about what we have planned for her. Please step forward Sheila so everyone can see you properly.'

Sheila somewhat bashfully stepped into the space in front of Ian, who greeted her formally with a kiss on both cheeks. 'Sheila. I first met you as Rachel's bridesmaid, and since then you have become an important figure in my family's life. We take this opportunity to thank you publicly for the great deed you did for all of us in 1992. Please accept these small tokens as our thanks.'

Rachel stepped forward bearing a beautiful portrait photograph of Ruth, commissioned specially for the occasion. It was large and in a gilt frame. Ian felt behind the sofa and emerged with a case of fine claret which he said was for both Sheila and David. Finally Ruth stepped up with a massive bouquet which she presented very formally before signalling for quiet. 'One of the nicer things that this change allows is for me to call you Auntie Sheila, please.' She smiled.

Sheila hugged her in assent, and then turning to the company, thanked everyone, saying that the evening was one of the happiest in her life, which it was, and that she only wished that all of her work had been so successful. She turned amidst great applause and left the room to compose herself.

Shortly after that weekend Ian and Rachel sat with Ruth to discuss her future education. GCSE level examinations were about to start and Ruth was confidently predicted to do very well. In particular she was very good at natural sciences and maths as well as music. As a pianist she already had a distinction at Grade 8 and was beginning the long hard road leading to a professional performing diploma. She was also singing very well, having lessons privately and doing quite a lot of solo work in the school.

Ian suggested that she follow the same path that he had taken some forty years previously and go from Uffculme School to Blundell's in Tiverton, a famous, old independent school offering a more academic upper school. Since in any event she had reached the top end of Uffculme School, which ceased at GCSE level, some decision was needed. The alternative would be East Devon College in Tiverton. Ian went one stage further and suggested that she apply for a music scholarship at Blundell's. He pointed out that her piano teacher was on the staff there, and therefore there would be no need to change.

Ruth was very unsure. She instinctively resisted change, especially change which might alter her friendships, especially with Jack and Sarah who might think that she was becoming snobby. Eventually she came to realise that opportunity was knocking at her door and that she would be stupid to decline, and so she nodded her acceptance.

36

1998/9 Tiverton

Life at Blundell's was very different. The company was much more confident, assured and socially adept; the teaching was more academic and intense; the outside activities more varied and challenging. The school had been boys only from its beginning several centuries previously, but the decline of empire and social change had led to girls being admitted. Most people thought this a good thing since it softened the regime somewhat.

Ruth was amazed at the performances on the sports field of both the boys and the girls. Blundell's had always been a big Rugby school but the sheer pace and vigour at which the game was played left her feeling bruised and breathless just from watching.

Also the campus was a lot larger than she was accustomed to with some quite imposing buildings, including a dedicated music school containing lots of practice rooms, with pianos in them, and other spaces big enough for orchestras and choirs.

After a few days being somewhat overawed, she began to realise that this place was not hostile or snobby at all, but was rather homely with a family feel. She did not know then that this was a recognised feature of the school.

There was no time to waste. The intensity of her A level programme and her music schedule alongside left little room for anything else. The pressure was on in a way she had not previously experienced. It seemed that every minute of the day was committed in some way. Even the weekends were not spared the rush. There were sporting or social events, quite a lot of visiting drama and, of course, concerts both small and large scale. She quickly made new friends, though mostly on a superficial basis, and formed healthy relationships with her tutors who rated her highly.

As part of this new life Ruth acquired a new singing teacher, Mrs Lucy Marsh, who for the first time in Ruth's experience began to teach her the techniques of singing, not quite in the long established manner, but with a major overlay of science, describing what the particular muscles do, and how the physics of sound in the human voice works. These were attitudes that had spread from across the Atlantic from American experimenters who sang with cameras in the air passages, and scanning machines exploring exactly what goes on when a fine singer is in full flow. This knowledge, available in the 1990s for the first time ever, had been grasped enthusiastically by Lucy Marsh and used to great effect. That is not to say that the old teachings were rejected entirely, just that they were steadily being modified, as the science of voice became more clearly understood. An excellent anatomical atlas was never far away during a singing lesson. Ruth felt very privileged.

She was at home most of the weekends however and tried to retain contact with Jack and Sarah who were now at East Devon College. Most Sunday afternoons Ruth would bike over to Hill Farm in old clothes to help with the milking or feeding, and then have some tea. There was plenty of opportunity for games both formal and informal in the farmhouse or surrounding barns. The hay loft was often a scene of some horseplay between them.

One icy winter afternoon it was too cold to stay outside and so they all went to Jack's room to watch a video. Soon the curtains were pulled shut; the old fashioned Belling electric fire was pumping two kilowatts of heat in to the spacious room, and they sprawled on a couple of easy chairs and the floor mat. Jack and Sarah were on very good form. Sarah had put on a lot of height so her heavy busted state did not seem so overwhelming, and she had a boyfriend at college who had quite obviously been good for her self-esteem. Jack was almost 6 feet tall and strongly built, as befits a farmer's son used to throwing bales of hay around. He was soft spoken with a dry humour which made both of the girls laugh. He was doing an agricultural course and would be going to Cannington before long. Just after 6.00 Sarah declared she had work to do and would leave them to finish watching the film, so she disappeared to her own room.

A little later, Ruth, sitting on the floor at Jack's feet became aware that his fingers were gently running through her hair. She pretended not to notice, since it was not in any way unpleasant, but then found herself pulled by her armpits onto the chair and onto his lap. He looked at her and said. 'This is how it all started Ruth, when you fell into my lap in the hayloft about two years ago'. Then he stifled her giggles by kissing her long and lovingly in a way she had not known before.

Eventually she eased him away and, looking into those remarkable eyes, said 'I too knew precisely that things had changed at that moment. In fact I remember what I said then. I have been reminded of it quite often and I could repeat it now, except you don't need to have it repeated, do you Jack?'

For answer he stood up with her in his arms as if she weighed nothing at all and walked to his narrow single bed lowering her onto it. Whilst she watched he stripped down to his underpants and joined her, gradually teasing more and more clothes off her, until she too had bare breasts and just a pair of rather chaste knickers on. They spent a delicious hour exploring one another with great care and sensitivity. There was no hurry, but there were frequent intakes of breath when a previously private sensitive part received its first ever touch from another being. Of course the underpants eventually came off, and they were naked as the day they were born. But, in some unspoken taboo there was no attempt on either part to have full blown sex. Perhaps they were saved by hearing Sarah's desk chair move in the next room. They rapidly got up and dressed, just managing to be where she had left them before the door opened. If she noticed the rumpled bed she made no comment.

Ruth left the farm that night on a real high. She felt more complete and happy than she had ever remembered. Coming down the long hill she peddled furiously in her joy. At the bottom of the hill she was going much too fast to take the bend in the icy conditions, her front wheel slid from under her, catapulting her into the base of a tree. As she flew through the air she thought, 'lean into bends you idiot' and then there was nothing.

Rachel looked up from her book to where Ian was doing the Times crossword in deep concentration. 'Ruth is late, darling, and it's a full school day tomorrow. I think I should ring the farm and get her to come home now.'

'Ok,' he muttered in the middle of trying to solve an anagram.

Jack answered the phone, his voice going cold when he heard Rachel's request. 'She left her well over an hour ago Mrs Plowman. She should have been with you long ago. No, there was nothing wrong, In fact she was in good spirits.'

Obviously something was seriously amiss, more than a puncture that would have allowed her to walk home easily in the time. It was agreed that the Wilsons would drive from the farm at the same time as the Plowmans came the opposite way.

Jim thought the tractor would be right and so father and son set off, using the very bright working lights on the tractor to show much more than ordinary car headlights would. The working tractor still had a small trailer hitched behind. Only half a mile down the road they saw the bicycle in the hedge, right on a road junction. It did not take long for them to find Ruth. She was lying very still on her face at the foot of a tree. Just as they spotted her Ian's car came along, and so all of them arrived at her side together.

Ian took over immediately and was relieved to find that she was breathing and had a good pulse, but she was deeply unconscious and her head was at an awkward angle. He refused to move her, but rang for an ambulance on his mobile phone. He knew full well that the paramedics had more experience than he of moving spinal injured accident victims, and that clumsy handling might make a bad situation even worse. Meanwhile he wrapped her in an aluminium foil blanket that he always kept in his car just in case he became stuck in a winter snowdrift at night. He little thought it would be used for his daughter. Then they could do nothing but wait. The ambulance was with them in about 15 minutes and took her to Exeter.

Ruth woke up several days later in hospital with a neck brace on and tubes everywhere. Rachel was at the bedside tearfully relieved to have her return to consciousness. In the days that followed it became apparent that there was no significant brain damage if any. Scans were normal and all her brain activities were quickly returning to their usual excellent level. Rachel was thankful she had always insisted on a bicycle helmet, believing that it had maybe saved Ruth's life.

But Ruth couldn't properly use her right arm. The surgeons said that the flexion injury to her neck had damaged the spinal cord. The scans showed some shadowing consistent with some bleeding at the seventh and eighth vertebra level on the right. It was not certain whether there was just a haematoma there in which case good, maybe full recovery would probably take place, or whether the nerves to the arm had become detached in which case there would be no recovery.

Ruth closed her eyes trying to suppress the tears on hearing this news. 'What about my piano!' she cried. 'Will I play properly again?'

'I do not yet know Ruth. If we are lucky you will get some use back and be able to play, but I cannot yet tell you how much recovery there will be.'

But recovery did take place and remarkably quickly. Ruth was up and about very soon and could manage herself in the bathroom and dress within a week of waking up. Right arm movement returned as did full function of the right thumb index and middle fingers. The ring and little fingers however obstinately did not recover fully.

Some movement returned but the fine skilled movement needed to play the piano to a high level never came back, as Ruth glumly remarked to her Dad. 'I am doomed to be a two finger typist.' This was not of course true since more than half of the fingers worked normally, but that was how she felt at the time.

Ruth was out of hospital quickly and back at school within a month, but not riding her bike for a while, not taking part in sports and not having her beloved piano lessons. The school decided that, though she was well behind with the course work, she was bright enough to catch up, and so she was allowed to stay with her peer group.

She felt enormously diminished and found motivation a real problem. The music department, suspecting this, surprised and delighted her by asking her to sing the soprano solos in a big school concert at the end of term. The result was magical. Her joy of living returned almost in full measure. She became a fully active member of school activities, and attacked her academic course with real determination. Lucy Marsh played a significant role in her recovery, coaxing and coaching her vocally and giving her belief in herself. She even tried to play some duets with Ian, and after leaving the piano in tears once or twice, did manage to play well enough for the sessions to be enjoyable. She returned to her piano lessons and got some benefit from them, but felt that this was more like physiotherapy than music training, and stopped finally once she had come to terms with her situation.

Young Jack found himself almost returned to the state of old friend as opposed to potential lover. This was not because Ruth had changed in her affection for him, but because opportunity was now greatly reduced. Jack, and sometimes Sarah, now came to the Plowman house to see Ruth, rather than her going to the farm. There were fewer private places and behaviour was consequently restrained. It would not be right to think they were like brother and sister, for their greetings and farewells, the snug way they curled up on the sofa together and their warmth of conversation were not those of siblings. But, apart from some slightly intimate groping, there was little sex in their doings together.

After a year at Blundell's School there was a major meeting concerning Ruth's future. It was decided to go for a place at Oxford, since her academic levels were very high. She was doing very well in sciences, especially chemistry and biology. She thought that this must be the direction to follow now that a concert pianist career was impossible for her. Lucy Marsh suggested that a Choral Scholarship would be very helpful, explaining that the system meant an audition for the Choral Scholarship before the result of state exams is known, even before they are attempted. The place would therefore be provisional upon the later academic exam results.

The journey north from Uffculme on a wonderful late autumn day in 2000 involved a diversion through the Cotswolds. Ian had decided to stay overnight at the venerable Randolph Hotel in Oxford so that Ruth could be well rested and relaxed for her ordeal the following day, whilst he and Rachel could have a rare day out sightseeing in the city.

Rachel and Ian both insisted that they accompanied Ruth on her trip to Oxford. It was not that they wished to interfere, indeed they had become very good at fading into the background, but the opportunity to combine a helping hand to Ruth with a small adventure for themselves proved irresistible.

On the way they visited Ian's old friends Michael and Maria O'Leary in their lovely Lechlade home. Michael had been a distinguished orthopaedic surgeon working in Oxford, but internationally renowned for his work on joint replacement and prosthetic materials in particular. Now retired, the O'Learys revelled in their wonderful garden and in their small but luxurious boat. This was normally moored on the Thames right at the bottom of their garden, but not long previously they had transported it to France and kept it there for a whole six months whilst they explored some wonders of France's inland waterways. A very happy lunch in Lechlade was enhanced by the presence of their son James, and his American wife, Josie, who were visiting from New York.

After lunch Ruth, not really knowing the O'Learys, and somewhat preoccupied by the hurdle she would face on the morrow, excused herself from the general conversation and took James and Josie's little boy, Joseph, into the garden to play on the swing. Although it was quite cold, the sun was bright and they both enjoyed the exercise. He was a delight, cheeky and fun, being quite uninhibited, as is often the case with American children. Ruth had flickering memories of playing with Kevin, ten years previously. She missed having her siblings living with her. The relationship with Bridget and Kevin, lacking sufficient contact, had withered, like any other plant, for want of water.

St Peter's College Oxford, one of the smaller colleges in the university, offered strong musical leanings and a number of choral scholarships not necessarily tied to a degree in music. Mostly housed in converted industrial buildings, the college was formed at the end of the 1920s to allow students of modest means to enjoy an Oxford education. Lacking the grand façade, gardens and colonnades of its more famous peers, St Peter's was a warm, homely place, in which everyone was made to feel important. It was therefore a perfect ambition for Ruth to study biochemistry there, whilst also conducting a high level interest in music. She envisaged a career in medical research whilst operating a lively amateur music life. She had not considered how close this path lay to that followed by father Ian 35 years previously.

Breakfast at The Randolph was a truly sumptuous affair and, since singing consumes blacksmith level energy, Ruth was encouraged to take full advantage. Afterwards she hugged her parents and, with their well wishes ringing in her ears, she walked to her audition.

Ruth had chosen to sing 'Deh vieni non tardar', one of Susanna's arias from Mozart's Marriage of Figaro. When she had finished the chairman of the panel smiled at her and asked if she had any plans to sing professionally. She had to admit that she had considered it, but thought that she probably was not good enough. He looked at her pensively for a moment before replying that perhaps that judgement could wait until the voice had matured for a year or two more. Meanwhile, assuming the panel decided to offer her a scholarship and that her academic results secured her a place, he advised her to find a good voice teacher in Oxford with whom to continue her studies, and he also suggested that she join a university chamber choir as well as the chapel choir at St Peter's. He recommended the Schola Cantorum of Oxford, the university's most prestigious chamber choir. Ruth later realised that this was an enormous compliment.

Her academic results were indeed good enough and Ruth accepted a place at St Peter's, beginning her new life in the Autumn term of 2001.

37

2001 Catastrophe

The beach was almost empty of people as the women walked together. They were right on the water's edge, wearing beach shoes to protect against sharp sand or cuts from broken shells, and had their skirts tucked into knickers to keep them from soaking in the waves. Despite the shallow shelving of the beach the waves splashed water up to their knees. On their heads they wore wide brimmed hats because here the sun was hot and, there being little pollution, would burn them easily.

More remarkable was that the two women were looking constantly downwards, their eyes seldom leaving that small area at the water's edge, where the object of their mission was most readily found. The little, older woman, would stoop every now and again to stare under the few inches of moving water, checking what she thought she had glimpsed. Each carried a plastic bag and a battered kitchen knife.

They were exploring one of the world's finest shelling beaches, the six mile length of Sanibel's Gulf Coast seashore, an amazing source of wonderful shells, from sand dollars to huge horse conch shells. Some, like the two inch wide sundial they had found yesterday, were rare, but others like the fighting conchs which they sometimes trod upon painfully were very common. Maria, the older of the two, loved the beautiful shark's eye shells which were quite plentiful. Every now and again one of them would plunge a hand into the gritty sand and emerge with a shell of note. There were facilities in the Island Inn to boil the shells of any adherent matter and then they would be lovingly polished. They had been firmly instructed not to collect live shells.

As they walked they were surrounded by hundreds of small birds, sand pipers mostly but white ibis too, and, just a few yards out to sea, the occasional pelican would swoop like a lumbering old flying boat into the water to claim its lunch. The birds were not quite tame, but were certainly not timid either, parting almost reluctantly to let them pass, and then closing ranks immediately after they had gone.

Maria had laughed when Michael, on their first day, had dramatically left the sea at the approach of a triangular fin, only to be told he had run away from a friendly dolphin.

They loved this island, reached over a long causeway, because of its contrast with tourist Florida. There were no high rise blocks, and space was carefully meted out by the Island authorities ensuring that overcrowding would never deprive the place of its innate charm. Approximately a third of the land constituted the Ding Darling Nature Reserve, a world class haven for bird watchers. Maria had never seen such amazing camera lenses in her life. To arrive here was in some ways to step a hundred years back in time, yet with proper first world plumbing and some very good places to eat. The Inn regarded September as low season because of the very hot, often sultry, weather, so there were fewer guests than would be the case in a month's time. This suited them very well.

The two turned for home well before dusk, and walked a bit more briskly than when looking for their prize. It was not good to be out, lightly clothed at dusk when the midges came, sometimes in large numbers. A previous holiday here had been almost ruined by hundreds of midge bites, all because good advice had not been heeded.

They arrived back at the Inn in good time to have a shower and change before sitting on the insect screened sun deck of their room with a gin, ready to chat and watch the magnificent

Sanibel sunset. Josie, whose family had been coming to the Island Inn for many years, told them that the establishment was traditionally a dry house, and even now there was no bar as such, but the guests all knew the drill and private parties on the verandas of rooms often became quite liquid in nature. It was, of course, Josie, or rather her parents who originally introduced Mike and Maria to Sanibel on their 'get to know you' visit prior to the wedding, and they had visited two or three times since.

Maria was sorry that her children had both crossed the Atlantic to find mates, because the access to grandchildren was less than she would wish, but she was delighted nonetheless for both James and Maureen in their choices. James had met Josie at a rock concert when in Boston on a Harvard Postgraduate Law Course. Josie had been working at the time as a microbiologist at MIT. Her father ran a much respected law firm in Massachusetts, and had had no small part in mentoring his son-in-law. In time, and after a number of internships, James had become a corporate lawyer, working for Morgan Stanley in New York. He and Josie had a lovely home in W 72nd Street and two glorious children. Josie, now in her prime, aged thirty seven was busy picking up her career again. She was a good mother and a stunningly beautiful woman, tall, straight and with a good figure, kept from being too ample by vigorous early morning work outs. She was also very attached to her mother-in-law, much to Maria's delight. Maria knew she was genuinely welcome in New York.

Josie left Michael and Maria to check that the children, with whom Michael had been swimming in the pool and playing endless games of shuffleboard, were preparing for the evening. They had decided to eat at Chadwick's that evening. Chadwick's, on the neighbouring island of Captiva, was rightly famous for its evening buffet, which was enjoyed by all, but especially by the children who could choose what they fancied more easily than from a formal menu. The variety of seafood, meats and vegetables all presented in a most attractive manner would stimulate the most jaded palate.

The short drive to Chadwick's over the bridge at Blind Pass, a neck of sea which is often quite violent, brought them to the South Sea Islands Plantation Resort. They dined well, despite the theme this evening being sea food, which seldom thrilled Michael. The Napa valley Merlot however, pleased him greatly. In fact the only imperfection of the day was that James had departed from Fort Myers that morning to attend a meeting in New York. It seemed that Morgan Stanley was engaged in a law suit concerning security in their New York Office.

James took a yellow cab home from the airport and spent the evening preparing for the following morning's meeting.

Terrorists had truck bombed the World Trade Center in 1993 and some three hundred people had died. The evacuation had been relatively inefficient; panic had dominated the proceedings sufficiently to cause criticism. Morgan Stanley's security chief, Rick Rescorla, a Cornishman, who had transferred to the American Army after service with the British in Africa, had been incandescent that his company had not followed his recommendations prior to that incident. His concern at the time had steadily risen since, to a level that can only be described as revealing a compulsive obsessive state, based on the conviction that sooner or later the terrorists would try again. He lobbied the board room, took advice from national experts and formed a committee nicknamed Team Rescorla. He had the whole workforce practising evacuation drills about every three months, an activity which did not endear him to those concerned, whose memories of 1993 were fading fast. Importantly, he had the firm install special lighting and smoke extractors. He was convinced that an attack would one day come from the air. His was an utterly lone voice. However, he had convinced Morgan Stanley that the Port Authority had let them down badly in 1993 and this was the reason for a series of meetings which concerned James, a corporate lawyer with the firm.

Next morning James was at his desk on the 72nd floor of World Trade Center 2, the South Tower, bright and early, getting everything ready for the nine o'clock meeting. At about a quarter to nine a bright flash and a physical shake of the building led him to look up and across to the North Tower very close by. He saw massive flames and a vast amount of smoke pouring out of the upper part of the building about twenty floors above his level and knew instantly that a serious incident was unfolding. Colleagues had obviously seen and heard the same thing.

There was immediate concern; alarms rang, mobile phones shrilled, and then could be heard the bull horn of Rick Riscorla. At about that time staff saw bodies falling from the North Tower, mostly normal looking people, some falling face down, others face up, one man clutching a woman by the hand. They realised that these were people who had chosen to die quickly rather than be consumed by smoke and flame. It was time to go.

Thus began the evacuation of the South Tower, around about 0855 that morning. Hardly was it under way when they were struck by a similar plane to that which had flown into the North Tower. There was just sixteen minutes between the strikes. The impact was just above James' office from the seventy fourth floor up to eighty two. The evacuation became a torrent, which continued until the tower imploded and collapsed some two hours later.

Many hundreds of miles away in the Island Inn that morning the guests were settling into breakfast when there was a loud shout of alarm from the Inn's small reception area. There was a commotion in the large communal area outside the dining room and almost immediately, the head of reception, stood in the doorway saying that there had been an attack on the World Trade Center. Michael looked at his watch, which told him it was just before nine. As one, the diners rose and rushed to the room next door where the TV had been switched on. They had just time to absorb the scene of the North Tower in the World Trade Center blazing when a large plane, a Boeing commercial airliner in appearance, flew across their screens directly into the South Tower, rather lower and, they thought, even more violently than in the North. Both towers were ablaze and absolute pandemonium reigned.

Breakfasts were forgotten as staff and guests together huddled and cried together as the dreadful events of that day unfolded. It was immediately clear that two planes crashing into the Trade Center could not have been some dreadful accident, but that New York was under attack. This was confirmed when a further plane struck the Pentagon at nine forty three and a fourth crashed into a field near Pittsburgh just after ten.

Josie was frantically ringing James' cell phone, but only got a loud hiss of static. They tried the land line, but that was futile also. All day they sat and watched, dreading the next announcement. Everyone in the Inn was shocked, but they all came to realise that this particular family were not just spectators to a horror, but were deeply personally involved. One of their number, the cement in their family, was in that terrible inferno and nobody could do anything but gape at the TV screen.

Refreshment was brought and ignored. The children were silent and overawed. Josie just sat, tears coursing down her cheeks, diverting only to take a call from her father, who had nothing encouraging to say to her.

Michael and Maria sat on a sofa, both arms around each other, heads touching, unable to speak except in monosyllables. Hope hung in the air, overlaid with despair.

Eventually at the end of that most awful of days they went, exhausted, to bed. The children crawled into Josie's bed and were welcomed. The three of them, drained of all emotion, slept late next day.

Mike and Maria also clung to each other, with Mike murmuring hope in Maria's ear until he slept. He awoke very early next morning, when it was still dark, to an empty bed. He found her sitting, cross legged, like an urchin, on the beach, watching the tide. There were hardly any waves and the air was eerily still and silent. He sat alongside her, reaching for a hand, and there they stayed until the sun was up.

The waiting was unbearable. Josie drove the children home to New York, feeling an overpowering need to be near the scene. It was a two day journey and Mike worried that she was too tired to do it alone. She gently but firmly declined the offer of help. Clearly she wished not to share her thoughts.

Mike and Maria stayed on in Sanibel a further week, praying for news, reluctant to return to England in case there was need to rush to a hospital side. No news came and so eventually they flew back to Lechlade, greatly diminished.

Three months later they learned that, of Morgan Stanley's huge workforce in the South Tower, nearly three thousand had survived, largely because of Rick Rescorla's foresight and diligence, as well as his unflinching brave behaviour on the day. Six Morgan Stanley people had died, including Rick and his two deputies. They never found James.

In the atrocity that has come to be called nine eleven, some three thousand and forty were known to have perished, about seven hundred more than at Pearl Harbour. Two hundred jumped to their deaths. Four hundred and eleven emergency staff died including three hundred and forty one fire fighters. September 11th 2001 had previously been designated the United Nations World Day of Peace. Nobody seems to have told Al Queda.

In the years that followed Maria and Michael regularly travelled to New York. They usually stayed with Josie, and visited Ground Zero, which was the nearest thing they had to visiting a grave.

Right alongside the site was a little church, close enough for the sycamore in its garden to have been burnt in the fires of the attack. St Paul's Chapel, though very close to the scene and covered with debris, became the refuge for rescue workers to have a drink, something to eat and even a brief sleep in the days after the attack. It also became an interim memorial with hundreds of messages, some in memory, a few in hope, from families and friends, who came to see for themselves what had happened. Much of this remained and, for Maria, it became a pilgrimage to visit regularly.

Michael and Maria tried to lose their grief by working in their lovely Lechlade garden. Michael had been retired several years and although he still loved to potter on the river in his boat he made a very special attempt to make the garden good enough to be opened to the public occasionally. He loved herbaceous borders and would lose himself all day tending to them. He cut a strange figure, this truly distinguished surgeon, in old corduroy trousers tied up with orange coloured twine, a pair of green Wellington boots, and a wide brimmed bush hat. In the winter he would wear an old oiled Barbour jacket to keep warm and dry.

In the evening he would read or watch television and had a bottle of Johnny Walker at his elbow. Maria noted that the bottle needed to be replaced much more often than before James had died. The truth is that they were both greatly reduced by the loss of James, but Michael seemed to have been even more troubled than Maria, complaining bitterly of stomach ache much of the time. Maria worried about this, asking him to seek medical help, but he refused to listen to her entreaties.

It was only when he became jaundiced that he finally accepted investigation. There was an inoperable cancer of the pancreas. He faded away quite quickly, leaving Maria a very sad widow in October 2003. He was just seventy, she was sixty eight.

Widowhood is never easy, but for Maria it was rather like being smothered in a suffocating blanket of grief. In twenty years she had lost both parents, a husband and a son, had endured the horrors of a high court case, which led to her early retirement, and now was almost alone.

She did have a lovely daughter, thousands of miles away in Canada, but she knew Maureen would be unlikely ever to come back to England to live. Her grandchildren were not close enough to be part of daily living, and since James' death she had not found it possible to be very sociable even with the old friends in Cirencester and Oxford. She had never relished the 'twin set and pearls' lifestyle, and did not play bridge. She was however reasonably well off, having two pensions and a considerable legacy from her own parents. She would travel.

On a glorious morning the next summer she woke with the sun pouring in through her window, so she breakfasted on the terrace, looking up at the mountains. The little B&B, just a few kilometres outside Bardi, was homely, but very welcoming with delicious homemade bread and honey. After breakfast she drove into the town with its magnificent Castle Landi, standing on a giant outcrop of red jasper. To Maria the whole ambience of the place made her think of her mother Rosanna, and Uncle Andreas, who had left here over seventy years previously, part of the great exodus of people from the Italian countryside at that time. After a brief look at the Oratory with its amazing altarpiece by Parmigianino she made her way to the Arandora Star Memorial, with its chapel commemorating the fifty or so lives of men from this town who had drowned on that fateful day in 1940. She was not surprised to meet a Welsh family there, part of the great bond between Bardi and the towns of the Rhondda Valley, in particular Merthyr Tydfil. It was to Merthyr that many Bardi people had emigrated in search of work, and it was the South Wales men who formed a large part of the internees on that disastrous voyage.

The Welsh were delighted to discuss their origins with her, revealing a passion for Rugby Football at the highest level of the game, jokingly saying that their family would be torn between playing for Wales or Italy. They were moved to learn that Maria had attended the dedication of the Memorial in St Peter's, Clerkenwell in April 1960. In the end they agreed to meet up later that day for dinner. There they told her that the Welsh link with Bardi remained strong even after almost seventy years and that regular visits had become a way of life for a lot of people.

Satiated at last with the homage to her past, Maria drove back to the coast the next day, eating great fish in Viareggio and listening to Tosca at the Puccini Festival in Torre di Lago, before flying home from Pisa.

38

2001 Oxford

The shadow of 9/11, as it had become known, lay heavy even upon a college in the city of 'dreaming spires'. The catastrophe happened just before Ruth went up for her first term and, because of the presumed loss of James O'Leary, was much discussed over the evening meal in Uffculme. Ian in particular seemed dreadfully cast down, Ruth supposed because of his closeness to the family, something she could well understand with her head, but clearly not feel so deeply with her heart since she had only met him the once.

To her surprise Oxford was buzzing with high emotion about the global diplomatic crisis. The general opinion seemed to be that the atrocity was mind blowing in its enormity and that no country, much less a superpower like America, could let the matter go without some retaliation. But here opinions were sharply different. No specific country seemed to be responsible for the crime. Rather it lay at the door of Islamic religious extremists who were in essence stateless, shadows of no fixed abode. The burning issue became one of what to hit and where to hit it. The name Osama Bin Laden spread like a stain over all of the media, but he was purported to be a citizen of western friendly Saudi Arabia, although not resident there. In fact it was rumoured that his family were in America at the time of the crisis and were quietly shepherded out to avoid further complications.

Eventually The World was told that the seats of terrorism lay in Afghanistan and in Iraq. Certainly there was evidence that Al Qaeda, the known terrorist movement spearheaded by Bin Laden did have bases within Afghanistan and did have links with the Taliban, an anti- Western Islamic government in that country. But in contrast Iraq was ruthlessly ruled by a despot named Saddam Hussein, at whose door many heinous crimes, including genocide, could be laid. However evil the regime, Saddam actually suppressed extreme religious sects of all sorts, running a secular state. Islam was no exception to this, and so it could be argued that Saddam was in fact the West's great buffer against extreme Islam, not its opponent.

The first matter, Afghanistan, was decided immediately. Operation Enduring Freedom, the American first response to September 11 2001 came on October 7th less than a month after the terrorist attack. Almost simultaneously Operation Herrick, the British equivalent joined in. They invaded Afghanistan and began to drive out the Taliban, and with them the terrorists, beginning a decade or so of messy attrition with an inconclusive result.

Thus, Ruth's arrival in Oxford in October of 2001 coincided with a superheated excitement concerning the rights and wrongs of the engagement, an excitement that would persist as a noisy background to most of her undergraduate years, dividing families and destroying lifelong friendships.

One evening the student club boiled over in angry argument and counter argument. It could hardly be called a debate since neither side was listening to the other. A loud, whiskery Scot leapt on a table top and harangued the assembly. 'OK, so George W has decided that someone must pay for the World Trade Center. Who came blame him for that? I certainly do not, and I do not think most of the world does either. What I blame him for is not first determining who the right target should be.

'Do we know that Bin Laden and his cutthroats are in Afghanistan? No.'

'Do we think the Afghan people made war on the USA? Again. No.'

'Why then should they, a poor people subject to many years of repression, starting with the English in 1870, right up to the Russians in recent years, and then being taken over by an extremist government, be made to suffer? They have done nothing wrong.'

'Why should those people be invaded by some excessively Gung Ho Army? The whole thing is wrong. What is needed here is a special strike like Mossad at Entebbe, or the SAS at the Iranian Embassy in London. We must not blame a whole population for a handful of madmen, who infect their people with their madness, by falsely cloaking it all in the name of religion.'

'Oh shut up and sit down Jock. We've heard enough tonight.' replied a large man whom Ruth had often noticed rowing on the river.

Despite the protest of Jock and large numbers like him, for the most part the American and British incursion into Afghanistan was understood and tacitly supported, because the public perceived that the 'evil' men needed to be brought to justice, and they were told that these terrorists were holed up in that country.

But Iraq was an entirely different matter. There seemed to be little if any evidence that terrorist attacks were coming from there, or indeed that Iraq sympathised in any way with Al Qaeda. Europe strongly suspected that American public opinion, having become markedly pro-Israel, regarded the whole region under the one umbrella as being anti-Israeli and 'Arab', and took no account of the vast distances and cultural differences between the countries concerned. How could they, since so few of them had any real notion of the world beyond their shores. Many in Europe however did not think the American government itself was so ill informed; rather that The White House had a different agenda, which had more to do with oil than with suppressing terrorism.

The President's father, George Bush senior, himself an oil magnate, had directed a previous war in Iraq, Desert Storm, less than a decade previously. There was a great suspicion that America viewed Iraq as unfinished business, and that Dick Cheney, the foreign secretary, was blowing up a storm in Iraq, using 9/11 as a pretext. The issue would dominate foreign affairs for many years to come. The debate raged throughout the whole of 2002 and into 2003.

On September 24th 2002, just one year after the attacks on the World Trade Center, arguments about the legality and morality of invading Iraq were reaching a climax in the West. The British Prime Minister Tony Blair, addressed the House of Commons, making a statement that would resonate all over the world. He observed that, in and after 'Desert Storm' in 1991/2, it had become apparent that Saddam Hussein's Iraq was engaged in preparing terrible weapons of mass destruction. Blair cited chemical and biological weapons, including a vast amount of Anthrax spores. There had also been a well advanced nuclear programme, not yet at nuclear weapon capability, but well along that road.

The Prime Minister reminded the house that after Desert Storm the United Nations had insisted upon a regime of inspection which they had backed with quite severe sanctions. Saddam's record of compliance with the United Nations had been poor, an attitude which had provoked a number of UN resolutions during that decade.

The Prime Minister observed that suddenly Saddam had indicated a readiness to be properly inspected. Mr Blair considered this change to indicate that, far from cowering in his bunker, Saddam's programme of weapons of mass destruction was now complete, and hidden.

In November 2002 the United Nations Security Council Resolution 1441 unanimously condemned Iraq for failure to comply with previous resolutions over the ten years since Desert Storm. The failure concerned not just the putative, unproved, WMDs but the illegal importation of arms and war like material.

Soon afterwards Blair was urging the House of Commons to vote in favour of war with Iraq, stating that Saddam had weapons of mass destruction that could be deployed within 45 minutes. Labour and Conservative MPs voted in favour of war. Liberal Democrats voted against. However it would be right to say that many Conservatives and some Labour members were privately grieved at the vote, and that they certainly would not have supported the proposition, but for Blair's rhetoric about Saddam's capability to strike at 45 minutes warning.

On February 15th 2003 sixty nations took part in a global day of protest against the proposed war. Three million are reputed to have marched in Rome and one million in London. Ruth and her friends were among them, bearing the support of Ian and Rachel. The BBC records show that up to ten million people marched that day, perhaps the biggest protest in history. It was to no avail.

The invasion took place on March 19th 2003. Saddam was toppled from power and disappeared, only to be found, tried and executed some time later. No weapons of mass destruction were ever found.

Meantime Ruth settled into the life of an undergraduate with enthusiasm. Some chemistry students at St Peter's were aiming for a career in industry, often in pharmacological research. Some wished to teach, whilst others were medical students doing biochemistry as part of a second MB course. All shared the same junior common room, living and dining together. There was a good campus social life, which Ruth embarked upon happily, revelling in the loss of restriction that came with leaving school and home behind. However these students were perhaps more serious minded than those reading arts subjects. Dissolute behaviour is a part of student life and her set at St Peter's was by no means immune from it. But in general, at a time when about a third of students regularly used soft drugs and the consumption of alcohol, particularly at the weekend, was extraordinarily high, Ruth's contemporaries were a relatively restrained group. Ruth herself could never quite forget her mother's addiction and was determined not to follow, so she never did drugs of any sort and used alcohol fairly sparingly.

That did not make her a prude in any way. She had a ripe and ringing humour with an infectious laugh, which, allied to her brilliant auburn hair, meant that she was always noticed in the common room, and soon became a very popular figure. In fact, quite unconsciously she was becoming a beautiful woman, one that others would never ignore. She was well above average height, had large intelligently enquiring eyes, and wore vibrant coloured clothes which set off her elegant, shapely figure to perfection. The whole ensemble was topped by that magnificent head of auburn hair, not bright ginger, but dark and very glamorous. She wore her hair a little long, so that it bounced alluringly as she walked.

Quite soon she was having man trouble. Other students pressed her into dates, invitations flew regularly, and in purely sexual terms she could easily have been having a high old time. However, despite her allure, Ruth was desperately man shy, and so resisted the approaches with charm and sensitivity so as not to appear unkind or, even worse, immune to men.

Apart from a few gentle flirtations at school and one very important, memorable, but short romance with her childhood friend Jack, of whom she remained very fond, she had never had any experience with boys, except in a purely social sense. From puberty onwards she had lived without siblings, and although sex and gender issues were certainly not in any way hidden at home, such matters were not a major part of conversation. Within her peer group she hid her sexual innocence behind her saucy sense of humour, and so it was assumed that she was as experienced as the rest of her friends. It did not occur to her that some of them were similarly disguising their virginity, under a show of worldliness. Also she could never quite forget that her mother had wanted to abort her, and all the implications that held. Along with her knowledge of Deborah's decent into prostitution, it was therefore not surprising that Ruth's attitude to sex and her own virginity were coloured by these aspects of her past.

One evening while walking along the river, Ruth was hailed and turned to find that she had walked past the rower she had noted before and who had been vocal in the student pub. He invited her for a drink after he had showered. Ruth waited in the bar, slightly apprehensive, having agreed so readily to spend time with someone she hardly knew. Marshall Dixon, for that was his name, stood 6'4" and was enormously strong, as is so often the case with champion oarsmen. Ruth knew that Marshall was greatly admired by a large number of the girls she knew, but she had never seen him out with any of them.

When he arrived, they sat and drank white wine and ate olives. The conversation flowed with great ease. Each discovered the complimentary sense of humour in the other. Ruth was aware of a magnetism she had not felt before and was both excited and alarmed by it. Marshall on his part behaved impeccably, seeing her to her door at the end of the evening, but did not indicate any wish or hope of crossing the threshold. Thus began many meetings on the riverside, often followed by visits to the city's plentiful supply of cafés and bars and to the happenings at Oxford's many venues of note. If funds allowed, this was rounded off by a proper dinner in one of Oxford's many restaurants.

Ruth found herself increasingly drawn to this man and so when one day he kissed her goodnight, she responded with a warmth that surprised both of them. That night, she pulled him inside the door and into her lodgings. There they sat watching a film on the sofa, glass in hand, with a free arm around each other. When the film finished they made their way to bed, almost like a married couple, so natural was their response. And there, Ruth very willingly gave herself to him, and really enjoyed the whole experience.

Their romance went on for some months, but eventually, perhaps because there was insufficient excitement, it cooled, until one day Marshall failed to show for a date and Ruth knew that it had come to an end. She grieved for a while, but not sufficiently to interfere with her studies and musical activities.

Getting around Oxford could be slow by public transport so Ian, somewhat anxiously, brought her bicycle up for her, and she rode this from lectures to choir practice, to Blackwell's music shop and to her regular enthralling visits to the Ashmolian Museum.

The Schola Cantorum of Oxford was formed in the 1960s by the distinguished musician Lazlo Heltay, who lived for some 35 years working in Britain and who undoubtedly raised the standard of British choral singing significantly. The choir rose quickly to eminence and under Lazlo's successor, Dr John Byrt, won the foremost of choral competitions 'Let the People Sing'. The choir numbered fewer than thirty singers, of whom just twelve or fourteen were sopranos. They were undergraduates, drawn from the whole university. Competition for admission was extreme, and the commitment was high, including, as it did, foreign travel and recordings with the cream of performers and conductors. But, as Ruth was to discover, having been successful in her audition, membership of that group, like any other high quality gathering, raised her own understanding and attainment to unexpected levels, which would mark her out for the remainder of her life.

Her introduction to the Schola Cantorum was quite stressful, since only a few weeks after her arrival they undertook a pre-Christmas tour to France during which they sang Tallis' wonderful 40 part motet Spem in Alium, which is scored for eight five part choirs. This meant a little augmentation of numbers, and all of the singers performing as soloists, one to a part, which is particularly demanding. But she found it a wonderfully bonding experience, which set her, both musically and socially, on her way in the choir.

Christmas at home in Uffculme that year was special. Rachel had learned that William Mason had been ill in hospital and, though recovering, was not yet back at work. So, after all the Plowman and Lindsay family had returned to their homes, she invited William to bring Bridget and Kevin to a festive meal and an overnight stay. Ruth loved Christmas and truly admired Rachel's drive and energy which had led to the Plowman home becoming the hub for a large number of people in the Festive Season. It was nothing for Rachel to feed twenty or more.

The visit however, was not a great success. William had clearly been diminished by his illness and was uncharacteristically negative. This allowed sixteen year old Bridget to be quite rude without contradiction, and fourteen year old Kevin to be sullen, uncommunicative and unhelpful. Ruth felt that they were on such divergent paths in life that she was regarded as an outsider by her own half brother and sister. In a peculiar way they made it feel as if she had betrayed them by entering a different way of life.

One positive thing that emerged from the visit came about when Ruth and William sat quietly alone in a corner whilst he was resting. She placed her hand over his and said. 'William, I know that you were part of my beginning, but you have never told me anything about my real father. I think I am grown up enough now to be told whatever it is you know. Please do that for me. It is very important to me.'

There was a long pause before William replied. 'I am not sure I should be telling you this Ruthie, but you are grown up now. I hear what you say and agree with you, so this is the truth as I see it.' He coughed, and a lot of nasty phlegm filled his handkerchief. When he had cleared himself he resumed. 'As you know, Debbie worked at the fruit farm in Tetbury when she became pregnant. Several of the boys working there were tested. In fact your father was Anatole Gennadi. He was a fine pianist and used to entertain us all at Tetbury. I guess that's where you got it from, my girl.' He smiled and squeezed her hand back before going on. 'I've seen the name quite recently in the paper. He's been over here doing some concerts. He's a professor in Warsaw now.'

'So he doesn't know about me?' she whispered.

'I shouldn't think so. You see Krystyna, the office manager was a Polish girl married to an Englishman. She was very good at her job, and generally kept an eye on things. She saw a lot. When Debbie became pregnant she chose the boss's son as the father, but Krystyna was not so sure, so she persuaded the boss to ask for tests. It was proved that his son was not the father but one of the students was. As soon as the tests were done Krystyna, realising there would be trouble, got the most likely students out of the farm and on their way home before the results were known. And, unless Krystyna told him, I don't know if he ever knew.'

'Do you ever see Krystyna now?'

'I don't go there now, Ruthie, and she is not working there, but I have a Christmas card from her. She might be able to get a message to him. But you should think long and hard before doing that. He might not welcome it after all these years, especially if he has no idea he might have a child.'

'Why did you marry Mummy, Daddy William if you knew all of these things? Weren't you put off?'

'I think of that often Ruth, especially now that it has turned out so bad, but I think we were in some ways like each other. We were both outside things you see. I don't read and write well and so feel different from others, and she was a wild one, and no mistake; but, like me, she was different, and that was an attraction. I think I liked her very much until the bad side of her really got going. By then I had you kids to worry about, so I had to go on, didn't I? I had no choice by then.'

A clamour from the kitchen with Bridget and Kevin fighting over some triviality brought the exchange to an end. Ruth and William both rushed to restore order. The remainder of the visit was difficult for all of them, especially for Ruth who was hurt and bewildered by the bad behaviour of her younger half-siblings. She accepted that an accident of fate had given her opportunities beyond those that they would experience, and that this had finally become an insurmountable obstacle to their understanding. They had nothing to say to one another. When they left Ruth felt that a cord to her past had finally snapped.

Ian, sensing her mood, put his arm around her as the Mason car pulled away on the late afternoon of the second day, and said. 'It's all right to mourn Ruth. We are all a mix of nature and nurture, and so we gradually change. You are experiencing great change in a short span of time. Many bright students find that there is pain in that. The Bible says something about it in Corinthians if I remember rightly, it goes something like, 'When I was a child I spake as a child, I thought as a child, but when I became a man I put away childish things.' That is what you are feeling and doing just now. Come inside with Mum and we will play some silly game together.'

The Plowman family, Ian, Rachel and Ruth, sat that late December evening, before the log fire, playing Trivial Pursuit whilst sipping a decent wine and raiding the Christmas chocolates. Sam, the spaniel, as always very sensitive to mood, curled up on the sofa next to Ruth, leaning on her in loving reassurance.

Esther Gruhn eased herself from her piano stool and shuffled slowly back to her desk. Breathing was difficult these days especially after any exertion. A world class singer in her day, she was now, though only seventy years old, as a consequence of allowing herself to expand to an enormous size, a physical mess, suffering from cardiac failure and diabetes.

But her mind remained sharp and she had become over the years almost as renowned as a teacher as she had been when singing. Pupils came great distances for a lesson with her. Quite a number were established professionals. Many of the best singers retain contact with a teacher, rather as a golfer or tennis player has a coach. The truth is that one does not oneself hear the sound produced in the same way that a listener does, so minor blemishes can easily become bad habits. The third ear is an important asset in the battle for perfection.

But Esther's teaching was not confined entirely to coaching established professionals. She maintained a busy teaching practice in her Maida Vale studio in London and rented a teaching room in Oxford for one day a week, simply because there was so much musical talent associated with the university.

That afternoon, having regained the safety of her enormous desk chair, she fixed the young woman who had come for a consultation with a piercing eye. 'That was a very good work out, very good indeed, Ruth.' She paused for breath. 'The voice is excellent. Maybe as it matures it will become even better. As yet, it lacks true maturity. That of course is wonderful for choirs, but not so wonderful if you want to sing the big stuff as a soloist.'

'But what impressed me more than the voice was the musicality. Your phrasing and dynamics were lovely, as was your understanding of the piece. Brahms Lieder are not the easiest things in the world to sing after all, but I found your interpretation exciting. Do you play an instrument?'

'Yes, I play the piano. I suppose I should say that, once, I had hoped to play very well, but I fell off my bike some years ago, and damaged my hand. I have never been quite good enough to play at the highest level ever since.'

Ruth showed Esther her right hand which looked fairly normal but had a stiff, slightly bent ring and little finger. 'They just don't respond fast enough now.'

'The piano studies, how far did you take them?' asked Esther.

'I was working for a performing diploma, when the accident happened. I was seventeen.'

'Ach, what appalling bad luck! How did you become so interested in music in the first place Ruth? You of course know that real excellence in anything is most commonly associated with early imprinting through one's environment. Great sports people, as toddlers, are often given a ball or a bat by skilful and passionate parents, so they evolve with the whole ethos as part of their being. Today, our young are often prodigious in their use of a computer. Their parents can never hope to catch up with them. Music is no different. Most of the Greats had some early influence from school or family. Tell me about your background.'

'Well, I had a difficult childhood. My Mum had me outside marriage and I did not know anything about my real Dad until quite recently. It turns out he is now a professor of music in Eastern Europe. My step Dad was a lorry driver but there was an old piano in the house and he taught me some basics. I remember loving it. Then, about ten years ago I went into care and was fostered by the couple who are now my adoptive parents. He is a country doctor with a passion for music, who plays the piano at a high amateur level. She is head of music at a school in Exeter and is a very good cellist. Both of them sing.' She shrugged expressively. 'So, I guess I have grown up with it. They made sure I had the best teachers in the area.'

'You see.' Esther wagged a stubby finger in Ruth's direction. 'You see, you fit the pattern perfectly. This, perhaps, is your destiny, if not as a career, then as an abiding passion. But tell me about languages Ruth. A proper singer must sing in several languages and have some understanding of, and feeling for, them. Do you speak German, French or Italian?'

'I only have schoolgirl French, but a bit more than that in Italian. A friend at school was Italian, and I have been to see her family in Tuscany several times. Her parents do not speak English much, and certainly not in their own home, so I had to learn some basic Italian very quickly. I have only a few words of German.'

'Well, that will come in very handy. OK Ruth, I have made up my mind. I am happy to take you on. Initially we both commit to a probation term. After that we shall see how we both feel about each other. You know,' said Esther, 'one to one teaching of voice is very much about getting on together.'

'Oh, and by the way I shall want to see you weekly to start with, and shall expect you to do some work between lessons. If I am in Oxford I shall fit you into my day here. Occasionally you might be asked to come to London instead, but not very often. I am quite expensive and so you have made a significant financial statement today. Is that going to be all right?'

'Yes, I am an only child and both parents are working, so they will happily fund me.'

39

2004 London

Ruth Kathleen Plowman gained a good second class honours degree in the summer of 2004 and was delighted to land a job in London in the research labs of GlaxoSmithKline, the giant pharmaceutical company. Her delight was partly due to the new and challenging environment, but also finally to put the relationship with Marshall behind her. However she and Esther Gruhn both noted she was singing better than ever. Esther teased her that she thought she'd had a love affair.

The company was a conglomerate formed by merging a number of venerable companies over a period of many years. Elements were provided by Smith Kline and French, Nephew, and Glaxo as well as a number of others. When Ruth arrived the company was just settling down from its latest series of mergers. It was among the world's largest pharmaceutical houses and one of the biggest companies on the London Stock Exchange. The headquarters were in Brentford, West London, on the Great West Road with the M4 motorway just behind, its vast building towering in a grand manner over the traffic. Communications to the West Country and to central London were very good. In fact, Hammersmith Bus Station was but a mile or so away, and from there Berry's Superfast Service went all the way to Tiverton. On Friday evening the bus left Hammersmith around six thirty and would have Ruth home for bed time. If Ruth had been home for the weekend she would catch an early coach up from Devon just after seven in the morning and be at Hammersmith by just after eleven, all for less than £15 return.

She found a small but delightful flat overlooking Brentford Lock and put her mind to becoming a successful industrial biochemist, working in an air locked laboratory in protective clothing. The work concerned vaccines, a subject which held fascination for her ever since she learned about Edward Jenner, the country doctor from Berkeley, Gloucestershire, who, in 1796, more than 200 years previously, had become interested in the country folk's observation that the farm workers, accustomed to cows, did not get smallpox. He concluded they were given immunity by having had the much milder cowpox and so he inoculated an eight year old boy with the pus from a cowpox pustule on a milkmaid. The boy did not get smallpox, even when exposed.

Prior to Jenner, a procedure known as variolation was commonly practised in which the inoculation was from a pustule of smallpox, not of cowpox. Variolation did greatly improve the survival figures from smallpox, but because the inoculation was of the potent smallpox itself, there was a death rate from the procedure of about 1% and many were quite ill. Fashionable European families conducted the inoculation by puffing infected material into the nostrils of the person to be inoculated.

Jenner was not the first to think of using cowpox. Dr John Fewster read a paper on the subject to the Royal Society in 1765; there were reports also from Denmark and Germany, and a farmer named Benjamin Jesty, in Yetminster, Dorset, had inoculated folk in 1774. Jenner may have known about that, but it was he, Jenner, who was responsible for developing and publicising the matter, in so doing probably saving more lives than anyone in history. The procedure became known as 'vaccination' from Vacca, the Latin for cow.

Ruth joined the company in the middle of its much publicised development of an antimalarial vaccine, a project continuing since the early 1990s. Since malaria was still the commonest cause of death in the world, Ruth was rightly very excited to be involved, no matter how small a cog in the wheel she would be.

In the evenings she managed to continue her music quite actively, visiting Esther Gruhn in Maida Vale every week and, armed with a recommend from the Schola Cantorum in Oxford, she joined the famous Vasari Singers, who have a busy concert and recording schedule. There was also the enormous variety of entertainment in London's great theatres and concert halls to be enjoyed.

Life was exciting and rewarding enough, but in May 2005, quite dramatically it became more so. Ruth's mobile phone rang one evening as she walked along the Thames enjoying a glorious sunset. It was Esther Gruhn who told her that a charity concert she was running in St John's, Smith Square in just a week's time, was in trouble because the soprano soloist had been taken to hospital with appendicitis.

'Oh my goodness, and you want me to stand in at one week's notice?'

'Yes, Ruth. I think you would do it very well, and there will be some folk present who might take notice of you for the future.'

'Well, there is very little time to learn anything new. What is the programme?'

'That is why I am ringing you. You will be singing solo numbers to provide the contrast to a small instrumental ensemble, so I would suggest you could manage from your existing repertoire. Perhaps some Brahms or Mahler lieder, a little Mozart opera, and a couple of light ballads would fit the bill. In fact it was remembering the Brahms you sang to me three years ago, that made me ring you first.'

'OK Esther, I'd be pleased to do it, but I need a session with you first, and we also need to sort out a pianist.'

'I will fix that for you. The pianist will be here when you come for the pre-concert session with me. Can we fix a time for that right now please?'

A few days later Ruth presented herself at Esther's studio and there, sitting at the piano, was a man of indeterminate age. He rose, smiling warmly, reaching out to shake hands. 'I am pleased to meet you at last Ruth. My friend Esther talks a lot about you, mostly in a very complimentary manner.' The smile emphasised his attempt at gentle humour. 'My name is David, David Cohen, and this lady persuaded me that we should do this concert together. I hope I shall please you.' He waved in the direction of Esther, who stood to one side laughing at his self-deprecation.

'Ruth, please understand that David is a very old family friend and happens to be one of the finest accompanists in London just now. We are privileged to have him, even if I did have to bribe him heavily with several glasses of good wine.'

They all laughed together, and so the meeting went off happily with good humour and turned into a fine rehearsal session. Going home on the underground, Ruth sat thinking about David Cohen. She found it hard to judge his age, but noted some greying at the temples and slightly weather beaten skin, which suggested a man of middle thirties or maybe a trifle more. She did not like to ask. He was tall and thin with a slight stoop, she thought from many hours bent over a keyboard. The hands were large and strong with long fingers, and his brow furrowed very deeply in concentration when negotiating the more demanding passages of the chosen programme. She felt that he was strong and powerful, his voice was gentle and quite quiet, but without much music in it. She also noted that, although he smiled in greeting, his face otherwise was not very expressive. He had not said anything much about his life, mostly confining himself to pertinent interjections on some musical point or other, always deferring to Esther's opinion. She was the teacher after all. But, somehow, Ruth had the impression that behind David's gentle humour there lay a very sad man, and that there was a sense of mystery about him.

They had all agreed to meet at St John's 90 minutes before the concert for a warm up for half an hour before the doors were opened to admit the audience. When Ruth arrived she was feeling sick with apprehension. This was not a school concert, nor even an exposure as one member of a high class choir. This was a very different matter, a solo experience in one of the nation's most high profile concert halls. She had 'warmed up' at home so diligently and energetically that she wondered if she had made her voice tired. But then she remembered the advice given by both of her teachers, that the voice, when produced properly, is a very robust thing. After hard rehearsals or concerts, one often felt able to do the whole thing again.

In the event the concert passed off better than she could have expected, given the limited preparation time she had been given. Esther rewarded them both by whisking them by taxi up to Charing Cross Road and then walked them into J Sheekey, the famous fish restaurant, in St Martin's Court. The three of them sat in a small section of the restaurant with about half a dozen tables only. A fine bottle of wine awaited them and the waiting staff were deliciously attentive. They were so high after their excitements that they were about half way through their main course before they realised that they were surrounded by many well-known West End actors.

David was much more relaxed than when they had first met, and spoke animatedly about his working life as a professional pianist. Ruth admitted to him that she had once entertained ambitions to follow the same career path, until the fateful accident. She showed him her limited finger, explaining that it was not a problem for ordinary life, but would be impossible for a top class pianist.

Soon after, David excused himself, kissing both ladies lightly on the cheek and disappeared into the night, leaving them to enjoy their coffee without him. A strange silence came upon the women, each engrossed in private musings, until Esther sighed and muttered. 'Such a nice man.'

'Yes, Esther, and he's such a wonderful pianist too. But he doesn't give much away does he? I know I have only met him a couple of times, but we did make music very well together; and yet I do not feel I know him at all.'

'Nor will you in a short acquaintance Ruth. He has always been inclined to be a private person but in the past two or three years he has often been uncommunicative almost to the point of complete withdrawal and silence, in which he fulfils his job and nothing else. In fact, if he were not so charming and polite, it could easily be interpreted as rudeness.'

'Tell me more about him Esther,' demanded Ruth, her interest piqued by the mystery.

'Well, like me, he is Jewish. His grandfather was a music professor in Germany and escaped Hitler in the late 1930s, coming to London with his wife and young family to teach. One of his children became a distinguished psychiatrist here. That was David's father. He worked in a major south London mental hospital, but sadly died quite young, leaving his widow to manage the children, none of whom had finished school. She did brilliantly, since all of the children have done well.' She paused to sip her coffee before going on. 'David became the major male figure in the family, and grew up with perhaps more responsibility than most. I think that made him a particularly serious minded young man, perhaps driving him to excellence in his chosen path.'

'And what was his path?'

'He wanted very much to be a concert pianist, and for some years, that seemed to be the way he was heading, but somehow he was always the consummate technician, who never truly lit the blue touch paper. In crude terms he lacked the bravura to succeed at the very top. There was no lack of musicality, just a constraint that meant that his work, though much admired, did not excite. Gradually he came to accept that his role in life was to be an accompanist, and since then he has been very much in demand.'

'Is he married?'

'He was, but his wife, Monica left him and they were divorced a few years back. She was charming, intelligent and beautiful but was not musical, and she resented his obsession with it, so I guess the marriage was doomed from the start.

Certainly none of their friends were surprised. She is a producer for the BBC now, with a good career of her own.'

The Times newspaper a few days later carried a critique of the St John's concert, which painted Ruth in quite favourable terms, an extremely rare thing for an amateur. The effect was to challenge her life choices. She determined to sing more, intensifying her teaching and eventually, with encouragement and financial support from Ian and Rachel, she became a full time student at the Royal Academy, where Esther was a professor.

There she truly excelled, winning prestigious prizes, and blossoming into a real performer. This led to quite a number of concert engagements in which, with Esther's connivance, she quite often managed to work with David Cohen. They gradually became good friends, despite his innate caution, which, she realized, stemmed largely from his previous hurt.

Post graduate opera work brought acclaim and, eventually, an invitation to sing in the renowned Verbier Festival in Switzerland, an internationally famous holiday destination, popular with Royalty and celebrities, which boasted first rate skiing in the winter and good walking in the summer. Verbier Festival was considered a proving ground for many of the world's best young musicians, both instrumental and vocal. Ruth sang Musetta, the great Puccini role in La Boheme, and received good reviews.

David could not resist her invitation to listen to her sing Musetta in such an environment and drove all the way from London, some 800 miles, for the last performance. He pretended it was just to enjoy a long summer drive in his beloved Morgan Plus Four motor. Perhaps it was, but whatever the motive, he agreed to come to Verbier and to drive Ruth back to London afterwards. He stayed at the Hotel Bristol, one of the older established hotels in Verbier. After the performance there was a party, before the cast all went their different ways. David played the role of consort perfectly, never once revealing that his was the more established music career. In fact he did not reveal that he had any knowledge except as a friend. It was almost as if he enjoyed being second fiddle to Ruth's triumph.

After the party they went to David's hotel room and drank a bottle of champagne in private celebration. Almost inevitably they ended up falling into his bed and there made passionate and deeply satisfying love. Years later neither could say for certain who had planned this, or even if it had been planned at all, but both recognized that the scene had been perfectly set. What could have possibly been better, a triumphal performance of a great role as a woman with a big heart but questionable morality, public acclaim from a knowledgeable audience, a good party and a good champagne in a beautiful alpine setting.

On the way home next day they diverted slightly to Lake Annecy in France, and stayed for three days in a lovely east bank hotel. Ruth was exuberant, almost intoxicated with life, and insisted that she be given the opportunity to paraglide from the mountain top over the lake. David, warmly engrossed in a good feeling closely related to smugness, indulged her every whim.

They were almost silent for the long drive back to Calais, and the channel tunnel. The weather was perfect so the hood was down, and the wind noisy in their ears, discouraging conversation. They had stopped at an 'aire' for a baguette lunch, when David looked up in the middle of chewing to say. 'You will move in with me won't you?'

She nodded her assent, meaning it with all her heart.

Back in England it did not take long for people to notice new qualities in the young soprano. She visibly filled out into a truly gorgeous woman, and the voice, so good before, enriched tremendously into a true operatic voice capable of managing the big roles in the repertoire.

A star was born.

40

2009 Resolution

A state of excited anticipation, mixed in almost equal measure with anxiety, consumed Ruth all the way from Waterloo to Devon. It was a beautiful autumn day and, as the bustle of London, the drab scenes of suburban rear gardens and small industrial plants, were replaced by rural England, she noticed how the low trajectory sun made the shadows of houses and trees seem peculiarly sharp. The leaves were mostly still on the trees, and had turned the world into a magnificent palette of reds, browns, and yellows, quite startling in their beauty. This particular train journey was slower, cheaper, but more picturesque than the equivalent Great Western from Paddington, passing through small villages and towns with attractive architecture. Most of the countryside and the habitations had a carefully manicured feel almost as if a landscape gardener had designed every corner.

She sat in a window seat, the bright sun on her face creating an illusion of warmth, allowing her mind to wander; but whatever thoughts it threw up to her, whether the sweetness of David's well-wishing as he dropped her at the station, or her anticipation of going home to Rachel and Ian and sleeping in her own room, albeit one she had not much occupied for almost a decade, she kept returning every few minutes to the magnificence of the Verdi and the artistic mountain she must climb tomorrow. In truth, she was somewhat disappointed that

David had chosen not to come with her for this, her first Verdi Requiem. But, as he said, she would be in good hands with her family. She wondered if in reality his decision had more to do with the text of the work, with which he admittedly had problems. Christian liturgical works did not sit easily alongside his modern atheism, especially with his Jewish background.

'Musical are you, dear?' enquired a plump lady with a broad smile, red cheeks and a large basket, who occupied more than her proper share of the seat opposite.

'I am so sorry,' responded Ruth with a hint of embarrassment, realising that she had gone into a private reverie and had clearly been humming, though not so very privately. Smiles were exchanged all around the compartment, the little tease leading to general conversation of the revealing sort only to be had on a train, with strangers that one will never meet again.

By the time the sun etched, old red sandstone of Devon's ploughed fields signalled the approaching end of the journey, they all knew that this striking young woman was to sing in their Cathedral the next day. She left the train, running into her father, Ian's, waiting arms, with their good wishes billowing around her, almost like some benign wind.

Ian was, as he always had been, welcoming, secure, and loving, with that dry, self-effacing humour which Ruth knew disguised a good mind, one which perhaps had not been stretched as much as it should. He never seemed to age, though he had needed a couple of new hips and walked with a slight roll, rather like a sailor. He drove home through the fading light in his elderly Jaguar, a rash retirement treat he had allowed himself, despite Rachel's mock scolding. Ruth remembered his pride when he first brought it home, new. It had been just as she left school and went to Oxford. 'My goodness, that seems a lifetime ago', she thought, but it was just nine years.

Rachel was on the front step as they came up the drive, hugging her as if her life depended on it; and then, talking and laughing all the way, with Ian carrying their daughter's case, they found themselves in the sitting room, warm with a log fire.

There, sitting, crossed kneed, with a magazine on her lap and spectacles perched rather low on her nose was a lady of mature years. She was small and rather thin with deep creases in her skin, and her eyes were somewhat deep sunk as if she had endured much sadness, but they were bright enough, and accompanied with a lovely warm speaking voice as Ian introduced them. 'Ruth, this is my dear friend Maria O'Leary, whom I have known since we were together at medical school. You must have heard us talk of her often, but I am not sure you have ever actually met.'

'Oh yes, we have Ian,' said Maria, 'surely you remember that you all visited us in the Cotswolds when you brought Ruth up for her Oxford interview. She was a pretty girl then, but I see she is a very beautiful young woman now.'

'Thank you for the compliment,' said Ruth, as memory flooded back, placing this lady in context, and wishing Ian had warned her on the way from the station. 'I am so sorry about your son. That was terrible. He was with Morgan Stanley wasn't he, and I seem to remember he had an American wife and a lovely little boy? I think he was called Joseph. Ah yes, and your son was called James, was he not?'

'I remember you played with Joseph all afternoon in the garden,' said Maria softly.

'Well, he was fun, and I was quite shy in those days, so we escaped all the grown up talk'. They laughed at the confession, and at the memory of a swing hanging from a tree, a lovely pond with large fish in it, and a golden retriever who never seemed to tire of chasing balls.

'What has happened to them since?' Ruth's voice trailed off in some discomfort.

'Since 9/11 you mean?' said Maria. 'Well, Josie, my daughter-in-law could never quite accept that they have never found anything of James, so she feels tied to New York, and has settled there, I guess permanently now. It is after all a wonderfully vibrant city. Her own family are not too far away up in Massachusetts, so it all makes perfect sense. I go to see them most years for a couple of weeks to visit James' grave site, and to keep up with Joseph mainly. My daughter is teaching in Canada, so I combine the visits.'

'Have you ever been to Ground Zero, Ruth? It is a remarkable place. There is a little church just beside the site which became the shelter and rest centre for the rescue operation. It is very moving, especially to those of us who have no tangible grave to visit. I went several times with Michael, especially when he was dying of his cancer. He found a degree of peace there which made the journey worthwhile.'

Maria fell silent after this, but fortunately they were interrupted by Rachel's arrival with a tray of tea and cream scones. No visit to this part of the world would be complete without a cream tea.

Over tea Ruth noticed that Ian and Maria had a lot to say to one another, mostly medical talk, so as soon as they had finished she readily accepted Rachel's invitation to exercise the dog together. They took Rachel's little Smart car, with long scarves and stout walking boots stowed behind, and with a towelling bag in which to wrap a saturated cold spaniel. Rachel and Ian had owned a spaniel since shortly after Ruth's arrival in their home. Originally it was intended as Ruth's pet, but they had become just as devoted, and had wasted little time in replacing the original Sam with another of the same name after he had died. It was already getting dark, so they could not sensibly go up to Culmstock Beacon, which was Rachel's favourite walking space. From the top there were views for many miles, and some pretty rugged walking; wonderful for a frustrated gun dog whose owners would not raise as much as a peashooter between them. He would put up pheasant and other wild fowl, running endlessly with his nose close to the ground and frequently cocking his leg to leave his calling card, saying with absolute clarity 'Sam was here'. Today however, the night had come early and was a touch frosty. There was a voice to protect for the morrow, and a celebratory dinner to finish preparing, so they settled upon a gentle walk along the Tiverton canal.

As the two women strolled, mostly arm in arm, Ruth asked a little about Maria, and teased her mother gently that Dad seemed very close to her.

'Rachel smiled perhaps a little ruefully. 'I do sometimes wonder if I was second best,' she said. 'Ian has been in love with her for 50 years I guess, but Michael got in first and Ian was left on the side.'

'Actually that is not quite fair, Ruth, because the real problem was not Michael but religion. You see Ian was a Methodist as a lad, becoming Anglican when a student, but the step to becoming a Catholic was one step too far for him, and Maria could never tie herself for life to a non-Catholic.'

'I suspect, although they would never say so, that there was a romance 50 years ago, which failed because of these things, and so they have happily settled for being very good friends.'

Ruth trudged in silence for some time, digesting this information about this woman she hardly knew, and who had not figured in her adolescence, before turning to her mother and asking, 'And how do you feel about having a rival in your husband's heart in your own house?'

'Almost always completely at ease,' said Rachel. 'Even if he were to visit her alone, which I hasten to add he does not. You see, they are friends who have looked at being lovers and have chosen another path, a path which permits an intellectual intimacy, and real affection without danger or threat to anyone, a path without guilt, for which they do not need to apologise. As the spouse of one of them, I am very grateful because she offers things I cannot offer and because her very existence makes my marriage more secure from any other outside threat. Ian has enough trouble coping with the two of us, you and me.' She laughed in genuine amusement. 'He certainly could not cope with three women, you understand. That is one reason why whenever they meet I try to give them some time together. In fact it was I who invited her for this weekend. It is unspoken, but we all know it.'

'So how is it that this important person has not figured at all in my life until now?'

'Well, I suppose mostly that has just been chance. Maria was very busy for years, then she was not well for a long time, and no sooner had she begun to get better than James was killed and soon after that Michael died. Life has not been easy for her, and she became almost a recluse for a long time, apart from trips abroad. I guess that is why you have only met her once and even that was brief enough for us to have forgotten.'

'OK, I understand that, but let me be clear about Maria and Dad. She seems lovely but I feel I should not like her if she is a threat to you and therefore to my family. I have had enough of that in the past. And this business of cross faith love is important to me. As you know David is of a different religion too. He is officially Jewish, although I consider him to be an atheist. Are you saying I must not marry him, but just keep him as a friend? I might find that terribly difficult, if not impossible now.'

'No Ruth, I would never presume to tell you any such thing. I did point out that Ian and Maria had settled the matter many years ago. I choose to believe that they were never quite lovers, merely that the question was asked, not that it matters any more. She is a wonderful woman who is my friend also. Since Michael's death we have seen much more of her and I have played my part in that. I think Ian has become even more important to her in the past few years, and in some senses we are a threesome, but of course Ian always comes into my bed, not hers, so that is fine. We are all very content with the way things are.'

They trudged on, the lights of the canal bridge and the car park showing them the way.

'I believe it is absolutely for the individuals to decide for themselves, though, as you must know, in some cultures to marry outside one's faith might result in terrible punishment, even death. There have been several, so called, honour killings in Britain this year.'

'Are you happy then Mum? You always seem to be, and so does Dad.'

'I would say that I am as happy as I know how to be. I am secure and content in my teaching. I have a wonderful husband, who understands my world, and is very accomplished in it himself. I have many good friends, including Maria, and I have the most fabulous daughter any woman could imagine, of whom I am very proud. I am therefore very rich indeed, even if the bank manager does not know it.'

Ruth sniggered at this last remark, for she knew that her parents had lost all their savings in the banking crisis and were in effect living on half of what they had expected. Bankers were the bottom of the feeding chain as far as the family were concerned, their behaviour an offence to all. Ian and Rachel were far from poor, but they were no longer as well off, their trappings of middle class affluence such as the fancy cars were really dinosaurs, things of the past which would not be replaced, like for like, when they were worn out. They did not complain, for many of their friends had experienced the same. This economic disaster seemed to have damaged the retired, and the folk living on investment incomes, more than most others, but the scar would remain and some banking names would, for ever, be held in disdain. Respect for institutions previously regarded as cornerstones of sobriety and reliability had been shattered. The problem was that the very people at the heart of the matter, the bankers themselves, seemed oblivious to the reaction that they had engendered in their own customers, and continued to milk the community of its wealth. The effect was being felt all over the world, and in some unlikely places. One tiny example was that tickets for tomorrow's concert had been much harder than usual to sell and a full house was by no means guaranteed. A few years previously, 'sold out' notices would have been put up days in advance.

With this sombre thought they turned for home and were soon engrossed together in the kitchen, except for about 30 minutes when Ruth disappeared to the music room in order to 'rev the engine' as she put it. Maria and Rachel, preparing the vegetables whilst Ian laid the table, stopped talking for a while to listen. Both were smiling when Ruth emerged, complaining gently that Rachel's Bechstein could do with a tune.

Ian's 8 year old St Estephe proved a great partner for the lamb joint. Eating would be relatively slight the next day, so Rachel quite deliberately fed them all very well. The atmosphere around the table was light hearted, and all were enjoying each other. Even the sad Maria had greatly cheered and was enquiring diligently into Ruth's blossoming career.

It was over the cheese, a particularly runny Sharpham brie, and some Quick's cheddar, that the loosened tongues returned to more personal things.

Ian was laughingly regaling them all with a story of some student indiscretion on Maria's part, in which he imitated Professor Davies, their anatomy professor. "Now Miss Bellini' he squeaked 'will you please repeat the structures in the knee from front to back'. Miss Bellini stands up and says 'Yes sir, it is 'Treeves was a very fine surgeon except in piles', accurately quoting the mnemonic by which we learned the sequence of structures concerned. Everyone fell about laughing that this girl,' he said, pointing his fork towards Maria, 'would actually give the Prof the mnemonic, not the real answer.'

He, Rachel and Maria giggled at the story and it was a moment or two before they each noticed that Ruth was not laughing. In fact she sat with her glass half way to her mouth staring at Maria with a completely stunned expression on her face.

'Miss Bellini? Did you say Miss Bellini, Miss Maria Bellini?' she demanded of her father.

'Why yes, of course,' said Ian. 'Bellini is Maria's maiden name. O'Leary is her married one.'

'And which name did you work with?' Ruth stared at Maria.

'Why Bellini of course,' said Maria. 'It is normal for a woman doctor to continue to work under the name she first registers with, even after marriage. Why do you ask, Ruth? It seems important to you.'

'And you worked in Cirencester?'

'Yes, we lived in Lechlade as you know, but I worked in Cirencester.'

'So the person I know as Mrs O'Leary, wife of Michael O'Leary of Lechlade is actually Dr Bellini of Cirencester?'

'Come on Ruth, what is all this about?' her father demanded. 'It is not quite polite to treat dinner guests to an inquisition.'

Ruth put her glass down and slowly stood to face the three of them. She said nothing at all for what seemed a long time, and then, as if making up her mind, said, 'Mum and Dad, there is something I have never told you. My first name has always been Ruth, but I have had three second names. My current one, the one I am proud of is Plowman, before that I was Mason, and that was my name when you first knew me. But originally my name was Ruth Troutmann and my mother was called Deborah.'

It was Maria's turn to react. It was as if she had been shot. She sat upright in her chair, a fearful expression on her face almost of a wild animal trapped by hunters, which is much as she felt herself to be, 'Oh God!' she said, 'Oh my God!' Her head dropped into her hands and she wept the tears of a lifetime of pent up feeling.

Ian and Rachel, completely puzzled, just stared at them both in bewilderment, not knowing what to say or do.

Ruth recovered first. She turned to her parents and said, 'You see, I had a very unhappy childhood with a mother who did not want me and did all in her power to let me understand that. When I was quite little she became pregnant and married the father of that baby, so my name was changed to Mason. He was very good to me but he had to be away a lot and my Mum used to drink heavily and do drugs as well. When I was about eight I found out my Mum was taking her old doctor to court because I had not been aborted. You may remember the case, especially as you have always been friends of Maria.'

Ian and Rachel nodded, understanding beginning to flood them.

'Mum just went on drinking and getting into trouble more and more often until Social Services got involved, which led to me being fostered. That's how I came to know you both. Then, later, my real Mum died and you adopted me, so my name changed again.'

'But why have you kept all this to yourself until now?' demanded Rachel.

Ruth paused and then faced Ian and Rachel squarely. 'The lady at Social Services whom I now call Auntie Sheila, said there was no need to tell you about all this unless I really wanted to, and it was never important enough until now.'

Turning to Maria she said softly 'This lovely lady is the doctor who did not kill me. I owe her my life.'

She crossed to Maria, pulled her to her feet, held her at arm's length and said simply 'Thank you, Maria. Thank you for allowing me to be.'

Then she too began to weep and all four soon found themselves having a great tearful hug together, a hug which went on for some time, until Ian extracted himself and insisted on opening a bottle of champagne over which they talked excitedly, Maria wanting to know all of Ruth's doings, and Ruth hers, whilst Ian and Rachel just became filled with a very great happiness. Eventually Ian reminded everyone that Ruth needed to go to bed sober and in good time, so they all retired, though Maria lay thinking how sad it was that Michael had not lived to be present this evening.

Exeter Cathedral was famous for its Norman towers and the imposing west facade which dominated a delightful Cathedral green. The green, fringed by fashionable shops, cafés, an Italian restaurant and by Exeter's venerable Royal Clarence Hotel with its fine dining. The bar knew a thing or two about gin, serving H&C (Hendricks and Cucumber) making it a favourite of the Plowman family. It was here, Ian had chosen to assemble his party for the concert. A merry party, of a dozen or so, mostly, but not entirely, of mature age, met at 6.30 for half an hour of reminiscence. Some were Rachel's music teacher colleagues, some were neighbours, some were family, and there were several of Ian's work colleagues, reminding him, once again, of the strong ties between medicine and music, Jack and Sarah, and one or two of Ruth's university friends. Sheila Green, Ian and Rachel's bridesmaid and Ruth's social worker, had brought her husband all the way from Brighton for the occasion.

Maria felt herself on the fringe of the group, not quite belonging to anyone except Rachel and Ian. Over the years she had become adroit at hiding her innate shyness and joining conversation freely, but tonight she was not quite able to give her whole mind to the social exchanges, and wondered if the people she spoke with had noticed that she was functioning in an automatic manner. In a few minutes she was going to hear the daughter of the woman who had come close to destroying her, sing one of the great works. The little girl that had not been aborted had grown up into magnificent womanhood.

She, Maria, felt very privileged to witness this small but significant step on Ruth's professional path, with all the vulnerabilities and uncertainties involved, and genuinely wished her well, but she could not entirely put on one side the traumas that Ruth's conception, birth and early life had brought to her door. The reminder was wholly unwelcome, opening the wound, like an exhumation, just when life on her own, lived on her own terms, was beginning to become manageable.

She had not slept well last night, replaying all the events around those awful years of legal wrangle and she was, today, conscious of her years in a way that she disliked. She moved stiffly, aching all over, even in the hip that had been so well replaced. There was a slight headache right between the eyes, and light seemed rather too bright. In plain terms she felt old. She felt every bit of her 74 years. It was a relief when, just before seven, Ian declared that they should cross the green into the great church to claim their seats.

When they entered the Cathedral it was already almost full, (so much for fears of the recession causing empty seats), but then it was the Verdi Requiem being performed, and that never fails to pull the crowds. Maria thought there were about a thousand people sitting expectantly, but was pleased to find that Ian had somehow managed to reserve seats in the nave, just a dozen or so rows from the front. She knew enough about this type of concert to realise that they were not so close as to be overwhelmed, and not so far way as to be blurred by the acoustic delay normal to great churches.

There were some 60 players in the orchestra and over 120 singers in the choir according to the programme. The choir was a great coming together of many smaller choirs throughout the county. She tingled at the most exciting sound on earth, that of an orchestra tuning up. It never failed to produce a frisson of excited anticipation, a falling away of care and a sharp increase in mental focus.

And then, all of a sudden there she was, this girl who might never have been. The choir stood, the audience clapped and the four soloists, followed by the conductor, came on to the platform, turned to the audience and took a smiling bow. Ruth, standing on the audience's left at the end of the row looked pale, but her auburn hair set against the shimmering green of her long concert dress made for a very striking appearance.

The conductor turned to face his orchestra and choir, picked up his baton, and the sepulchral sound of the hushed bass strings with the awed whispering of the great chorus seemed to come from deep in the earth, so quietly at first that one was not quite sure they had begun. Gradually the volume rose, and then suddenly so did all of the soloists, each in turn crying 'Kyrie Eleison'. Maria felt the tenor strike through her, responding to him almost in a primeval way, as if her body recognised the quality and sheer bravura of her native land and its music. And then Ruth in her echo of him soared like a bird into the upper reaches of the human voice, so apparently effortlessly that all of her family and their friends smiled in acknowledgement, knowing that all would be well tonight.

And so Verdi's masterpiece, written more than a century previously, once again captured the very essence of those who heard it. 'It may help to be a devoutly religious person, but it is in no way essential to be so in order to be deeply moved by this music,' she thought. Rachel, sitting next to her, was totally engrossed, her eyes glittering in the awesomeness of the Dies Irae, especially when they were suddenly surrounded by the sound of four offstage trumpets echoing the four in the orchestra, joining up with horns and trombones to make the most amazing introduction to the great duet between bass soloist and the chorus. Somehow the conductor made the music ebb and flow like some mighty river, taking everyone on some sort of inevitable journey towards a great conclusion. At times he seemed to hold the sound on the end of his fingers so that all in the audience found themselves with a collective holding of breath.

There was no interval, just a brief pause for the conductor to mop his brow, the orchestra to re-tune, the audience to shift in their chairs and for those so inclined to have a cough. The mood did not change, and focus from all present was undiminished.

The final movement begins with a dramatic, plainsong like, declamation from the soprano soloist and then expands into a fantastic chorus topped by the single voice of the soloist who at one point climbs through the voice right up to a top C to tower over both chorus and orchestra. This is a very special moment for any Verdi soprano. Many do not have the voice and strength to do it justice. This night brought no such doubts with it.

Libera me Domine de morte aeterna in dies illa tremenda

Free me Oh Lord from death everlasting

The great passion poured from Ruth with enormous authority and power. She shook the very cathedral and all those within it, so that when the work came to its fearful muttered close, the whole assembly was still and silent for what seemed a long time.

And then, suddenly, there was pandemonium. The audience was on its feet, calling and clapping till their arms and hands hurt. The soloists, choir and orchestra stood to take their bows, but as the ladies were given their bouquets it was noticeable that the volume of clapping rose to even higher levels when Ruth received hers.

Rachel and Maria stood there in the middle with tears pouring down their cheeks. Maria crossed herself and said very quietly.

'Thank you, Oh Lord. I am free at last.'

As they all left the cathedral nobody noticed the elegant man of Eastern European features. Professor Anatole Gennadi, the famous pianist, remembering a summer spent fruit picking in Tetbury, was overwhelmed by a mix of pride and sorrow.

Footnotes

* The age of majority

Until the latter part of the 20th Century, a doctor would be obliged to inform a parent of any medical intervention until the age of 21. In 1969, The Family Reform Act reduced the age of majority from 21 to 18.

Subsequent reformers, notably the Gillick case, have led major debates on the rights of doctors to prescribe and treat young people of certain ages. For a long time it was considered that parents had a right to veto treatments of under 16 year olds, but more recently the Courts have regarded the concept of competence as the guiding principal, so that a young person passing the 'competence test' may receive medical care against parental wishes.

The notion of 'competence' also applies to the right of a minor to deny parental access to his or her medical records.

* Termination

For many years, a child born after 28 weeks gestation was regarded as a human being, and whether born dead or alive was accorded the formalities associated with that status. Thus a stillborn baby born after this time would have a birth certificate, a death certificate and a funeral.

Pregnancy ending prior to 28 weeks was regarded as unviable and the process labelled an abortion, whether natural or induced.

Prior to 1967, the induction of an abortion was illegal in the UK. After 1967 it became legal in certain circumstances, including maternal distress, up to 28 weeks of pregnancy. That age was reduced to 24 weeks gestation in 1990, and there has been continuing discussion about reducing this limit further.